FRAYED:
Surviving the Zombie Apocalypse

SHAWN CHESSER

ISBN: 978-0-9864302-7-5

CONTENTS

ACKNOWLEDGMENTS

For Maureen, Raven, and Caden ... I couldn't have done this without all of your support. Thanks to all of our military, LE and first responders for your service. To the people in the U.K. and elsewhere around the world who have been in touch, thanks for reading! Lieutenant Colonel Michael Offe, thanks for your service as well as your friendship. Shannon Walters, my top Eagle Eye, thank you! Larry Eckels, thank you for helping me with some of the military technical stuff. Any missing facts or errors are solely my fault. Beta readers, you rock, and you know who you are. Thanks George Romero for introducing me to zombies. Steve H., thanks for listening. All of my friends and fellows at S@N and Monday Old St. David's, thanks as well. Lastly, thanks to Bill W. and Dr. Bob … you helped make this possible. I am going to sign up for another 24.

Special thanks to John O'Brien, Mark Tufo, Joe McKinney, Craig DiLouie, Armand Rosamilia, Heath Stallcup, James Cook, Saul Tanpepper, Eric A. Shelman, and David P. Forsyth. I truly appreciate your continued friendship and always invaluable advice. Thanks to Jason Swarr and Straight 8 Custom Photography for the awesome cover. Once again, extra special thanks to Monique Happy for her work editing "Frayed." Mo, as always, although you have many pokers in the fireplace, you came through like a champ! Working with you has been a dream come true and nothing but a pleasure. If I have accidentally left anyone out ... I am truly sorry.

***

Edited by Monique Happy Editorial Services
www.moniquehappy.com

Prologue

The man shifted his gaze from the thin band of blue sky up ahead to the rearview mirror, where he saw nothing but angry clouds and darkened countryside. Seemingly following him on the same northwesterly tack, the pewter smudge was depositing big heavy flakes on the rolling hills and abandoned farmhouses and rust-streaked silos whipping by on both sides of the winding State Route.

Thinking ahead, just after traces of the first snowfall of the season began to stick, the driver had stopped on a zombie-free stretch of road a few miles back and engaged the four-wheel-drive. Now, negotiating the snow-dusted rollercoaster-like two-lane cutting between Wyoming to the east and Utah to the west, all the driver had to concentrate on as he approached his destination were the clusters of walking dead making yet another slow motion sojourn north. As he halved his speed and zippered between the staggering human husks, he noticed that their movements seemed sluggish—more so than usual—their already diminished motor skills seeming to degrade before his eyes in pace with the rapidly dropping mercury.

As the rig passed within arm's reach of another slow-moving group—where normally the younger and more agile specimens would at least crane and get an eye lock on him or, if the conditions were right, manage a clumsy swipe at the vehicle—there was a delayed response, their maws opening and arms extending only after the SUV was well past them.

"Well, well," said the man, flicking his eyes to the rearview. "*That* is what I was hoping would happen. Levels the playing field, a little." Despite the task at hand, a grin spread across his face and he rapped a ditty on the steering wheel. "Bite me biters ... aren't such the bad asses now are we?" Though he wanted to stop and take out thirty or forty of the things in one fell swoop, he didn't want to expend the energy clearing their carcasses from the road would require. As he swept his gaze forward, he saw off in the distance the north-moving herd he'd first seen two hours prior and a number of miles south.

Spitting a string of expletives, the man slowed the vehicle and grabbed his binoculars from the seat next to him. Then, knee-steering, he risked a couple of glances at the shambling mass, only pressing the field glasses to his eyes for a couple of seconds at a time, which was all he needed to learn that the main body had just passed his turnoff, leaving only a loose knot of walking corpses and the few lone stragglers bringing up the rear for him to worry about.

Knowing the distant herd would soon crest the small hill and then be on the downslope and out of sight, he slowed his ride to a crawl, swung wide right, and hauled the wheel hand-over-hand. The sun-dappled horizon swung a one-eighty across the windshield's wide curvature and the tires squelched on the far shoulder as he straightened the wheel and looped around the listless pack of dead he'd just bypassed. A hundred yards south around a bend in the road where he figured the vehicle's silhouette would be masked from the dead, he eased off the gas and let the rig coast until its forward momentum bled off. Now, with two hundred yards or so and a grass-covered hillock between him and the biters, he jammed the SUV to a stop on the solid yellow centerline and put the automatic transmission in *Park*. For the sake of comfort, he took his boxy semi-auto pistol from its holster on his hip and placed it on top of the dusty dash within easy reach. Eyes threatening to close on him, he kicked his seat back, elbowed the door lock down, and flicked on the stereo to start the soothing sounds of *Johann Sebastian Bach* flowing from the speakers.

***

The man's respite was cut short just minutes into his powernap when the half-dozen dead not fooled by the coast maneuver caught up to the inert vehicle and began raking their nails against the sheet metal. Though the late German composer was being all but drowned out by the keen of bone against metal and hollow moans of the dead, the man tolerated the sneering creatures batting the window just inches from his face for ten long minutes.

Once the ten minutes had passed, for good measure the man stared at the second hand's sweep and allowed five more minutes to crawl by. Finally, convinced most of the dead would be far enough away to the north so as not to key in on the growl of the diesel engine, he jacked his seat up and started the motor. Fighting the wheel and clunky gearbox, he conducted a three-point-turn and was rolling north at a fair clip.

Seconds later, he arrived at the crest of the hill where he had first spotted the herd which, in the thirty minutes since, had only shambled a half a mile beyond his turnoff and into a veil of falling snow. Closer in, however, was the smaller knot of biters that inexplicably were still within eyeshot of his turnoff, which was a narrow dirt road shooting uphill and to the right off the paved State Route.

Practicing what he preached to his kids—*better safe than sorry*—he gently pressed the pedal to start the SUV rolling forward over the hill's crest. Once gravity grabbed the three-quarter tons of American iron, he jacked the transmission into neutral, manhandled the transfer case out of four-wheel-drive, and then killed the engine. Without the boost of power steering, keeping the SUV's squared-off grill guard aimed at the throng of dead took considerable effort.

Halfway down the hill, the wind whistling through the half-dozen bullet holes in the driver's side door alerted the dead to his approach and, sluggishly, as if in slow motion, they turned in unison and faced the noise.

A beat or two later, the sickening sounds of the coasting SUV plowing through the picket of corpses made its way through the rusted floor pan and again the soothing string work of another Bach masterpiece was drowned out. Before the remaining corpses could scrape themselves off of the roadway, the man had set the brake, grabbed his weapons, and was unfolding his massive frame from the high clearance vehicle.

Standing on the road in the midst of the crushed and mangled corpses, he slipped his Glock back into its holster. Then he donned his faded knee-length western-style duster, leaving it unbuttoned. Finally, he cracked his back and neck then slipped the corded nylon rope over his head and adjusted the scabbard it was attached to so that the pommel of his ancestral blade was within easy reach behind his head.

"Come to Daddy," he growled, a wolfish grin spreading on his face as he began wading through the leaking corpses to get to the throng of dead vectoring toward him.

Chapter 1

Cade Grayson's undead welcoming party on Utah State Route 39 consisted of two horribly decomposed first turns. In a can't-see-the-forest-through-the-trees type of way, he would have missed them entirely had the colorful tatters of wind-whipped clothing clinging to their bodies not drawn his eye to them through the picket of lodgepole pines. And as he ground the big Ford pickup to a halt just inside the Eden Compound's foliage-covered front gate, it became clear that prior to hearing the vehicle's approach, the Zs had been trudging along on an easterly heading. Which was a good thing. Because it meant that the wall of logs blocking the two-lane a few miles west of the compound was doing its job.

Dreamed up by another Eden survivor—former Bureau of Land Management firefighter Daymon Bush—the barricade provided a buffer between the compound and both the herds of dead finding their way along the State Route from the burned-out towns of Huntsville and Eden and the larger hordes of rotten corpses migrating from the more densely populated city of Ogden twenty miles further west of there.

So far the blockade had done exactly what Daymon had promised it would. However, much to the small band of survivors' collective surprise, the feat of engineering brought about by a week's worth of precision chainsaw work was inexplicably doing double duty. For no matter the size of the group of walking dead, upon hitting the wall of trees and finding no prey there, invariably, either jogged by some snippet of memory or driven by the primordial urge to hunt buried deep down in the reptilian part of their atrophied brains, they would about-face and shuffle back from whence they'd come. But, unfortunately, there was an exception to the rule. If the dead saw or heard anything—talking, engine noise, sometimes an animal or bird's call—while near the roadblock, the urge to hunt in them would be triggered, resulting in a moaning assemblage of death. Which was a whole 'nother can of worms which necessitated the tedious and dangerous task of a great deal of up close and personal killing followed by the back-breaking labor disposing of the putrefying bodies entailed.

Messy work that Cade wanted no part of, that was for sure. The latter more so than the former.

Keeping one eye on the dead through the trees, Cade killed the engine and set the brake. He fished the long-range 40-channel CB radio from a pocket and adjusted the volume up a couple of notches. He looked out the windshield at the snow falling faster now, keyed the Talk button and hailed Seth, who was manning the security desk inside the nearby subterranean compound. "I'm going east to the 16 junction and then north from there," he stated, looking down at his Suunto and noting the time. "Figure I'll be gone for a couple of hours at most."

"Heading out *solo*," Seth came back, wryly. "You got some kind of a death wish there, Grayson?"

"We've all got to die sometime," Cade shot back. He reached over the center console and scratched Max, the brindle-colored Australian shepherd, behind the ears. "No need to worry, though. I've got my wingman, Max, by my side."

Seth said, "That's already been established in spades ... on both counts. Watch your back. There's nobody at the overwatch to help you with the gate. And remember ... there won't be anyone there when you return either."

"Roger that. I have eyes on two Zs. Are you seeing anything else on 39?"

The radio in Cade's hand broke squelch, then Seth's voice emanated from the tiny speaker. "I've got a bad case of CSS down here."

Max yawned and swung his head in Cade's direction, cropped stub of a tail beating a steady rhythm on the passenger seat.

Furrowing his brow, Cade thumbed Talk and asked, "C-S-S?"

"A bad case of *can't ... see ... shit.*"

Cade shook his head. "Are we talking or texting?"

"A bit of both, old man. Can you wipe the camera domes for me before you leave the ... *wire*?" Still not used to using the military lexicon adopted by most since Duncan took control, and used more frequently since Cade's arrival, Seth sometimes found himself struggling to recall the proper words, second-guessing himself, and often fearful that he was misusing them.

"Roger that." Cade stuffed the radio inside his MultiCam parka and plucked his suppressed Glock 17 from the passenger seat. Acting on years of training, he ejected the magazine and pulled the slide back to verify that a 9mm round was in the pipe. Satisfied, he seated the full magazine in the well and, knowing that the dead and locked gate were tasks he'd have to tackle alone, shouldered the door open. With one leg in space and about to step down from the cab, the radio in his pocket emitted a low hiss. Cade froze, one foot on the running board and one hand holding the grab handle, as he listened to Seth ask him to keep an eye out for cheese.

"Any kind of cheese," Seth went on. "Moldy sixty-day-old parmesan. Those little bastards hermetically sealed in red wax. Hell, at this point I'm a beggar. I'd even settle for processed cheez-whiz-in-a-can." The radio never left Cade's pocket and soon Seth's desperation-filled voice trailed off and there was a heavy silence in the cab. *No moans. Damn.*

With a firm set to his jaw, Cade lowered himself to the ground. He clucked his tongue ushering Max out, then, intent on making as much noise as possible, reached behind his head and flung the door shut. The resulting metallic clang resonated loudly for a beat, but without a wide-open expanse for the sound to expand and travel, it died off quickly.

Already alerted to the presence of fresh meat by the Ford's rumbling engine and throaty exhaust, the eastbound Zs, now frozen in place and eyeing the forest, heard the door slam and immediately set off at a fast lope in the gate's general direction. Their moans growing loud, the pair refined their search by homing in on the noise of wet gravel crunching underneath Cade's boots—and with their own bare feet slapping a cadence on the cold asphalt, traversed the road on a collision course with the realistic-looking wall of foliage.

Before Cade had taken a dozen steps beyond the truck's bumper, the Zs' dry raspy calls had risen in volume. A beat or two later, the gate was rattling against its hinges and crooked and bloodied digits were probing the nylon netting holding the carefully arranged saplings and vegetation in place.

"Keep your pants on," Cade barked. He stopped a yard back from the gate and paced left and then right to make sure two was the magic number.

And it was. So he holstered the Glock and withdrew his Gerber Mark II fighting knife from its scabbard on his right thigh. Carefully he probed the fence head-high with the honed black blade until he saw a flash of white through the warren of interwoven branches. He widened the opening a bit and saw a pair of cracked and shredded lips. They were drawn taut over a mouthful of yellowed teeth, all jagged shards parked in a jaw hinging slowly up and down. The little snippet he saw through the fence reminded him of an expectant grouper inspecting a pane of aquarium glass. The narrow face and bloated lips, even the swollen black hunk of flesh for a tongue looked as if it belonged in the mouth of a fish instead of this shell of a former human being.

Guessing where he thought the shorter of the two creature's eye socket would be, he banged on the fence there with his free hand and held the dagger's tip perpendicular to the inner netting. Seconds passed and then the fingers withdrew and disappeared and a tick later probed the fence a foot to the left. Meeting Cade's expectation, the fence bowed in a couple of inches. Palm on the Gerber's pommel, he leaned in and thrust the dagger through the barrier left-of-center of the steadily growing human-head-sized impression. There was a bit of resistance at first, but the attempt yielded nothing but a fresh inches-long-gash to go along with the roadmap of lesions and scratches already criss-crossing the Z's alabaster face. Enticed by Cade's presence, but confused by the gate, the two Zs wavered, their heads bobbing tantalizingly close yet still just outside of striking range. So Cade searched the ground nearby and found a wrist-thick foot-long piece of tree branch. He scooped it up, peered over his shoulder at Max, and waggled it over his head. After catching the shepherd's multi-colored gaze, he threw the stick overhand to the right and watched it sail twenty feet or so and land on the spongy ground inside the fence with a hollow thud.

Stub tail a blur and eyes fixed on Cade, Max sat on his haunches waiting for permission.

"Get it boy."

Instantly gravel shot from under Max's paws as he gave chase.

The flexing at the gate stopped as the rotters, keying in to the out-of-sight sounds and sudden flurry of movement, released their grip. A tick later the wet slaps of rotted flesh on pavement started anew.

Gerber still clutched in his right fist, Cade followed Max. After traversing a dozen feet, he stopped near the gate's edge where a gnarled wood post was buried in the ground and the barbed wire fence separating the roadside ditch from the dense tree line began its westward run. He shifted his weight to the balls of his feet and bent his knees, going into a partial combat crouch while keeping his upper body coiled tight, like a spring under pressure.

Max paralleled the barbed wire fence, picked up the sun-weathered length of wood with his mouth, and began working it between his teeth, pulverizing it into a hundred little pieces in seconds.

With the usual eye-watering stench preceding them, the Zs staggered from behind the blind. Fixated solely on Max and unable to feel pain, they hit the fence at full speed and continued their hunt, with rusty barbs tearing chunks of flesh from their emaciated frames.

Cade waited behind the blind for the faster of the two to pass him by and then let out a soft whistle, causing the trailing creature to stutter step and turn clumsily to its right.

"Peek-a-boo," Cade said, as the Gerber flashed black against a growing white background and penetrated the rotter's right eye socket with a soft squish. Instantly, like a snipped marionette, the thirty-something female rotter folded to the ground where it settled face down, ass up—an unmoving heap of skin and bone. Resting there on the cold ground, with the knuckles of knobby vertebra and sharp pelvic bones straining against the pale bruised dermis, the thing could have easily passed for a concentration camp victim.

Before the first flesh eater had been stilled, Max had already destroyed the stick and was sizing up the remaining creature, teeth bared and hackles raised.

Still unaware of Cade's presence, the second Z leaned hard into the chest-high strand of wire, bowing it inward half a foot, and gouging a foot-long, inch-wide chasm into its pale skin. Eyes fixed only on Max, and with its own teeth bared, a guttural, seemingly hate-filled sound escaped its maw.

"I got this," muttered Cade, approaching the abomination from its blindside. Without pause, he reached across the wire and wrapped one gloved hand around the thing's scrawny neck. Simultaneously he lifted and tightened his grip, closing off the hissing creature's windpipe. With silence returned to the lonely stretch of road, and hatred burning hot behind his eyes, Cade thrust the dagger deeply into the patch of soft flesh an inch in front of the male cadaver's right ear.

Like its *off* switch had been thrown, the Z went limp, its toes swaying an inch off the ground. Milky eyes rolled back, retreating into hollow sockets. And then, held aloft an arm's length from Cade's face, its jaw slackened, revealing a maggot-addled tongue and mouthful of crooked teeth still home to ribbons of flesh and sinew from its last kill.

Cade released his grip and let gravity take the dead weight. Then, cursing his decision to lay hands on the dead, and feeling a tinge of discomfort from the sight of the yellow pus sullying his glove's padded leather palm, he added baby wipes and hand sanitizer to his mental grocery list.

"Come on boy," he called to Max. "You get to watch my six."

Seemingly aware of his appointed position, Max sat on his haunches, peering through the fence at the twice-dead humans. He panned left down the road then held steady for a moment, ears perked, nose sniffing at the cold air. Then the multi-colored shepherd swiveled his head right and fixed his gaze on the shadow-covered road to the west.

"I'll be damned," said Cade. "You're hired."

Max yawned and lay flat, his graying snout at rest on his outstretched forelegs. Then with his eyes, one brown, one blue, moving left and right, he issued a split-second throaty growl which Cade took as an affirmative.

Cade swung the gate away, then called Max and ushered him inside the truck. He hopped in after, fired up the big V10, wheeled the F-650 through the gate and onto the smooth two-lane where he left it facing east, and set the brake. Again he grabbed the suppressed Glock off the seat next to him and checked his surroundings for Zs. *Better safe than sorry doesn't count any longer.* In the new reality brought on by the swift-moving Omega Virus, sorry meant dead, and Cade wasn't about to chance the latter. He'd seen way too much of it recently. One instance in particular hitting more closely home than others.

Seeing nothing moving, east or west, he hopped out on the road and quickly closed and locked the gate behind the matte-black truck. With its low engine rumble fracturing the morning stillness and wisps of gray exhaust hanging above the road, he adjusted the foliage affixed to the camouflaged entry. Then, remembering his earlier conversation with Seth, not the part where he was begged to seek out a Hickory Farms and return with a holiday cheese log, but the request to clean the CCTV domes, he hurried past the gate and down the tree line. It took him a second or two of scrutinizing a trio of firs before he located the two half-domes ubiquitous in nearly every store and bank and eatery before the fall. The *eye in the sky* as it was not so affectionately called by some Vegas casino players. Only these cameras weren't looking for card cheats. They were trained on both approaches to the entry. The east-facing camera viewed a short stretch of the road that was relatively straight and included a steady uphill grade and then nothing but low hills breaking up the distant horizon. The camera trained to the west had a little bit of a warped view of the entire curving length of 39 through the dip in the road on up to where it disappeared into a tunnel created by the encroaching woods.

Cade stood on a fence post, stretched out his full length, and ran a microfiber cloth over both onyx-colored domes, bringing a shine that lasted only a moment before the flakes started sticking again.

He hopped down, landing purposefully with most of his weight on his recently healed left ankle. He felt nothing abnormal. No flash of pain from compressing scar tissue. Not even the twinge of discomfort he'd experienced after fast roping from a hovering Osprey and sprinting over the sloped clearing upon returning from a recent snatch and grab mission to Southern California. *So*, he thought in Ranger parlance, *the ankle is one hundred percent, good-to-go*.

Retracing his steps, he stopped and dragged the Zs, one at a time, into the ditch, figuring he'd send Wilson to dispose of them later. Finished, he boarded the idling truck which had come into his possession in a crazy roundabout way shortly after the dead began to reanimate and walk the earth. After having been stolen from a mansion somewhere in Colorado, the oversized vehicle—which had obviously been custom-built for the long dead NBA basketball player whose underground multi-car garage it had been liberated from—was driven to Schriever Air Force base in Colorado Springs, a homicidal killer named Pug behind the wheel.

Nudging the details of the truck's crazy odyssey from his mind, Cade inadvertently gazed uphill and caught sight of the disturbed ground. Though not entirely evident unless you knew precisely where to look, the replaced sod, newly green from recent rains yet still stunted from the shock of being peeled away from the dirt, marked the location of the graves containing the fallen.

Cade saw them in his mind's eye, from left to right: a ski instructor and friend of Logan's named Sampson. A man whom, embarrassingly, he didn't remember ever meeting. Then there was the former Salt Lake Sheriff named Gus whom he had barely gotten to know before the *event* at the quarry stole him and Jordan and Duncan's brother Logan from the earth. Capping the right side were the three recent additions, the grass atop them greener, the feeling of loss to Cade and the entire group still stinging like a freshly opened wound.

Shoving those thoughts down where they belonged, tucked away in the place where they would be less apt to resurface at an inopportune time and possibly divert his focus or cause him to forget something as small in detail yet still very important like cleaning the CCTV domes for Seth, he racked the transmission into Drive and accelerated east. Eyes forward, hands gripping the wheel tight, he kept his speed under thirty the entire length of Utah State Route 39, up the hill, then on down the slight dip and into the first turn, where the two-lane became crowded again on both sides by towering firs.

As the wipers beat out a cadence on the windshield, and the heater finally began to warm the truck's frigid cab, Cade cast his gaze at the rearview mirror and watched for a second as the season's first snowfall, disturbed by the rig's passing, was sent into a frenzy, the big flakes jinking and swirling away hypnotically in a thousand different directions.

Once the right-hand curve straightened and the trees had fully closed in around the road, he stilled the wipers and, to beat back a forming band of condensation, set the heater blowing on the windshield. Having made hundreds of trips to Mount Hood's ski areas — at first either with his dad or by himself, and then later with Brook and Raven—Cade was no stranger to driving in snow and ice. However, though the F-650 had four-wheel-drive and was shod with tires that looked capable of tackling all that Antarctica could throw at it, piloting a behemoth such as this was nothing to be taken for granted. The growling V10 possessed the kind of power he'd never been exposed to. On pavement the thing handled like a dream, eating up bumps and powering through herds of zombies without missing a beat. But the old adage—four-wheel-drive can't help you stop—had been drilled into Cade's memory by his father starting in his teens when the two of them would make the hundred-and-twenty-mile round trip from their home in Portland, Oregon to the Timberline Lodge ski area in the family's venerable Jeep Grand Cherokee. So at the next snow-covered straightaway he came to, with his hands in the proper ten and two (also influenced by his father), he gripped the wheel even tighter and stood on the brakes. Instantly the foot pedal hammered back against his lug-soled boot as the four-wheel anti-lock brakes brought the beast's forward momentum from thirty miles-per-hour to a complete juddering stop within an astounding three truck lengths.

Impressive came to mind as Cade looked back at the chevron patterns pressed by the tires into the dusting of freshly fallen snow. At first the two laser-straight tracks behind the rig took a slight jog right then, presumably, when the hammering had first hit his foot and technology took over, they righted and showed no further deviation.

Time to see what Black Beauty (as Raven had named her) *can do accelerating from a standing stop.* Still clutching the wheel in a way that would've made Dad proud, Cade released the brake and pinned the pedal to the floorboard. Instantly the truck was pulling strongly ahead, and in the next beat the white emptiness of the snow-dusted meadows on both sides of the road was blazing by in his peripheral. Attempting to break the rear end free from the road's surface, he jinked the truck sharply left and then right to no adverse effect.

***

A handful of minutes after taking the rig through the impromptu Truck-Trend-Magazine-type of cold weather test, the stunted hill on which the abandoned quarry was located passed by on Cade's left. Due to the inclement weather, the top third, which was notched flat where the sheds and massive garage resided, was hidden behind a gauze-like veil of clouds.

The feeder road, however, was not. The bushes flanking it were beaten back by multiple vehicles making dozens of trips to empty the compound of its worthwhile contents. The muddy road was now partially snow-covered and easy to follow with the eye. The white stripe clinging to the side hill rose and fell and then disappeared to the right before reemerging and then vanishing again into the clouds.

Leaving the quarry road behind, Cade hit the straightaway bordering the Ogden River and upped the speed. Moving at a forty-mile-per-hour clip, in under ten minutes the Ford ate up the distance from the quarry road to the juncture where State Route 39 bisected State Route 16.

He tapped the brakes well before the crossing and then a football field's length short of the junction brought the Ford to a complete stop with the engine idling and heated air hissing through the vents. He trained the Steiner binoculars at the convergence of State Routes and glassed the area from right-to-left. He saw the jog in 16 where it went from a north/south run, took a right angle turn west and ran straight for a short distance before swinging back northbound again. A stone's throw north of the jog in driving terms was the intersection and the wrecked yellow school bus where a Z had literally gotten the drop on Brook and rent a baseball-sized bite of flesh from her back. The rear end of the bus was facing him and the wheels jutted out horizontally to the left, leaving a scant few yards of road on which to squeeze by.

Both Chief Jenkins' patrol Tahoe and a second vehicle that Cade expected to see here were gone. Instantly a tingle shot up his spine. He felt the combat juices begin to flow, sharpening his focus and slowing his heart rate.

Momentarily finding himself caught in a break between the slow-moving clouds, Cade lowered the field glasses and decided, despite this new development, to continue on into Woodruff and get this *shopping spree* over with.

Chapter 2

Cutting the air behind a big overhand swing, the razor-sharp blade created a faint whistle before embedding in the putrefying creature's skull. The honed steel, pre-treated with a liberal amount of gun oil and now slickened by a viscous mixture of congealed blood and lumpy gray matter, retreated easily from the six-inch chasm and in the next beat was tracking on a horizontal plane, backhand, towards the monsters vectoring in from the man's right. A deft back step and guttural grunt later, the former humans crumpled to the gore-slickened roadway like a couple of stunned boxers, their heads bouncing and spinning away, jaundiced eyes in the sockets still scanning the surroundings for fresh meat.

Overhead, a murder of crows, having been disturbed from their early morning feast, cussed and muttered, their shrill caws echoing off the cold metal skin of a nearby cluster of inert vehicles.

Hearing a dry rasp at his back, the man tore his eyes from the swirling black mass overhead and leveled his gaze at the sword clutched firmly in his two-handed grip. Reflected in the blade's polished surface, he watched a half-dozen biters round the SUV he'd left parked near the shoulder several yards north of him. He stood stock-still and waited for the dead to come to him. Energy was his friend. Especially with the temperature sitting somewhere in the low thirties and food high in calories and protein a dwindling commodity. Wait, watch, and at the last second uncoil like a bear trap was an energy saving technique he'd adopted early on.

The zombies doddered across the recently crushed mess of rotting flesh and bone. Protruding from the putrid morass, wisps of hair still attached to half-moons of crushed and shattered skull waved in a wind gust stout enough to cut through his oiled leather duster. Still he didn't move. With nothing to his fore, he watched them shamble closer, their stunted clumsy steps accentuated and clownlike as reflected back to him in the black blood dripping down the unwavering blade.

Once free from the obstacle course of human detritus, they picked up speed, moving in an almost lock-step fashion.

He remained still as their spindly arms elevated, straining for him.

Getting closer. Ten feet, he guessed, judging by the growing size of the leering faces mirrored back at him.

The raspy hisses rose over the wind and then morphed into hungry sounding guttural moans.

Five feet.

He imagined their crooked fingers kneading the air and the hairs on his neck sprang to attention. And though already chilled to the bone, gooseflesh rippled like an electric current up his ribcage.

Still he didn't move. He felt alive now more than ever.

Three feet, now.

Excitement building, his body shivered against the stiffening wind. Finally, with the calls of the dead in his ear and his toned muscles under incredible tension, he spun counter-clockwise, straightened his arms and locked his elbows, bringing the nearly invisible blade—now horizontal and reflecting sky—around like a natural extension of his body. Breaking his wrists just before impact enabled the razor-sharp edge to cleave cleanly through two skulls and enter a third before coming to rest against the female cadaver's ethmoid bone. She had been big in life, and her twice-dead weight nearly ripped the weapon from the man's calloused hands as gravity instantly yanked all two-hundred-plus pounds of her vertically to the pavement.

Three things happened near simultaneously as the man backpedaled left, still in control of the wildly vibrating blade. First off, the initial victim of his roundhouse, suddenly minus the top third of its skull, staggered forward, the final impulses sent from the now-bisected brain urging pustule-covered arms to grasp the meat that was no longer occupying the last place registered in its dead gaze. A fraction of a second after the first to meet the blade—arms outstretched, crooked fingers still blindly probing thin air—crumpled to the pavement, the rotten interloper to its right, bald head cleaved clean through on a forty-five from ear to crown, tumbled sideways over the plus-sized corpse, the energy from it meeting the ground still rippling through its decay-ravaged blubber.

Three down, three to go, crossed his mind even as he was acting on muscle memory and dropping them one at a time behind three efficient downward strokes, separated by a barely perceptible right to left pivot, and only a half heartbeat's time between each lethal blow.

Chapter 3

On the LCD screen in the F-650, north/south-running State Route 16 was represented by a thick yellow line intersected by eastbound 39. As soon as Cade turned north onto the straight stretch of two-lane, he saw a sign indicating 16 would soon turn into Main Street, which bisected the blink-and-you'd-miss-it town of Woodruff. On the screen, the name change was already indicated in blue font and, like seedlings growing in time-lapse photography, smaller yellow lines representing side streets began sprouting left and right off the main drag.

He drove on for a few blocks and, seeing nothing but a burned-out mom and pop store and fields in the distance, shrouded by a gray haze of falling snow, he decided to double back and work his way east, starting with the nearest cross street.

He made a quick U-turn and, nearing East Center Street, turned his attention to a mid-sized passenger car that had been pushed up onto the curb. It was wedged tight nose first between a light pole and a mature oak, the latter doing considerable damage to the passenger side and creasing a sharp V into the roofline. The sheet metal reflecting the image of Cade's ride was dented and dirty and scratches marred the once-shiny black paint. There was a long dead corpse behind the wheel, its skeletal hands still clutched the misshapen steering wheel and, like a big white tongue, the deflated airbag draped from the torn leather housing and onto the unfortunate victim's lap. And speaking to the considerable forces that delivered the large Cadillac DTS and driver to their final resting place, all of the glass in the doors was blown out and it sat on four flat tires. On the ground, refracting the newly fallen snow and looking oddly out of place, shards of safety glass thrown under the vehicle's rockers and bumpers sparkled and shimmered as he let his foot off the brake and started the truck moving again.

Half a block south of the mangled luxury car, Cade's eye was drawn right to the waist-high hedge paralleling the sidewalk and separating an automotive shop from Main Street. Something about the entire run looked odd, like it had been trampled recently. From the corner of Center to the block's midpoint, the dense, squared-off shrub angled sharply away from the street, and the snow that dusted everything else—nonexistent.

On the expansive but nearly empty parking lot to the lee side of the shrubs, a dozen or so cars waiting for service they would never receive were pushed up tight against what appeared to be the shop's office and an adjacent rollup door, which was battered and bowing inward.

Cade stopped the truck, swung his gaze back to the road, and suddenly the cause of the damage dawned on him. Where he was sitting, Main and Center, was *the* chokepoint on the dead's migratory route where State Route 16 narrowed, and the roaming hordes, due to their size and mass capable of moving vehicles and shoving houses off their foundations, came against the most resistance. Further scrutiny revealed more damage from the shambling masses. A trio of power poles on the east side of Main were leaning away from the street at about the same angle as the hedges opposite them. The lines once supplying power to the fix-it shop and nearby business were all stretched laser-straight overhead under great tension and looked as if they might give way at any moment. Cade's eyes touched upon the sidewalk and he couldn't decide if the upheaved concrete at the base of the poles was keeping them from toppling completely or if the taut supply lines were doing the job. At any rate, sitting in the idling truck anywhere near the listing poles was asking for a Darwin Award, so he continued on and hooked the next left at Center.

A little baffled that so far he hadn't spotted a single Z in downtown Woodruff, he drove walking-speed east for a full block. At the next intersection, he spied the business where Brook's foraging foray had nearly been derailed. The words on the shingle hanging over the front door read, "Back in the Saddle Rehab." Although he knew the major details of the ill-fated stop just off of Main Street, he'd been spared the minor ones, the first of which he now found to be false advertising, because it was here where Wilson had been nearly *bucked* out of the reversing Raptor and into the arms of the dead. And it was also here where Chief was bit in the *saddle,* so to speak.

Secondly, the building looked much smaller in person than Wilson's description of it. It struck Cade as more *residence* than business. Just a little two-story house on a quarter of the block surrounded by a big unimproved parking lot. A sea of gravel, in fact. Therefore, Cade decided to swing by on his way out of town to procure the items on the list he presumed would be there. A quick in-and-out. Crossing T's and dotting I's.

Two minutes.

Tops.

Cade scanned all points of the compass and still nothing was moving. Seeing that Woodruff suddenly ended three blocks east, he brought the Steiners up and swept his gaze over a cluster of buildings just up the road beyond the edge of town.

On a knuckle of land and set back south of the road were a trio of prefabbed homes. The unremarkable single-story items were made from two halves constructed someplace else, trucked here, and then hemmed up on site. They were placed on side by side lots and had identical snow-covered driveways leading up from the road to flatly graded rectangles all white with snow and large enough to accommodate a pair of vehicles. Probably a family plat divided for siblings, Cade guessed.

He snatched up the CB and hailed Seth, who for the day was acting as Chief of Security, a position created by Duncan not only to instill a certain sense of pride in the job, but also to make the solitary experience attractive to others besides just Heidi, who, through the marvels of modern pharmaceuticals, was quickly bouncing back from her month-long malaise and could only be pried off the shortwave radio using the jaws-of-life.

Seth answered at once and, after a brief back-and-forth, assured Cade, save for the wet snow having already accumulated on the CCTV domes, that all was well at the compound.

"I'm going dark for a few minutes," Cade said. "I want to check out some mobile homes east of the Woodruff main drag."

"On Main Street?"

"No. About a half a mile east on"—he craned around to see the sign—"looks like I'll be six or eight blocks east of Main on Center Street. Woodruff isn't exactly a sprawling metropolis."

"Roger that," replied Seth. There was a clicking sound that Cade took to be the younger man's thumb releasing the switch on the microphone attached to the base unit. Then, out of the blue, the silence in the cab was broken when Max let out a low guttural growl. Cade looked to see the shepherd—ears drawn back and teeth bared—on the seatback and looking focused on something through the truck's smoked rear window.

With the volume knob trapped between thumb and finger, Cade was about to power off the CB when Seth's voice came through the speaker. "You still there?" he asked, a sense of urgency in his voice.

"Roger that. What's up?" Listening for a response, Cade again scanned his surroundings, only to find that he'd drawn some unwanted attention. Attracted to the idling engine, a small group of walking dead had just emerged onto Center Street roughly a block east of Main. After a couple of seconds of dead air, during which Cade kept his eyes locked on the rearview mirror and watched the dead spread out shoulder to shoulder across the yellow line, Seth finally came on and promised he would be right back as soon as he found the list of new requests he had misplaced.

"You gave me the list."

"These are *additions* to that list."

"Make it quick, Seth. I've got Zs on my six and I've got work to do," Cade answered back irritably.

Seth made no reply to that. So Cade let his foot off the brake and, driving one-handed with the CB in the other, covered half the distance to the trio of structures on the hill. He soon grew impatient and was on the verge of silencing the radio altogether, more so to conserve the batteries than from a reluctance to talk to the kid, when Seth beat him to the punch. "Glenda wants to know if you can read the writing on her list."

"I learned cursive in school," Cade replied.

"You *are* old," said Seth.

"Spit it out."

"She wants to add some things to it."

"Go ahead, I'll commit them to memory."

"You sure?"

"Can't write, I'm driving. And Max isn't growing an opposable thumb any time soon, so spit it out."

"Suit yourself." Seth rattled off a laundry list of stuff Glenda thought of after compiling her first fairly lengthy list. Then Seth tacked on a couple of things for himself: magazines, a handheld video game, batteries—which were already on the first list as well as Cade's own mental list. There was a pause and then, in a soft voice, as if he was asking for the world, Seth requested a Snickers bar if Cade came across one.

"Who would run from Zs and leave their last Snickers behind?" Cade said, incredulous.

"Good point," Seth conceded. "In that case, then. Any chocolate will do."

"Gotta be aboveboard with you, Sport. If I come across a Snickers ... I'm keeping it all to myself," said Cade, smiling. "Finders keepers. Spoils of war. Besides, what you don't know, won't hurt you."

"Come on," replied Seth. "That's not fair. I've got a sweet tooth and I'm sick of *frickin* MRE pound cake."

Max issued another ominous rumbling warning.

"Any Mounds Bars I find have Seth written all over them," Cade said, laughing.

"Keep 'em. Those and Baby Ruth are the worst," Seth fired back. "Especially after watching *Caddyshack*."

Cade wheeled the truck right, muscling it one-handed onto the driveway. "I thought you had a *cheese* tooth," he said, eyes scanning the squat dwelling's darkened windows.

"Fine," Seth said, dejection evident in his tone. "I'll take the crumbs."

"Roger that," said Cade. He switched the radio off and stowed it in a cargo pocket. He stuffed the yellow sheet torn from a legal pad and completely filled with handwritten requests in another. With the sound of gravel crunching under the rig's off-road tires, he halved his speed and covered the last thirty feet to the empty parking pad, never taking his eyes off the curtain-shrouded windows, of which there were three. The two windows bookending the dwelling looked to be four foot tall by six wide and situated between them, but closer to the one on the left, was another half their size and frosted. In his mind, working left to right, Cade paired each window with a room: *bed, bath* and, to the right of the garish-looking bright-red front door, *living.* Presumably he would find the kitchen at the right rear corner opposite the living room. And if that was the case, then no doubt a hallway and closet and second bedroom, in that order, would finish off the back half of the prefab.

Easy enough.

Cade reached to the passenger side footwell and retrieved the red Kelty backpack he'd borrowed from Daymon. Forgoing the carbine for now, he plucked the Glock from the center console and looked over his shoulder at Max. "Coming or staying?"

Max moved toward the open door, stub tail twitching furiously.

"Coming, obviously," Cade stated. "I want to check something first." He toggled out of the navigation system and then fooled with the buttons below the truck's LCD display. After a few seconds of trial-and-error, he called up a screen displaying the current outside temperature and saw that it was thirty degrees and probably dropping. He sat there for a bit, listening to the soft patter of snow hitting the metal roof overhead. Saw big fluffy flakes alight on the windshield, break apart and begin the slow slide toward the static wipers. The flakes landing on the warm hood, however, didn't stand a chance, some melting away at once and running off in all different directions, while others collapsed instantly, creating dime-sized pools on the flat portions of the black slab of sheet metal.

He watched the temperature drop another degree from 30 to 29 then climbed from the Ford, waited for Max to bound by him, closed the door and locked the truck using the key.

Max beat Cade to the black *Welcome* mat in front of the contrasting red door and was sitting there, tail twitching, and staring over his shoulder as his master-for-the-moment approached.

"All clear?"

Max pawed at the mat.

Cade pounded the door with a closed fist, calling out, "Anyone home?" He pressed his ear to its cold surface and listened hard. A handful of seconds passed. He craned and checked the windows for movement then, raising his Glock, flicked his eyes to Max, who was peering up expectantly. "Sounds empty inside."

As per usual in the zombie apocalypse, the door was locked. So Cade put the sole of his size nine desert boot to work delivering a solid kick just left of the knob and deadbolt. On impact an electric shiver ran up his right shin, a mild ache started in his ankle, and there was a sharp crack as wood split and the door flung open. A second dull thud reverberated about the front room as the inside knob impacted drywall, producing a nice-sized dimple there.

Fingers tented, Cade met the rebounding door, stopping it mid-swing. "Anyone home?" he asked again, the earlier tone of formality gone from his voice.

Nothing.

Once he'd crossed the threshold and was standing on the dingy white square of linoleum passing as the foyer, the former Delta operator cocked an ear toward the back of the house and sniffed the air. Hearing nothing, he shrugged off the pack and, with Max sitting on his haunches and facing the hall to the left, closed the destroyed door and barricaded it with an overstuffed loveseat.

"Smells like mold," said Cade, the running commentary unnecessary but helping to pass the time. "Much better than death ... eh, boy?"

He pulled the curtains to the living room window and instantly the front room and kitchen was awash with flat white light cast off the fallen snow outside.

The nearby kitchen was small by most standards. It contained the usual stove and fridge in white enamel, but no dishwasher. The sink was filled with soiled dishes and contained an inch of water, the source of the sour smell. In a drawer he found two packages of Duracell batteries, D and C cells, four of each; not enough to satisfy that portion of the list, but a good start nonetheless. He stuffed the batteries in the pack and proceeded to rifle through the cupboards, spilling anything resembling a spice or seasoning into the Kelty's gaping top opening. A long winter was ahead of them, he figured. The deer meat Tran had dried and squirreled away from the *grazers* in the group wouldn't last them long, and the considerable stores of beans and rice Logan had stockpiled in the dry storage would get old real quick without the added kick of the scavenged spices.

In the cupboard were a few cans of various types of soups and vegetables. *Strike one. No cheese, Snickers, or chocolate.* Done in the kitchen, Cade shouldered the pack, pulled out Glenda's personal list, and saw that most of the items on it were the kinds of things you'd find in a bathroom. So he walked past his four-legged sentry and down the hall, but not before peering out the picture window dominating the wall above the back of the sofa. He saw the Ford had collected more snow and was now two-tone, white over black. Beyond the truck, still a number of blocks away, the cluster of Zs trundled up the slight grade, seemingly leaning into the driving flurries, looking every bit like they were on the verge of being stuck fast in quicksand.

He turned from the window and padded down the hall to the bathroom, which was only as wide as the tub/shower combo built into the back wall. Compared to the front room this one was a cave, the outside light barely penetrating the frosted window and opaque shower curtain.

On the moldy tile floor was a pile of paper wrappers and the slick backings from a dozen Curad bandages. An empty and partially crushed box labeled "STERILE GAUZE WRAP" sat amongst the hastily discarded wrappers. The sink was empty, but the previous waterline was a crusty reddish-black stripe, and below it the white enamel was tinted pink. Cade was no Sherlock Holmes, but it was clear, based on the evidence, that someone had cleaned a wound and prepared a makeshift field dressing here.

Feeling around the mirror, he found a catch. Pressing it let the door swing away from the wall, which revealed the contents of a recessed medicine cabinet. Three shelves. Lots of antacids and creams but only four opaque orange bottles, all with childproof caps and instructions and warnings—both in writing and portrayed by symbols—printed on the labels.

After a cursory glance, and finding that only one of the bottles contained some kind of a drug with a long multi-syllable name that matched Glenda's cursive, he tossed them all, along with the creams, into the pack.

The bedroom at the end of the single-wide screamed bachelor. There was an unfinished lodgepole pine twin bed pushed against the outside wall. A matching nightstand and dresser flanked the bed, which was lit up by horizontal bars of light spilling in through the dust-coated venetian blinds. Nothing he saw from the earth tone covers to the antler lamp on the nightstand suggested a woman lived here.

He rifled through the clothes left behind in the dresser and crammed anything made from fleece or wool into the pack. There was nothing of interest in the closet. He checked under the bed and found only dust bunnies. Lastly, he lifted the mattress off the box spring and looked there only because it would nag at him later if he hadn't.

"One room to go … where is everybody, Max?"

Nothing.

"You bark when you hear 'em. OK, Max?"

Still nothing.

Max yawned wide and then rested his head back down on his outstretched front legs.

Before leaving the room, Cade skirted the bed, parted the horizontal blinds and took a peek. Though the snow cut down on the visibility, it seemed the Zs trudging up Center Street had geared down, going from barely moving to statue still. The ramifications of what he was witnessing hit him like a ton of bricks. Apparently freezing temperatures coupled with the wind-chill was doing to the walking dead what up until now only a quick double-tap or dagger to the brain could accomplish—render them immobile. Though only temporary, he guessed, he would take it nonetheless.

The second bedroom left Cade wide-eyed. It was one part office containing some of the things on his list and two parts science fiction geek nirvana complete with sculpted statues of popular and, not so, superheroes. Mostly Marvel and, ironically, the first one he recognized was of Captain America with his red, white, and blue shield raised and at the ready. The statue next to Cap was Wolverine in his trademark pre-battle pose, hunched over, arms curled with the razor-sharp adamantium claws fully extended, their angular tips nearly touching up front. There were numerous homages to Star Wars: figures on a shelf and spaceships hanging from the ceiling. For a moment Cade was twenty and naive and the world was back to normal. No walking dead. No opportunistic bandits. Just a full life ahead of him and Brook.

A hot tear traced his cheek as he reminisced.

In the front room Max growled at something then came padding into the man cave slash shrine assembled by an adult unwilling to let go of days gone by.

The dog gave Cade the usual head tilted sideways look that seemed to be saying: *Hurry the hell up.*

"Just like a good wingman … reminding me to quit crying and get the lead out." Cade relieved the office of the laptop on the desk. Stuffed it, the power cords, and a stack of software CDs and DVD movies that he didn't bother to inventory into the bulging pack.

Turning to leave, he caught sight of himself in the mirrored closet doors. Simultaneously he looked ten years younger and ten older. The former impression was due to body mass alone—he was now more muscled up top and slimmer in the waist. Just about how he'd been put together at twenty-five years of age. The latter, however, he based on the newly formed wrinkles on his forehead and prominent, deep crow's feet in the corners of his eyes. Wearing a combination scowl and thousand-yard stare, the face staring back looked more forty-five than his chronological age of thirty-five. Hell, he thought, in a matter of months the zombie apocalypse had prematurely aged him. If things continued the way they had been going, in a few more people would be mistaking him for Duncan.

Shaking his head at the mere thought of looking anything like the old Vietnam vet, he slid the closet door open and was instantly rid of the stranger staring back at him.

In a box at the bottom of the closet, he found a handheld video game of some sort and a dozen tiny cartridges to go with it. They went in his pocket and he pushed both mirrored doors to the right. What he saw there defied all logic based on the rest of the pieces of the puzzle already revealed. Belying the bare bones nature of the dwelling, secured to the back wall of the closet was a gun safe more at home in a McMansion than a doublewide. He tried moving the circular wheel affixed to the thousand-dollar-item's door. It didn't budge, and he had no heavy tools nor the time to crack the thing. If only Tice were here with his high-tech toys, he thought as he slid the door shut and found himself once again staring at his aged visage.

After flipping his scraggly bearded reflection the bird, he called Max and retraced his steps through the house and stopped before the closed door leading into the attached garage.

Chapter 4

In the span of a couple of minutes, less time than it takes to boil an egg soft, the man and his blade had reduced all of the zombies within sight to motionless forms, their blood black and pooling on the pristine blanket of white. Here and there a severed head or arm or leg lay where it had fallen after meeting ancestral steel.

With a grim look on his face, the man ran a scrap of oiled cloth up one side of the blade and down the other. Satisfied, he dropped the sullied rag to the ground, where it landed with a soft squelch and left a vibrant halo of red on the virgin patch of snow. Acting on the assumption that the main column of dead was well out of earshot, he shrugged off the gilded scabbard and slipped the edged weapon home. He stowed it behind the driver's seat and clambered into the SUV. Wanting to spend as little time as possible exposed on the open stretch of road, he quickly turned the engine over. Working the wheel hand-over-hand, he turned a tight right and eventually had the rig crawling eastbound up the winding, snow-covered drive toward the house and big red barn.

The diesel engine growled and chugged, fighting both the incline and the semi-worn tires' inability to maintain traction in the slushy muddy mixture churned up by them. Passing by on the left were the remains of what once were beautiful animals. Reduced to bones and tufts of fur by the hungry birds, the carcasses looked ghostly wearing the fresh layer of snow.

The man's only reason for driving this tired old war wagon was its familiarity to the handful of survivors still residing in the border area between Wyoming and Utah. Its official-looking appearance carried with it a certain psychological edge. But why in the world his new son-in-law favored this throwback to the Cold War over all of the newer unmanned vehicles standing silent sentry over failed roadblocks on the Interstates and State Routes leading into and out of Salt Lake City was a mystery never to be solved, he conceded after a moment's thought. And he supposed so was his daughter Lena's decision to pick the man as her husband from the pool of dozens of worthy candidates she had grown up alongside.

He heard the transmission slipping as the truck made the final turn and the two-story house and looming red and white barn door filled the mud-spattered windshield. He wheeled the SUV around a rusted piece of antique farm machinery partially blocking the drive and pulled to a halt, nose in to the fence surrounding the massive pasture now devoid of anything living.

The man stilled the engine, shifted his gaze to the front porch and, just like clockwork, the silver-haired old man was emerging from the screen door with a long-gun held at a low ready.

The driver again unfolded his considerable frame from behind the wheel. Without acknowledging the older man, he hinged the driver's seat forward and reached in and came out with a large white cylindrical object. Set it on the snow-covered gravel and reached in and withdrew a second identical item. Unarmed, the man walked the distance from his SUV to the porch, one cumbersome propane cylinder swinging from each of his baseball-mitt-sized hands. "Ray," he said, forcing a smile. "And Helen's upstairs with the crosshairs on my head, I presume."

Squinting against the snow glare, the man on the elevated and covered porch lowered his shotgun and, with one arm outstretched, beckoned for the monster of a man to join him on the porch. "Alexander Dregan, propane baron, scholar and a gentleman." *Switzerland*, thought Ray in direct opposition to his words. He went on, "Helen and I weren't expecting another visit from you until ... week after next."

"I wanted to get ahead of the weather," Dregan said. He stopped at the stairs and effortlessly lifted the propane tanks and displayed them, arms outstretched like a T. "I brought Helen refills.

Hope she has pie. And a few boxes of five-five-six. We've been doing a lot of foraging east, and strangely enough, the pickings in the ammo department are slim to none. And *none* seems to be taking over the neighborhood."

Ray trapped the shotgun in the crook of his arm. He held the screen door open and stepped aside. "As they say ... timing is everything. Five hundred rounds are yours if you keep the cylinders coming through winter. And Helen just so happened to have baked a pie. Had me two slices last night. Almost went in for a third—"

"I had to slap Ray's hand away," said a voice from somewhere inside the house.

"Old Ray's still getting frisky with you, eh Helen?" Dregan said, craning his head in the door before crossing the threshold. "Where do you want these?"

Stepping from the gloom, stubby scoped carbine in hand, Helen replied, "I'm the *randy* one." Then, abruptly, her tone going all business, she added, "You can put those out the kitchen door with the others. And take the empties with you when you leave, won't you please, Mister Dregan."

Ray followed the caller inside and, before closing the doors, cast a furtive glance over his shoulder at the camouflaged SUV and the driveway winding out behind it.

The door lock snicked shut behind him and Dregan heard Ray ask how the hunt for his daughter's killer was going. To which Dregan grunted and said, "Sore subject. My sons ... they want me to arm up and hunt them down. Me, I am more inclined to wait until spring and let them come to me. That way we're not fighting the weather and vehicle breakdowns."

"Not to mention the *deaders*," added Helen, opening the door leading out to the enclosed back porch for the hulking man.

Again Dregan grunted, but more from the exertion of easing the tanks down softly than a preamble to voicing a thought. He said nothing and stepped back into the kitchen, rubbing his calloused hands together.

Shutting the chill out, Helen closed the back door and rearranged the thick sheet of plastic weatherproofing to keep out the drafts. Then she shuffled over to the propane-fired heater and warmed her hands. Finally, without making eye contact, she said, "Almanac is predicting a doozy of a winter."

Nothing but small talk, thought Dregan. He said, "Farmer's Almanac didn't predict the scourge of dead, did it?"

"No … but it was kind of inevitable the way we were treating our Mother Earth."

Dregan rolled his eyes. He said, "About Lena's murderers. Have you seen any sign of them or that big truck since I was here last?"

"No, we haven't," answered Ray immediately. "Again, you're jumping to conclusions. Helen made it abundantly clear the last time you were here … and every time prior … that we *only* offered them harbor from the dead. Nothing more. Nothing less. For all *we* know … they had nothing to do with the ambush and killings. Maybe it was coincidence."

"That's alright, Ray. Believe what you will"—the big man cracked his knuckles—"I've got the patience of Job. One way or another they'll show their faces around here again and you'll call me and then we will find out once and for all."

Helen wrapped the remains of the pumpkin pie in wax paper and placed it on the counter near Dregan. She looked up at him and said in a soft voice, "They didn't seem like killers. Not by a long shot."

"We told you … most of them were kids," said Ray. "You're educated, Alexander. You knew who Nietzsche was when I first met you. One of the few who has. What would those folks with the nice vehicles and weapons have to gain from killing a couple of teenagers driving *that*?" And though he couldn't see it, he hooked a thumb over his shoulder in the direction where the surplus Chevy was parked.

"Because, Ray," Dregan said calmly. "*That* vehicle was stripped of supplies. Food. Ammunition. Their packs and weapons."

"Could have been the bandits from up North," said Helen, the bun of hair on back of her head coming loose and bouncing with each nod of her head. "I told you that the woman and kids were just out hunting for medical supplies for her daughter."

"Yes … you … did," said Dregan. "And to your credit, that story hasn't changed. But those people"—he clucked his tongue and looked Helen in the eye—"they were the only ones in the vicinity when the crime occurred. And the Judge says that's sufficient evidence to bring them to trial."

"Can't you just give them the benefit of the doubt?"

"No, Helen, I can't. I've never believed in coincidence. And blood ... it's always been thicker than benefit of the doubt."

Helen pulled a chair in from the dining room, sat down and stared up at the bearded man leaning against the doorjamb. "If they do come back and we call you, what are you planning on doing with them?"

Dregan said. "*I* plan on letting my gut be the judge and jury—"

Helen finished "—and executioner." She pursed her lips, eyes unwavering.

The big man nodded. "Magdalena *was* my baby girl. If it comes to that, I'll make sure the punishment surpasses the crime."

Switzerland, thought Helen. She said, "We have the CB you left us." She steepled her fingers and looked into his blue eyes. "But first we'll let *our* guts decide whether we're calling you or not."

Dregan smiled and turned back to face Ray, who had retrieved the shotgun while Helen had the big man's undivided attention. He stared down and met Ray's eyes. Then slowly lowered his gaze to the shotgun aimed at his gut. "I can't commute a sentence If I've no gut to listen to." He reached out and with one finger gently moved the barrel a few degrees right until the blast would destroy the plastic-ensconced porch door and not his breadbasket.

Ray didn't reacquire.

Détente, thought Dregan. He was still alive. So he reached inside a pocket, slowly, and came out with a package of batteries, which he tossed onto the cutting board. "For the radio. Just in case for some reason it's not working when they return."

Ray's eyes narrowed, then he handed over the sizeable brick of ammunition they'd promised the self-professed propane baron of Salt Lake City.

Butcher knife now in hand, Helen smiled and motioned with it toward the front door. "Thanks for the propane. Best not forget your pie on the way out, sweetie."

Chapter 5

The single-car garage was nearly empty and illuminated only by slivers of flat light working their way between the horizontal slats of a set of aluminum blinds. The owner of the house, definitely not a car guy, used the space exclusively for storing lawn beautification and gardening items. A workbench was covered with bags of fertilizer and other growth aids, all emblazoned with big colorful eye-catching font touting optimal PH levels and assorted added minerals and the like. *No use.* However, there were several tired-looking boxes, stressed and filled to overflowing with scores of small packets filled with all manner of seeds. Upon closer inspection, Cade was displeased to find the ratio of flowers and vegetables leaning more towards the former column.

Under the bench was a lawnmower, trimmer, rusted rototiller and industrial-sized plastic spray bottles with marks for calculating measurements and handled pumps for pressurizing the mix. Save for the meager supply of vegetable seeds which got dumped into the pack, and a nearly full fifty-five-pound bag of dry dog food which Max had shown keen interest in and Cade had promptly heaved over his shoulder, there was nothing else of use to either of them.

Recalling some items not on the list but logged into his memory earlier, Cade grabbed a paper sack with stiff and sturdy handles from under the sink in the kitchen. Nose wrinkled against the stench from the sink, he padded through the front room and transited the hall to the bedroom. Without hesitation, he went straight for the bookshelf he'd spotted earlier and emptied two rows of paperbacks into the grocery bag. As they tumbled from the shelves, the titles and author's names on the spines and covers registered: *Tolkien, Heinlein, Bradbury, Sagan, Asimov, Niven, Goodkind.* The list went on and the bag grew heavy as all of the greats passed in front of his eyes and vanished inside. He snatched a trade paperback off the top shelf and examined the cover. Saw the book was by an author named *Forstchen* and the title was *One Second After.* The blurb on the back cover revealed the book was about an EMP attack on the Eastern Seaboard of the United States; a catastrophe he'd gladly embrace over the current widespread Omega outbreak and resulting armies of flesh-seeking walking dead. But the reality of the matter for both the book's content and what was happening all around the world was that there was no reset button for either. No way to bring those already turned back to the side of the living. And where Omega was concerned, time was of the essence. So, making himself a mental note to crack it open later, he tossed the book atop the others and, bag in hand, retraced his steps down the hall.

A quick glance out the window told him the temperature had fallen since he'd been inside. The big, fast-falling flakes had seemingly been supersized and were now floating to earth like goose down. The kind of snow he and Brook sought out in their youth. Oftentimes elusive in the Pacific Northwest, deep fluffy powder was his favorite surface to ride in the world. The waist-high stuff his petite wife plowed through wearing a wide smile.

Youth *not* wasted on the young, he thought, focusing on the dead down the hill. The further drop in temperature seemed to have affected them greatly. Though they were still moving his way, uphill, their pace was glacially slow. That was the good news.

Grabbing his attention a tick later was a sight that wouldn't have even registered on his give-a-shit-meter had it been moving at a normal pace. However, it wasn't. In addition, the sheer numbers involved were staggering. Hundreds, if not more than a thousand migrating flesh eaters—which in Cade's mind after having seen the hordes in Denver and Los Angeles and at the Conex roadblock standing between Ogden and Huntsville, still constituted a herd—a grouping not large enough to move cars and topple poles, yet still a force to be wary of. Under normal circumstances, he would lay low and let them pass on by, but this turn of events was far from normal. Trying to wait them out as slow as they were moving might get him snowed in and trapped outside the wire overnight. The former he could dig out of. The latter was unacceptable. The last time he'd been trapped in a house by the dead his life had been spared by the appearance of a Black Hawk helicopter with Duncan at the controls. This time, however, if the slow-moving train of death somehow got wind of him and encircled the home, these flimsy pre-fab walls wouldn't last an hour under the kind of force numbers like that were capable of exerting.

But he had a plan. So he pushed the loveseat aside, opened the broken door, and let Max outside first. Forgoing the keyless entry for fear the dead might hear the alarm chirp, he opened the Ford with the key and let the dog in. The overstuffed Kelty, unwieldy bag of Purina dog chow, and paper sack full of reading material all went into the backseat area with Max. After spilling out a liberal amount of dog food onto the floorboards for the shepherd, Cade gently closed the rear passenger door, climbed behind the wheel, and pulled his door shut with care.

Acutely aware of how fast and far sound could travel in the open, before firing the big V10, Cade planned his egress route from the vantage the higher ground afforded. By the time he came to the most obvious conclusion, the dead had seemingly ceased all forward movement and appeared frozen in place due west of the rehab place.

Adding a mental wrinkle to his plan, which he figured would be doable only on account of this newfound turn of events, he started the motor and jockeyed the truck around on the patch of snow-covered gravel.

Fear the reaper, crossed his mind as he wheeled the F-650 down the narrow gravel drive and what he hoped to be a quick in-and-out stop at *Back in the Saddle Rehabilitation.* And if all went as planned there, hopefully an uneventful meet-and-greet with the unmoving zombie herd.

Chapter 6

The first missile came extremely close to taking out Daymon's eye. However, just as he was reacting to the first near miss, the second whizzing projectile, coming from the opposite direction, caught him full force on the top of his head. He let out a yelp and a plume of his own breath enveloped his face as he went to the ground on all fours, numbed hands feeling around blindly for something to fight back with.

"Incoming," bellowed Wilson as he dove, joining Daymon on the crushed grass where he instantly began pulling armfuls of heavy snow close to his body.

Keeping his head down just below the bent grass stalks demarking the edge of his and Duncan's sad attempt at creating an alien crop-circle, Daymon slowly walked a three-sixty—still on all fours—and was able to locate both enemy positions.

A blur of white shot by a foot over their heads from the direction Jamie and the others were holed up.

By the time Daymon was back to facing Wilson, the scrappy redhead had already produced half a dozen perfectly formed snowballs each the size of a navel orange. Then Daymon noticed the twenty-year-old's breath billow up around his ever-present camouflage boonie hat and knew instantly their position was given away. So he grabbed two of the snowballs, winked at Wilson, and laid flat. Tucking his arms in, he logrolled a few feet left and came up to his knees, throwing arm cocked, eyes scanning for a target. Which he found a few feet left of where he'd initially spotted movement.

Daymon raised up on his knees, arm cocked and the target in his crosshairs. He let fly with everything he had in him, but before he could see if the snowball had found its mark, there was an explosion of pain behind his eyes and he fell back down onto his stomach, uttering obscenities and trying to blink his eyesight back so he could go kick the shit out of the headhunting waste of skin who had beaned him.

North of Ray and Helen's Home

Dregan drove north on 16 with the venerable Chevy dropped into four-wheel-drive and Helen's mirthless smile still etched in his mind's eye. The snow was sticking hard to the road now, and though the military version of the K5 had a fairly strong engine under the hood, keeping it from fishtailing around the corners while rolling on worn tires was a full time job.

So he took the curves like he imagined Helen would—slow and cautious. On the straightaways, however, trying to make up for lost time, he kicked the speed up a bit. And it was on one of these stretches, moving at a clip above the posted limit, when a sudden gust threw the snow horizontal at the windshield and visibility was reduced to only a couple of car lengths.

Dregan doubled down on his grip on the wheel and was easing off the accelerator when a human form materialized fast out of the clutter. Facing away dead center in the road, the oblivious biter made no move to acquire the engine noise that Dregan was certain it could hear. Instead, in the few seconds during which he had a decision to make, Dregan saw the thing take only one sluggish step forward. Then, the reaction severely delayed, its head began a slow sweep left in the general direction of the rapidly approaching SUV.

Turn evasively to avoid the thing and risk driving into the ditch, or mow it over like the ones by Helen's place?

Grimacing, Dregan chose the latter. The impact juddered the vehicle to the frame and the unsuspecting shambler folded under the bumper like it had been sucked up by a gigantic Hoover. There was a chorus of bangs and bones crunched as a hundred and some odd pounds of frigid flesh ping-ponged between the undercarriage and road. A tick later the noises ceased and it was spit out, arms and legs windmilling until it finally came to rest face down on the shoulder.

Cursing himself for choosing the Blazer over the Tahoe or one of the military vehicles, he pulled over to the shoulder, more so out of habit than the possibility a vehicle would rear end him if he chose to do so on the centerline.

He dropped the transmission into *Park* and, in the sideview mirror, watched the dead thing for a moment. In its futile slow-motion attempt at standing, hands and feet slipping on the slickened road, its drunken movements made Dregan think of a newborn foal trying to stand—not a biter recovering from a catastrophic collision it neither felt, nor cared one way or the other about.

Clearly the weather was affecting these things more by the minute. He reached for the stereo and kicked the volume up so he could hear the string section over the buffeting wind. When his gaze swung back to the mirror, the biter on the road behind him was lying flat and not moving. *Either it was giving up*, he thought, something he had never witnessed the dead do, especially with prey in sight, *or the cold shocked it into suspended animation.*

He spent a minute staring at its reverse reflection. One elbow, bent at an impossible angle, jutted out from underneath its body and was pressed against its cheek. Dregan remembered Lena sleeping in her crib all funny like that, oh so long ago. Only her legs hadn't been twisted around one another, feet pointing skyward like some kind of a freak show contortionist.

Dregan pushed the memory of his second born from his head and, just about the time he'd been sold on the cold-shocked theory, the abomination pushed its upper body off the road and again started in on the baby foal routine.

"Fuck me," Dregan said, banging his palm on the steering wheel. "Shit, shit, shit."

After a prolonged effort, somehow the battered creature made it to its knees. A single rib bone, curving unnaturally outward, protruded through its threadbare shirt. A gust of wind kicked up, ruffling the thin fabric and with enough force to topple the creature back to the road where, exhibiting the same blind determination, it began the arduous process of picking itself up again.

Seeing the tenaciousness on display brought to mind the herd that was somewhere up ahead. *No reason to catch up to them just yet*, he thought. *No matter the effect the dropping mercury was having on them.* Handling a dozen semi-sluggish biters by himself, no problem. Being near several hundred all by himself—sluggish or not—that made his skin crawl. Even inside the warm truck he could feel the imagined crush of clammy flesh and the wanting frigid hands tearing at his clothes in search of firm purchase.

He had seen some of the dead play possum so, until he was sure what he was up against, discretion would have to win out over valor. No reason to go rushing headlong down the State Route. He had nowhere to be. So he turned up the volume a little bit more and, with Bach serenading him, cast his gaze to the east and stared longingly at the thin band of clear blue sky sandwiched between the distant mountains and tail end of the storm.

Seeing the biter start to crawl hand over road-rashed hand, he locked the door and peered down at the gas gauge, seeing that it was showing three-quarters full. *Good!* The need to stay warm trumping a few ounces of wasted diesel, he opted to let the engine idle and again kicked his seat back and savored the Mozart flowing out of the aftermarket set of speakers.

Chapter 7

Cade sat in the warm truck at the end of the long drive and watched the herd inch down Main Street. After twenty long minutes it became crystal clear to him that they were going nowhere soon. And at the pace they were moving—if in fact they were still ambulatory at this point in time—the Second Coming would likely occur before the entire column made it north of Main and Center. So with his next stop no longer being dictated by the fear that he might become trapped anywhere by the herd, he hooked a right out of the driveway and onto Center and then headed east instead of west, taking him away from the rehab place. He drove for a short distance, a block or two if measured in the city, and turned right at the next drive.

The Ford's tires printed a fresh set of tracks in the new snow and Cade parked it on an identical white rectangle in front of a modular home the same in every way to the one he'd just left save for its exterior paint color.

Up close he noticed this house *had* been touched by a woman. There were flower boxes full of drooping brown stalks attached to the siding just under the larger two of the three windows gracing the front of the place. Colorful garden gnomes and Bambi-type deer were arranged around the base of a nearby tree, and a birdbath was erected on the lawn dead center to the large picture window.

Max growled at something on the passenger's side, causing Cade to lift up off of his seat and follow the dog's gaze. Next to the garage, partially obscured by a knee-high burn pile, was an early-model mid-sized sedan. Closer scrutiny revealed it was minus a rear wheel and canted sideways, away from the house. Next to the root-beer-brown vehicle's rear bumper, Cade spotted a hydraulic jack lying on its side, as well as the poor soul who had become pinned and died there as a result of its obvious failure. On the undead man's arms, raised purple bite marks stood out in stark contrast against the pallid skin. The Z, whom Cade instantly nicknamed *Jack*, on account of his unfortunate demise, was flailing its chewed-on arms and swatting at the falling snowflakes. "Good job, boy," Cade said. He reached back and gave Max a good scratching behind the ears. Still eyeing the trapped creature, he rattled the transmission into *Park,* stilled the motor, and exited the truck.

With Max on his heels, Cade skirted around a generic-looking SUV hybrid that, sitting beside the Ford, looked like something from the future. A byproduct of a mini-van's fling with a Jeep, perhaps. It was bulbous up front and sat a little too low to the ground considering the off-road tires wrapped around the rims. The front windshield was spidered and protruding from it dead center was the lower half of a long dead person. Hips to toes, though the impact with the van's bumper had left its mark, the bare legs were shapely, pale, and all woman.

Intrigued as to what the legs' owner looked like, Cade swiped the snow from the driver's side window and found himself staring into the clouded lifeless eyes of a long dead Z that had registered in life, in his humble opinion, somewhere between a solid seven or eight on the easy-on-the-eyes scale.

The passenger door was unlocked, so he quickly searched the mutant SUV and found only the usual: maps, registration, proof of insurance, and papers showing it'd passed the last smog check. There was no chocolate. *Strike two.*

He called to Max, "Let's go." Then together they made tracks in the snow to the modular home's front door, where he performed the same routine as before.

He banged once on the door and called out. *Nothing.*

Hackles up and growling, Max pawed at Cade's right leg.

"We got us a Wal-Mart Greeter somewhere inside of there?"

Again, Max with the guttural growl.

"All right, wingman. We go in hot then." He rapped on the door again while drawing his Glock. With Max still voicing his displeasure, Cade listened hard for another second and, when there was no discernable sound from behind the door, he delivered the kick, but with his left leg this time.

The result was the same—but different.

Equal and opposite reactions happened next as Newton's Third Law came into play and the door blew inward. Instantly he caught a face full of air heavy with the stench of rotting flesh. However, instead of the knob drilling a fresh hole in the drywall like the house before, this door's vertical edge hit the source of the stench full on and, after a split-second hitch, continued its inward swing. Cade got a quick glance at the Z as the door began to shear away from its hinges. The hissing thing was massive and female and thoroughly decomposed. It also had caught the door and the full energy from his kick across the sternum and forehead and, like felled timber, had slowly keeled over backwards. A tick after glimpsing the hideous face, Cade felt a thud course through the joists, floorboards, and carpet and vibrate the sole of his boot that he'd just planted on the aluminum threshold plate.

Wanting to preserve the advantage, he shouldered open the remains of the door and put a boot on the struggling creature's chest. As he watched his tan combat boot sink into the nightgown-covered folds of flesh there, he started to swing the Glock on line with the enormous target the pasty-white forehead presented. And like clockwork, as it always did when he entered into combat and the fight component of his hardwired fight-or-flight instinct kicked in, time started to crawl. Sights and sounds became more acute as his adrenal glands flooded his body with endorphins.

Behind him he heard Max growling.

To his right, a grandfather clock was ticking; then a click sounded and suddenly it began to announce the time with a series of long, sonorous gongs.

Between the first and second chime, the morbidly obese undead woman was wrapping both meaty hands around his ankle and calf. Before the second chime had dissipated, there was a pair of neat little holes punched into her forehead and both clouded eyes were rolled back. And by the time the clock had finished alerting everyone and everything within earshot that it was ten o'clock in the morning, Cade had swept the house for more dead, returned to the front room, and was eyeing the closed door leading into the garage.

A sudden wind gust carried some light flakes in through the open front door. So Cade dragged the leaking three hundred pounds of dead weight away from the blood-slicked four-by-four square of taupe vinyl flooring, closed the buckled door as best he could, and then dumped the offending grandfather clock over on its side, effectively barring entry to dead and breathers alike—the latter of which concerned him more than the former at the moment.

With Max watching his every move and slinking after him through the prefab like a shadow, Cade went to the kitchen and scavenged a box of heavy-duty Glad garbage sacks from under the kitchen sink. He made his way to the bathroom first and raided the medicine cabinet, throwing everything of use into one of the sacks. He opened the cabinet door under the sink and took all of the feminine products there. What he wouldn't give for the days when Brook would force a *mission* to the Safeway on him. There was a time in his life when he would gladly have accepted an excursion behind enemy lines over a trip through the Express Checkout with a pink box emblazoned with butterflies or feathers containing items he didn't quite understand, nor pretend to. Now, however, considering the state of the world, he'd gladly run naked through Safeway stating his mission proudly while waving a bottle of Massengill's in one hand and the biggest box of Kotex he could find in the other.

Still pining for normalcy to return to the day-to-day, he stalked from the bathroom and checked out both bedrooms, looking in the closets and under the beds and their mattresses. Finding nothing of use save for a couple of fleece blankets, which went into the bag, he made his way to the kitchen and started emptying everything from the cupboards into a second garbage bag. The big woman had a huge appetite in life. That was for sure. Especially for candy. But not Snickers. *Strike three.*

Somewhat crestfallen, Cade dumped a sealed bag of hardened marshmallows (added to the list in Raven's handwriting) into the second bulging black bag, tied the drawstring, and then promptly peeled a fresh one from the thick Costco-sized roll.

Empty bag in hand, he approached the door leading into the garage. Performed nearly the same routine as he did on the front. Bang. Call out. Listen hard. Max wasn't growling at this point and the door was unlocked so kicking it wasn't necessary, which was good, because now there was a sharp pain stabbing his left leg a few inches below his knee. The beginnings of a shin splint, no doubt. *Getting old sucks*, crossed his mind as he opened the door, leveled the Glock, and took a quick step back.

Chapter 8

Nothing undead or living rushed him, so Cade holstered the Glock and entered the garage, which he found utilized in a vastly different manner than the other. There were a couple of grease stains on the concrete pad, but no cars, because they were both parked outside, one speared through with a twice-dead corpse, and the other atop what had presumably been the dead woman-of-the-house's husband.

Against the rear wall, he spotted a pair of multi-speed road bikes, both gently used. Next to the bikes was a pair of modular shelves, the plastic stacking type, brimming with automotive products. It appeared from the diverse selection assembled on them like soldiers at parade rest, that the man liked his car as much as the woman liked her food. And with the weather over the coming months forecast to be worse than normal—at least according to the pre-recorded opinions of some long dead farmers—that was a good thing, because the Black Hawk and other vehicles needed to be winterized. So everything went into the bag. There were bottles of lubricant, spark plugs, air cleaners, two cans of Fix-a-Flat, and cans both of starting fluid and windshield deicer.

On the way out with the newly filled bag, Cade spied a spare car battery still hooked to a deep cycle battery charger. After depositing the stretched and misshapen Hefty Sack near the door with the others, he returned for the battery and charger.

He stacked the final two items by the other stuff, padded to the picture window behind the sofa in the living room, parted the horizontal slats and peered out. Due to the blowing snow and the hulking F-650 in his line of sight, he couldn't see anything beyond the end of the driveway.

He made a bigger portal in the blinds, pressed his face to the glass and looked left. He saw *Jack* still trapped under the car and still swiping at the snow with his gruesome bite-riddled arms. As if it sensed Cade's scrutiny, the corpse suddenly ignored the falling flakes, lay back, stretched out on the snow as far as possible and fixed its glassed-over eyes on the house.

What a way to go, thought Cade. He pulled his head away and let the slats snap shut. Moved the clock aside and hustled the scavenged supplies out to the truck, heaving everything into the load bed. Then he whistled and opened the driver's door. Once Max was inside the cab, Cade shut the door. With snow collecting in his beard and every exhaled breath creating big white plumes that slowly rose and roiled away, he stood there shivering and thinking. To anyone with a shred of imagination, concluding that he looked like a Viking or Mongol raider contemplating which city to sack next would not have been much of a stretch.

After a few seconds, apparently having made up his mind about something, he hurried back to the house. Crabbed past the broken door and stepped over the clock and twice-dead woman and went straight for the garage. Once inside, he reached over his head and pulled the pin that disengaged the drive chain from the overhead motor. With visions of the dead-filled parking garage in Los Angeles still fresh in his mind, he rattled the door up in its tracks and turned back to the pair of bicycles.

One at a time, beginning with the larger of the two, he wheeled the bikes to the Ford and heaved them both in back, where they settled with a whoosh of disgorged air atop the bed of plastic garbage bags.

With Max watching him from behind the steering wheel, and looking every bit like he was about to start the rig up and drive the thing, Cade went back inside the garage through the open overhead door. He entered the house again and made a bee-line to the vanity on the wall opposite the front door. He reached high and snatched the depression-era glass vase there, removed a bouquet of silk flowers from it, and without thought dropped it to the linoleum floor. Flowers in one hand, Glock in the other, he hurried back the way he'd come.

Outside, he closed the garage door and zippered between the sedan and the hybrid SUV. He stopped near the burn pile just out of arm's reach from Jack.

Saying a silent prayer, Cade holstered the Glock and set the flowers on the car's trunk. Then he drew the Gerber and gripped the creature's left wrist with his free hand. With little effort on his part, he trapped the arm under his knee. Finally, after making the sign of the cross and reciting the Holy Trinity for the unfortunate man, in one fluid stroke—a move performed too many times to count and perfected in the months since the dead began to walk—he slid the blade into his left eye until he felt the high-carbon stainless-steel tip meet bone. At once the trapped Z went limp. Cade withdrew the black blade, dragged the dagger through the snow, and then finished cleaning it on the twice-dead Zs tee-shirt.

Again clutching the multi-colored bouquet of fake roses in one hand, and the Glock in the other, Cade made his way back to the Ford. He hopped inside and caught Max looking at him the way dogs are wont to do. Head cocked to one side as if saying, *Are we done here yet, or what?* To which Cade said, "Don't get any ideas, Max." He tossed the roses on the console. "Those aren't for you. They're for Raven."

Realizing he was talking to the dog way too much, Cade dug the CB out from under the flowers and switched it on. He looked over at Max and said, "We better—" but cut himself short and instead pressed the key to talk and got Seth on the other end. He quickly filled him in on the news, good and bad, the former being that he had procured a fair amount of the items on the lists, and the latter being the scarcity of a certain brand of candy bar wrapped in brown and made by a certain company bearing the same name as the Greek God of War. After listening to Seth go on about how badly he *needed* chocolate, Cade needled him further. "Do you want some cheese with that whine?" he asked, already knowing the answer. That prompted another full minute of bellyaching out of Seth before Cade was able to get a word in edgewise and detail his next two planned stops.

Once Cade finished, Seth asked, "If anybody inquires, when should I say you'll be back?"

Cade looked at his watch. "I can't see being outside the wire past noon."

"Roger that," said Seth. "Call in when you get close."

"Still having problems with icing on the camera domes?"

"Yep. Both of them on the State Route and the one on our feeder road are getting it good."

Cade removed his camo ball cap and banged it against the floor mat to rid it of melting snow. "We'll have to get Foley working on a fix for that." He paused. "The ones trained on the clearing ... how are they?"

"Fine. They're inside the tree line. In fact I'm watching a ferocious battle taking place up there."

Cade snugged his hat on. "Come again?" he said.

"Daymon, Wilson, and Foley are going up against Duncan, Tran, Jamie, and Taryn."

Watching the snow intensify outside the truck's windows, Cade suddenly caught on. "Oh ... a snowball fight. Who's winning?"

"Believe it or not, the Old Man's squad is taking it to Daymon's crew. Don't know how he does it, but Tran melts in and out of the tree line like a little ninja."

"Jamie's no slouch, herself."

"Copy that," Seth said. "Wouldn't want her sneaking up on me"—he went silent for a long beat—"unless, of course, *Lev* was out of the picture."

Detecting a trace of humor in Seth's voice, Cade said, jokingly, "Easy, cowboy."

Seth laughed. "You know I wouldn't wish ill will on him."

"Roger that," Cade answered back. "I'll see you in a few." He consulted his Suunto and noted the time. Ten after ten. He put the truck into as tight a U-turn as the big 4x4 would make. Still, he had to reverse it half a truck length before transiting the drive to Center Street where he went left and, making new parallel tracks where the old ones had already filled in, finally wheeled west towards the rehab place.

***

Two minutes later, after using all of the shoulder to pass by the trio of near-frozen Zs, and with his silent wingman curled up into a ball on the passenger floor in front of the heat vent, Cade pulled to a smooth stop a block east of Main. Gripping the wheel with both hands at twelve o'clock, he leaned forward and rested his chin on his knuckles. He blinked his eyes in disbelief at what he was seeing. "They're immobilized," he said, taking his eyes from the herd and regarding Max. "This, my furry four-legged friend, is a game changer."

***

A minute after seeing the phalanx of dead rooted in their tracks, some in mid-step, many more toppled over onto their faces or sides or backs, arms and legs twitching minutely but not fully responding to the neural commands issued, Cade was alone outside of the truck.

With Max nosing the passenger window and watching him, Cade stole one last look down the sidewalk at the dead, then mounted the back steps to the rehab place.

The rear door was ajar and a small snowdrift had accumulated just inside on the scuffed wood floor. Forgoing the normal routine, he entered silently with his Glock leveled, the black cylindrical suppressor leading the way. There was a rich odor of decay in the air that grew stronger as he crept down the short hallway.

From where the hall opened up to the front of the business, the floors were covered by the kind of blue tumbling mats usually found at a wrestling match or gymnastic event. On the right wall were a series of doors, all hinged open. Drawers and plastic containers had been ripped from within, their contents—paper brochures detailing therapeutic exercises, resistance bands fashioned into different lengths, and rubber balls of all sizes and colors—littered the floor.

He bent to pick up an item and caught a flash of movement to his left. He turned and saw the reflection of a Z in the floor-to-ceiling mirror affixed to the south wall. In one fluid motion, he spun to his right and brought the Glock on target, its tritium sights lined up with an imaginary spot between the rotted thing's roving eyes.

Having a hell of a time picking its way through the clutter near the back stairway, the Z emitted a screech that instantly sent the hair on the back of Cade's neck to attention. "That's not right," he said aloud, hoping that all of the undead weren't going to sound like this after the temperature buoyed back up. He didn't remember Nash mentioning anything about the cold's effect on the dead other than the fact that they didn't ever completely die. However, he did know that early on, after the outbreak, Sylvester Fuentes froze some recently turned specimens solid. And when he had thawed them out, inexplicably, within a very short time they were ambulatory again. For all Cade knew, the notes detailing those first experiments had been in the computers and were lost in the fire set by Pug. Moreover, if the thumb-drive found by Taryn contained anything other than the doctor's notes on the Omega antiserum, Nash had decided, for whatever reason, to keep that knowledge to herself.

Moving with a locked-knee type of shuffle, the high-pitched squawking still emanating from its constantly moving maw, the creature caught a 9mm round to each milky eye, fired by the man whose pistol prowess had earned him the nickname *Wyatt* early on in his Special Forces career. *They don't call it a silencer for nothing*, he thought to himself as the screeching pusbag went silent and fell in a heap, partially blocking a gloomy stairwell leading up.

Finished '*shopping*' in under a minute, cargo pockets bulging with liberated goods, Cade hurried back to his truck.

He popped the door and climbed in, saying, "Mission accomplished, Max." He trapped the Glock under his thigh and transferred some of the liberated goods from his pockets to the deep center console.

Max growled as soon as the motor turned over. "Yeah ..." Cade said in response, "I don't want to drive through them either. But it's what we're going to have to do in order to get back to 39. And Max, when we return to the compound"—the dog looked up from the floor, regarded him with multi-colored eyes, and yawned—"do not let on to the others that I talked to you so much." Another yawn confirmed acknowledgement as the truck rolled slowly over a handful of withered and gunshot Z bodies and then bounced and lurched as Cade drove it off the curb.

As Cade angled the F-650 toward the column of dead, he detected no movement whatsoever. They were rooted in place like life-sized figures in a museum diorama. Or those terra cotta soldiers on display in the Forbidden City in China, the country responsible for this entire mess.

"Domino time," said Cade, intending to put the wide steel bumper to use like a cowcatcher on a locomotive. He turned left onto Main and drove south, weaving slowly left and right, pleased when his spoken assumption came to fruition. The impacts with the Zs sounded through the sheet metal like hollow thuds, which were a far cry from the usual resonant slaps and screeching of fingernails digging into the paint. Instantly a chain reaction was started and, domino-like, the dead began toppling into each other, cascading away from the Ford like dual waves pushing out from the bow of a ship. Gunshot-like cracks of bones breaking under the tires competed with the same shrill noise the Z in the rehab place had made. Only here, in the midst of scores of immobilized flesh eaters, the noise soon rose to a deafening peal and suddenly Cade was driving through a scene from his childhood nightmares. In the next instant, with the windows vibrating slightly from the sonic onslaught, in his mind it was *Oldies Night* and he was at the Moreland Theater in Portland ensconced in the comfortable love seats in the back of the house. He wasn't alone and there was this ethereal feeling of being wary and excited all at once. He was on the precipice of stealing a kiss from his first real girlfriend when *that* sound belted out of the speakers directly above them. He let go of Barbara's hand then, took his arm from around her slender shoulders, and clamped his palms over his ears just like the people were doing on the movie screen. Who knew the body snatchers screamed when they were onto you? Until then, sitting through it in the theater, he'd had no idea. That God-awful noise ruined the moment and the screaming pod people returned in his sleep regularly in the form of nightmares that lasted nearly a year until another *Oldies Night* featured *Alien* and a whole new cast of baddies took their places.

The mental side trip lasted a millisecond and then, for the first time Cade could remember, he heard Max whine. Not one and done, but a long, drawn-out series of plaintive yelps ending in a final shuddering whimper. Concerned for the poor fella, he took his eyes from the road for a second and saw the shepherd burying his snout into the carpet and pawing at both ears.

"I'm with you buddy." Feeling his chest rising and falling rapidly underneath his body armor, Cade swallowed hard and said, "Almost through them, boy." Then he looked a few blocks over the heads of the slack-faced ghouls to the point where Main widened and intersected State Route 39. There he saw the rounded snout and road-grime-coated underside of the overturned yellow school bus standing out like a sore thumb against the snowy white background. On the upturned side was a thin layer of snow that from this distance looked like frosting atop a slab of lemon pound cake.

He tapped the brakes and walked his gaze over the rear of the blocks-long column of death and noticed that their eyes were not facing in the direction of the march. To a Z, all eyes were focused on the cab of the truck. The strange noises continued and the dead kept toppling.

Then it hit him like a mule kick right then and there that those eyes must have been shifting subtly, imperceptibly, from the moment the noisy Ford entered their midst a couple of hundred yards north and had been tracking the fresh meat—*him*—elevated and displayed behind glass like a rack of lamb at the butcher's, all the way to this point.

An uneasy feeling washed over him and he threw an involuntary shudder as the realization that once the horde thawed out and reanimated, the ones leading the procession would invariably end up about facing and following the ones presently eyeballing him down 39 where eventually they'd pose one hell of a problem for the Eden Compound. So possessing only enough ammunition to put down a tiny fraction of them, he did the next thing that came to mind. In hopes of concealing his egress from watchful eyes, he steered the rig at the nearest of the leering monsters and mowed down a dozen of them. He reversed and repeated the process a number of times until the rear echelon of the procession was bent and broken, their blood and fluids trickling onto the snow.

"That should keep them from following," Cade said aloud, mainly for his own benefit. Then, as if he had just driven into the vacuum of outer space, the cacophony of the dead was gone, in place of it the V10 roar and metronomic swishing of the wipers.

Max sniffed the air and then, one paw at a time, crawled back onto the passenger seat.

Cade felt his breathing return to normal and the whoosh of blood rushing between his ears begin to ebb.

Finally, intent on making the junction before the few dead still left standing could track him with their eyes, he focused on the narrow band of white bracketed on the left by the bus's protruding tires, drag chains, and snaking exhaust pipes and on the right by the soft shoulder he knew was there somewhere underneath the snow.

He took a breath, held it, and finessed the pedals, heel-and-toeing them to simultaneously cut speed and power drift through the turn in a vehicle designed for towing and hauling—not high-speed maneuvers on snow.

The result was acceptable—barely. The shoulder was under there, but both passenger side tires fell off it, sending the truck into a hard list on that side and the road sign marking the 16/39 junction airborne, broken off like a matchstick and tumbling end-over-end.

In the next half-beat, three things happened near simultaneously.

First, Cade hauled the wheel hard right, stabbed the gas pedal, and the dull gray horizon shifted right-to-left in front of his eyes when the truck started into a slow speed sideways slide.

Then, rivaling the din the dead had been making, there was a metal-on-metal screech when the truck glanced off the bus and a fair amount of black paint and road grime was swapped between the two vehicles.

Finally, as he tromped the gas, the front wheels pulled straight and the school bus flashed by in his left side-vision, while the ground-hugging shrubs and Jersey barriers bordering 39 blazed by in his right.

Once clear of the choke point, Cade risked a quick glance over his right shoulder. Barely visible, even from his elevated vantage point, the prone dead looked small and inconsequential. Whether they had or had not seen the truck turn onto 39 was the sixty-four-thousand dollar question. Even if they had, thought Cade, he doubted the seemingly aware among them would remember enough to hunt him after the thaw. Which could be a day, a week, or longer. At any rate it amounted to an unknown window of time that the Almanac didn't mention and led to another thought that really set the gears in his head to spinning.

Chapter 9

Less than a mile southeast of the 16/39 junction, Alexander Dregan was fighting off sleep, the battle made all the more difficult by the layer of snow shrouding the windows and the soothing melody filling the cab compliments of the Kenwood head unit and strategically placed woofers and tweeters. *One thing the kid did right.*

He rubbed his eyes then started the wipers moving. Not wanting to roll the window down and get a lap full of snow, he banged a fist against the driver's side glass so he could see out, starting a mini-avalanche cascading off the outside surface. He leaned over and cleared the passenger window in the same manner.

Dregan consulted both side mirrors, then flicked his eyes to the rearview. *Nothing.* It was still only him on the lonely road. Parked nearly equidistant between the old couple's home and the hallowed ground he was intent on visiting. The only place where he could think clearly. Perhaps it was because when he was there he was away from the constant din of responsibility. The gravitational tugging at him by his boys for approval, answers, permission, and affection, the latter of which he didn't know how to dole out—unless it was Lena who sought it.

But more likely the reason he felt whole where he had found Lena's lifeless form was because he could in a way sense her spirit there. In fact, he'd made the pilgrimage there so many times over the past few weeks that his older son had on one occasion even gone so far as to question his sanity. Like a Muslim to Mecca—he was drawn. Maybe he *was* going crazy as the judge had also insinuated to him days ago. But wasn't the whole world? After all, the dead were walking and wouldn't stop. Their decay rate was agonizingly slow. Some of the survivors he'd been trading with in the outlying camps were even beginning to turn to cannibalism to survive. He had heard they were holding lotteries. A morbid and deadly version of *shortest straw* in which the loser wasn't assigned some kind of unenviable task or forced to sleep on the couch or forgo riding shotgun for the day. The unlucky loser became *dinner.*

Savages, he thought, and threw a shudder at the prospect of eating another human. With a reflux of acid tickling his throat, he yanked his sleeve up and consulted his watch. Half past ten. Wanting to return to the walls before noon in order to confront the judge before the big man became too bogged down with hearing grievances and issuing rulings, he rattled the shifter into Drive and started out slow, the vehicle shuddering as the accumulated snow was packed down and forward momentum was established.

To the west, riding low over the foothills and presumably enveloping the Wasatch Mountains farther away still, the dark roiling clouds scudded along at a rapid clip. He came to a short straightaway, briefly shifted his gaze right and saw over the craggy red mountains a thin horizontal gash in the storm, brilliant blue sky showing through it. But behind the brief respite the break represented was another foreboding gray smudge.

Directly ahead, before the State Route became Main Street in the town of Woodruff, it made a sharp left and then a short distance later an equally sharp ninety-degree jog right. From here the road shot razor-straight north, the low buildings and canted telephone poles of Woodruff cluttering the horizon in the distance.

Closer in, Dregan saw the toppled bus. Snow covered the dozens of upward facing right-side windows and more was swirling in the air, cutting the visibility. He halved his speed as the hallowed ground drew nearer and suddenly the wind took a break and he caught his first glimpse of the biter herd he had succeeded in avoiding hours ago and many miles south.

Instantly his gut clenched and he jammed on the brakes, Pavlovian responses both. The SUV slewed sideways, coming to a stop roughly a quarter mile short of the road to Huntsville and Eden—both on his short list of towns ripe for foraging.

The knot in his stomach tightened and the usual butterfly flutter there brought on by the mere sight of this many monsters in one place commenced. He silenced the music so he could think. He drew a deep breath to calm his nerves then snatched the binoculars up and held it in as he glassed the column.

A few seconds passed and he exhaled slowly, causing the image to judder. "I'll be," he said aloud, liking what he was seeing. "The dirge has ceased and so has the dead."

Interest suddenly piqued, he threw the volume back up and continued north with a million unanswered questions muddling his thoughts.

***

Tooling along 39 a couple miles west of Woodruff, Cade was glimpsing snippets of the retreating storm through the snow-dusted trees. Shifting his gaze from the road ahead to the rearview mirror, he saw the widening band of blue sky to the east and liked what it represented. Though he was no meteorologist, he figured, based mainly on all the time he'd spent in higher elevations on Mount Hood and other places around the world, the clear sky and low sun would drop the temperature into the lower twenties. Optimum conditions for what he planned to be doing the rest of the day.

But first, he had an unplanned side trip to make and then a promise he *had* to deliver on.

The quarry turnout was partially overgrown and easy to miss if one didn't know where to look. Cade watched the digital mile counter tick over as he rounded yet another corner on the twisting serpent that was State Route 39. After a quick calculation in his head, he slowed the Ford to a crawl and stopped on the straight midpoint of a gradual S-turn. He leaned right of the steering wheel, over the center console into Max's personal space, and craned his neck. The mist and low clouds present earlier had burned off, letting him see clearly the hillside rising up and away. Using the peak above and behind the quarry as a reference point, he moved his gaze down the rocky bluff and located the access road climbing steadily up, a hard-to-miss whip of white consisting of multiple switch-backs and a handful of steep straights.

He let the idling engine pull the truck and located the break in the brush just before the road dove into a shallow right-hand sweeper. Branches raked the Ford's flank as Cade wheeled it off the State Route. Instantly, the four-wheel-drive proved its worth as the tires bit into the feeder road, churning up an icy mixture of mud and gravel that pinged and thunked off the undercarriage—all out-of-place noises that caused Max to rise up off the seat after each loud report.

In no time the grade lessened and the final turn before the gate was in sight. To the left, the road fell away sharply for hundreds of feet. To the right, a vertical wall of snow-mottled red soil passed close by the window, giving the sensation the Ford was static on an ice floe and an icebreaker's rust-spotted bow was pushing slowly by.

Straight ahead, Cade spotted a lone Z, shoeless and shirtless and standing stock-still. Its atrophied arms were outstretched and both gnarled hands were clutching the wheeled gate. Twelve feet from the ground to the strands of rusty barbed wire strung atop it, the gate dwarfed the seemingly immobilized ghoul.

Leaving Max in charge, Cade stepped down from the truck and shut the door. The air was much colder here a couple of hundred feet from the road, and every inhaled breath was a reminder of that fact.

"Hey Z," he said, feeling the burn in his lungs. He whistled and received no perceptible reaction to the stimuli. The Z didn't flinch or waver or turn its head to get a fix on the source. It was as if it had somehow been granted final death while gripping the fence.

Holding the key to the new padlock in his gloved right hand, and training the Glock on the Z with the other, Cade approached the gate. Wary of the potholes no doubt containing Great-Lake-sized puddles underneath the clean blanket of white, he picked his way along the pronounced ridges. *Better safe than sorry*, he thought. No doubt the half-dozen pools of muddy standing water were now sheets of ice waiting to send him to his butt. Last thing he needed was to break his tailbone and miss out on the golden opportunity laid out at his feet.

When he finally arrived at the gate with his coccyx still in one piece, he saw that the Z still hadn't budged. So he leveled the Glock and jabbed the suppressor against its bony shoulder blade. It swayed forward a few inches along with the slight give in the fence before returning to its initial stance.

"Thank you, Lord," Cade said, dropping his pistol in its holster. He leaned against the fence and regarded the thing face-to-face. It was one of the first turns, that was for sure. The adverse effects of nearly three months spent outside in the elements was showing. Its gray skin was mottled and sloughing off in places, revealing the corded muscle and tendon just under the surface. The forty-something man had been short and lean in life. Five foot tall, maybe. One hundred pounds, max. In death, the nearly nude and graying being looked more circus oddity than walking dead. Cade imagined the Barker saying, *Step right up and see the human skeleton.*

He leaned in even closer, face hovering just inches from the Z's, and detected a slight twitch in its left eye. A few seconds passed and that bloodshot orb rotated his way, achingly slow. Then the scratchy moaning started. Low in timbre at first. Then it rose in pitch and volume, until the awful peal sounded identical to the calls of the dead making up the Main Street herd.

With visions of Body Snatchers returning to his head, Cade drew the Gerber. With no hesitation, he raked the dagger's jagged saw-like edge across the Z's neck just inches above its breastbone. Two sawing back-and-forth strokes and the Z was silenced—but not dead.

"Much better. Now let's see what you can do." He pried the cold undead hands from the fence and turned the stiffening corpse towards him. He saw a trio of purple-ringed dots below its solar plexus. A tight triangular grouping made by small caliber bullets, .22 rimfire, presumably. The skin around the entry wounds was dappled with tiny black dots. *Powder burns.* Whoever had fired the weapon that had left them there had done so at close range and likely hadn't survived the encounter. Looking into its listless eyes, he said jokingly, "Shall we dance?" The thing remained silent, its cold-affected vocal cords now severed. And as Cade lowered it to a prone position on the frozen ground, its head hinged back like a Pez dispenser, revealing the damage the blade had inflicted while releasing a viscous dribble of nearly black blood onto the snow.

Cade grabbed a handful of wispy gray hair, twisted the head towards him, and stuck the Gerber in the waifish Z's open maw. He rattled it around in there trying to get a response. *Nothing.* However, the dagger's tip clinking against molars and canines did create a macabre symphony nearly as cringe-inducing as the thing's utterances prior to having its throat cut.

"We're done here," Cade said. He cleaned his blade in the snow and slipped it into its scabbard. He knelt and grabbed the Z by its ankles. It was incredibly light, probably weighing closer to eighty pounds than one hundred. Then, retracing his own serpentine trail of footsteps in the snow—which had stopped falling for the time being—he dragged the corpse toward the ledge, its head, attached by only vertebra and a few strands of muscle, bouncing and twisting violently along the ground the entire way.

There was no countdown when he reached the edge with the undead corpse. No kind words for whoever it used to be. Just a grunt and burst of steam from Cade's nose and mouth as he heaved the dead weight into the misty void. The sound of breaking twigs and dislodged rocks and pebbles cascading down the steep face reached his ears as he turned and walked purposefully towards the gate. Along the way, he imagined the thing cartwheeling all the way down, pasty appendages flailing, the nearly severed head flopping madly, speed increasing exponentially until finally the inevitable, and hopefully fatal, rapid deceleration against a very firm and unforgiving terra firma.

At the gate, Cade again drew the Glock and fished in his pocket for the shiny key to the new Schlage lock. With his black pistol trained on the blind spot to his right, he cut the angle and confirmed visually that the padlock Duncan had snapped shut last time they were here was still in the closed position and the thick chain was wrapped through the fencing, seemingly undisturbed.

Seeing nothing waiting for him on the other side—living or dead—he used the key in the lock. He pocketed the keys and lock, unwrapped the chain, and let it fall to the ground. With little effort, he got the wheeled gate moving and kept pushing until there was room for the truck to pass on through.

On the way back to the Ford, he paused and looked at the recently stripped electrical wires dangling near a mount where a shiny black CCTV dome used to reside. The mount was secured to the far right fence post and was partially protected from the elements by a small alcove etched into the side hill. Whether the depression was due to erosion or a byproduct of the blasting that had taken place in order to open up the road, he hadn't a clue. What he did know, however, was whoever had removed the dome and then the camera had left behind the umbrella-shaped shroud installed directly above it.

It took a little finessing to get the Ford tucked in close to the soaring red wall. In the process, he scraped the right front fender against the waist-high rocky outcroppings protruding from the side hill.

Satisfied, and not the least bit concerned about the rig's finish, he put it into *Park* and set the brake. Grabbed a multi-tool from the glove box and leaving Max inside and the truck idling, he hopped to the road.

He stepped onto the heavy-duty bumper and then crawled up onto the slick hood. Hand over hand, gripping the fence to keep from slipping, he made it to the corner post and went to work on the oval shroud with the Phillips drive. In a couple of minutes he had defeated the trio of fasteners and tossed the liberated part to the ground.

One down, three to go.

The shroud went behind the seat and Cade climbed in and began jockeying the rig around. Once through the gate, he hopped out, rolled it closed and locked himself in.

He clambered back behind the wheel, maneuvered the rig past the quarry's still black waters, and parked it near the enormous rust-streaked building, complete with its destroyed office and attached multi-vehicle garage. The dozens of bullet holes punched into the steel siding were instantly evident, each one punctuated by its own vertical streak of rust. At first glance Cade got the impression that the building was weeping and, given the savagery that happened here just weeks ago, that impression came as no surprise.

He sat in the cab with the heater blasting and took the entire scene in. Straight ahead, sitting atop a series of carefully hidden underground chambers, the recently retrofitted steel building looked as much forgotten relic as the weathered mining equipment scattered about the property. In addition to the newly created bullet holes marring the building's west facing façade, Cade recognized high up on the siding the circles of fresh paint that had been exposed when Foley or Seth—he wasn't clear on whose undertaking it was—relieved the building of the west- and south-facing camera domes. He also noticed they had initially been mounted flush and tucked under the eaves, therefore there were no shrouds like the one up front to be had here.

Cade shook his head and pounded the steering wheel gently. "What now, Max?"

The shepherd yawned.

Not one to give up so easily, he shifted his gaze left. Settled it on the trio of swaybacked outbuildings sitting in a neat little row jutting off at a right angle from the left side of the main building. All of the windows were darkened with grime and, showing signs of forced entry, all three doors had been reduced to splintered boards hanging from rusted hinges.

Though Cade wasn't here when the place had been stripped of its essential items, on a visit since, he had poked his head into each building and learned that they contained mostly specialized tools useful only to miners and roughnecks.

He looked a circle around the property searching for anything Foley might fashion into a shroud like the one he'd just liberated from the front gate.

Finishing the three-hundred-sixty-degree sweep, he returned his attention to the shed and saw them in an altogether different light. Saw them for what was useful on the *outside.*

Rust … nature's camouflage, thought Cade as he shut the motor off. Armed with the Glock and multi-tool, he exited the truck and, with Max on his heels, went straight for the nearest of the three dilapidated sheds.

Chapter 10

With the motor off and Mozart silenced, Dregan spent ten minutes sitting in the truck watching the stalled horde through a pair of binoculars. During that time, with the snow still falling lightly and the delicate flakes alighting on the camouflage hood, he witnessed many of the dead making up the horde toppling over. At times only one stiff corpse would fall to the road with all of the grace of a knocked-out fighter. A handful of times he witnessed one of the biters lose out to gravity and fall into another, starting a domino-like chain reaction. In fact, he found it quite humorous seeing a daisy chain of rigor-affected corpses bang into one another and end up tangled on the road like some kind of undead orgy gone awry. Whoops, he'd thought morbidly at the time. Looks like somebody forgot to holler their *safe* words.

***

Now, having deemed it safe enough to venture outside amongst the overwhelming numbers of dead, Dregan could see his breath *inside* the truck, and nearly two-thirds of the horde were horizontal on the road, arms and legs akimbo, not a sound coming from their rotten mouths.

He grabbed his sword and a suppressed AR-15 from behind the seat. The carbine he slung over his shoulder. Then the sword, which he intended to use on the assembled monsters, came out of the scabbard with a metallic *snik*.

Dregan closed up the SUV and marched solemnly down the State Route, keeping to the middle of the snow-covered road right where he imagined the yellow centerline to be. Twenty yards north of his parked Blazer he came upon the exact spot where he'd found Lena's lifeless body. As it always did, his proximity to the scene of the crime brought back the mental image of her cratered face. The bullets, a trio of them he guessed, had done precisely what they were designed to—break apart on impact and tumble. The initial impacts shredded her angelic features. He figured the bullet that entered below the bridge of her nose had killed her instantly. The kinetic energy punched everything, nose and all, inside before the bullet broke into pieces and shredded her brain. The other bullets only added insult to the lethal injury created by the first. The skin and muscle and flesh that was her left cheek had been peeled back, one big bloody flap revealing shattered teeth, most of them blown into a thousand splinters scattered on the road and now buried somewhere here under the snow.

Dregan crossed himself and recited a prayer. With tears forming and a lump welling in his throat, he trudged ahead. He ignored the school bus. He walked right over the particular spot on the road at the junction with 39 where they'd found the Jackson Hole Police Department Tahoe parked on top of dozens of mashed corpses.

He paused a few steps beyond the bus and looked at the ground near his boots. Standing there with the duster flapping in the wind, he wiped the tears and ruffled his bushy black beard.

Then, in his mind's eye, he saw through the snow and was looking at the skid marks on the gray asphalt. The black chevron patterns left behind were unusually large and appeared to have come from the tires on a military vehicle or commercial truck. The distance he had paced off between the two parallel black stripes told the same story. Add the numerous shell casings found here and Dregan had many clues to the puzzle that was her death. A puzzle he was still far from piecing together completely.

Now, just past the intersection, walking head down, eyes sweeping the road, Dregan picked up on two faint parallel lines imprinted in the snow. They tracked off to the north toward the herd. And if not for the emerging sun he would have missed them entirely.

Stooping over, he probed the top quarter-inch of snow with the sword. He inhaled and held the breath. Set the sword aside and went to his knees. Gently he brushed the fresh layer of snow away and saw the same thick chevrons compacted into the base layer of snow. Like metal shavings to a magnet, his eyes were drawn north.

Still staring down the road, he reached into his pocket and drug the iPhone out. He swiped through the photos and came to the series he was looking for. Wincing, he bypassed the postmortem shots and stopped the scroll on the evidentiary pictures.

"Perfect match," he said, looking down the road. In the ensuing couple of minutes the dead hadn't moved at all. The snow had stopped falling and, as if Lena were sending a message, shafts of golden light were bathing the roadway ahead. The phone went back into his pocket and he lapsed into a moment of deep reflection.

***

A couple of minutes later, after calculating the snowfall at roughly an inch an hour and estimating the new coverage over the tire tracks to be a quarter to half an inch, he concluded that the vehicle responsible for leaving them had passed by sometime in the last half hour or so.

He stood up and paced off the distance between tracks and found it to be a perfect match. Smiling at his good fortune, he followed the tracks north past the sign proclaiming to any northbound traffic—of which there had been very little in the last few months—that *State Route 16* was now *Main Street* and the speed limit a *Strictly Enforced 35.*

With his labored breathing producing a seemingly constant white cloud that swirled around, shrouding his face, he marched on, emboldened, until he was standing on the center of the road, the nearby telephone poles lining it canted at odd angles and the road smeared with pulped biters everywhere he looked.

It was obvious that the southbound vehicle responsible for the tracks had also cut a swath through the middle of the dead and apparently took the time to run these ones over.

The dead on the road made not a peep, standing or fallen. However, as he followed the trail of battered bodies north on Main, he *did* detect the slightest of movements at times. Mostly action in his side-vision that he wrote off as blowing snow or tattered clothing flapping in the breeze.

He didn't believe his own intuition until he spun a one-eighty and noticed that the hundreds of pairs of lifeless eyes he had made contact with as he hiked north into the belly of the beast were now inexplicably fixed on him. Not all of them. But the ones still standing at an angle where they could see him as he had moved through their midst *had* tracked him. And it pissed him off. He thought the freezing cold and the wind chill had killed them. He prayed it had. The first frost of the season was yesterday and they seemed slower then. And now, miraculously, Utah and Wyoming had been blessed with a very early first snow.

But they weren't truly dead in the sense of the word. So he raised the sword and held it two-handed, vertical in front of his face, and belted out a war cry that echoed off the nearby buildings.

The full-throated wail had no noticeable effect on the dead. There was no movement whatsoever.

He remained rooted, staring at the upright biters. Watching the final tiny flakes drift down and settle on their heads and shoulders, adding to the snow already accumulated there as silence returned to Main Street.

In a fit of rage, and projecting a generic man's face on the biters—the face he'd arbitrarily assigned to Lena's killer— the big man waded into the stalled-out herd, swinging the sword in wide-reaching arcs. In a frenzy that lasted only a couple of minutes, he'd relieved two dozen of them of their heads, stabbed a dozen more through the temple where they lay, and came to the conclusion that though they still hungered for his flesh, they were of no threat to him so long as the weather held.

Stooped over and panting, he dropped the bloodied sword between his splayed-out feet. Planting his hands on his knees, he started to cry. His back heaved and the tears flowed hot as he contemplated the hard uphill slog he and his family had before them.

***

He stayed in that position for a couple of minutes; then, with tears freezing to his cheeks, he scooped the sword off the ground, stalked over to one of the prone creatures and wiped the double-edged blade off on the thing's tattered white and blue *BYU* tank top.

On the way back to the camouflaged Blazer, Dregan contemplated the tire tracks. He wondered what their being here near Woodruff implied and quickly concluded that none of it could be good. With those boxes checked, all that was left was the hard choice he needed to make.

Near the intersection, he glanced up and read the road sign facing him. There were three towns listed and the distance between the nearby junction. The first entry read Huntsville 49, then in descending order vertically, Eden, 53, and lastly, Ogden, 63.

Standing at the junction, he began to feel Lena's presence and slowly the rage that was still bubbling under the surface receded. And as if she were pointing the way from the afterlife, his gaze was inexplicably drawn from the ditch where he had found her faceless body to the shoulder just off to his right bordering 39 westbound.

Incredulous, he asked himself, "How'd you miss those, Dregan?" There, on the ground where southbound 16 swooped to the right, the sloping edge beyond the shoulder was partially collapsed. He covered the distance in a hurry, knelt on the road and discovered the true nature of the disturbance. Pressed into the soft gravel were the same bold chevron patterns as the ones cut into the off-road tires responsible for the southbound tracks.

Hands shaking, he dug out Lena's phone and compared the pattern in the photo with the ones in the freshly churned-up gravel. Again they were a perfect match.

Following the tracks with his eye, he came to the conclusion that the vehicle that made them

had also sheared off a nearby sign, leaving a two-inch splintered nub sticking up through the snow on the shoulder.

With yet another piece of the puzzle tumbling into place, he rose and turned to the west, fixing his eyes on 39 winding away into the distance. And though he couldn't see the tracks because of the effects of the flat light on the snow, he knew in his heart of hearts they were there somewhere.

"Gotcha," he said. Out came an old wallet-sized school photo of Lena. He kissed her on the forehead and hustled back to the Blazer. Along the way, he unshouldered his AR and untied the sash securing the sword and scabbard to his body. With his heart breakdancing in his chest and a smile spreading on his face, he piled into the Blazer behind his weapons and started the engine.

Chapter 11

Inside one of the rundown sheds, Cade had found a rickety wooden box on which the words TNT and HANDLE WITH CAUTION and NO SMOKING had been stenciled in warning-red. He placed it in front of the broken door of the first shed and, using it as a makeshift stepladder, was able to reach the gooseneck lamp affixed to the weathered siding. Finding his multi-tool of no use on the screws that had been fused tight by age and rust, he grabbed ahold of the tubular neck two-handed and stepped off the dynamite box, letting his hundred and eighty pounds do what the Phillips attachment could not. Instantly there was a sharp crack, a horizontal fault line formed in the gray clapboards, and he was back to earth holding the rusty light standard and base plate complete with the stripped-out wood screws still sticking from it.

Under Max's watchful eye, he repeated the process, tearing the lights off the other two decaying buildings, and when he was done there were three fixtures lying in the snow and heavily insulated wires protruding from the three fresh wounds atop each door.

The fixtures, bases and all, went into the Ford's bed with the bikes, garbage bags, and other odds and ends.

Back inside the truck, Cade started the engine and spent a moment warming his hands in front of the heater vents. Meanwhile, Max had regained his place on the passenger floor and was licking snow and mud from his paws.

Outside the truck, the snow had tapered to just a few scattered flakes and, as Cade had assumed would be the case, the thermometer built into the truck's trip computer told him the temperature was still falling.

Scratching the shepherd behind the ears, Cade said, "The day is young, Max. What do ya say we get back to the compound?" To which Max, eyeing the curved plastic ball launcher Cade had snatched from the house with the dog food, thumped his stub-tail excitedly on the floor mat.

"When we get back to the compound, I'm sure someone'll throw the ball for you, boy," Cade said, wheeling the rig around in the quarry lot. "Unfortunately, Old Man Winter has left no time for R and R in my immediate future."

As always, Max offered up an indifferent yawn and rested his muzzle on his paws.

***

Fifteen minutes after monkeying the first fixture off its outbuilding, the quarry gate was chained and locked up tight and Cade had negotiated the winding feeder road with no issues.

With a thin sliver of blue peeking through the cloud cover directly overhead, he bumped the Ford back onto 39 and proceeded west toward the Eden Compound.

***

Delaying the inevitable conflict at the end of the freshly printed tracks, Dregan sat in the truck with the engine stilled and rooted in a pocket for a power cord. He plugged the USB end into the stubby 12v lighter adapter. Then he reached into his parka and pulled his battered business iPhone from an inside pocket. He hadn't made or received a call with it since three days after the dead began to walk. It had been in the console of his truck along with the charger for most of the forty days leading up to Lena's murder. In the days since it has been with him always.

He snugged the large end of the white data cable into the phone's charger port and powered it on. "I'll be ..." he said upon seeing the device light up.

He tapped out 9982—Lena's birthday: month, day, and year—and the phone unlocked and he was presented a screen cluttered with colorful application tiles. He navigated to the video playback app, sorted through the videos until he found the one shot only a week before the Great Fall. Hit the opaque arrow on the screen and started the three-minute snippet running. He watched Lena and Mikhail—Michael to everyone outside his close circle—exchange vows. Saw the camera waver for a few seconds on the priest as he finished reciting the nuptials and then in a sing-song nasally voice proclaim the young couple *man and wife*. Feeling his face flush, he cursed at Lena for choosing Mikhail for her husband—an opinion that resided only in his head and heart until the two of them were dead.

After spending fifteen minutes watching mostly older videos from *before,* he noticed that the snow was tapering off and a wide north/south band of cobalt sky had appeared off to his left. The low mountains to the east were no longer indiscernible from the gray clouds, their white peaks standing out sharply against the brilliant blue backdrop. Behind the peaks, however, another storm front consisting of snow-heavy black clouds was forming.

He turned the key and listened to the rattle clatter as the ancient diesel motor surged to life. While the power plant worked up to a proper operating temperature, he powered on the CB and raised his eldest son, Gregory.

The second Dregan stated his intentions, a heated argument broke out with both men pleading their cases, the son's coming across heated and emotional, and the father's relayed calmly and rationally; when Dregan didn't capitulate and agree to wait for Gregory to join him before proceeding, the connection was terminated abruptly on the son's end.

Dregan shook his head. "Fools rush in," he said in a low voice. That the boy had even dared question his decision to follow at a standoff distance and gather as much information as possible before striking only served to solidify it. Weeks of perceived inaction on his part had caused a rift that was threatening to widen and break them all apart.

With a bevy of emotions tugging his heart every which way, he drove slowly to the junction with 39, hooked the sharp left there, negotiated the gap between the school bus on the left and the low Jersey barriers on the right, and then picked up the faint tire tracks spooling out to the west. Keeping his speed to half of the posted fifty-miles-per-hour, he followed them a number of miles through canyons of snow-flocked trees until there came a point in the road where there was a deviation in the westbound tracks. There they abruptly veered hard left into the oncoming lane, looped back and disappeared through the low bushes flanking the right side of the road. Beyond the point of entry were identical but opposite tracks from the maneuver being repeated when the vehicle he was following had emerged back onto the road and resumed its westbound tack.

Dregan ground the SUV to a halt. He looked right and saw that the shoulder was churned up from the comings and goings. His eye traced the snowy white straights and switchbacks up the side hill.

With every intention of following the road upward, he cranked the wheel right and was nosing the rig through the underbrush when the CB crackled to life. Derailing his plan, his youngest son said in a voice strained and emotion-filled, "Don't do it, Dad. You know Judge Pomeroy has forbidden us from taking the law into our own hands."

Forbidden. Dregan absolutely hated that word. *Fuck Lucius Pomeroy.* Dogs were *forbidden* from jumping on furniture. Kids were *forbidden* from playing with matches. Adults were free to choose their destiny. Always had been, within limits. And now with the world gone to shit, he believed men and women should have even more freedom. He especially hated how the judge from Salt Lake had sidled onto the scene shortly after the fall and started throwing his weight around, quoting old laws and exerting his authority on even the most mundane of issues. It was as if Dregan had been thrown back into the business world, where every little peon with a government title reveled in keeping him under their thumb through inane rules and regulations.

Feeling his face flush hot with anger, Dregan snatched up the CB. He paused briefly to collect his thoughts then spoke. "This is none of Pomeroy's concern, Peter. I don't know what Gregory has been telling you, but you need to remember one thing … this is a *family* matter."

There was silence for a moment. Then a rustling in the background followed by an unmistakable voice emanating from the CB. "You're not the one to dole out judgments, Dregan," said a deep male voice. "I am. The people"—*Sheeple*, thought Dregan—"elected me and don't you forget that. A jury will decide what happens to Mikhail and Lena's killers when they are caught."

"Bullshit. It's my score to settle," Dregan shot back. "Not yours or twelve or a hundred of my *peers*." He spat out the last word.

"That's not how we did it before," came Pomeroy's banal reply. "And that's not how we do it now."

Like a fork of lightning, it hit Dregan where the judge was. "Why are you in my home?" he spat.

"I'm not," replied Pomeroy. "I'd never make it up that ladder of yours. So I'm standing in your yard next to your Tahoe and talking to your boy. Where are you?"

"None of your business. Now put my boy back on and go bother someone else."

"I came to speak with you," replied Pomeroy. "Someone said you were snooping around Helen and Ray's place again."

"Providing a service."

"Now I'm *really* looking forward to seeing you in my chambers when you get back from your little sojourn," Pomeroy said.

Through gritted teeth, Dregan said, "Me as well." He paused. "Now give the CB to my boy."

There was a rustling and a grunt and then the radio went silent.

"Peter?"

"I'm sorry, Dad. I was playing in the snow when he drove up. He saw your truck in the drive. He didn't believe me when I told him you were gone."

Knowing Pomeroy was probably still within earshot, Dregan lied to Peter. "When your brother gets back, tell him that I changed my mind about going to Huntsville. I figure since the biters are slowed down I'm going to continue on north and snoop around Randall."

"When will you be home?" Peter asked.

"Before noon," replied Dregan, truthfully.

"Love you, Dad."

"Love you too, Peter."

Standing in the snow in the front yard of the Dregan home, Peter put the CB in his coat pocket and swung his gaze to the big man dressed in black. "Don't be mean to my dad," he said, voice wavering.

In turn, Pomeroy smiled wide and said, "If your dad continues to walk the line, you have nothing to worry about." He turned toward his full-sized Chevy Suburban, took two steps through the snow and turned back. "You did the right thing, Peter. You kept your dad safe by telling me the truth."

Peter stuck a spindly branch in the middle snowball of the three making up the scrawny-looking snowman's body. Unsure of what to say, wisely, he said nothing and watched the black SUV reverse from the drive and motor off toward the center of town. When it turned from view, he looked over both shoulders and, upon seeing the coast was clear, threw a pair of upthrust middle fingers after the SUV.

Chapter 12

Eager to spill about the new development, and wanting to do it in person so as to accurately gauge the reactions of the other survivors, Cade threw the truck through the corners and met the speed limit on the straightaways. A handful of minutes after leaving the quarry road he was through the main gate, had negotiated the middle barrier, and was pulling the Ford in tight next to a row of snow-covered trucks and SUVs.

The moment Cade rattled the transmission into *Park* and set the brake, he realized something was not right. Across the clearing, near the compound entrance, wearing parkas and hats and bulky snow boots, Taryn, Wilson, Sasha, and Raven stood in a rough semi-circle over a prone form that, judging by the muscular physique, had to be Lev.

Cade shifted his gaze to the near side of the clearing, just beyond the motor pool, and saw Daymon sitting in the Black Hawk's open door. The dreadlocked man was doubled over with his face planted in his gloved hands and to Cade it looked as if he was real close to throwing up. And to further complicate the already confusing scene, Duncan was kneeling on Daymon's left side, head craned and apparently trying to establish some kind of eye contact.

Leaving the motor running and his door hanging open, Cade hopped down from the truck. "What's going on?" he mouthed to Wilson.

Wilson pointed toward the Black Hawk across the clearing. "Daymon's what's going on."

"Is Lev OK?" Cade asked.

Answering the question, Lev sat up and started massaging the left side of his face.

Wanting to hear it from the horse's mouth, Cade hustled the thirty yards to the Black Hawk, where he found Heidi sitting inside on one of the canvas benches, sobbing, her eyes red-rimmed and puffy.

Daymon peeled off his gloves and looked up. Hands curling into fists, he said, "I'm going to kill that mother—"

"It was an accident," said Duncan, cutting him off. He was still on bent knee and trying to make eye contact.

Cade stood there, neutral, his head panning back and forth.

"*This* is no accident," Daymon shot back, pointing at his right eye. "It's going to be one hell of a shiner." He bent at the waist, scooped up a handful of snow, and pressed it to the eye in question.

"To be honest," proffered Duncan. "I've never seen a snowball fight that *didn't* devolve into fisticuffs like that."

Daymon ripped off his stocking cap, releasing the rubber-band-bound dreads that were just beginning to grow back. He chucked the cap on the ground by his gloves. "He was *aiming* for my head."

"Looked like it to me," chimed Heidi, dragging a sleeve across her eyes.

"I'm sorry," Lev called over the distance. "It's not like I packed rocks inside of them. Besides ... the way you and Wilson were laying low like little pussies, your ugly mug was all I could see."

Daymon threw his hands in the air, a wan smile curling the corners of his mouth. "I would have *checked* my fire."

"Just like you *checked* that right cross?" blurted Sasha, stalking towards the Black Hawk, Raven at her elbow trying unsuccessfully to slow her advance.

Daymon hopped down from the helicopter. He tossed the handful of snow to the ground, revealing the beginnings of a wicked shiner. "Okay, okay," he said, arms up in surrender. He fixed his gaze on Sasha. "You're right. I should have *checked* my anger. I'm sorry for overreacting."

"Late to the fistfight, I see," Cade said.

"Not much of a fistfight," Duncan drawled. "You just missed Urch here *not* connect a haymaker on Lev's chin. Hit him on the jaw and temple instead. Shoulda seen Glenda step in like Larry Steel and break them up."

Nearby, arms crossed over her chest, Glenda nodded.

Seeing this, Cade quietly said, "Sounds like you each landed a blow. Makes it even in my book. I don't care who started it. And I need you both to drop it. Forget it ever happened, because truthfully … with what I'm about to tell you we can't afford to waste any time on blue-on-blue engagements." He turned and faced Lev and the others and waved them over. Once everyone who was currently topside had assembled in the shadow of the hulking Black Hawk, starting with Raven, Cade looked each person in the eye, letting his gaze linger for a half-beat on each face before moving on. Finishing where he had started, he threw Raven a covert wink and described what the weather was doing to the dead. Looks of amazement were exchanged all around. There were a couple of muted high-fives. Then Cade answered all of their questions—most of which centered mainly on the sonic tempest he'd endured while in the midst of the immobilized herd.

Finished, he took Raven's hand and, with a subtle nod and arch of the brow, summoned Foley and Duncan to follow him away from the babbling crowd.

At the Ford, he boosted Raven up and into the cab with Max, who was still on the floor in the front and still enjoying the air blowing from the heater. Then he looped around back, dropped the tailgate, and proceeded to unload. He set both the shroud he'd removed at the quarry gate and the gooseneck lights from the outbuildings at Foley's feet and asked him to get with Seth and rectify the problems with the cameras.

"Me ... MacGyver?" Foley said. "I specialize in software and computers. Not tasks fit for a building superintendent."

"That's the attitude," Cade shot, a hint of sarcasm in his voice.

"You're right," Foley said. "It's just that I'm not looking forward to being cooped up all winter."

"The snow is our friend," Cade said. He smiled and gestured at the Eddie Griswold Winnebago parked under the trees by the road. "Maybe Daymon will let you bunk with him to cut down on the monotony."

"No thanks," Foley said. "Heidi's got that job now. Besides ... I've smelled one of his farts."

Feigning incredulity, Duncan said, "Worse than mine? Oh, goody." He rubbed his palms together. "More ball-busting ammunition."

"Just don't tell him I said it," Foley begged.

Pantomiming locking his lips and throwing away the key, Duncan said, "Secret's safe with me."

Foley flashed a thumbs-up and scooped up the shroud and gooseneck light standards.

"You do know there's fifty thousand of those dead things in Ogden. And according to Glenda, several thousand more in Huntsville and Eden," Duncan said, watching Foley lope off to start work on the new project.

"So we've got our work cut out for us," Cade said, matter-of-factly.

"And then some," Duncan added.

"Can you see to rounding up the necessary bodies, weapons and supplies?" Cade asked.

Duncan chuckled. "Can-do. Should I invite Rocky Balboa and Apollo Creed?"

"Your call."

"What are you doing?"

Cade nodded at Raven in the Ford. "I've got a promise to fulfill."

"I'm on it," Duncan said, and ambled off toward the compound entrance whistling the theme from the old Western *The Good, the Bad, and the Ugly.*

Cade climbed up and slid behind the wheel and in seconds had the F-650 angling for the feeder road.

***

With the widening swathe of blue sky renewing his energy, Dregan threw the aged Blazer through the turns, slowing only for the sharpest of hairpins and on the long uphill sections where the engine left him no other choice.

Around every corner he imagined the phantom vehicle would be sitting broadside, blocking the road, a half-dozen armed men with angry faces waiting to greet him.

Thankfully, a dozen minutes removed from the previous stop, so far, each blind corner had disappointed.

He could see the storm through the slot in the trees. It was moving west towards Huntsville and Eden, the east wind hurtling it towards a collision course with the craggy Wasatch Range where they would be ripped open and deposit whatever snow they harbored.

Once again, his sixth sense prompted him to slow down. Only now, it was more than a feeling of foreboding in his gut than an imagined vision of his demise.

A quarter-mile ahead the rig slowed, involuntarily though, as gravity and Mother Nature and the flagging diesel made it unavoidable.

Eyes glued to the two bluish-white stripes printed in the snow, Dregan held his breath until the shallow hill's curved apex, where the road widened slightly into a gentle right-to-left sweeper that eventually was swallowed up by the distant gloomy hole in the forest.

Both sides of the road were hemmed in for the first twenty yards or so. On the right side, a combination of thick undergrowth and dense forest was shot through by a sturdy-looking fence being slowly overgrown by it all. Paralleling the State Route to the left was a long run of triple-strand barbed wire. Rusting and sagging, it was secured every ten feet or so to gray and gnarled chest-high wood posts that formed a picket following the contour of the land all the way to the forest up ahead.

There was a meadow white with snow beyond the barbed wire fence where he half-expected to see deer or elk loitering. However, that wasn't the case as he slowed opposite it and came to a dead stop, the only sound the ticking of the diesel.

He swept his gaze around again and suddenly realized something was missing. A cold chill broke out all over his body as he dropped the transmission into Reverse and slowly backed up a few feet. Caught up in the suddenly changing scenery, he missed the fact that he had stopped the Blazer directly atop the point in the road where the wide set of tracks took an abrupt right turn. At first he couldn't fathom how the phantom vehicle had passed through the fence and parted the forest without leaving a like-sized hole and knocking every flake of snow off of the diverse flora as it had during its previous off-road deviation. Then he walked his eyes along the fence and several things dawned on him. Attached to one of the gnarled posts was a sturdy vertical hinge. In addition, behind the vegetation, which was real and had been living at one time, he could just make out a trio of horizontal bars, about as thick as a man's forearm and apparently made of steel tubing.

Everything was arranged so that to a passerby it looked just like a natural part of the scenery. Then, in his peripheral, a dozen feet above the shoulder, he picked up a pair of plastic half-domes each about the size of a softball and standing out only because of the hazy white rime clinging to them.

Suddenly his intuition was no longer just a distant voice urging him to pay attention. It was telling him he likely no longer had the element of surprise and had taken an instant one-eighty turn and was screaming ambush and urging him to flee.

Because Dregan had listened to the inner voice and acted immediately by throwing the truck into gear and backing away, he never heard the growl of an engine approaching from somewhere in the forest to his right. White-knuckling the steering wheel, he tromped the pedal to the floor. The diesel coughed and there was a tinny whine coming from the transfer case as all four wheels tried to obey the command relayed from the action of his foot.

Trailing a wide plume of gray-black exhaust, the rig fishtailed down the hill in reverse until reaching the run-out, where Dregan wrenched the wheel, put the gearbox in neutral, and spun it around in a sloppy one-hundred-and-eighty-degree bootlegger's reverse.

Heart pounding a hole in his chest, more so from the crazy maneuver than the words *ambush* and *flee* that had popped into his head, he engaged *Drive*. Wincing from the obstinate clunk of gears not exactly meshing perfectly, simultaneously he goosed the throttle and flicked his eyes to the rearview mirror, where he saw not so much as a single vehicle in hot pursuit nor a forest full of winking muzzle flashes announcing lethal lead being thrown his way.

Chapter 13

Cade pulled the F-650 up to within two truck lengths of the hidden gate. "Stay here for a second, sweetie."

Raven nodded. "Jawohl, kommandant."

With the driver's door partway open and just about to leap to the ground, Cade arrested himself with one hand on the A-pillar grab bar and looked over his shoulder. "What? Who taught you that?"

Raven began, "Taryn has a couple of episodes of an old show called—"

"—Hogan's Heroes," Cade finished, incredulous. "I can see Taryn liking it. She marches to her own drummer. But you?" He adjusted his ball cap and gave her a double take. "You like it?"

"Not really. But it's all we have."

"Not anymore," Cade responded. "I brought you something back from Woodruff that should keep you and the gang busy for a long while."

Raven instantly switched to Kid-on-Christmas-Eve mode and began needling Dad for intel.

"I'm not sure what titles I grabbed," he conceded. "When I take you back to the compound you can dig in and see for yourself."

"Is it an iPad?"

"Just wait."

"A TV and PlayStation?"

"Patience." He took the truck out of gear and set the brake. "Stay here," he said, reaching behind the seat. He came out with her Ruger rifle and grabbed his M4. He exited the truck, crunched thirty feet through the snow and then stopped behind the gate to look and listen. Seeing nothing there, he walked back and helped Raven from the truck, closed the door for her and handed over the little rifle.

Clutching the silk flowers in one gloved hand and the Ruger in the other, Raven followed behind Max to the gate. Once there, she cast a confused look back at the idling truck.

"Screw the gas," he said. "It'll be toasty inside when we're finished up there."

Nodding in understanding, Raven propped her rifle on the backside of the fence and held both arms out.

Cade leaned his M4 by the Ruger and then effortlessly lifted his daughter over the fence and settled her lightly on the other side. Gripping the Ruger by the forestock and aiming its muzzle away from his face, he handed it over the fence. He did the same with the M4 then said to Raven, "Watch our backs while I come over." He pulled up on the bottom strand and ushered Max through. Then he padded a few feet to his right and scaled the fence himself.

Standing on the shoulder in an ankle-deep snowdrift, Cade looked the length of 39. He let his gaze linger west for a few beats, then did the same looking to the east. "Clear," he called out more from habit than to tell Raven something she could obviously discern herself.

Once they'd crossed the slickened road, the process was repeated. Raven went over first. Then the guns and the dog. Lastly, after once again checking their six, Cade climbed up and over.

"Here," Raven said, handing over half of the bouquet.

Guns and flowers in hand, father and daughter tramped up the hill, and once they had reached its approximate center, Cade stopped briefly to get his bearings before changing course to his right by a few degrees. Another dozen yards and they were standing before the row of graves where the fallen were buried, the last three of which hadn't fully settled and stood out slightly from the rest.

Head down and moving slowly, Raven formed up on Cade's hip and handed him her rifle.

Without a word, she approached the first of the three snow-covered mounds. Stood at the grave, wavering for a moment before placing a red flower on the spot where she guessed the foot to be.

"We miss you, Chief," she said. "We're all very sorry that we had to bury you up here. None of us knew where your special place was. Lev had an idea … but he wasn't totally sure, so—" She went silent and wiped at the tears with the back of her gloved hand.

"You going to be alright, Bird?" Cade asked.

Raven said nothing. She merely nodded and shuffled a few paces to her right.

Even with a persistent inner voice telling him that this supposed attempt at closure was reopening old wounds, Cade decided to refrain from further comment and let her do this how she wanted. So, after looking over his shoulder at the road and then scanning the tree line for threats, he followed in her footsteps and again stood silent sentinel off her left shoulder.

At the second grave Raven knelt and arranged two flowers, one red, one white, in the shape of a cross, at roughly the same location as the red flower on the previous grave.

"One for you, Chief Charlie Jenkins. And one for ..." Her voice broke and she went silent for a tick.

Cade stole a glance and saw her jaw trembling. Still, he restrained himself. *Let her feel her way through it.* Better here and now in a controlled environment, than later somewhere foreign and all by herself.

"And one for Pauline," she went on. "She knows you tried. And she knew you loved her."

Strangely composed, Raven stood up straight and made her way to the final mound in the row of many. Stopped in front of the lonely looking grave on the periphery and placed on the ground near the foot what remained of her half of the bouquet of multicolored flowers. She removed a glove and reached into the front of her coat and came out with the slender aluminum cylinder hanging around her neck on a length of olive-colored nylon cord which contained the Omega antiserum auto-injector that as far as anyone knew—based on its short historical performance—had at most a thirty percent chance of saving whomever it was used on.

Worrying the cylinder with her delicate fingers, she said, "I'm sorry Duncan and my dad didn't get to you in time. Duncan liked you

... even though he said you wouldn't stop talking long enough to get a word in longwise."

Edgewise, thought Cade.

"Edgewise," Raven said, quickly correcting herself. "We're all going to miss you, Phillip." She went quiet and snugged her glove on. Adjusted it so that her trigger finger protruded through the cut off tip and took the Ruger back and held it at a comfortable low ready position.

To say Cade was pleased at how his twelve-year-old had conducted her *business* would be a gross understatement. Furthermore, he was heartened to see her know enough to free her trigger finger and fetch her weapon. Smiling inwardly, he asked quietly if there was anything else she wanted to say.

Wagging her head side-to-side, she said, "Nope," then knelt and scratched Max behind his perked ears.

All business, thought Cade. *Just like her mom.* He walked to his left and divided the rest of the flowers among the other graves. One each for Logan, Jordan, Gus, and Sampson. Just as he finished, the clouds parted overhead and the meadow was awash in blinding sunlight.

Shielding his eyes against the instant and overwhelming glare, Cade fumbled in his jacket pocket and came out with a pair of scratched and abused Oakley sunglasses, which he donned just as an epic sneezing fit wracked his body.

With Raven's repeated *bless you's* trailing off, he wiped his nose on his sleeve and looked uphill towards the break in the trees where the hidden overwatch was. He regarded Raven for a moment then, in a voice meant to leave nothing open to interpretation, said, "I want you to stay right here with Max while I take a quick peek at the old hide."

Raven said nothing. She just nodded and stomped her feet, trying to keep warm.

"Be right back." Cade turned and hiked a couple of dozen yards up the hill and when he finally arrived at the hide he found the place undisturbed. Apparently, in the weeks since the position had been abandoned, nothing, dead or alive, had found its way here from the nearby fire lane. Whether that last incursion by the dead that precipitated Phillip's death could be chalked up to just dumb luck or cunning creatures on the hunt, Cade hadn't a clue. However, the decision to abandon it afterward had nothing to do with the attack. Manpower issues and the changing weather were the driving factors. And the vote to do so was nearly unanimous, with Cade and Lev being the only dissenters.

Shaking his head, he gazed at the back of the hide where the creatures had entered. The undergrowth was trampled and the branches that had gotten broken in the struggle were now hanging limp, the leaves on them wilted and brown. The red clay soil ringing the abandoned shooter's position was scarred from the struggle. And as if to punctuate the life and death battle that took place here just a week prior, the lake of blood that had drained from Phillip's body at a lethal rate was still evident, albeit dried to black and reflecting the tangle of branches and snippets of blue sky overhead.

"Come on, Dad," Raven called. "I'm freezing my you-know-what off. And so is Max. His tail is *not* wagging."

Cade looked downhill and saw her kneeling and draping the shepherd with the bottom of her woolen army surplus coat.

"One more second, sweetie." He went to one knee and double-checked for new footprints, anything indicating the place had been visited—by the dead or the living. *Nothing.* He hustled back to Raven, shouldered his carbine, and gripped her gloved hand. He gave it a soft squeeze and helped her stand. "Feeling any better?"

"Yesh," she said, the word coming out garbled as she wiped her nose off on her shoulder. "I'm still real sad about Phillip, though. He was funny."

"I lost that bet," Cade conceded, hanging his head.

"What bet?"

"Oh ..." He looked at the State Road for a beat. West and east before meeting her eyes. He saw a steely determination in them—just like Brook. Finally, he went on, "The bet I made with your mom. I thought you wouldn't make it past the Chief's grave without losing it. Bottom line, Raven. You're a lot stronger than I give you credit for. You're a lot stronger than I think even you know. You're a survivor with ... as Mom used to say ... *an old soul.* Just like my pal Mike Desantos. Only he *was* old."

Raven stopped and fumbled around for the antiserum canister. Once she grasped it with her glove, she stuffed it back inside her coat and zipped that up to her chin.

"No reason to be embarrassed you have that," Cade said. "I earned it for you. It's yours. And yours, only."

She said nothing. Didn't stop walking. Didn't look up. Kept her eyes on the white ground.

He put his hand on her shoulder and in a somber silence—a silence possessing an almost physical quality—walked side by side with her down the hill. They climbed over the fence, crossed the road and were back at the truck and ensconced inside with the heater blowing on them before either of them spoke.

Raven said, "I won't tell Mom that she was *totally* right. Cause' she'll never let you live it down."

"You got that right," said Cade. "And that's mighty big of you." He rattled the transmission into gear and started reversing to a spot wide enough to turn around. They drove in the same silence, through the inner fence—which Cade closed and locked behind them—and almost all the way to the clearing before Cade, unable to help himself, asked, "So, *what* are you going to tell her?"

"The truth," Raven said. "I wanted to run but my legs wouldn't work."

So you toughed it out?"

"Yep."

That's my girl.

***

By the time Cade was wheeling the F-650 toward the compound motor pool, Alexander Dregan was passing by the quarry entrance and no longer looking in his rearview every few seconds. Moreover, the more miles the still-grieving father put between himself and his recent discovery, the more the anger that had trumped patience and driven him to follow the tracks in the first place had diminished. And when he finally made it to the junction with 16 and the scene of Lena's death, he was feeling a Zen-like calm and in the first stages of planning his long awaited revenge.

Chapter 14

Save for Brook, Seth, Heidi, Raven, and Sasha, the rest of the Eden survivors were topside and enjoying the sun's emergence.

Lev was in the process of hoisting a large black duffel bag into the bed of Daymon's Chevy pickup when Cade nosed the big Ford in next to it. As Cade killed the engine, Daymon, sporting a nasty shiner, his stocking cap pulled low, heaved his Stihl chainsaw into the Chevy's bed. The moment Cade stepped from the truck with Max shooting by him like a furry missile and nearly causing him to fall, he was fielding a flurry of questions. The first of which was Daymon inquiring as to how Cade knew for certain that the two vehicles on the far side of the roadblock were going to start.

Holding a finger up to both Daymon and Lev, an act that instantly stilled the verbal barrage, Cade clambered up onto the Ford's left rear tire. "Raven," he said, stopping her as she passed behind him. He leaned into the bed and, under the watchful gaze of Lev and Daymon, and with no attempt on his part to conceal the items, handed Raven two powder-blue boxes with no heft to them. "That's all for your mom."

Daymon looked to Lev and mouthed, "*Tampons*" and cracked a smile.

Shooting the pair a sour look, Raven started to walk away.

"Wait a second," Cade added. "There's more." He leaned back in and there was the rustling of plastic and the sound of something small rattling against hard plastic as he transferred some items from a garbage bag to a smaller paper bag. He jumped to the ground and handed the bag to Raven. "The medicine goes to Glenda."

Arms full and with her rifle slung on her shoulder and banging against her backside, Raven started off for the compound entrance.

"Tell your mom I'll be there in a minute," Cade called after her. He pulled a navy blue exercise ball from another pocket. It was about the size of a lemon and made with a rubber whose compound was just firm enough to provide forceful feedback when squeezed and kneaded. Though it was intended to be used by victims of stroke or paralysis for strengthening their hands and forearm muscles, Cade figured it would keep Max busy for a while. He got the plastic whip-like doo-dad from the truck and nestled the ball in the cup on one end. He cocked his arm then flung it forward and watched the shepherd come from out of nowhere to give chase. He handed the ingenious and nameless (to him) invention to Wilson, then walked between the truck beds, around the Chevy's tailgate, dropped it down and planted his butt on it.

Exhaling, he regarded Daymon and Lev with a steely gaze. "You two kiss and make up yet?"

Daymon grunted.

There was a whirring noise and scratching of paws and claws on the ground as Max tore off after the hurled ball.

Lev tracked its path for a second then dropped his gaze and said, "He's the one who swung on me. I'm waiting."

Like a little kid, Daymon mumbled something unintelligible under his breath.

Lev shook his head.

Cade did the same. He cast his gaze at the ground beyond the tailgate. "The price of greatness is responsibility," he said. "Sir Winston Churchill."

Daymon waited until Cade looked his way then stared him down. "Finished?" he asked, irritation evident in his tone.

With a sweep of the arm, Cade said, "You have the floor, my friend."

With no sorry to Lev, or thank you to Cade, nor millisecond of hesitation, Daymon said, "I want to go to Huntsville."

"Done," said Cade, to looks of amazement from both men—Lev more so than Daymon.

"That was easy," Lev said, wagging his head.

"One condition—" Cade began.

Daymon arched a puffy black-and-blue eyebrow, then grimaced from the pain.

"You have to bring Kindness," he said. "I think *he* ... *she*, whatever you call a machete, is going to see lots of action."

Daymon smiled and rested his hand on the machete's Day-Glo green handle. "It'll be just like cutting back a fire break. Only more rewarding."

Lev put his elbows on the edge of the truck bed. Looked Cade in the eye and said, "Me too? And Jamie? Because we want to *get some* ... for Phillip, mainly."

Right away, Cade nodded. "You can come. And Jamie too as long as she brings her attitude and that war tomahawk of hers."

"Done," answered Lev, smiling.

"We're going to need to bring Duncan," Cade added.

A disembodied voice behind them said, "What's that Old Man good for ... exercising the mutt?" Then a cackle filled the air and Duncan materialized from the nearby tree line. "By the way, the inner fence is clear. Not a single frozen rotter to be seen."

"Sneaking up on us like that is likely to get you killed," said Daymon in a near whisper, his voice taking on a gravelly rasp.

Duncan let loose another burst of grating laughter. Wiping away a stray tear, he said, "Son, if that's your best Clint Eastwood, you better go back to the drawing board. Cause you sounded more like Fred Sanford than ol' Dirty Harry. I bet somewhere the old boy is probably rolling over in his grave."

"He's probably holed up in a mansion somewhere in L.A.," added Lev.

"Los Angeles is *toast*," interjected Cade. "Load up. I'll round up the Kids and we're Oscar Mike."

From across the clearing, someone bellowed, "Cade Grayson ... I have got a bone to pick with you." A thin band of gray clouds parked in front of the low sun. Cade removed his Oakley's and steeled himself against Glenda's fast approach. "In private," she said, stopping a few yards short of the testosterone-filled huddle.

Something in the older woman's tone led Cade to believe that if he didn't capitulate and join her pronto, she'd march right over, take his earlobe in a death grip, and drag him to a place more suitable for interrogation.

"Go on," drawled Duncan. "She don't take no for an answer."

Cade twirled his shades in his hand, thinking.

"I don't like that broad," Daymon whispered.

"I heard that," Glenda said. Her hands went to her hips. "*Now*, Mister Grayson." She turned and walked a dozen feet toward the center of the clearing.

Leaving the three men chuckling in his wake and stepping clear of Wilson, who was winding up to chuck the ball again, Cade marched across the snow and stopped a yard away from Glenda. "Yes?"

"No bone to pick. I just wanted your attention."

"Well, you certainly got it."

"Three things," said Glenda. smiling at the admission. "If you make it as far as my house on the hill, will you go inside and bring me back some pictures of my boys? Maybe one of Louie, too. Duncan doesn't have to know."

"Mums the word. And …?"

"There were survivors on a sailboat anchored in the east end of the reservoir. I was keeping tabs on them through Louie's old field glasses. They didn't look too good then—" Her shoulders rolled forward.

Remembering seeing the boat she was alluding to on the trip out to Grand Junction, Cade said, "I know the one. I'll make it a point to check on them. And …?"

She began, "Don't take this weather for granted. Here today—"

"—Gone tomorrow," Cade finished.

Glenda nodded. "Exactly," she said, "and … you better bring Duncan back to me … in one piece. He's got to read his Fourth Step to me."

"Fourth Step?"

"A.A."

"Ah," Cade said.

No," shot Glenda, her brow furrowed. "A ... A. Alcoholics Anonymous."

Cade smiled and nodded dumbly. He asked, "How many days has it been?"

"Twenty-one," answered Glenda, beaming. "Not a detectable drop. Doesn't he look good?"

"He dropped some pounds. That's for damn sure. Not quite to fighting weight, though," Cade said with a wink. "That's three questions. Are we done here?"

"The question part, yeah," she said. "I wanted to thank you. There's some stuff in the bag Raven brought me that Heidi will benefit from. At least a couple of things that will keep her out of the *booby hatch* and sleeping topside in the Winnebago with her man."

Liking the sound of that, Cade said, "Then I'll be sure to keep my eyes peeled for more."

"You're a good man, Cade Grayson. No matter what Brook says." She laughed at her joke then looked past Cade and blew Duncan a kiss. Without another word to Cade, she about-faced and strode off toward the compound.

Cade turned and slinked back to the huddle. "Is she gone?"

The men craned and looked past him and nodded in unison.

The clouds scudded away to the west, leaving the sun's rays lancing down with a vengeance.

Cade donned his Oakleys and pulled his hat down low. "Load up the truck," he said. "Food, water, and ammo. Someone grab the battery and cables out of the F-650. I'll be right back."

"I'm driving," Daymon stated. "It's my truck."

Cade said nothing.

Duncan stared hard at Glenda's backside until she entered the compound. The second she was gone from view, he said, "I like her comin' and going."

Shaking his head, Cade tossed his rucksack in the Chevy's bed and hustled off towards the compound. He passed Tran and Foley along the way, the former clutching a handful of tools, the latter carrying the shroud and all three of the shades from the quarry outbuildings, now minus the gooseneck poles and light fixtures.

Cade nodded.

Tran reciprocated while Foley, displaying the fruits of his labor, held the fixtures up in front of him and said, "Superintendent is on it."

Chapter 15

Cade stepped inside the foyer, closed the plate door at his back, and suddenly couldn't see a thing. Pausing to let his eyes adjust to the change in light seemed to have no discernable effect.

"Sunglasses," said a voice from down the shadowy hall.

Cade said nothing. However, flashing a sheepish smile, he removed the Oakleys and stuffed them in a pocket. He transited the Conex and paused at the makeshift plywood security desk where he whispered *thank you* to Seth, who was grinning and staring at the flat panel monitor. Smile fading, Cade reached past the man's head and with one hand grabbed the thin black satellite phone, its green missed call light still steadily pulsing. With the other hand, he worked the charging cord loose and tucked it out of the way.

Seth looked up from the monitor. He flicked his eyes to the phone and asked, "Aren't you going to see what Nash wants?"

"Not right now." Cade quickly stuffed the phone into his pants pocket.

There was a long pause during which both men stared at the monitor and watched Tran man the middle gate while Foley wheeled the white Dodge Ram on through. Finally, Cade shifted his gaze from the monitor, met Seth's eyes, and whispered, "But maybe later."

***

Topside at the motor pool, the six people joining Cade on his impromptu excursion had already checked and rechecked their weapons and stowed their full magazines in pouches affixed to their load-bearing MOLLE gear.

Jamie was sitting on the open tailgate and methodically running the gleaming blade on her black hatchet across an oiled whetstone, the rhythmic rasp interrupted by Duncan and Daymon debating the merits of a machete over a Gurkhas' khukuri, with the older man, of course, extolling the value of the latter primarily only to push Daymon's buttons.

A few yards away, in the Black Hawk's shadow, Taryn and Wilson took turns throwing the ball for the thoroughly exhausted Australian shepherd.

***

Roughly a hundred yards away and ten feet underground, in the Grayson's quarters, Cade set the overflowing garbage bags on the floor. He propped his carbine by the door. He shed his pack and coat and put them on a chair by the door. Greeting Brook with a kiss, he reached in a cargo pocket, came out with the second stress ball and handed it to her. She nodded then gave it a squeeze with her right hand and promptly deemed it "*perfect*". Then, looking like a magician performing an impromptu trick, Cade pulled the balled-up elastic bands from his pant's pocket, one at a time. Green, red, yellow, then another green band, which was followed by a final red one.

"Where's the rabbit?" asked Brook, the left side of her face lighting up with a smile, the opposite showing a touch of paralysis.

"Daymon ate it."

Raven's head popped up. She put her book down and scooted to the edge of her top bunk, eyes wide, jaw slack.

Seeing this, Cade said, "Joking. Daymon only eats squirrels. But don't tell him I told you so."

Raven's headlamp beam cast crazy shadows on the back wall as she pantomimed zipping her lip before inching back to the center of her bunk.

"You break down and listen to the message from Nash yet?"

Cade shook his head side-to-side.

"I'm impressed. That's got to be a record. What's it been ... five days?"

"Seven. But who's counting," he said.

"How long you going to hold the need for adrenaline hostage, Cade Grayson?"

"We'll have to wait and see if my plan goes accordingly."

"If it does?"

"Then it depends how you're feeling about me heeding the call." He took a bottle from the chair by the bunk and squirted some liquid from it onto his palm. Held it for her to see. "Vitamin E?"

She nodded. Turned away from him and slowly hiked her shirt up in back.

"It's looking better and better every day," he said, enthusiastically. "Is it feeling any different … still tight?"

"It's tolerable. Doesn't feel like a bear trap clamping down on my skin today."

He rubbed his hands together to warm the oil. Worked it into the thick scar tissue near her spine where the crawler had rent a chunk of flesh from her.

"Oh ... shit, *that* smarts!" she exclaimed, as he worked the nutrients into the angry red nodule.

"No pain—" Brook began.

"No gain," Raven finished, a soft blue glow now edging out the gloom above her bunk.

"Limit your time on the computer," said Cade. "You'll ruin your eyes."

"With all that's going on out there, Grayson," Brook said, hiking her shirt back down. "And that's the nit you're choosing to pick?"

Cade faced her and shook his head. He squirted a bead of oil on his index finger and worked it into the pink scars peppering her face. "Those bullet fragments sure did a number."

"Last I checked I wasn't trying out for the Miss America Pageant. Besides ... better the fragments than the whole chunk of lead."

"Roger that," Cade replied, nodding. "And to think there'll never be another Miss—" Suddenly cutting off his thought, the radio in his pocket hissed and in his familiar syrupy drawl Duncan was imploring him to *get the lead out.*

"Gonna answer him, Dad?"

Cade shrugged and kissed Brook on the forehead. Then, looking her in the eye and with a vertical finger pressed to his lips, he rose up from the bunk, snuck over to the far side of Raven's perch and grabbed the dainty foot dangling over the edge—a move that elicited a shriek and burst of laughter. He let go, poked his head above the bunk, and then blew her a kiss. "See you in a while, Bird."

"Dad," she said.

"Yes?" he answered.

Raven said nothing. Instead, holding it by its nylon cord, she dangled the canister containing the last dose of Omega antiserum near his face.

He reached up and took it from her. Turned it over in his hand once before rising and stepping up onto the bottom bunk. And though she was recoiling away playfully, he gently grabbed her wrist, pulled her near and coiled the cord into her open hand. Gazing into her eyes, he placed the canister in her palm and closed her fingers one at a time. "It's yours and only yours." He wrapped an arm around her neck and kissed the top of her head, noting to himself that she was sticking to her guns and no longer wearing her hair in pigtails. *Too girly*, she had said the day before. And par for the course lately, in solidarity with her mother, her brown locks were pulled up into a high ponytail that stuck out back of her ball cap like a mare's tail.

Saying nothing more lest he get all maudlin on his girls, Cade traded the ball cap for a black knit item, scooped up his carbine and coat, and ducked out the door.

"When should we expect you back?" Brook called after.

Poking his head back inside, he replied, "Before dark, hopefully."

She blew him a kiss and then he was gone, the heavy door clanging audibly in his wake.

***

The sun was back behind the clouds when Cade exited the compound, so the Oakleys remained in his pocket. Halfway across the clearing, he saw that the truck bed was loaded down with more gear and people had already taken their places inside. To his amazement, though Taryn was arguably their most capable driver, she was sitting in the back seat between Wilson and Duncan. Seeing this display of humility, given her young age, had Cade marveling at how far she'd come since being plucked from the jaws of death on that body-strewn runway in Grand Junction. How in just a few short weeks she'd morphed from college student working a summer job as an airport barista to an orphaned but capable member of a small group trying to survive hell unleashed on humanity.

As Cade neared the truck, he saw through the back window that Lev was riding *bitch*—as Cade's fellow Delta operator Jorge Lopez was fond of saying—and, curiously enough, Jamie had gotten her wish and was riding *shotgun*, with her head leaning against the passenger window.

So, left with no other seating option, Cade threw his carbine in the bed, snugged his hat low on his head, and climbed over the closed tailgate.

Cade donned his glasses to ward off the slipstream to come, cleared a space for himself amidst all of the gear, and cast a quick glance at the side mirror, where he caught sight of Daymon flashing him a toothy grin. Knowing full well based on past experience what was coming next, Cade clamped a gloved hand firmly on the side of the box bed and worked his boots under Daymon's overstuffed Kelty backpack. And he was right in doing so, for a tick later the engine revved and Daymon was reversing out into the clearing much faster than necessary, *testing* the 4-wheel drive no doubt. Suddenly the truck slewed and lurched to a stop—a move that quickly reorganized everything in the bed, Cade included. Through the sliding back window Cade saw a two-way radio in Duncan's hands. Then the grizzled aviator craned back, met Cade's gaze and mouthed: *We're waiting for Foley.*

***

A couple of minutes passed and then Cade detected the faint sounds of the approaching vehicle. A handful of seconds after that the white Dodge Ram burst from the narrow feeder road, looped around and parked in the vacated spot. And as Daymon wheeled the Chevy towards the road, Cade watched Tran and Foley exit the Dodge simultaneously. Then, before they were lost from view, he caught sight of Foley flashing him a thumbs up. *Mission accomplished,* thought Cade just as the heavens opened up anew and big fat flakes filled the air all around him.

***

Less than a minute's travel down the bumpy road, the truck came to an abrupt stop and Cade hopped out and opened the middle gate. He stood aside and let Daymon pull the truck through, then shut and locked the gate. Instead of immediately climbing aboard the idling truck, he hustled over to the tree with the security camera attached to it and inspected Foley's handiwork. He watched big flakes settle on the newly installed lampshade and promptly slide from its steeply angled surface. Liking what he saw, he climbed back into the bed for the short ride to the hidden gate.

Along the way, with the truck dancing to and fro about the rutted gravel road, he stared up through the narrow gap in the trees at the thinning band of blue demarking where the previous storm ended and the next began. And as he did so, near his feet, Wilson's Louisville Slugger was doing a crazy dance on the truck's bed. By his head someone's pack was vibrating madly, loose rounds in a side pocket jangling away. To his left, making a racket of their own from impacting the metal bed was the spare battery and jumper cables. Adding to the cacophony that suddenly reminded him of a Big Easy one-man-band was a rattling chainsaw, fuel and oil for it, plus gas for the pair of SUVs awaiting them on the other side—the latter of which was sloshing around in a half dozen plastic cans.

In no time the truck came to a smooth, rolling stop and there was silence. Cade hopped out and checked the main gate for Zs. Finding it all clear, he swung it open and watched the truck roll through.

Chapter 16

Once the Chevy was on 39 and pointing west, Cade closed the camouflaged gate and cast a cursory glance at the CCTV domes. Superintendent or not, Foley had come through again. The shroud above the domes seemed to add ample protection from the elements without adding much to the entire unit's profile. Which set him at ease, because if a person didn't know where he or she was looking, the likelihood of it being spotted from the road was slim to none. And those were the kind of odds Duncan was always crowing about, so Cade figured they were the kind he could live with.

Before boarding the truck, he removed a glove and dug the Motorola from his pocket. He called up Seth and asked him how the view was.

"Crystal clear," came the man's reply.

"Is the external audio mic working?"

"I can't hear you and you're what … ten feet away?"

"About," Cade replied. "Can you hear the truck's engine?"

"Nope."

"One thing at a time, I guess," Cade conceded. "Can't expect Foley to work miracles considering the circumstances."

"Roger that," Seth replied.

"We'll be switching over to the handheld CB soon. Make sure yours is powered on with fresh batteries."

"Copy that," Seth called back. "And you guys all come back, ya hear. *Stay frosty* out there."

"Roger that," Cade said. "No pun intended, right?"

"I'm not that witty," said Seth.

Cade listened to the younger man's laughter then heard him say *Over and out* like some kind of trucker and the connection finally went silent. He stood there for a three-count then pocketed the radio and crawled in the bed with his back against the cab. And as the truck pulled strongly to the west, his eyes were locked on the flowers up the hill and he realized how they were more than just an acknowledgement of the dead. That they were also more than just a device to pretty up the ground while simultaneously punctuating their passing and gaining some kind of closure in return. To him, at that moment, the flowers represented the vibrant and bright souls of the survivors he was glad to know and surround himself with. And, conversely, the stark white snow was the perfect metaphor for the cold cruel world closing in on them.

***

At the intersection with 16, Dregan turned left, drove a short distance and parked a dozen yards south of the herd. He regarded the dead that had obviously been run over. Then he looked at the ones he had culled with the sword. Finally he wielded the binoculars and swept the head of the column. Though he couldn't be a hundred percent certain, the monsters there looked to be just how he saw them last, albeit sporting a little more snow on their heads and shoulders where the standing ones were concerned.

He saw a murder of crows strutting about the ground, hopping upon the fallen corpses, but largely staying away from their gaping maws.

He exited the truck and slammed the door, causing the birds to take flight in an explosion of black feather and excited chatter. As he crunched forward, sword in hand, he watched a pair of pissed-off raptors alight on an upright corpse and their combined weight start a massive chain reaction. When all was said and done, the crows were again airborne and twenty or more of the semi-frozen monsters had clanked together and were settling on the roadway in various poses. Some reached skyward with gnarled fingers. Others had settled almost board flat, their mouths ajar and readily accepting the falling snow.

Dregan approached one of the standing creatures, drew the Viking steel and slid the scabbard between his hip and belt. He stopped an arm's reach from the biter, brought the sword over his head and held it there, two-handed. "Fuck you," he muttered and delivered a vicious chopping blow that split the leering abomination vertically from skull to breastbone, where the sword stuck fast. He tugged once and the corpse remained upright and wavering, the sword wedged firmly. *When all else fails*, he thought. *Put the boot to them.* And he did, his size thirteen boot in front of an explosive kick to the stiffened flesh-eater's chest sending it crashing to the road. *One down, millions to go.*

Curious as to how the cold had affected its brain, Dregan moved around to its head and probed the gray matter with the sword's tip. Expecting to find the outer lobes frozen solid, the opposite was true. Like the inner core—cerebral cortex is what he thought it was called—the outer matter was moist and soft and he hadn't a clue why. A light jab from the sword's tip to one eyeball was met with much resistance. Upon further probing he found that it was beginning to freeze.

Having seen enough to confuse him completely, Dregan returned to his vehicle, tossed the sword on the passenger seat, and climbed behind the wheel. A tick later, after performing a tight U-turn, he was motoring south with the soothing sounds of Bach and thrum of rolling tires serenading him.

***

At that very moment, sixteen miles to the west as the crow flies, Cade was clambering out of the Chevy with his fully loaded ruck on and the suppressed M4 in hand. He checked that the spare magazines for his carbine were snugged securely into their slots on his chest rig then zipped his parka up around his bearded chin and watched the others gear up and assemble.

Daymon shrugged on his battered Kelty, which was bulging in odd places because the bulky car battery and jumper cables were now shoehorned inside along with the rest of his gear. He wore Kindness, his aptly named machete, strapped to his right leg. The stubby shotgun Duncan had bequeathed him weeks ago was dangling off his left shoulder by a short nylon strap. And as if he wasn't already loaded down enough, the lanky former BLM firefighter snatched the Stihl chainsaw off the truck's open tailgate and manhandled it over his shoulder, where he balanced it horizontally and held it there with one gloved hand gripping the business end of the flat guide bar.

"Got the kitchen sink anywhere on your person?"

"No, Cade. I left that at the compound," Daymon shot back. "I've got a Snickers bar in here somewhere, though. Carry the saw and you can have it."

"I like 'em," Cade replied. "But not that much. And thanks—"

One-handed, Daymon snugged the Kelty's waist belt tight. Finished, he looked at Cade and said, "Thanks for what?"

Cade reached into his jacket pocket and came out with something in hand. He unwrapped it slowly and when he was finished, displayed the faded brown wrapper with its easily identifiable logo facing Daymon and took a big bite, chewed slowly and swallowed. "For reminding me this was in my pocket. That's what," he said through chocolate-stained teeth. "It's been in there for weeks."

Sitting a dozen feet away and loaded down with a pack and shotgun of his own, Duncan called, "Holding out on us, huh Cade?"

Cade said nothing. He just finished off the candy bar and stuffed the wrapper in a pocket.

"Let's go," said Wilson, impatience evident in his voice. His Todd Helton was perched on one shoulder and he was standing shoulder-to-shoulder with Taryn, their matching Beretta pistols on opposing hips and nearly touching.

Meanwhile, back at the truck, Lev and Jamie had just finished splitting up the group's food and had stowed it in their matching desert-tan soft packs.

Daymon and Duncan were already on the other side of the roadside ditch and passing the time ribbing each other. Cade interrupted the grab-assing and said, "Felix. Oscar. Why don't you two go ahead. We'll catch up with you."

Duncan flipped Cade the bird but there was no questioning the request. Daymon turned and melted into the forest. Duncan shrugged and smiled and then followed the boot prints in the snow.

Daymon pushed through knee-high ferns and ankle-grabbing undergrowth and when he finally emerged from the first layer of forest, he halted and leaned against a freshly cut stump to wait for the others.

Meanwhile, back on the road, Cade was telling the others to go on ahead of him.

"You sure?" asked Jamie.

"Positive. I want to hang back and cover up our tracks."

Seeing the wisdom in that, Wilson said, "Need a hand?"

"I got it."

"You can't carry our water forever," Wilson said.

"No, I can't. Nor do I intend on doing so." Then, without realizing he was regurgitating a line favored by his late mentor, Mike Desantos, Cade added, "This isn't my first rodeo, Wilson. You all can go ahead and catch up with Frick and Frack. I'll bring up the rear."

There was a moment of indecision on Wilson's part. As big flakes fell silently on the cedars and firs blocking the road, the redhead went quiet and stood staring at Cade while a fair amount collected on his floppy boonie hat.

Cade pointed to the break in the forest, in the general direction the sounds of breaking branches was coming from. "Go," he said, in a firm fatherly tone.

Holding their matching AR-style carbines at a low ready, both Jamie and Lev nodded and without a word entered the forest.

Cade made a shooing motion that finally got Wilson and Taryn to follow after the others. He waited until they were out of sight then moved off the road and crouched down among a drooping clutch of ferns, his suppressed Glock locked and loaded.

***

After remaining still for a handful of minutes with his collar covering his mouth to keep evidence of his breathing from giving him away, he concluded they were all alone. He stood and brushed the accumulated snow from his hat and shoulders. Then he looped around the truck, locked the doors and stowed the key in his back pocket. Reaching across the hood, he hinged both wipers up and away from the windshield—an old trick to keep them from freezing to the windshield he'd learned back in his skiing days. Then, just to set himself at ease, he searched for a suitable fallen limb with a fair amount of branches and needles. Knocked the snow from the five-foot item to lighten it up some and walked a zig-zag pattern backwards from the Chevy to the spot on the shoulder where the others had entered, sweeping the branch back and forth the entire way in order to cover their tracks.

Chapter 17

Bach's concerto finished and the next track on the CD Lena had burned for Dregan the day before her wedding began playing. It was a pop number from a band she adored. Some young guys calling themselves *Marooned Five*. He shook his head, thinking the group should've dispatched with the mysterious and just gone ahead and called themselves *The Gilligan's Island Five*. Or *Tom Hanks and the Castaways*. Maybe even some funny play on *Lord of the Flies*. If anything, at least the latter would appeal to the British teenagers. Then, just as quickly as the inane train of thought entered his mind, he forgot about the band and his mind drifted to Lena.

Cursing, he ejected the CD, switched hands on the wheel and rolled the window down with the hand crank. Fucking U.S. Army contracting with Chevy and buying the cheapest base model available. No power anything. Cut its balls by dropping an underpowered diesel power plant in it to save a buck and then turned around and spent the savings on heavy-duty bumpers and a fresh coat of brown, black, and green paint.

He chucked the CD out the window and then shook his head, thinking it quite ironic how he—an immigrant and naturalized citizen from the Ukraine—was now driving a perfect example of how Ronald Reagan duped the old Soviet Union into spending themselves out of World Super Power status.

Doing his best to forget Lena for the time being, lest he let his rage get the best of him again, he rolled up the window and let the engine noises replace the pop band, and hopefully the emotion it had dredged up.

He felt the transmission searching for a lower gear as the Blazer tackled the next hill head on. Then the engine took on a lower tone—going from the usual rattle-clatter to a kind of labored growl as the apex drew near. At the top, he stopped and set the brake. Still a good distance from the turnoff to Helen and Ray's ranch, he grabbed the binoculars off the seat and glassed the property from left to right. Dotting the pasture were dozens of snow-sprinkled alpaca carcasses, the wisps of hair still clinging to them jumping and dancing along with each new gust of east wind. Beyond the pasture, he saw the turnaround in front of the two-story farmhouse and fifty feet south of there the red and white barn looming over them both.

The windows of the buildings were darkened, which was to be expected since the power was still out and might never be restored. He noticed the old couple's battered pickup wedged tight against the house, and for a brief second thought about stopping and sharing his good fortune with them. Maybe tell them where the tracks had led him and pick their brains and see if they knew what type of people inhabited the valley between Woodruff and Huntsville before the walking dead did to the United States in weeks, what all of her enemies had failed to do in the two hundred and thirty-five years prior.

***

While Dregan was in the truck on the hill and looking down on the farm, Ray was just to the right of the dining room picture window, holding the curtain back with one hand, and looking off to the northwest through narrowed eyes.

Cradling the antique shotgun in the crook of his arm, he craned towards the stairway and said, "Is it him, Helen?"

"I'm not sure," she answered, her voice echoing down the gloomy stairwell. "What do you see?"

Squinting against the glare and unable to bring the dark shape on the distant road into focus, Ray said, "A black blob. Hell, all this snow makes it so bright that it seems like I'm staring down an oncoming train."

Upstairs, Helen spun the focus ring on the field glasses, bringing the vehicle into sharp focus. She said, "It's him again, alright."

"I was afraid of that," Ray called back. "I'm starting to think he knows we aren't telling him everything."

"I sensed it earlier," conceded Helen. "He seemed on edge. Like a climber whose last rope is beginning to fray."

"Well," Ray said. "If he comes up the drive I'll walk out and greet him. If I sense any bad intent I'll give you the signal and distance myself from him."

"If I shoot him dead," Helen called. "We're going to find ourselves dragged up before Pomeroy."

"Better to be judged by twelve than carried by six," replied Ray.

***

Staring intently at the house on the hill, Dregan mulled over the possibility that the group the old couple gave refuge to the day Lena and Mikhail were murdered might return on less friendlier terms than before. And if they did, what would the geriatrics do? The fact that he didn't truly know where the couple's loyalty fell was troubling to say the least. On one hand, since Helen and Ray had been beneficiaries of Bear River's charity when their Alpacas were decimated by the dead, the probability of them calling right away as promised, Dregan figured, was highly likely. However, if the murderous gang surprised them before they could get to the radio, they would probably be forced into giving up the nearby community in order to save their own skin. Sad thing was, Dregan couldn't quite blame them.

So with more questions than answers kicking around in his head, and drawing up battle plans and acting on them before the element of surprise was lost first and foremost on his *docket*, he took his foot from the brake and, to save gas, let gravity pull the Blazer forward. Snickering at the play on words, that he was certain Judge Pomeroy would find no humor in, he let the rig coast all the way down the hill, past the road leading up to Helen and Ray's house and another couple of hundred yards beyond and then eased his boot down on the gas pedal.

***

Helen propped her carbine in the corner next to the bed. She walked to the doorway and, projecting her voice down the hall, said, "He's gone." She shuffled back to the bed where she sat down and listened to the stairs creaking under Ray's weight as he came up to join her. A minute later he entered the room, sat on the bed next to her and, shoulders rounded from the stresses of their new existence, said, "He's got to grow tired of the constant searching."

"Put yourself in his shoes. You'd be searching too."

"The way that poor man talks about Mikhail, I would have *never* given that boy my blessing."

"Not even if *she* was smitten?"

Ray said nothing. Just shook his head and sighed.

Staring towards the window where big flakes were swirling and pattering the glass, Helen said, "We're going to weather this storm, Ray. Just like we always do ... together."

***

A quarter-mile away Dregan was beginning to curse the new storm moving in when the answer to his dilemma suddenly dawned on him. Shaking his head side-to-side and angry at himself for not seeing the obvious until now, he wrangled the transmission into *Drive* and accelerated south in the northbound lane. Steering one-handed, he snatched up the CB and, speaking in his native tongue in case anyone was eavesdropping, hailed his oldest son. There was a long moment of silence during which the sky really opened up, instantly cutting visibility down to a couple of hundred feet. So Dregan flicked on the wipers and halved his speed. Finally a voice answered in Russian and, skipping all the preliminary pleasantries, Dregan bombarded his son, Gregory, with a flurry of orders, delivered rapid-fire and also in Russian.

With the smile on his face growing wider, and oh so ready to savor the sweet taste of revenge, Dregan signed off and began filling the roster in his head with the names of men he knew who—for a price—would help him move forward with his plan.

Chapter 18

When Cade first caught sight of the rest of his party, all six of them were standing shoulder-to-shoulder on the same fallen length of moss-covered old growth, taking in a sight that apparently had rendered them all speechless.

Cade padded down a beaten path flanked by chest-high stumps on the left and a wall of logs on the right. A few yards later, he came to a steep drop-off and found himself peering down on a creek bed littered with no less than a hundred stiffened corpses, their faces frozen in death grimaces, many of them staring straight up at him. Arms and legs, bent and broken, jutted at odd angles from a thin stratum of wind-drifted snow. It was what he imagined the killing fields of the Chosin Reservoir or Battle of the Bulge might have looked like to the heroes who survived those examples of Hell on Earth. And as he marveled at the sheer number of Zs that had ended up down there on account of too many bodies crowding the two-lane crossing, it dawned on him that no way in Hell could all of the corpses tangled together down there be dead in the real sense of the word. But as awful a scene as it was, it appeared that whatever the others were gaping at had it beaten hands down.

Interest piqued, he picked his way right along the edge of the cliff, stepped up onto the log and, standing next to Daymon, finally got his first unobstructed look at the crossing. And what he saw there, as hard as it was for him to wrap his brain around, easily dwarfed the assemblage of death below.

Breaking the all-encompassing silence, Daymon turned to Cade and said, "Got a God-sized weed-whacker on you?"

Cade said nothing. The sight of close to a thousand Zs clogging the bridge and crowding the group's two vehicles, all seemingly staring the meat from his bones, had stolen the words from his mouth. The only thing going for the group was that the wall of corpses was stationary and not belting out that spine tingling sound he was exposed to earlier. And no sooner than the thought had crossed his mind, Duncan said, "So Cade ... strangely enough, I'm not hearing all of the Pod People screams that you described?"

Still, Cade remained silent. He was performing a quick headcount using a trick taught to him by the President's former head of protection, Adam Cross. It was in no way scientific, but by dividing the area occupied by the crowd in question into little parcels and then estimating the number of bodies in each parcel, the task could be boiled down to a simple math problem. And a handful of seconds after seeing the static column in all its gory glory, Cade came up with a number. And that number was worse than he thought.

"Seven hundred … give or take."

"Captain America speaks," Daymon said.

"I say *give*," proffered Jamie, eyes glued to the monsters and hefting the tomahawk in one hand.

"There can't be *seven hundred* rotters over there," said Wilson, his voice cracking.

"I'm leaning on the *give* side as well," added Cade. "Let's get at it." He edged by the group, grabbed a wrist-sized branch sticking vertically from a fallen old-growth fir, and hauled his hundred and eighty pounds—two-forty total, including the full rucksack and weapons—up onto the next log over, where he found solid footing and proceeded to help the others up.

"Seven hundred," said Lev, shaking his head as he accepted Cade's offered hand.

Cade smiled. "Plus several dozen that seemed to have gotten themselves in a pickle and are stuck fast to Daymon's sharpened branches."

"My idea," said Duncan.

"Those are not *punji* stakes," countered Daymon. "Whole different concept. You can take *all* the credit for those poo-dipped things."

Cade gave Taryn and Jamie a hand around a jagged clutch of branches, then watched them follow the men who were slowly picking their way lengthwise along the fallen log. With Daymon leading, they crept along single file, putting one foot in front of the other mindful of the shadowy crevices, all the while battling vertical branches with a propensity to snap back and deliver a stinging reminder to the unaware that this was no proverbial walk in the park.

"Be careful when you jump down," warned Cade even before they reached a suitable spot to do so. "There's sure to be crawlers trapped under there."

Eventually the seven survivors had made it unscathed to the midpoint of the first hundred-and-fifty-foot-tall tree Daymon had dropped across the road weeks ago and found themselves looking down on the front row of Zs, where a myriad of different contorted faces and frosted-over eyes stared back. It seemed as if all walks of life were represented here—whites, blacks, Hispanics, Asians—the Omega virus didn't discriminate whom it infected. And once infected, the dead saw everything as meat. Packed in against the barrier, like a bustling crowd leaving a subway train car, were a mix of men, women, and children—the majority of them once able-bodied males, and all of them suffering from the elements and in varying stages of decay. A good deal of the dead were badly burnt, their dermis blackened and contrasting sharply with the blanket of white that had settled over everything.

Cade swept his eyes over the static crowd and spotted an undead farmer still wearing frayed overalls but sans the ubiquitous straw hat. He saw twenty-somethings in skinny jeans and concert shirts. A gangly soccer mom had died and reanimated and come a long way from home judging by the bloodied tee-shirt declaring her son an honor student at Joseph Smith Middle School in Salt Lake City. There were preadolescents, the elderly, and everything in-between represented there on State Route 39. Also on display were the defensive wounds suffered by many in the herd that spoke loudly of man's incredible will to fight back. A high percentage of them had suffered horrible bites to the neck and torso—raised purple rings dappled with pale tooth marks. And the craters where mouthfuls of flesh had been viciously ripped away were now crusted with blood, frozen black and shiny. Cade noticed how a large number of the monsters were missing digits, or parts thereof. And standing out from the crowd, flashing macabre toothy grins like the worst nightmares imaginable, were the ones who had lost all of the soft fleshy bits from their faces to the dead before turning and joining their ranks.

Mercifully dragging Cade from his momentary daymare, Duncan said incredulously, "Where in the hell do we start?"

Elbowing Wilson in the ribs, Daymon said to him, "Why don't you jump on down and let Todd Helton start the conversation?"

Brow furrowed, Taryn craned and shot Daymon a sour look. In the next beat she turned to face Wilson, hoping to hear a strong rebuttal.

"Eff that," answered the redhead. "I'll jump down after *you've* killed enough with *Kindness*. Besides ... what if we're all down there and they suddenly reanimate?"

Jamie delivered a look to Taryn that said *it'll be all right*. Then she regarded Wilson and said, "It's too cold for them to reanimate. I'll go first and show you *all* how it's done. Figure a good place to start would be freeing up the vehicles so Duncan can work on getting them running. Then we just hack our way across the bridge."

Daymon nodded. He kneeled and set the chainsaw down, balancing it crossways between two fallen trees. He rose, leaned forward to look at Cade and suddenly the weight from the top-heavy pack started him on a one-way trip toward the mosh pit of death. But Lev's arm flashed out and he got a handhold of Kelty just before the point of no return. Clutching the ripstop nylon in a death grip, he held on long enough for Cade to spring to action and together they reeled Daymon back from what would have amounted to a back-wrenching fall—at the very least.

Without missing a beat, Daymon nodded a thanks to Lev then reacquired eye contact with Cade and asked, "So Sarge, are you going to answer Duncan's question?"

Purposefully Cade shot him a dumb look and shrugged as if saying *I don't follow.*

"Where are your screamers?" Daymon cupped a hand to his ear and said in a cartoonish voice, "I can't hear you *screamers*. Cat get your tongues?"

"Good thing we can't hear them," Cade said. "I figure when these things start screaming again it'll mean they're thawing out, and by then if we're anywhere near a whole bunch of them—" He paused to let the words sink in. Looked over the faces of the others and finished his thought. "We might as well all kiss our asses goodbye."

"Enough talk," said Jamie, throwing a visible shudder. She turned to face Cade. "Where should *I* start?"

Cade gripped her right shoulder. Took the tomahawk from her hand and slipped it into the sheath attached to her belt. Then he looked down the line both ways, first at Jamie then Duncan and lastly Lev. Then he shifted his gaze and met eyes with Wilson, Taryn, and lastly Daymon. Once he had their undivided attention, he filled them all in on the next part of his plan.

Chapter 19

The closer Dregan got to the fortified community called Bear River, the fewer dead he encountered. However, now and again, drifts of snow on the road concealed the random corpse that when run over broadcast the sickening crackle of breaking bones through the truck's floorboards. Save for herds and the occasional mega horde transiting north to south and back again on nearby 16, the community had made great strides in keeping the roamers culled. Frequent trips outside of the walls were now the norm. Over the last few weeks, the judge had the foraging patrols pushing farther out on a daily basis. They'd made the most gains south and east, clearing and searching every building they came across, and returning with trucks filled with food, water, firearms, and all manner of useful goods. *We're taking our valley back from the dead and any lawless that we catch in our noose will be questioned and tried by a jury of their peers* was the judge's response to Dregan after denying his initial request to form a posse of sorts to track down Lena's killers. That was the first time of many when the judge had made it clear that under no circumstances were the citizens to take the law into their own hands. An edict that Dregan didn't agree with. '*Rulings*,' is what Pomeroy called his decrees. Of late, after having assembled a sizable group of men he had armed and appointed as court bailiffs who answered only to him, he was acting as if he were a Supreme Court Justice and, like the prestigious nine of the old world, was preparing to *rule* for life over the burgeoning community.

Cursing the man under his breath, Dregan turned east off of 16 and followed a meandering tree-flanked two-lane that rose and fell gradually before dog-legging right and cresting a rise, where he brought the Blazer to a crunching halt. Looking at the walled community of Bear River from afar, he saw the squared-off tops of the perimeter guard towers rising up above the trees they'd been constructed in. Though the hard edges and whip antennas sprouting from the nearest were a dead giveaway as to their presence, the heavy weapons hidden behind walls constructed from precast concrete noise-reduction panels sourced from the freeways to the south had already proven adequate to repel even the most determined breathers coming with bad intentions.

Dregan slowed and brought the Blazer to a halt in the center of the road on the final rise before the long downhill run-out to the turnoff to the front gate. Knowing he was being watched, and that one high caliber sniper rifle was trained on his upper torso and another chambered to fire a much larger round was targeting the Chevy's engine block, he switched to the guard channel and announced who he was.

To Dregan, good OPSEC (operational security) meant following these necessary formalities. There was a saying an old veteran and mentor back home used to recite that best described who he was before, during, and after the *Great Fall*—as he and others in the community called the rapid worldwide spread of Omega and the even faster fall of law and order. *There are three types of people in the world: sheep, wolves, and sheepdogs. The sheep cower when confronted with danger, accepting their demise with a banal indifference. The wolves—murderers, rapists, thieves, and child molesters—are the predators who take advantage of the sheep. Then, young Dregan, there's me and the men like me who are the sheepdogs*, the man had said at the time. *We were born with an innate ability to harness and channel aggression. We feel the need to protect the flock from predators, the wolves. You'll know who you are early in life, Alexander.* What he said next eventually started Dregan on a quest to prove him wrong. *It isn't necessarily imbued through training or experience. It's a feeling ...* Dregan remembered the man saying while tapping a finger firmly on his breastbone. And as he sat in the truck thousands of miles from where it took place, he remembered the moment as if it had happened yesterday. He recalled the fragrant flowers blooming next to the parade grounds. Heard the Hind helicopter beating the air far off in the distance.

Yes, though softened around the edges over the years, Dregan was still one of them. And this old sheepdog missed the man who had taught him so much. He wondered if Yuri had ridden out the Great Fall, thinking maybe the old warhorse, a foot shorter and twenty years older, had found an island off the Crimean Peninsula and was surviving just like him.

With the memory of his friend fading back into the ether, a burst of static followed by a voice requesting the password came from the radio's speaker.

Dregan keyed the CB to talk. "Jack," he said with a wan smile.

"Jill," came the scratchy reply.

Jack and Jill, thought Dregan. Easy enough to remember, but not as clever as yesterday's *Bart* and *Lisa.*

Dregan set the radio aside and drove down the slight decline, past a copse of stunted trees, and caught sight of the south gate, which was nothing more than a Jackson County school bus, all thirty feet of its passenger compartment filled to the windows with hardened concrete. Through the mesh screen covering the front passenger window he saw movement and then slowly the bus reversed to create an opening just wide enough for the Blazer to pass through.

Parked inside the entry, flanking the narrow road was a pair of desert-tan Humvees sprouting turret-mounted machine guns. A dozen men milled about, their reflections rippling in the Hummers' green-tinted blast-resistant glass.

Dregan saw a knot of men clothed in civilian attire standing next to a copse of firs. Two of them were smoking and all were carrying carbines slung over their shoulders.

He pulled up close and rolled his window down. Looked to the rearview and watched the bus move back into position, sealing them all inside. Flicking his gaze back to the men, he put the truck into *Park* and fished out a cigarette of his own, the first of the day.

He flicked a disposable Bic, lit the Camel and, barking out their first names, called three of the men over.

Chapter 20

The house Dregan had initially claimed for himself and his two sons was one of those you'd find built on an abbreviated lot in a growing city. In-fill was what he had heard them called. Two-and-a-half times taller than it was wide, and with a single-car garage taking up most of the downstairs footprint, the three-story place was perfect from a defensive standpoint.

The main living area, once accessed by a steep stairway rising from the cement pad fronting the garage, was home to an average-sized sofa and pair of overstuffed chairs. Next, divided by a wide granite bar, came the dining room and kitchen. And at the rear of the house on the left was a small bedroom and opposite it, a half-bath. A sliding patio door led out to a deck overlooking an overgrown backyard. Secured to the sturdy cedar railing with three-inch decking screws was an emergency fire ladder ready to be unrolled in a moment's notice to effect a quick escape if need be.

Two more bedrooms were on the third floor: the master, with the balcony over the parking pad facing north, and the other, diametrically opposed at the rear of the house, facing south, its deck affording a sweeping vantage looking out over an orchard with a clear view of 16 snaking off into the distance.

Dregan parked in an alcove of sorts. Stacked haphazardly against the wood shake wall rising up in front of the rig were dozens of rust-streaked propane tanks commonly found under most outdoor barbecues. Rising to the top of the driver-side door were a pair of industrial-sized propane tanks, the kind normally exiled to the periphery of your local gas station and emblazoned with all kinds of OSHA-approved warning stickers. Partially strangled by creepers and host to a thin veneer of snow were the remains of the front stairway, brown pressure-treated treads and risers and stringers all cracked and twisted from being physically rent from the house by a vehicle with a tow chain.

He killed the engine and grabbed his belongings. Exited the Blazer and looped around front of the captured Jackson Hole patrol Tahoe. He slung his carbine and sword over his shoulders, letting them cross behind his back. Removed his gloves and stowed them in a pocket. Then, commencing his least favorite part of coming home, took ahold of a freezing cold rung and began to scale the telescoping ladder propped up where the stairs used to be attached.

He hauled his considerable bulk hand-over-hand to the front porch, making it there a little out of breath. He worked his keys in the trio of locks on the door and once inside could still see his breath coming in blossoming plumes. He rubbed his hands together and called out, "Gregory!"

Nothing.

"Peter!"

Still no response.

He closed the door and crossed the foyer to the base of the stairs. "Anyone home?"

A sleepy voice called down. "Yes, Dad. I went back to bed."

"Is that all you do … sleep?"

"No. I play video games but it's too cold to go outside and start the generator."

"Get your lazy butt up, Peter," bellowed Dregan. "It's nearly noon."

"Who cares. I don't have to go to school. Or work. Sleeping passes the time."

"Get down here. We need to talk."

A bunch of grumbling and bellyaching filtered down the stairway. Then heavy footsteps crossed the floor followed closely by the hollow clunk of a toilet seat hitting the tank.

"Damn right it's cold, boy," Dregan said, crossing the room. He knelt on the tiles in front of the jury-rigged natural gas fireplace.

There was a braided steel hose running from a tank outside through a hole in the wall and across the hearth, where it disappeared behind a steel grate. In the center of the hose Dregan had spliced a valve with a wheel. He palmed the wheel counterclockwise, starting a slow hiss of gas from behind the clouded glass. Acting quickly so the gas couldn't build, he clicked the Piezo igniter, producing a whoosh and instant warmth that he felt on his face.

***

A handful of minutes later, the fake logs were glowing and Peter had come downstairs and was prone on the sofa, wrapped up in multiple blankets and peppering his dad with questions.

"We'll have to see," replied Dregan to Peter's third inquiry as to how many people the *other side* had. At twelve, the boy tended to still see conflict as if it were a first-person-shooter game and not the life and death equation the apocalypse often presented.

"The only way I'll know the answer to that question is if they pay a visit to the ranch before we move on them."

"The old couple?"

"No Peter. We can't rely on them. I dropped in on them this morning and they seemed a little standoffish—"

"What's that mean?" asked Peter.

"They didn't seem too friendly."

"Oh."

"You have to learn how to read people, Peter. You get that down … you've won the battle before it begins."

Sitting up, Peter asked, "They were mean?"

"No … they just weren't as inviting as before. I felt like a stranger in their home." Dregan stopped pacing and leveled a serious gaze at the boy. "For all I know they're trading with the kids too. So I've hatched a plan to make sure I know if they venture back into our part of the valley by this time tomorrow."

"What happens this time tomorrow?"

"I'm going hunting."

"What about me?"

"I need you to stay here. If the judge comes sniffing around again you are not to talk to him. Think you can you do that this time?"

Peter nodded.

Dregan smiled. He could no longer see his breath and had removed his gloves. However, even with the radiant heat slowly warming the family room and working its way upstairs, the house remained cold and uninviting. Nothing like the *home* the dead ran him and his family out of, forcing them to leave behind everything including decades of fond memories.

He walked to the kitchen and looked out the window. Across the street, fronted by a ragged hedge, was the house Lena and Mikhail had recently taken as theirs. The grass not beaten down by the snow was drooping away from the hedge and crowding the narrow cement path leading to the front door. The curtains were pulled closed and the driveway was empty. Just looking at it infuriated Dregan and shot a cold chill through his body.

Turning back towards the warmth, he looked down at his watch and realized he was not going to make the agreed-upon meeting with Pomeroy at the makeshift courthouse.

Chapter 21

To a person, the Eden survivors thought Cade's plan was doable until twenty minutes or so in, when all of the dragging and lifting and pushing it took to toss the corpses into the void began to take its toll on all of them.

"We need help," Wilson said.

Daymon cleaved a rotter's head from crown to brow, then paused and shot the redhead a cold stare. "You're beginning to whine like your sister."

Coming to Wilson's aid, Taryn shot back. "That's harsh. He's pulling his weight."

Saying nothing, Daymon took hold of a corpse that the cold had shut down mid-stride, jaw leading the way, in a pose suggestive of forward motion. Still making no comment, he hauled the stiffened body across the eastbound lane to the railing, where he released his arm from around its waist and left it like he'd found it—standing, skin as white as the snow its bare feet were planted in, and looking more like a store mannequin preparing to take a leap than something carrying a virus deadly to them all. He let his gaze linger on the male corpse for a second then looked down the length of the rail and addressed Wilson. "My moms told me it's easier to get your work done when your gums aren't flapping."

Finding a strange sense of confidence after hearing his girl stand up for him, Wilson toppled a Z into the void, turned, and said, "My *moms* was fond of saying if you can't say anything nice, don't say anything at all."

Taking a handful of the creature's soiled blue jeans, and wrapping the fingers of his other hand in its oily hair, Daymon rose with a grunt, twisted at the waist, and heaved the shirtless creature over the edge. He watched it bounce and come to rest atop the pile then turned back to Wilson, lip curled into a sneer, and hissed, "You taking my effin inventory ... *boy?*"

After shifting his gaze from Daymon to Wilson and then quickly back to the dreadlocked man, Duncan dropped his corpse like a sack of potatoes. "Daymon ... you been readin' my Big Book?"

Already kneeling next to another corpse, Daymon looked up, brow furrowed, and said, "Your what?"

"Never mind," drawled Duncan. He held Daymon's gaze for a beat then went on, "You already gave Lev a shot to the jaw. Now you and Mister *needs-to-grow-a-pair* here are jawbonin'. To me it sounds like something's eating at you. Shall we talk about it?"

Daymon flashed Duncan the bird, then, for a beat, as snowflakes danced across the road on a gust, regarded the middle-aged female staring up at him. Looking like he had come to some kind of a decision, he finally grabbed a fistful of natty blonde hair and plunged a gloved thumb into the Z's eye socket. Smiling, he worked it around like he was churning butter, then dragged the dead thing to the railing and, without pause, added it to the growing mound directly below the bridge.

"Guess that answers my question," muttered Duncan, snatching a child-sized flesh-eater off the ground by its stick-thin arms and giving it a flying lesson.

"Halfway there," bellowed Cade from across two lanes as he watched a limp body cartwheel down the cliff wall and smack the rocky creek bed below with tremendous force. "Keep it up. We'll rest when we clear a path to the west end."

***

Heeding the sage advice of Daymon and Wilson's long dead mothers, the group put their heads down, their differences aside, and worked in silence. Thirty short minutes later, the narrow bridge was cleared of the dead and the group had gathered mid-span.

"Five hundred down, two hundred to go ... is that about right Cade?" Duncan asked.

"I'd say you're in the ballpark," Cade replied. "You want to take charge of getting our wheels up and running?"

Duncan took a pull of water from a Nalgene bottle. "I'm on it," he said, dabbing a sheen of sweat from his forehead with a faded handkerchief. He put the damp rag away, finished the water, then walked the length of the gore-spattered bridge to the overgrown spit of land hemmed in by a drop-off on the left and the tree blockade on the right. He knelt down and fumbled around in the snow until he found the flat rock Cade had hidden the keys under. He wiped the dirt off the two sets and thumbed the unlock button on the black fob.

Success.

The 4Runner's lights flashed and he heard the soft double *thunk* of the door locks actuating. He opened the gore-streaked door, climbed behind the wheel and, half-expecting to find the battery dead since the vehicle had been sitting idle for weeks, was delighted to hear the seatbelt warning chime when he inserted the key in the ignition.

Two for two, he thought.

"Be gone, Mister Murphy," he said, as he turned the key. At first, *not* sounding like *success*, there was a faint clicking that didn't sound at all good; then, as if his plea had been heard and heeded, the V6 motor churned to life.

Leaving the engine running to work up the charge, he made his way to the Land Cruiser with the plastic doodad in hand that looked nothing like a key or a fob. He simultaneously waved the device by the door handle and depressed the button there. The sound of the locks popping was much quieter than the 4Runner. *Oh the refinement an extra fifty grand could buy a fella in the old world.*

Once he was sitting on the supple leather driver's seat, he set the smart key in the console, pressed a foot on the brake, and depressed the *Engine Start/Stop* button. At once the dash lights dimmed and went dark entirely. That was it. No seatbelt chime. No starter ticking away futilely. Just silence interrupted now and again by the faraway sounds of the others dispensing of the dead.

Duncan pounded a palm on the wheel and without conscious thought snaked his hand into his inside coat pocket—an autonomous action learned from years of dealing with his problems the only way he knew how. Glenda called it *coping by numbing out.* And it caught him *completely* flat-footed.

He sat straight and took a deep breath. Thankfully, there had been nothing in the pocket. No smooth metal flask. No pint of Jack. Not even a dainty airline bottle crafted perfectly in scale to resemble the full-sized item.

He had been coping without that liquid crutch since the first time he sat down with Glenda in the clearing at the fire pit weeks ago and poured every drop of Jack he possessed into the ashes. In fact, he hadn't had so much as a nip since Chief and Jenkins went into the ground and he'd even succeeded in white-knuckling it through Phillip's ordeal. *Fake it til you make it*, Glenda had said at the time. And though he was the one who had been sent to the hide to check on Phillip and found him in a different state altogether than he had expected—wandering around the clearing with half of his neck ripped away and all of his guts missing—he couldn't do what needed to be done. At least not at that stage in his sobriety. So, all the while fighting the overwhelming urge to find a bottle and check out—he waited by the fence until Cade arrived and then, with a feeling of utter worthlessness hanging over him, watched the steely-eyed survivor stick a dagger in the snarling beast that used to be their friend.

He made it through the funeral, cursing Phillip for losing his life even while he sensed he was one drink away from losing his own.

So that night, with Jack Daniels and the ghosts of the recent dead sharing equal space in his head, he had dropped to his knees beside Glenda and repeated a prayer he thought hokey and old-fashioned at the time. Instantly the weight from living the way he had been for the last decade—a weight that had increased tenfold since the dead began to walk—was suddenly lifted.

Seeing this recent knee-jerk reaction for what it was—a learned response to stress he would probably never be rid of and thankfully didn't ever again have to rely on—he bowed his head and closed his eyes and said in a low voice, "God grant me the serenity to accept the things I cannot change; the courage to change the things I can; and the wisdom to know the difference."

Feeling a thousand times better, Duncan opened his eyes and fixed his gaze on the far end of the bridge. There he saw Cade moving through the dead, stopping here and there to stab into them with his blade.

Nearby, Wilson was still swinging away at skulls with his bat, wasting way more energy than necessary, culling only one rotter to Cade's half-dozen.

A couple hundred feet beyond the stretch of road Cade and Wilson were clearing, Taryn, Lev, and Jamie were dragging corpses already granted a second death off the road and into the woods.

Meanwhile Daymon had been working a knot of dead between the other two groups, swinging *Kindness* at the standing corpses and felling them like wheat to a combine.

Duncan watched the former firefighter cull the last of the ones that were standing; then, as nonchalantly as if he were taking a union-mandated break, sit atop one of the larger specimens and then start running his whet stone back and forth along the machete's blade.

"That's my boy," Duncan said, in front of a sad-sounding chuckle. Then, having seen enough heads being chopped to last ten lifetimes, he hinged over and popped the Land Cruiser's hood. He hauled himself out of the driver's seat, made the long walk to the mound of gear, and returned, schlepping the tools, cables, and battery.

He connected the jumper cables between the rigs, slid onto the Cruiser's cold leather seat, and commenced the wait necessary to determine if the battery would take a charge. Bored and cold, he opened the center console and dug around in the contents. Passing on the manual and spare bulbs and fuses, he came out with an official-looking document, unfolded it, and determined it was a dealer's shipping and sales invoice. He perused the specs, got to the small print indicating the sales price, and took a deep breath. "You've gotta be effin kidding me. Seventy-nine grand for this trailer queen." He knew it was a pricey ride, but not closer to a hundred grand than fifty. Shaking his head, he refolded the piece of paper, put it back inside the console, and closed the leather-wrapped lid. Then he leaned over and punched open the glove compartment. Trimmed in fake walnut and skinned with the same leather as the rest of the rig, the lid opened slow and quiet, revealing in all of its black and white glory a full and sealed fifth bottle of Jack Daniels.

"Fuck me running," he whispered. He wracked his brain and couldn't recall placing it there. But then again, as he thought back, he was always prone to finding bottles he had stashed away during a blackout.

What he did next was totally unexpected and involuntary. Causing the rig to shimmy and consequently the amber-colored liquid to ripple in the bottle's neck, he recoiled and sat ramrod straight.

With a knot twisting in his stomach, he sat there staring straight ahead and listening to the nearby 4Runner's V6 purr away. After another minute or two, during which he stole a couple of quick guilt-filled glances at the bottle, he worked up the courage to lean over and, as if the yawning glove box was harboring some kind of venomous snake or brimming with skittering jumbo-sized scorpions, quickly slam it shut.

With the elephant in the Land Cruiser now behind closed doors, he let out a deep breath and thanked God he wasn't tilting Old No. 7 to his lips and making bubbles. However, in a perfect world and to another person, *out of sight, out of mind* would probably suffice. His first instinct after the split-second recoil should have been to crack the seal and pour it out on the snow outside—the operative words being *should have*. But a beat after seeing the label, he was no longer driving the bus, metaphorically speaking. And the little voice in his head, the one currently taking fares and issuing transfers, had already convinced him that shutting it from view would be adequate for now.

He drew in a deep, calming breath, reached over with his right hand, knuckles still showing through the skin from gripping the wheel tight, and once again depressed the *Engine Start/Stop* button. There was a different sound this time, like a starter turning. A tick after there came a promising shudder from the engine then absolute silence.

"Bastard." Duncan slapped the wheel and flicked his eyes to the exotic wood-trimmed glove box door.

Fighting the urge to give in to the little voice in his head telling him he could get away with *just one*, and knowing that one *always* tasted like *more*, he muttered under his breath and stepped out into the cold.

Chapter 22

Ten minutes of playing mechanic, a couple of busted knuckles and half a book's worth of expletives later, Duncan had the dead battery from the Cruiser swapped with the one from Daymon's backpack.

Doubting the swap would lead to instant success, he trudged back around the open door, got in and punched the all-powerful *Engine Start/Stop* button.

The starter whined and the engine turned over. *Victory*. Hard as it was for Duncan to believe this tired-looking thing was basically new off the lot a few short weeks ago, the motor sounding as strong as it did gave him confidence that—despite its thoroughly battered exterior—the thing would make the relatively short round-trip to Huntsville and back.

As he sat in the Cruiser monitoring the voltmeter's needle on the dash cluster and basking in the tepid air now filtering through the vents, he could feel the compulsion welling up within him and, before he knew what he was doing, the glove box door was open and his fingers were caressing the smooth glass bottle.

Nearly rocketing out of his skin as a result of three sharp raps on the glass to his left, Duncan slammed the door shut and turned that way, no doubt wearing a kid-caught-with-his-hand-in-the-cookie-jar kind of look on his face.

"Cade Grayson … you trying to give a fella a heart attack?" he drawled, punching the power window the rest of the way down.

"If Glenda hasn't killed you yet," Cade said, wearing a grin. "Nothing I do is going to hasten your trip to the grave."

Hoping Cade hadn't seen the bottle, Duncan changed the subject. "Well, the 4Runner started right up. This princess ... not so much." He thrust both hands out the window, displaying his knuckles. "I put the new battery in. Good call bringing it."

"Looks more like you got into a street fight," Cade said. He took hold of Duncan's hand. "Are the shakes back?"

Duncan made a face. Pulled his hands in through the window and folded them in his lap. "No . . . why do you ask?"

Cade said nothing. He studied his friend's face and deduced that if the two of them were standing nose-to-nose the older man would have probably crossed his arms defensively and most likely shifted his gaze away and up prior to spewing that last line of bullshit.

"How long have you been standing there?" Duncan asked, his voice barely a whisper.

"Long enough, Old Man," Cade answered.

Duncan sighed. It was a remorseful from-the-gut kind of sound. "I was just about to pour it out," he lied.

Cade leaned forward and placed his crossed forearms on the Cruiser's roof. "Looked to me like you were giving it a hand-job."

Duncan removed his glasses. Tossed them on the dash where the air from the vents gave them a quick fog. When he turned back, in a serious tone he asked, "Did I ever tell you how much I *loathe* that nickname?"

Cade turned his head and looked at the rest of the crew, who were now sitting on the road and passing around MREs. He started drumming his fingers against the roof. "Did I ever tell you how I loathe being called by my full name? My mother did it ... and when she did, I knew my ass was grass."

Duncan chuckled. "Brook does it too. Doesn't she?"

Cade nodded. He said, "Look at it on the bright side, Old Man. Every time someone calls you by the nickname your brother coined, he's being remembered in a small way."

Duncan said nothing. Unconsciously he broke eye contact with Cade, passed his gaze over the other survivors who were now standing in a loose circle in the center of the road, and then fixed a hard stare on the glove box containing the fifth of booze.

Seeing this, Cade said, "I'll leave you two alone to talk things through." He pushed off the vehicle, turned, and walked away.

Duncan wanted to say something. Anything. But his innate ability to conjure up a witty quip or think of a prescient observation to get the conversation moving in another direction failed him. The proverbial cat had his tongue and was swallowing it whole.

All he could do was stare at Cade, who had already covered about a dozen paces. Saw him shift his carbine to his right hand and glance at the ever-present black Suunto on his left. Then, saving him from doing something he would regret, the former Delta operator said in a booming voice, "We're Oscar Mike in five."

Still watching Cade close the distance with the other five survivors, who were now policing up their gear, Duncan leaned over and snatched up the bottle of Jack. He closed the glove box door and, muttering under his breath, twisted the cap ever so slowly. The paper tax-label tore; then, with a practiced chop of the palm, he spun the cap off and caught it one-handed mid-flight. Instantly the scent of sour mash, heavy with charcoaled oak, hit his nose and froze him in a moment of indecision that lasted all of two seconds.

"God grant me ..." he stuck his arm out the window and, finishing the prayer in his head, turned the bottle upside down.

Chapter 23

The bailiff, if you could call him that, was a skinny little runt of a man with a prominent forehead made all the more noticeable by the thin ring of gray hair riding up high on his misshapen skull. Why Pomeroy hadn't scrounged up an official-looking hat and uniform for the guy had Dregan wondering how serious the self-important prick was taking his new approach to justice.

As the bailiff's bugged eyes trolled the room, first scrutinizing the gallery where Dregan sat among a half-dozen other Bear River citizens, then passing over the jury of twelve, he couldn't help but think how much the guy, who had to be pushing sixty, reminded him of the late actor Don Knotts. Not the younger Barney Fife version, even though, like the *Shakiest Gun in the West* in Andy Griffith's Mayberry, the bailiff's Colt Python revolver also wore him. But more so like the older, shifty-eyed, Ralph Furley character of Three's Company notoriety.

Though a trio of propane-powered heaters worked hard to heat the converted bookstore, Dregan couldn't get warm. Shivering on the folding chair, he passed the time waiting for the show to get on the road by watching his own breath roil from his open mouth.

At 11:59, a murmur rose from the jury seated left of the judge's large wooden desk and a shadowy form eclipsed the frosted glass of the storeroom door immediately behind it.

Furley's body went rigid when the doorknob rattled. Then, as the door swung inward on well-oiled hinges, a little more enthusiastically than need be—in Dregan's opinion—the Don Knotts lookalike put a cupped hand to his mouth and called out, "All rise for the honorable Judge Lucius Pomeroy."

The rustle of fabric mingled with the steady hissing of the heaters as nineteen people rose, and though Dregan's arthritic knees were suffering horribly from the sudden change in weather, he followed suit.

The judge entered first, followed closely by an African American bailiff who was almost twice the size of the first, yet still gave up a hundred pounds and a couple of inches to the judge. The bailiff wore a tag that read: *Mason.* He pulled a chair from the kneehole and stood rigid and silent while the rotund judge plopped some papers on the desk, looked up over the top of his square-framed glasses, and gave the room a cursory glance. Finally, as the first bailiff closed the door, the judge adjusted his black tent-sized robe and sat down with an audible grunt.

As the chair's springs groaned in protest to the three hundred pounds settling on it, Mason stepped forward and said, "You may *all* be seated."

The Don Knotts look-alike bailiff remained standing, left hand perched on the Colt, while Mason walked the aisle between the folding chairs and exited through the papered-over front door, closing it quietly behind him.

Dregan sat back in his seat with an audible groan, the pain seemingly going in equal opposition in real time to the falling mercury. For a long minute, the judge didn't look up. Maybe he was praying, thought Dregan as he tried massaging the blood back into his knees.

Finally, Judge Pomeroy scooped a manila envelope off the desktop, opened it, licked one sausage-like finger and began flicking through a dozen sheets of what looked to Dregan like ordinary printer paper.

***

A few minutes went by before the judge finally looked up to address the jury and give instructions. Fighting the urge to nod off, Dregan listened half-heartedly as the judge went over the evidence and testimony that would be admissible in the case.

The oration was short; once the judge finished, the front door opened and Mason was back, leading the accused in with the help of another of Pomeroy's recruits—a younger man Dregan recognized but didn't know by name.

What was wrong with the way they'd been doing this? Dregan had asked anybody who would listen, in the days prior to the court system being brought back by popular vote. *Busy work*, he decided, after seeing that first trial drag on for two days and end exactly as it should have, with the thief losing a hand and then immediately being taken kicking-and-screaming to the State Route and exiled as a reminder to all of what would happen if one of the Ten Commandments was broken.

One less mouth to feed, Dregan supposed as the bug-eyed bailiff called the plaintiff's name and read off the charges.

Dregan winced as each horrendous offense read aloud created a visual he couldn't purge. Towards the end of the long list he was seeing Lena's face transposed on the shocking images in his mind, and it took every ounce of self-control in his body to keep from walking forward ten feet and throttling the cannibal baby raper himself.

The prosecutor, who supposedly had been a real honest-to-goodness lawyer at a big firm housed in a mirrored tower in Dallas, Texas, before everything fell to pieces, rose and adjusted her rumpled navy pantsuit. One at a time, she called two credible witnesses, let them say their piece, asked a couple of questions and then rested her case.

Next, the witnesses were cross-examined by a reluctant-looking town member acting as defense counsel. *For fuck's sake, get on with it*, thought Dregan, as the man droned on, not totally into it, but still going through the motions.

Finally, the defendant, a twenty-five-year-old malcontent who had allegedly grown up in a boy's home and escaped from a correctional boot camp after the dead began to walk, threw his hands up and said, "Let's just get this fucking joke of a trial over with so you can banish me and I'll be on my merry way."

"What are you trying to say?" asked the judge, steepling his fingers, a gleam in his eye.

"I did it. It was done to me and therefore I do it to others." He laughed. A kind of high-pitched squeaking that went on until the judge struck the desk with the square-headed meat-mallet acting as a gavel.

"Order," the judge said.

"I guess that settles that," said counsel, nervously adjusting his loosely knotted tie.

"I have nothing to add," stated the lady lawyer.

Thank God. Dregan sat up and his chair creaked, drawing nervous glances from the jury and a woman on his right who had been knitting an infant-sized jumper.

Judge Pomeroy raised his makeshift gavel and again pounded the desk with it. "The prosecution rests. Defense?"

The man in the tie nodded and organized the papers in front of him without regard to the slack-jawed defendant to his right. "Defense rests," he finally said, and took his seat.

Out of his side vision, Dregan saw Bailiff Mason move forward from near a carousel filled with used paperbacks and take up position behind the self-confessed cannibal and habitual child rapist.

"Having been found guilty by your own admission, I, Judge Lucius Pomeroy, on behalf of the good people of Bear River, do hereby pronounce you, Dewey Ford, guilty of *coveting,* thereby breaking the Tenth Commandment. I hereby sentence you to death—"

Ford bristled when the judge said *'coveting'* and then rocketed from his chair when he heard the severity of the sentence. In a flash, Mason had drawn a bright orange gun-shaped item from the holster on his hip. Before Ford could shove his chair back, the smaller bailiff was rushing to protect the judge from the front and fifty thousand volts were coursing through Ford from the rear, the charge being delivered through a thin filament stretched a dozen feet between the TASER in Mason's hand to the metal barbs lodged firmly between the condemned man's shoulder blades.

As the defendant's limp form lay on the floor, pants soiled in front, Judge Pomeroy finished the sentencing spiel. "Dewey Ford, I hereby sentence you to death by biter. And I hope they start on your privates."

"They're not *active* right now," said Mason, still holding the TASER.

The judge rose and looked a question at Dregan.

Dregan nodded, corroborating what the bailiff said.

"Bailiffs ... I want him held in custody until such time as the sentence can be properly administered."

As if he was trying to make a second break for the door, Ford started to twitch. Then the soles of his shoes made a cringeworthy squeaking noise against the floor tiles as his legs spasmed uncontrollably.

Staring daggers across the desk, the judge motioned Dregan forward.

Dregan nodded, then rose on legs half-asleep and shot through with pins and needles.

"My chambers," said the judge.

The back room of Armchair Family Books, corrected Dregan in his thoughts. *Pretty far removed from the United States District Court for the District of Utah.*

Chapter 24

The fallen tree roadblock and patch of discolored snow where Duncan had emptied the fifth of Jack Daniels on the roadside was four miles behind the Land Cruiser when he stabbed its brakes and pulled over to the shoulder.

"What do you want to do?"

Cade craned around and watched the 4Runner pull up even and stop. "I say we push on and tackle the root of the problem. That was hard work back there. I can only imagine how longshoremen feel after a day's work."

"I've done some of that kind of work ... in my youth." Duncan smiled at the memory. "We mostly hit the bars after shift. Closed the place down. Rinse and repeat after a bowl of Wheaties."

Daymon poked his head between the seats. Looked at Duncan. "You didn't do much if *any* of the heavy lifting back there, Old Man."

"Yeah ... but against all odds I got this here demolition derby victim running."

"True dat," said Daymon, offering a fist bump, which Duncan regarded for a second before leaving it hanging in the air over the center console.

Saying nothing, Daymon disappeared into the back seat all by himself.

Duncan looked a question at Cade. The same one he had offered on dozens of occasions since his brother was murdered, leaving him the sole Winters at what had at times informally been called the Winters' compound. A reluctant *why me* look that meant a vote was in order.

Cade nodded. "So we vote."

Duncan powered his window down. He nodded at Wilson and addressed Taryn, who was driving. "You guys need to vote on whether we cull these rotters here and now, or finish them on the way back. Cade's of the opinion we need to push on."

Taryn nodded. Duncan watched her twist around and talk to the back seat passengers, Lev and Jamie.

"Three of us want to push on to Huntsville now," Wilson said. "Jamie"—he nodded toward the back seat—"wants us to put down as many as we can before the weather turns."

"I kind of agree with the lady," said Daymon. "Glenda did say the temps can make wild swings this time of year. I've seen a little of it in Idaho and Wyoming."

Cade had been listening, but he was also walking his gaze over the herd of Zs spread out across the road thirty feet off the Land Cruiser's bumper. "There's less than two hundred here," he said. "We *need* to move on."

"Yep. I'm with Cade," Duncan drawled.

Daymon said nothing.

"Five yay, two nay," Cade said, stating the obvious. He shifted and met Daymon's stare. "Don't worry. You'll be killing more of them with Kindness before the day is done."

Duncan chuckled. "Poor Urch." He mouthed, "*Follow me*," to the Kids in the 4Runner and eased off the brake.

It was slow going, but by keeping to the shoulder in places—the path of least resistance—Cade and Daymon only had to dismount a couple of times to clear a swath of road through the dead wide enough for the bigger Land Cruiser to pass.

In the 4Runner, Wilson was leaning as far away from the passenger window as possible. Even though he knew the abominations gliding by just outside his window weren't an immediate threat, it still seemed as if they were all being consumed alive by their vacant stares.

Every so often he would muster the courage and steal a quick peek and see what effect the elements, raging fire, and decomposition had on the human body. It quickly became clear to him that many of the monsters had caught bullets during the course of their travels, the damage presenting as mostly just pencil-sized entry wounds to the arms or torso. One in particular stood out from the others and would probably be visiting him in a nightmare later. Powder burns dappled the middle-aged rotter's pallid skin from hip to neck. There were frozen streamers of dermis and scraps of flesh dangling in semi-permanent stasis from the periphery of a basketball-size hole in its gut. And further evidence of a run-in with a shotgun blast were the connect-the-dots patterns peppering the flesh around the empty chest cavity, where hundreds of shot pellets had entered and stayed just under the skin.

Finally having seen enough, Wilson tipped his head back and closed his eyes.

The group burned thirty minutes navigating through the herd and had just gotten going again when they came upon a scene that begged a dismount and further investigation.

Chapter 25

Dregan had cut to the chase. No pleasantries. No small talk. It was clear the two men didn't see eye-to-eye and there was no reason for either of them to put up a front.

First Dregan voiced his displeasure for the judge's unannounced visit and contact with his minor son, a move the judge explained away as a simple I-was-in-the-neighborhood type of thing. Then Dregan cut to the chase and told the judge that his visit with Ray and Helen had been to deliver propane, nothing more. After all, how was the judge to corroborate the story when he hadn't set foot outside the wall since he'd arrived. This the judge didn't protest. A kind of quid pro quo, since Dregan hadn't pressed him further on the house call issue.

When they finally got around to the matter of Lena and Mikhail, all Dregan had to do to convince Pomeroy he was content to wait was lavish a little praise on the way *justice* had been handed out to the Ford kid. And as an exclamation point to the matter, Dregan blew a little more smoke up the man's fat ass by adding how he believed—after all he had seen during the last hour—that the wheels of justice would soon catch up with Lena's killers.

And finally, in response to the judge questioning him about how he was coping with his loss—a query Dregan believed to be from the mouth and not the heart—Dregan had said simply, "Time has a way of healing old wounds."

In the end, Dregan had the judge's promise to not visit without prior warning. And in return, telling a bald-faced lie, Dregan promised to not take the law into his own hands.

"We're going to crawl back out of this," Pomeroy had finally said after a pregnant pause. *Bullshit*, thought Dregan as he rose and shook the man's clammy hand. And as he did, he thought to himself, *Justice will be swift and final.*

Suppressing a smile, Dregan left the musty room, closing the frosted glass door at his back. Letting the smile curl his lip, he slow-walked through the deserted bookstore where the cannibal rapist had just gotten all that he deserved.

Outside, he stood on the raised wooden sidewalk and marveled at how, under the gray light of afternoon, the snow-covered main drag lined with one and two-story buildings reminded him of the faded old photos of Deadwood or Tombstone or Silverado. Then it struck him how those towns had fallen, not to the rampant crime prevalent at that time in history, but to the advent of Mister Ford's assembly-line-produced four-wheeled steed that in part had made the Iron Horse serving the frontier towns, of which Bear River was one, as obsolete as the venerable Colt Peacemaker.

He chuckled at the irony. Him standing here thinking about one Ford's deeds when perhaps a direct descendant of ol' Henry himself was about to get his privates gnawed off on account of his own misdeeds.

Suppressing a chuckle, Dregan stepped into the street at about the same time a red Jeep with more rust streaking its squared-off body than paint rounded the corner. Noticing the vehicle approaching off his left shoulder, he gave the driver a wave and stepped back onto the curb just as the rig crunched to a stop inches from his toes. The driver's side window whirred down and instantly Dregan received a hot blast of fart-laden air to the face.

"Let me guess," he said to the man driving the Jeep. "Breakfast was venison jerky and Smirnoff."

The man's lined face stretched tight and he smiled wide, revealing a mouthful of cracked stumps for teeth. "Just Smirnoff," he replied.

Why did all the dentists have to get eaten? thought Dregan, wincing from the added stench of halitosis. "I'm glad you came, Cleo," he said. "I need a favor from you."

The man held Dregan's gaze, took one hand from the steering wheel and rubbed his fingers together briskly, universal semaphore for: *It's going to cost you.*

Dregan offered a conciliatory nod. "It's just a little recon job," he began. He laid it all on the table. The where's, why's and how's. Once he got to the how he wanted the job done part, Cleo shook his head. He wasn't having it. Dregan pushed the issue and Cleo said, "Keep me in propane for two winters."

Figuring the man's liver wouldn't hold out that long, Dregan nodded. Didn't matter if it did. He had squirreled away enough propane since the fall to keep all of Bear River going for two winters. And he also knew where more could be found.

Unfortunately, Cleo knew this too. "*And* a case of vodka and two cartons of cigarettes," he added.

"*Two* cartons?" said Dregan, almost yelling.

"And vodka." Again Cleo showed off his rounded teeth, sharing his bad breath in the process.

Exasperated, Dregan took off a glove and ran his fingers through his beard. The vodka was nothing. He had cases stashed in the garage. The cigarettes, however, were damn near worth their weight in gold. But then again, so was maintaining the element of surprise. And the only way to ensure that was to know the comings and goings of everyone in the valley.

"You are raping me, Cleo. You know that, right?"

Another big smile as Cleo extracted a small notepad, the coiled wire pinched in places and the paper curled up. Still grinning ear-to-ear, with intelligent—though bloodshot—blue eyes sparkling, Cleo licked the tip of a pencil and wrote hard on the lined sheet until it was full of tiny scribbles looking more like something from a Pharaoh's tomb than words taught in school. The smile disappeared and, after underlining the last sentence twice, pressing hard enough to break the pencil lead, he handed the contract along with a pen taken from his flannel pocket to Dregan.

"Sign it please," he said, eyes narrowing to slits.

A vehicle slid by on the opposite side of the Jeep, heading in the general direction of the main gate.

Dregan glanced up at the truck carrying a foraging party of six in the back, then, looking like a man about to score drugs, he conducted a recon of his surroundings, two slo-mo jerky sweeps, one over each shoulder. Satisfied he wasn't being watched, he read the words jotted on the pad. After spending an inordinate amount of time deciphering the barely understandable prose, he read the heavily underlined words again. "The fee is up to three cartons now?"

Cleo nodded. He loved having *anybody* by the short hairs—especially the former wannabe sheriff of Bear River.

Dregan signed on the line and fantasized about throttling the little fucker. Picking him up off the ground and holding him aloft until he shit himself and his legs twitched after receiving their last ever orders from his dying brain. But that would get him nowhere closer to his end goal. Telling himself this was just business and he'd make up the loss elsewhere, he drew in a deep breath.

"Two cartons and a roll of chewing tobacco," he said over the exhale.

"OK," Cleo conceded. "Camels and Copenhagen. And handwarmers … it's going to be cold tonight."

Dregan shook his head. "All of that *and* the vodka."

"Stolichnaya," added the man, straight-faced.

Dregan sighed and gazed up and down the street. Then he looked skyward as the snow started coming down in thick sheets full of big flakes. "You know, Cleo," he said, flipping the collar up on his coat. "I'm just glad you didn't ask me to give you a blowjob."

The nubs for teeth reappeared and, after delivering a coquettish wink, the pencil reappeared in Cleo's hand and he played at amending the contract.

Dregan put his hands up in mock surrender and backed away with the Jeep already moving forward and Cleo's face sporting a wide grin. He kicked the pile of snow pushed up by the Jeep's tires and watched the boxy rig circle back around and head off the way it had come. In the next instant, he started calculating how many favors were owed to him by others that he could call in at such short notice.

Where there's a will, there's a way, crossed his mind as he stalked off for his vehicle.

Chapter 26

The dead baby girl was swaddled head-to-toe in a pink blanket and clutched tightly to the young mother's bosom. A placid expression was frozen on the child's delicate features, and if not for the presence of the blue jump rope knotted neatly around her impossibly thin neck, Cade would have thought death had come as a result of the firm one-armed embrace—not strangulation by ligature.

Sitting on the bench seat in back, shoulder-to-shoulder—small, medium, and large, like empty cups on display at a fast food joint—sat three other corpses, all grade-school-aged boys, separated by about a year or two chronologically and about half-a-head each in height. The boys were dressed in winter attire and wore blindfolds fashioned from an eco-friendly grocery bag—not quite fabric or plastic, but some kind of marriage of the two. Unlike the infant, each of the boys had one neat little entry wound about the diameter of a pencil eraser dead center on their foreheads.

Up front in the center console, partially concealed underneath cereal bar wrappers and balled-up tissues, was the weapon the woman, who Cade presumed to be the mom, had used to kill the boys: a chrome .22 or .32 caliber semi-auto pistol by the looks of the grip and mag well width.

Next to the pistol were a couple of well-worked-over pacifiers and a bottle half-full of a pinkish-looking liquid. And laying on its side by the baby bottle was what looked like some kind of over-the-counter kids' cough-medicine. It was brilliant red and looked high in viscosity, like pancake syrup. Cade guessed Mom used the medicine and formula or some kind of canned milk to make the cocktail in the bottle. Though the defenseless little former bundle of joy would never see a first birthday, Cade felt better about the whole thing knowing the baby probably hadn't suffered—much.

He craned and looked closer at the kids in back and saw very little blood; he guessed—based on the lack of visible bugs or maggots—they had suffered from perhaps a day's decomposition.

The mom on the other hand, like the dead man on the road, had taken no chances. It was clear she had not wanted to come back and spend eternity thrashing around inside the van with her dead daughter in a baby carrier on her chest. The gun she'd used to relocate her brains from inside her skull to the windshield and headliner was a black 9mm semi-auto that was still clutched firmly in her dead hand. Closer inspection would divulge that it was poorly made and inexpensive, like the chromed number between the seats.

Cade worked the scenario through his head. Judging by the twenty or so Zs ground into the pavement underneath the van, the occupants had probably come upon the herd up the road and then, either acting out of fear or hubris, decided not to turn back toward Huntsville and instead took a chance at bulling their way through. And once the driver had committed and the low clearance minivan became inexorably stuck, he dismounted and shot a few and then tried rocking the vehicle off the writhing pile of death with the lady behind the wheel.

However it went down, the result was crystal clear. Trapped inside, the mother did what any parent facing that many flesh eaters would do. Maybe to make it easier on all parties involved, Cade thought, she had proposed a game that required the boys to wear blindfolds before ... at least that was how he hoped it had played out. But he'd never know, because, as the saying went, dead men—and women and their four kids—tell no tales.

The sound of a door opening and closing snapped him out of his funk. He looked towards the other Toyota parked a dozen feet behind the Land Cruiser and saw Taryn on the road and approaching the scene. He watched her step over the partially eaten corpse of the man whom he had already pegged as the dad. There was a bullet entry wound on the right temple and most of the left side of his face was bulged out and misshapen—like a grapefruit squeezed of all its pulpy goodness. Only there was nothing good about what Cade imagined lay under the snow, scattered on the roadway in a radius around the same side of the body the bullet had exited. Suddenly he was reminded of a bumper sticker popular with the pro-Second Amendment crowd before the fall—a group of like-minded folk whom he had proudly counted himself one of. *You can have my gun when you pry it from my cold dead hands*, was how it went, and that's exactly what Taryn did. She planted her boot on the cadaver's wrist and pried the desert-tan semi-auto free from the rigor-affected fingers. She patted down the body and came out with one empty magazine; the rest, Cade figured, were somewhere near the body, but covered with snow and brains. Pocketing the mag and what looked like a handful of cereal bars, the lithe brunette picked her way through half a dozen fallen rotters and approached the high side of the mound of unmoving Zs the family's van was high-centered on.

For a second, Cade contemplated letting her see what was inside the death ride and then enlisting her help in searching the contents. Instead, as she was craning and skirting the vehicle's driver's side, like a cop stopping traffic, Cade held his gloved hand up palm out and turned her away with a slight nod to the 4Runner.

She froze in her tracks and shook her head. Matching his gaze, she blinked first and turned a one-eighty. She made it one pace back toward the vehicles, then paused as if in thought and performed a pirouette, finishing a complete, albeit rather sloppy, three-sixty.

"When do I get to be part of the decision-making process?" she asked, standing her ground and glaring back at Cade.

"You just were," hollered Duncan, who was in the nearby Land Cruiser with his window partway down and warming his hands in the air coming out the heater vents.

"Come on then," Cade said. "If you can handle Cobain there ... I'm sure you can stomach"—he gestured at the van—"what's inside there."

Without warning, big flakes began falling all around them.

Cade looked to the sky, and far off to the southeast, in the band of blue left by the clouds that had already passed them by, saw a number of contrails. Though he'd seen them thousands of times in his life, from this distance there was no telling what made them, nor which way the jet aircraft that had were headed.

There was a squeak and then a rapid *thwopping* as Duncan toggled the wipers too high for the conditions. Cade swept his gaze to his right and watched as Taryn skirted the bent and broken appendages sticking out from under the minivan. She approached him and stood on her toes, with one hand gripping his shoulder for support.

In the background the wiper noise died down to a manageable *thwop* every three seconds or so.

The mom's destroyed upper palate and shredded lips and cheeks were the first things Taryn saw as her eyes broke the plane of the bottom of the driver's door glass. She flicked her eyes up and saw the clumps of brain and hair and bloody shards of white bone stuck fast to the once cream-colored headliner.

Taryn was feeling the first tingling in her salivary glands when her gaze swept the dead baby. Then, the knotted jump rope and what it represented registered in her brain. She didn't even get a chance to look in the back seat before her jaw had locked up, and she lost her grip on Cade's shoulder and pitched back off of the crushed bodies she had been standing on. In the next instant, her hands and knees went cold as she landed in the snow on all fours. A tick later, pound cake and applesauce mixed with the pint of water she'd just consumed painted the ground a foot from her face. It steamed coming out and melted the snow on contact, creating a color strikingly similar to the detritus dried onto the van's headliner.

"Seen enough?"

"Fuck you," she said to Cade, dragging a hand across her mouth. "You could have warned me about the *baby*."

"I could have also told you about the three boys, aged six to ... ten, I'd guess. They're in the backseat blindfolded and sitting shoulder-to-shoulder, each with a bullet hole to the head most likely courtesy of Mom there." He shrugged and stood in front of the lift gate, examining the stick figure family on the back window: Dad, Mom, three boys and the infant represented as if it was already a crawler—on all fours—which Cade doubted. It had probably just barely perfected rolling over and doing that seal thing Raven used to do—up on her hands, back arched, head on a swivel checking out her new world. Simultaneously as he searched the lift gate for a latch, he smiled at the memory and his eyes misted over. Dragging a sleeve across them, he added, "It's a cruel world, Taryn."

Wilson skidded in the snow, through the debris field from the man's destroyed head, and went to his knees beside Taryn.

"I'm OK," she hissed, not looking at him. "Let's just take what we need and get going."

"I'm looking for tire chains," Cade said matter-of-factly.

Knowing her cars, Taryn said, "Don't bother. That van has different series tires than the SUVs."

"You're the expert," said Cade. He opened the hatch and stepped back while a mini-avalanche of loose sleeping bags, cans of food, bottled waters and various toys—mostly sports-themed—spilled from the back. After the items stopped pouring forth and settled in the snow, Cade stepped over a mini-basketball and waded through the colorful—though soiled—sleeping bags and started policing up the food, putting it all in the smallest of the bags, a Mutant Turtles-themed item rated for summer nights, not surviving winter temperatures.

Without needing a prompt, Wilson helped Taryn to her feet, had a couple of private words with her, then proceeded to rifle through the van, checking the side pockets, cup holders, and center console before finally striking pay dirt within the glove compartment. Coming out with a smile and several boxes of ammunition held aloft, he suddenly started feeling queasy himself. Something about finding fortune on account of a young family's tragic end unsettled him more than the baby's bugged-out lifeless eyes and Mom's gray matter frozen to the inside of the passenger window.

Chapter 27

Four miles West of Bear River, Cleo nosed his late model Jeep Grand Cherokee between two trees and jockeyed it around until it was under cover and facing perpendicular to the road. Off to the left he could see his tire tracks but wasn't too concerned; with the rate at which the snow was falling, any evidence of his passage would soon be erased.

The copse of trees he'd chosen would serve two purposes: keep the Jeep from being easily discovered and save him from having to dig the rig out in the morning should the steady snowfall continue.

He killed the motor and pocketed the keys. Took a small canister from the same pocket and, holding the hockey-puck-sized item in one hand, thumped the tin lid with a finger to pack the granular tobacco inside. He popped the lid and got a big whiff of the earthy-smelling tobacco then put a generous amount between his cheek and gums. He brushed the particles from his silver moustache that hadn't quite made it into his mouth, and then stuffed the snuff can into his breast pocket. He figured the nicotine buzz of a fresh dip every couple of hours would help him stave off Mister Sandman.

His lengthening ghost of a shadow told him the sun was up there somewhere, but the diffuse light it was throwing lent little in the way of definition to the rolling countryside and even less to the Bear River mountains off in the distance.

Forgoing the fur-trimmed hood for now, Cleo zipped his white parka to his neck. He slipped a compact semi-auto pistol along with two spare magazines full of 9mm into a pocket. Next, he checked to see that his handheld CB radio was switched off and then put it and a sealed package of new batteries for it into the other pocket. No way he would hear it over his footsteps anyhow. Finally, he nudged the door open and stepped out casually onto the soft, needle-covered ground, dragging a desert-tan-colored carbine after. His eyes passed over the snowshoes resting on the back seat and, after half a second's contemplation, decided bringing them would be a good idea. They went on the outside of his small rucksack, held in place by a couple of bungees. He shrugged the pack on, drew a deep cleansing breath, and grabbed his carbine from where he'd propped it against the Jeep.

He stepped from cover and continued north on foot through the pasture. To his left, he saw small, snow-covered hillocks rolling away to the west. Twin runners of fencing stood out against the snow. They stretched off to the north, bordering the State Route as it undulated away, twisting and turning like a big white snake.

Keeping Cleo company off of his right shoulder was a wide expanse of grazing land that eventually butted up against low foothills, normally scrub-covered red rock but now just a hazy white blur.

Fifty paces into his trek, he spat a big ugly black hole in the snow, then watched the warm tobacco-juice-laden saliva burn all the way through to the grass as he passed it by.

***

Ten minutes had passed since leaving the little oasis of trees behind, and off to the northwest Cleo could see the big metal dome on the silo and the steeply pitched roof of the red barn, the two big white X's on the southwest-facing hayloft doors marking the spot.

Running right to left, almost as crooked as the road beyond was the Bear River, which he would be crossing rather reluctantly when the time came. As he trudged ahead, he worked up a good sweat. The high-end hiking boots he'd scored from an abandoned house in Bear River were treating his feet well. They were dry, blister-free, and his Plantar Fasciitis, usually aching to the point of being debilitating, was only a low-level current of pain arcing between the big toe, along the arch and into the soft flesh of his heel.

He continued north for another quarter-mile until he came to a low spot in the pasture and cut a sharp ninety-degree left turn. The tack he chose took him between two large mounds, usually bright green and host to cows favoring the high ground. Now they were white with snow and the cows, having fallen victim to the corpses roaming the countryside, were but rib bones and an occasional skull poking through the vast carpet of white.

As the land sloped away toward the narrow river—actually little more than a creek—he said a prayer of thanks for the weather presently keeping the dead at bay. Though the momentary respite would allow the residents of Bear River to shore up defenses and cull many of the dead things currently in a state of stasis, he held no reservations the world was out of the woods yet. In fact, if his last run to the towns on the periphery of Salt Lake City was any indication as to what the future held for him and the others, he wanted this snow to be the first of a new Ice Age. Dying cold and hungry, he mused, was far better than the alternative.

The image of the dead streaming out of the overhunted metropolitan areas in droves was forever etched in his memory. He'd even heard talk of a mega horde, in the hundreds of thousands, pushing across the Great Salt Lake and completely razing Wendover, a little gambling town on the Nevada side of the border with Utah.

Though he had his doubts, there were other rumblings that said the lights were working in Colorado Springs, Colorado, but that experiment was drawing the dead there from Pueblo and Denver like bugs to a zapper.

Lost in thought, Cleo nearly walked right into the slow-moving water. He stopped short of the bank and emitted a low whistle.

"Almost got wet there, Cleo."

He picked up a rock and chucked it into the crystal clear water and counted slowly as it sank, stopping the count only when it finally settled on the bottom.

Two seconds. Over the cuff.

"Dammit!" He pulled a handful of plastic garbage sacks from the front pocket of his white ski pants. He placed one on the riverbank and sat on it. Then, using care not to puncture the thin black plastic, he double-wrapped his boots with the sacks, duct taping the tops just over his knees.

Good to go.

Grunting from exertion, he pushed off the ground and started fording the river.

Aside from a couple of slick rocks trying their best to pitch him into the drink, he arrived on the other side dry, wiggled his toes, and proclaimed his makeshift waders a success.

He sat down and ripped off the plastic sacks. Still sitting, he cast his gaze left and right and back, settling on a distant clump of brambles roughly twice as wide as it was tall. After tucking the sacks away in a pocket, he rose, covered the thirty yards up the gently sloping hill, and approached the tangle of vines from its west-facing side. He stepped into them with no hesitation and stomped a man-sized patch in the bare vines. Finished with that, he dropped his rifle and pack, and took a seat atop the latter.

"Home, sweet home," he muttered as he dug out his binoculars.

From his vantage on the stunted hillock he could see the entire rear of the two-story farmhouse and a portion of the south-facing elevation, where a small porch had been tacked on opposite the side door going into the two-car garage. In addition to being able to see comings and goings from the rear of the old couple's house, he had a view of 16, the front drive and level gravel parking area where an old truck sat, and the barn's north-facing doors.

Cleo settled his gaze on the house. The four ground-level windows facing him were dark, as were the pair on the rear of the garage. Upstairs, more of the same: four windows with the curtains closed, not a sliver of light showing.

He lowered the field glasses and looked behind him, quickly determining the gnarled runners rose at least a foot over his head and would hide his silhouette from prying eyes as well as afford a modicum of cover from anything or anyone approaching from behind.

Satisfied with the hide, he started clearing the snow in a semicircle in front of where he would be camped out for the next dozen hours. After a few minutes' labor he had exposed a refrigerator-door-sized rectangle of browned and matted grass and built ramparts on three sides with the snow he had displaced. The sides were roughly a foot in height, while the front he built up until it came up to his sternum when he was seated. Lastly, he pulled the plastic bags from his pocket and sat down on them.

Breathing hard from the exertion, and wanting nothing more than to light up a Camel, Cleo instead fished in a pocket for his snuff and freshened up the gobstopper-sized plug bulging his cheek.

All squared away, with a pair of hand warmers activated, one stuffed into each glove, he pulled the white blanket from his pack and draped it over his shoulders. Tucked the corners into the top of his parka and pulled the fur-trimmed hood up over his head.

Snug as a bug in a rug, and just catching a small buzz from the chewing tobacco, he put the binoculars to his eyes. There was movement now on the ground floor, and when he adjusted the focus ring, from nearly the length of a football field away he saw the woman of the house flitting back and forth in front of the ground floor windows.

Chapter 28

Big heavy flakes, suggestive of a slight bump up in temperature, were falling all around as the two-vehicle convoy hung a right off of Route 39. Making parallel tracks in the untouched field of white, the Toyotas cut a sweeping left-to-right arc in the parking lot and stopped side-by side in front of the partially burned-out Shell gas station.

On the passenger side of the 4Runner were nearly a dozen corpses. Partially obscured under six-inch drifts and with limbs poking through all akimbo, they reminded Wilson of National Geographic pictures he had seen of the bodies of abandoned climbers frozen in place on the inhospitable slopes of Mount Everest. He stepped out and closed his door, and as he did so he heard a chorus of thumps from all around as the other survivors dismounted, Taryn the first among them. Ignoring the bodies and oblivious to the metal rollup door to his right, which was bowing in and out minimally as if the garage itself were a living thing, he looped around front of the 4Runner and met the young brunette's stare.

"Are you going to be able to shake that visual ... the baby and the boys, I mean?" He put his arm around her shoulder as they walked by the Land Cruiser's warm grill.

"Yeah," she said. "In a year or two ... maybe. If I'm one of the lucky ones who doesn't get bit or blow my brains out first."

The prospect of either happening to the woman he was growing to love instantly numbed Wilson to the core.

"How about you?" she asked. "You looked a little green around the gills when we pulled in."

"Those rottercicles by the garage? Nope, they didn't even register. The herd we drove through, though … *that* was disconcerting. However, nothing, and I mean *nothing* has come remotely close to trumping my first couple of kills ... *yet*." And as he was saying it, in his mind's eye he was seeing the snarling faces of the undead parents he was forced to brain with his Todd Helton. Running over the vivid memory, like a macabre soundtrack broadcast in full on Dolby, he heard their undead toddler repeatedly ramming the baby gate behind closed doors. That day back in Denver was as surreal as a memory now as it had been then in person. The sound of wood on bone echoing in the hall outside his apartment, however, would never leave him. Nor would the *thunka, thunka, thunka* and what it represented emanating from the next door apartment ever be forgotten.

Approaching from the couple's blind side, Duncan said, "Sorry to spoil your Hallmark moment."

"If you only knew," Wilson replied.

Duncan grimaced. He said, "Taryn ... *come on down*," trying his best to mimic that long dead game show announcer from *The Price Is Right*. Then he nodded at Wilson and shifted his gaze to Lev and Jamie, who were just exiting the 4Runner. "The rest of y'all stand guard out here while we search the garage."

Wilson nodded and walked towards the road, head tilted, eyes scanning the yellow and red vacuum-formed sign. "Three oh three for Supreme. What I wouldn't give to bitch about rising gas prices again ..." he said, his voice trailing off as he neared the skeletal carcasses of the burned-out gas pumps.

Meanwhile, Jamie and Lev had split up, each taking a corner of the station—Lev to the east, by the corpses and static hulks of burned-out cars, and Jamie to the west, amid a sea of vehicles all singed by the fire that had consumed the contents of the minimart, yet inexplicably spared the high ceilinged double-garage.

Watching the three move out in pretty much the directions he had hoped they would, and without needing any extra input from him or Duncan, suddenly elevated Wilson, and to a lesser extent

Jamie—who could pretty much hold her own by now—a few notches upward on Cade's *there's-hope-for-them-yet* barometer. He waited until Wilson was kneeling on the cement island between pumps before motioning for Taryn, Duncan, and Daymon to follow. Once all four of them had ducked under the locked panic bars, Duncan having the most difficulty on account of the weather's effect on his decrepit knees, they skirted the burned-out shelving and formed up at a door on their right, its sooty surface all marked up and sporting a road map's worth of squiggles from the previous week's torrential rainfall.

Duncan traced his finger over the remains of the warning Glenda had etched there weeks ago. "Supposed to have read something like *danger, dead inside*," he pointed out. "At any rate, it don't now. And I figure by now the critter she said she left trapped inside there has been reduced to nothing but a *starer* like all the others."

"Definition of assume?" said Taryn, regarding the three men, one at a time.

Duncan smiled. He said, "Touché, young lady."

Shrugging, Daymon put his palms up and looked a question her way. *And your point is?* is what it seemed to convey.

"Ass. You. Me. *Assuming* makes an *ass* out of *you* and *me*," said Cade. He banged a fist on the metal-skinned door.

Nothing.

He turned the knob.

Unlocked.

Taryn worked her way next to Cade. She looked up at him, head tilted to one side. "Let me go first," she said emphatically.

"Something to prove?"

"No, *Daymon*," she answered, throwing him an over-the-shoulder glare. "You trying to get your ball-busting Merit Badge? Always talking shit." She looked away, shaking her head.

"Stand down," said Cade. He let his carbine hang on its center point sling and glared at Daymon. "First *you* and Lev. That dustup ended in fisticuffs"—Daymon tried to protest—"and now *you* and Taryn going at it." Cade looked at Taryn and half-joking said, "My money is on her."

Duncan said, "I want in on this action."

"That was a joke," Cade replied.

"Better work on your delivery then, Wyatt," Duncan said, flashing the man a toothy grin.

Daymon glared at the three, who were seemingly standing together in opposition to him.

"However, my man," Duncan added with an extra syrupy drawn-out drawl, "a hundred simoleons says she can take Urch. And a hundred more says Wilson can take him ... if she won't."

"We're all under a ton of stress. Nerves are frayed ... I get it," Cade said. "But we need to work together if we're going to make the most of this blessing the weather dropped in our laps." He looked at them one at a time and got nods from two out of three. Daymon didn't make eye contact. Shaking his head, he stalked off down the aisle toward the counter, kicking cans and piles of drifted snow as he went.

Also shaking his head, Cade turned the knob and pushed the door inward by a degree, listened hard and heard nothing. So he nudged the door inward another three inches, letting in a sliver of light that illuminated the nearly pitch-black interior. The first thought that entered Cade's mind as Taryn edged past him and into the gloom was a positive one. Maybe her mounting displays of bravado weren't a false façade as he kind of suspected. His next thought, however, as a pair of black hands grabbed the ponytail snaking from under her stocking cap and began dragging her inside was: *Cade, you've just officially made an* ass *of yourself.*

Taryn's shrill scream shattered the silence and then there came a dry huffing sound from the inky black.

To avoid becoming stuck when both he and Duncan stormed the narrow door simultaneously, Cade shifted his body sideways—an impromptu move that caused him to miss the initial step down and turn his left ankle on the garage's concrete pad.

Thanks to Cade's half-pirouette, Duncan squirted through the doorway a fraction of a second after, his near two hundred pounds hitting the door full force near the middle hinge and sending it sweeping inward, quietly, on soot-lubed hinges.

To Daymon, who was now skulking back down the aisle, watching Duncan following Cade through the door just as Taryn's shriek died away was like viewing a rocket launch on television with the volume on mute. As he reacted, rushing toward danger as Cade and Duncan had, there was a loud clap and the door rebounded, knocking Duncan off axis as if a giant hand had come from nowhere and slapped him down.

Recovering from the bone-jarring shiver that started a dull ache in his previously injured ankle, Cade released his grip on the carbine and drew his Gerber. And as he lunged for the black apparition draped over the struggling young woman, looking like a drunken superhero in flight Duncan passed in front of his eyes, nearly horizontal with the floor, arms flailing and hands clawing for something to arrest his fall.

The dull ache now a shooting pain, Cade, canting sideways, focused on the picket of white teeth inching near Taryn's nose and thrust his left forearm into the creature's widening maw. Just as the pressure of the teeth clamping down registered in his brain, a string of curse words blasted from Taryn's throat near his left ear. Then, as the three of them fell as one, he saw the immolated creature's eyes, wide and lidless, sweep for him, right-to-left. Next, his forward momentum ripped the creature off of Taryn and carried them both away from the door to a cold and unforgiving impact with Portland cement.

As they rolled around on the floor, the listless creature was working its fingers into Cade's back and continued gnawing hungrily on his left arm. Cade craned around and noticed Duncan recovering from his fall and crabbing along the floor toward Daymon, whose silhouette was now filling up the open door. And as motes of carbonized skin and flesh knocked off the creature during the ongoing struggle filled the air near his face, Cade simultaneously dug the Gerber's serrated edge into the Z's spine from behind and pressed his forearm forward with all his strength. There was a crackling noise. Then he heard Duncan lamenting the fact that he was a dead man as simultaneously the Gerber severed muscle and windpipe and the head came away from the body with an awful, wet, tearing sound. Finally, with Duncan still going on about them not having any more antiserum on his right, and Taryn sitting on the floor to his left and wailing about how sorry she was for barging in ahead of them all, Cade rolled out from under the thing's lifeless body and pried the jaws open with the Gerber. And though the head was no longer attached to the body, the eyes still scanned the room and the teeth chattered on, producing an unnerving *clicking* noise that rode the cold air inside the metal echo chamber. The noise continued on even as Cade got to his feet and placed the twenty-some-odd pounds of pure nightmare on the workbench, where the neck continued oozing black congealed blood. With the thing's jaw thumping a morbid rhythm on the oily bench top, Cade met Duncan's wide-eyed stare, drew back his tattered sleeve and showed off the magazines he had taped there in the morning before venturing out to Woodruff. "Looks like these things' trial run paid off, huh?"

Taking her hands away from her face, Taryn blurted, "Thank you, Lord."

After he finished crossing himself, Duncan whispered, "You are one lucky mo-fo, Grayson. And so am I ... I was *not* looking forward to breaking the news of your demise to Raven and Brook." Then, knees be damned, he crossed his legs, and clasped his hands limply in his lap.

A flashlight beam lanced into the room and there was a murmuring of voices coming from the doorway as the others, reacting to Taryn's scream, crowded around Daymon and started shooting questions Cade's way.

"Everything is under control," Cade said. "Go on back outside."

As Lev and Jamie complied, Wilson remained rooted and looked a question at Taryn.

"Cade's right," Taryn said. "It's under control now. I'll tell you about it later."

Wilson opened his mouth as if to say something, then, seeing Taryn's expression go serious, wisened up and ducked away from the door.

Cade pulled his sleeve down and then helped the young woman to her feet. "Murphy must have been napping," he said.

"I'm sorry," Taryn said, her eyes starting to go moist.

"What's done is done," Cade said. "Just know that from here on out we're all going to have to be extra careful entering and clearing buildings." He stuck the Gerber's black blade into the thing's mouth. The tinkling sound produced by the teeth coming down on it was ten times worse in the enclosed space than them chattering together.

"I'll never get used to a severed head doing that shit," Duncan said, brushing pea-sized briquettes of blackened detritus from his jacket and fatigue pants. The stuff was everywhere. There were smudges of black on the floor. On Cade. On Taryn. It was almost as if the zombie had shed its bark-like skin on everything it came in contact with.

Cade pulled a small flashlight from a pocket and illuminated the head, then walked the cone of light over the floor and the rest of the crispy critter, revealing pink flesh showing through the black shell in places, mostly around its joints.

"So Cade, tell me this," called Duncan as he rose to his feet. "Why wasn't this one in a state of suspended animation like the others?"

Taryn poured some water from a bottle onto her hands. Then she splashed it on her neck and face. Finally, looking like she'd just spent a day in the coal mines, she leaned forward, hands on knees, and regarded the head on its level, nearly eye-to-eye. "Better yet," she butted in, a sense of wonder to her tone. "Why didn't it start making noise until I was inside? Was it waiting to ambush us?"

Cade ran his dagger through the head's eye socket, silencing the chattering teeth and stilling the one good roving eye. He pried a piece of sooty matter away from the scalp and rolled the head under the workbench out of sight—but not out of mind. He turned the specimen over in his hand. It was about the size of a credit card and had all of the properties of one of those dry cedar chips folks scattered around their hydrangeas and rhododendrons back home. He passed the chunk of dermis off to Duncan and knelt next to the prostrate corpse. With the dagger's tip, he probed the creature's skin, which had partially solidified, becoming like a cross between a rhino's hide and suit of armor. It was brittle outside, and flaked off as he poked around the distended midsection. And as he inserted the blade a couple of inches deeper, he found the resistance more sponge-like than anything.

Once Cade had finished his impromptu dissection, he made a face and said, "This thing's skin is acting like natural insulation. And to answer Taryn's question—" he looked at Duncan, then Taryn, "—it *was* lying in wait for us, no doubt about it. These things are still learning. The longer they stay alive ... dead, whatever. The more of this kind of behavior I think we're likely to see."

"We better get busy culling them then," Daymon said, the bars of light slipping around his frame, rippling in the turbid air as he shifted in the doorway. "Kindness wants to eat."

Taryn was up on her feet now and switched on a flashlight of her own. She paced the perimeter of the garage, walking the beam over the products—air cleaners, oil filters, serpentine belts and all other manner of car parts—stored there, only pausing when she got to the partially disassembled early model pickup. "Nice Fat Fender Ford," she said to no one in particular. "Dad would have loved it."

Cade stowed the dinky mag-lite in a pocket. Then he took his carbine in hand and thumbed the button on the foregrip, bringing the tactical light online. He struck out on his own, illuminating the floor and walls and shelves with the cone of white light.

***

Duncan chatted with Daymon, offering up a half-hearted apology for busting his chops and promising he'd probably do it later but if not then certainly tomorrow.

A couple of minutes after disappearing into the gloom, Cade and Taryn had both completed a clockwise sweep of the garage, her returning loaded down with two plastic boxes containing tire chains, one pinned tightly under each arm, and him with pockets bulging with the type of spray cans usually containing auto lubricants of some kind.

"Mount up," Cade said, unslinging his rifle. He watched Duncan and Daymon turn back into the store and crunch through the snowy aisles. Once they were out of earshot, he turned and stood in the doorway, barring Taryn from leaving the garage.

She regarded him and spoke first. "I'm well aware of how stupid that was."

Cade said, "It's OK to have a little fear. In fact, it's healthy. Keeps us on our toes. That was partially my fault. This is all new to me. These things don't act like any enemy I've ever seen ... and that they're constantly pulling new tricks out of their asses doesn't help."

She said nothing. Then, as if the realization of how close she'd come to being bit dawned on her, she began to shake.

"It was a close call … sure. But look on the bright side, we're both still breathing." He reached for the door jamb and came back with her carbine. "Chalk it up as a freebie. A hard-earned learning experience." He handed her the rifle and stepped aside.

Taryn ducked by and said, "I'm done assuming. I'll take the blame there. I let Daymon get under my skin and as a result I made an ass out of myself." She sighed and shook her head. Fixed her eyes on his. "And for that I am truly sorry."

"I forgot about it as soon as the dust settled and I saw we wouldn't be burying you. We don't have any antiserum with us. And I don't know when or if we will get anymore. So you've got to—"

"Stay frosty," she said, cutting him off. "And I'll try and give Daymon a little slack. All of Heidi's ups and downs are probably taking a toll on him."

Cade had no reply for that. He was no shrink. He figured he'd leave all of that stuff to sort itself out. God knew there'd be plenty of time for it once the snow stuck around for the long haul. "Let's go," he finally said, fearing this snow event to be fleeting and that the dead would be walking again, sooner rather than later. "Time is of the essence." He followed Taryn through the door, both of them ducking under the panic bar. Once outside with snowflakes darting around his head, he looked to the others. "Mount up. According to Glenda our next stop is about a half a mile down 39 and then another half a mile north down a side road. Keep your eyes peeled for it."

Chapter 29

Though it was a tolerable fifty-five degrees in the Graysons' quarters, beads of sweat had formed on Brook's forehead. She was sitting hunched over in a folding chair and clutching a rectangular olive drab ammunition canister in her right hand. The metal canister was partially filled with dirt and the metal handles had been wrapped with a few lengths of silver duct tape. She was in the middle of the second of three sets of fifteen and feeling a burn near her trapezius and deltoids, not so much from the muscles being overexerted, but from the thick slab of still-mending scar tissue being stretched to its limit.

She counted: "Twelve, thirteen, fourteen," grunting between each repetition. At *fifteen* she let the ammo can down easy and sat up straight in the chair, the beads now sheeting down her face as she breathed in deep and listened to the soft sounds of whatever DVD Raven and Sasha were watching now.

Taking up the stress ball Cade had brought back from the rehab place, she worked it hard, squeezing the life from it until the fingers of her right hand ached and then kept going. Like the ammo can exercise, she did three sets of fifteen with the ball, afterward feeling as if she had milked a herd of cows with it.

"Raven," she called.

One of the girls silenced the laptop.

"Yes Momma?"

"Can you get me a water, sweetie? And when you come back I'm going to need you to stretch me out."

"Yes Momma," she said again.

A moment later Raven emerged from the gloomy rear section of the container with a canteen in one hand and a cotton towel in the other. She handed her mom the canteen and folded the towel in on itself until she had a tight square of fabric.

Before twisting the cap on the canteen, Brook pressed its flat side to her forehead, then cheeks, and finally rested it on the base of her neck for a moment. "Only good thing about this weather," she finally said.

"Cold water," Raven answered back. Then, like the world's smallest corner person tending to a tuckered-out boxer, she put the towel to use, dabbing the sweat from her mom's face with delicate stabbing motions, starting with the underside of her chin and working up to the constellation of scars on her cheek. Finished with that, she squeezed a pearl-sized bead of the vitamin oil onto the damp washcloth-sized towel and began working it into the pink and purple scar on her mom's back, wincing each time she encountered one of the deep indentions caused by the crawler's incisors.

"Can I get you anything?" asked Sasha. She was standing partly in shadow and gripping the bunk bed post like a subway rider expecting the train car to suddenly take a wild lurch.

"Just keeping Raven occupied helps me more than you know," answered Brook. "Wish money still had a meaning. I'd pay you handsomely by the hour."

Though it wasn't evident to Brook or Raven, a wide smile spread on the redhead's face and stayed there.

"I figure you girls can help Tran cook dinner again. If you're both up to it." In her side vision Brook saw Raven nod enthusiastically. "That will also get you two out of dish detail. What do you think, Sash?"

"Whatever you say, Mom—" Sasha caught herself the second the word she hadn't uttered in a long time rolled off her tongue. She went silent and sat down hard on the bunk, her expression gone tight and cloaked in shadow.

"It's alright, sweetie. You can call me that if you want. Might as well ... these last few weeks you and Raven have become so close an outsider would peg you two as sisters."

"Right, Mom," Raven said. "Me with my brown hair and eyes and perpetual suntan and her with red hair, greenish eyes, and totally opposite skin tone. I don't see it. Not by a long stretch."

"I agree with Raven," said Sasha. She rose from the bed and stepped around the end of the bunk and into the cone of light thrown from the hanging sixty-watt bulb. She fixed her gaze with Brook's. Had trouble holding it because Raven was now vigorously rubbing the muscles running vertically up the woman's right side. "You're just trying to make me not feel embarrassed, Mrs. Grayson. My mom is still out there ... somewhere."

"I'm sure she is," Brook said, nodding. "I won't be mad if it slips again. In fact I'd be honored. I'm sure your mom is a very tough lady."

Was, thought Raven. She capped the bottle and set it on the floor by her feet. "I'll share my mom with you until yours comes back," she said.

Sasha said nothing. Her chin dropped to her chest and tears rolled off her downcast face. They made little ticking patters striking the floor near her feet, and soon the silhouette cast there by her full head of hair was dotted with fallen tears.

***

Southeast of the Eden Compound, Helen was standing in front of her kitchen sink, looking absently out the window there, slowly scrubbing Ray's lunch plate with a Brillo pad. And as she made lazy counter-clockwise passes over the stuck-on bits of hash he had failed to lick clean, something just above her line of sight dead center in the backfield caught her attention. She froze instantly, every muscle seizing involuntarily and, without peering down, dipped the plate in the numbingly cold rinse water and snatched up a dishtowel. Still fixated on the unmoving lump sitting just at the edge of her vision, she dried the plate and put it aside then wiped the watery suds off the backs of her hands.

"Ray," she called, the word, uttered like a halfhearted stage call, carrying no weight. Keeping her eyes locked on the gray smudge a few degrees above the window's mid-point where the narrow excuse for a river made a westerly bend, she called his name again.

"Yes, dear?" he called back.

"I think there's something out in the field."

"A deader?"

From the dining room came the screech of a chair's legs giving way, wood scraping wood. It was followed by a half-dozen plodding steps and Ray's harried breathing.

Helen looked over her shoulder just as her husband filled up the doorway. He looked tired to her. Stooped, more so than usual.

"I don't know what I saw," she conceded. Then, something she should have done before calling Ray—which was usually her first inclination because she gathered it went a long way towards making him feel useful—she plucked her glasses from the sill, looped the diamond-cut leash over her head, and perched them properly on her nose. "Come on over and see what you think?"

And he did. He shuffled around the chair pushed in against the small bistro table left of the doorway and came up behind her. Placing a hand lovingly on her shoulder, he asked her to point to what she had seen.

With his naked eye, he followed the length of her arm to the tip of her finger and beyond. He took a deep breath and chuckled. "Oh, Helen. That's that old bramble mound I was going to hit with Ortho and it kept slipping my mind. And then the *thing* happened."

"That's what you've been saying about the rock *underneath* those brambles five years running now. When these dead things finally die off you better get the Deere running and pull it out once and for all."

Not having the heart to tell her those things were likely to be around and walking when both of their hearts gave up the ghost, he merely mumbled something agreeable and made his way back to the dining room and the task at hand.

Helen said nothing. She pulled her plate from the cold soapy water, gave it a wipe, and put it in the frigid rinse.

"Ray."

From the dining room, softer this time, because there was no weight on it, there came another scraping noise, still wood on wood, and then, "Yes, Helen?"

Wishing she had broken down and bought that snazzy combination shelf organizer/lazy Susan from the city slicker on

QVC, she continued moving cans around in the cupboard and let out a sigh.

"What strikes your fancy for dinner ... Vienna sausages and sauerkraut or ... Vienna sausages and sauerkraut?"

"Sounds like we had one too many *last suppers*, eh Helen," he called from the other room.

"Yep. Made the last canned ham for Alexander and his boys two Sundays ago. We still have a year's worth of those MRE things upstairs, though."

Concluding Helen was bored out of her wits—hence the planning for dinner so soon after lunch—Ray said, "Why don't you bring some downstairs then. I don't think there's any chance of us getting in trouble for purloining them at this juncture."

"*Juncture,*" she said. Just the one word delivered all nasally, as Ray oftentimes finished a sentence, caused her to snort. "Say that again, Ray. Sounded like a former Republican president from Texas." She wracked her brain trying to remember whom.

"Say what?"

"*Juncture*, Ray. *Juncture*." Just thinking about the old world seemed so absurd to her, seeing as how the first snow of the season was on the ground, the pantry was near empty and the front pasture was dotted with alpaca carcasses. She laughed like she was going crazy. A high-pitched warbling.

"I don't know, Helen. Why don't you go up and see?" he called again, not really hearing the question, but appeasing her with an answer anyhow.

Why don't I? she thought, casting another glance toward the brambles.

***

Three hundred yards due east from the farmhouse, Cleo shifted his weight from his left butt cheek to the right. There was no feeling in either now and he couldn't decide whether a minor case of frostbite was setting in or they were numb from lack of blood flow. After a few seconds spent in the new position, it became abundantly clear that the latter was the case when it started feeling like an army of sprites armed with pins and needles were attacking the area in question.

Adding to the sharp stabs and nettle-like tingling, the mother of all headaches was settling behind his eyes. Nicotine withdrawals, he thought. By now he'd be three-quarters of the way through his first pack of the day and it wasn't even mid-afternoon yet.

He shook his head, spit the spent plug of tobacco into the snow, and loaded a fresh dip. From another pocket, he took out the long-range CB radio and upped the volume a couple of notches.

As he took a scrap of paper from a pocket and double-checked the channel on the CB, a wave of nicotine hit his brain, producing a sudden pain negating euphoria.

He thumbed the Talk key. "Are you in place yet, Gregory?" He took his thumb off and for a long moment there was only a soft hissing coming from the speaker. He tried again. "Gregory?"

Chapter 30

Ended up being that Glenda was pretty accurate with her directions. The turnoff from 39 to the secondary road leading to the Utah Department of Transportation facility *was* half a mile west from the Shell station. However, the UDOT facility itself was another two-thirds of a mile due north at the end of an unmarked road Cade presumed was gravel based on the random pings resonating through the Land Cruiser's undercarriage.

Situated diagonal from the entrance on the far right corner of the neatly graded plot of land were two outbuildings the size of double-car garages. Fronting the two outbuildings was a thirty-foot-tall structure with a shallow pitched roof that was open to the air on all four sides. Sheltered from the elements on the center of the immense poured concrete pad were two gigantic mounds of pea gravel.

A twelve-foot-tall hurricane fence topped by rolled razor-wire surrounded the entire affair. Signs warning that the premises were monitored 24/7 by closed circuit television cameras were attached to the fence chest-high about every thirty feet. And displayed prominently on the front gate was another sign; on it was a crude caricature of a dog and underneath that, in big red font, were the words GUARD DOG ON DUTY.

Duncan parked the SUV nose to the gate and gestured to the white rectangle with the dog on it. "You think?" he said to no one in particular.

"No way in hell," replied Daymon. He looked at Cade. "Who is gonna cut the lock?"

"I got it," answered Cade. "Pop the hatch." He stepped out and, walking gingerly on his tweaked ankle, made it around back just as the rear door reached the bump stops at the top of its travel. Not wanting to dig out his lock gun, he instead fetched the mammoth pair of bolt cutters lying out in the open and made his way to the gate. It rolled left-to-right on what looked to him like a pair of Radio Flyer wagon wheels. A heavy-duty chain was looped twice around the gate's vertical pole and secured with a heavy-duty padlock.

A quick bite from the cutter's sharpened maw and the lock was defeated.

Cade let gravity take the chain and watched it coil like a metal snake near his feet. He grabbed a handful of fence, leaned into it, and rolled the door all the way open. He waved the two vehicles inside then shifted his weight to his right foot, wiggled his toes on his left, and rolled it in a slow clockwise circle. Once both the SUVs were inside the wire, he blocked out the breaking waves of pain and ran the gate into the closed position.

Grimacing in pain, he hobbled back to the Land Cruiser, opened the passenger door and fished a near-empty bottle of Tylenol from the side pocket. And while he worked at foiling the childproof feature, he caught Duncan looking over at him. "May I?" he asked.

"Go right ahead," Duncan said. "I won't be needing them."

Daymon was hauling his frame out from behind the driver's seat when he heard the exchange. Pausing with one leg out the door, he craned around. "You still a quitter, Old Man?"

"It's none of your dang business ... but . . . *yeah,* I've been sober since Glenda rolled into town."

"That's *bullshit.*" Daymon motioned towards the dash. "What's with the fifth of Jack in there?"

Duncan popped open the glove compartment to show that it was empty.

"You were getting *loaded* while we were chopping skulls and hurling bodies into the canyon?" Daymon asked, incredulous.

Shaking his head, Duncan said, "With Cade and God as my witness ... I swear to you I'm sober." He balled his hands into fists, reached over and pounded the glove box shut. "Damn it Daymon . . . you gotta believe me here. I won't lie to you ... I was thinking about drinking it. Only *thinking*, though. I did not take one sip. I poured *all* of it out on the bridge."

"Poured it down your gullet is more like it," muttered Daymon. He stepped out, slammed the door and, without a backward glance, stalked off toward the heavy equipment.

Realizing that Lev, Jamie, Wilson, and Taryn were all out of the 4Runner and had been watching the drama, and knowing that he was losing all control of the mission at hand, Cade threw his hands up and in the immortal words of Rodney King—as the story would later be recounted—said, "Can't we all just get along?"

His question was greeted by mostly dumb looks. Duncan and Daymon, however, were trying their best not to laugh.

Knowing how stupid the plea had sounded, Cade put his hands on his hips, and in his best Mike 'Cowboy' Desantos baritone, started issuing orders.

The rectangular area inside the fence was roughly the size of two football fields laid end-to-end. Where the nearest goalpost would be, off to Cade's left, close to the gate, was a boxy building about the size of one-half of a doublewide mobile home. The shallow pitched roof was white with snow and the horizontal blinds drawn tight. That was where he sent Taryn and Wilson to look for keys, but first he drew back his left sleeve and showed off the deep bite mark on the magazine taped there. A gentle, yet effective nonverbal way of reminding them to look before they leaped.

He walked his gaze over the yard. Backed in against the north run of fencing was a long row of heavy machinery. There were huge snowplows and graders and bucket trucks, a pair of the latter with wood chippers still hooked to them. Trucks attached to trailers hosting huge spools of wire were nestled in with line-painting equipment and steamrollers of different sizes. It seemed to Cade as if all of Utah's maintenance and road building chores were dispatched from this little plat of land.

Every piece of equipment on the lot was painted the same traffic-cone-orange and dirty from sitting in the elements unused since that Saturday in July when giving a shit about road improvements and public works projects took a back seat to surviving the dead.

Parked side-by-side to Cade's fore were a dozen boxy dump trucks made by Mack. They had chrome grills the size of a dinner table and a shiny cast metal bulldog perched atop the hood. Each one was equipped with a massive curved blade out front currently mirroring the white yard back at him. Built to operate on all types of surfaces the big rigs each sported ten huge all-weather tires distributed between three axles—two wheels up front on a single and four wheels each on the tandem axles supporting the rear-mounted dump box. *Two birds, one stone*, was his first thought. Clear the snow from your path with the blade while scattering gravel on your finished work from the spreader attachment out back. Pretty ingenious. And he currently had Daymon and Duncan vectoring for them, jumper cables in hand, with orders to choose the three best candidates among them based on how well-maintained they appeared and the amount of fuel presently on board.

Meanwhile, Lev and Jamie had moved out along the south fence line, carbines in hand. He had stopped at the midpoint southeast of the gate, out of sight yet still able to see the road beyond. She had continued on to the far northeast corner, and was scrutinizing the dense woods there.

Cade shifted his gaze and watched Taryn and Wilson enter the trailer. The pair remained inside for only a couple of minutes before exiting and jumping down the stairs, each with a pocketful of keys that jangled as they hustled back to the pair of Toyotas parked just inside the gate.

A handful of feet from Cade and still approaching, Taryn pulled the keys from a pocket. "Looks like there were people here after the outbreak. The chairs in there are all pushed around an old television and the garbage can is overflowing with about a week's worth of food wrappers and empty water bottles and beer cans."

"But I got these," Wilson said, bringing his right arm around from behind his back in a grand sweeping gesture. Clutched in his fingers was a six-pack of Diet Cokes. He pried one loose and handed it over.

Cade smiled. Cracked the top and took a long pull. "And it's cold," he said. "Been a long time since I've enjoyed one of these."

Wilson followed suit, swallowed, scrunched his face and burped, long and loud, drawing attention from Daymon, who had his machete in hand and was already jimmying the door lock on one of the big plows.

"Feel the burn," Wilson said, scrunching the can under his boot. He belched again, eliciting a hostile look from Taryn.

Still shaking her head at the juvenile humor on display, Taryn called ahead to Daymon, "We found the keys."

He jumped down from the truck. "Take 'em to Duncan, please."

"The maintenance chores were listed on a white board inside," Wilson exclaimed. "It says the plows were all prepped for winter in June. The front loader, however, was due for service the weekend all hell broke loose."

"That's OK," answered Cade. "We only need it to run long enough to fill the trucks with gravel."

"Who's going to operate it?" asked Wilson, the words dripping with skepticism.

"The surly one," Cade said. "As time goes I've come to learn he's got a pretty impressive skill set."

"Oh ... I see," Taryn shot. "That explains why *he* gets a pass."

"I try and treat everyone the same," Cade said to that. "So far nothing he's done warrants any kind of punitive action in my book. He has his trailer and he's supposedly working on his issues."

"He needs some of the same medicine Heidi is taking—"

Cade raised his hand, silencing Wilson. "We need to get a move on." He looked to the sky. "I figure we have five or six hours of light left, max. And quite a bit of work yet to do."

Thankfully, having been designed to sit for weeks at a time and then be ready to go at the first signs of inclement weather, the four pieces of heavy equipment necessary for Cade's plan to succeed started right up.

Having used earth-moving and clearing vehicles only sparingly on the fires he had fought, Daymon fumbled his way to figuring out the front loader's controls. After brushing up on the basics of maneuvering the back-asswards-steering vehicle, he spent the next ninety minutes filling three of the Mack trucks with gravel.

When the last full bucket was deposited in the truck driven by Lev, Daymon shut the front loader down on the patch of concrete he'd just cleared of pea gravel and hopped aboard the Mack for the short ride to the front gate, which he saw was already sitting open.

"Raring to go, aren't they?" Daymon said, a flat affect to his tone.

"Cade spent less than ten minutes getting acquainted with his truck. Since then he's been muttering and pacing back and forth waiting on you to finish."

Daymon shook his head. "Hell, there was only one loader," he said, the hard edge entering his voice. "I'm a firefighter who has used heavy machinery … not a certified heavy machinery operator who has fought fires. There's a *huge* difference."

"Don't kill the messenger," Lev said. "We couldn't have done it without ya." As the gate drew near, he made a fist and held it up. A conciliatory act that was his unspoken way of burying the hatchet with the other man.

Daymon reciprocated the fist bump. "We're cool then?" he asked.

Lev pulled up next to the Land Cruiser, the Mack easily dwarfing the SUV. "I'm over it," he said. "From now on let's take our aggression out on the dead."

"Agreed." Daymon opened the passenger door. He looked back with a grin and added, "Don't worry, we'll be back to culling them in no time."

Lev smiled at the other man's enthusiasm for taking the fight to the dead. Once the door closed, he waited for Daymon to walk clear of the truck then drove it off the UDOT yard.

By the time Daymon had climbed behind the wheel and punched the Land Cruiser's Start/Stop button, all three fully laden plow trucks had rumbled through the gate and were moving at a good clip down the feeder road. He waited until Jamie had wheeled the 4Runner through the gate and stopped on the right shoulder; then pulled out and parked in the center of the road a length ahead of her.

With the bulk of the convoy growing smaller off in the distance, Wilson and Duncan closed and chained the gate, after which the former sprinted to the 4Runner and climbed in on the passenger side, and the latter, rather reluctantly, crunched a path through the snow to the waiting Land Cruiser and hauled his old bones into the passenger seat.

"Gotta hand it to Captain America," Daymon said, waving Taryn around. "He sure knows how to strike while the iron is hot."

Clicking his belt, Duncan said, "I'm worried this *iron* you speak of is going to go cold before we have a chance to make much of a dent in the rotters waiting for us in Huntsville."

Daymon thought about that for a second then cast a quick glance at Duncan. "First things first, as Glenda likes to say"—an obvious, though subtle dig at the fledgling relationship—"we've got to get these plows to the barrier."

Like his mom had also taught him, for once, since he had nothing good to say, Duncan bit his tongue. In the side mirror he saw the Toyota creeping by on the right and unconsciously pulled his lap belt tight.

Inside the 4Runner, Wilson was basking in the warm air coming from the vents as Jamie steered the smaller SUV onto the snow-covered shoulder, around the idling Land Cruiser and then back onto the road, where she gunned it in order to catch up with the three plows. A few short seconds and a controlled power slide around the first bend later, the plows were in view and Wilson saw the blade on the first Mack lower slowly and then the truck, which he guessed was being driven by Cade, judder ever so slightly when the massive wedge of polished steel bit into the gravel under the snow. A tick later, like some kind of preplanned maneuver, the blades on the following plows lowered slowly but surely, and simultaneously there were three dirty rooster tails consisting of gravel and soil and snow pummeling the trees lining the right side of the road.

"I'd hate to be on the receiving end of one of those," Wilson said, trying to make small talk.

Eyes fixed on the road ahead, Jamie replied matter-of-factly, "Keep watching and I'm sure you'll get to see what happens to something that is."

Chapter 31

Once habitually clean-shaven, thirty-three-year-old Gregory Dregan now hid his lean facial features behind a black beard beginning to show some gray. Underneath the tangled whiskers, Gregory's cheek bones were high and angular and when his thin slit for a mouth parted in a smile—which it hadn't in the three weeks since his sister's murder—his eyes narrowed and a picket of uneven yellowed teeth was put on full display.

Though a dismal amount of snow had settled on the undergrowth-choked fire road he was on now, the Yamaha snowmobile he was jinking around rocks and fallen branches was having no problem rocketing his hundred-and-sixty-pound frame and backpack full of forty pounds of gear due west at an impressive rate of speed.

Branches reached out threatening to tear him from the seat. So, thankful he had not inherited his father's stature, he tucked his six-foot frame closer to the hurtling machine and tightened his grip on the handlebars.

Forty minutes prior he had secured passage from the Bear River compound with promises of favors payable by the Dregan family at a later date. Leaving the freshly bribed guards and gate behind, he pushed the snowmachine hard down a little-used feeder road much like the one he was on now to where it merged with Highway 16 half a mile north of the old couple's spread.

Fifty minutes into his trek, he was skirting the overturned school bus and blazing west on State Route 39, which twisted and turned all the way to the small town of Huntsville. Then, a handful of miles from the Woodruff junction, he had nosed the Yamaha left off 39 and followed a switchback gravel drive down to the north bank of the narrow Ogden river, where he crossed the single-lane cement bridge built by the Smith Mining company back in the eighties when he was still in grade school.

The abandoned mine had held nothing of interest to him, so he continued on through the facility, passing a dozen outbuildings of different sizes all with sagging roofs and corrugated metal siding sporting vertical tendrils of rust.

A mile west of the forever-idled Smith venture, the gravel road took a sharp right-hand turn straight to the south bank of the Ogden, where it went left and charged off west again.

With the snow pelting the abbreviated windscreen in staccato little bursts, Gregory steered the whiny machine along the road as it faithfully followed the river's twists and turns.

Before long, the lane veered left and began a long, steep, southwesterly climb away from the river. The trees crowded in quickly, shutting out the flat light of late afternoon, and just when Gregory thought the lane was about to become impassable it leveled off and the trees gave way to a stunning vista.

Now, thirsty and having to pee, he eased off the throttle and let the sled come to a stop in the center of the fire lane. With the acrid smell of exhaust threatening to spoil the moment, he quieted the burbling 4-stroke and reveled in the instant and absolute silence. He sat there enjoying the heat drifting up from the hard-working motor until the exhaust stench was replaced by the heady aroma of pines and damp earth. The urge to go building to an unpleasant pressure, he removed the matte black full-face helmet and hung it from the throttle. Slipped the rifle off of his back and shrugged the cumbersome pack to the ground. Why his dad insisted he take so much gear was beyond him. The rifle, pistol, and knife was a given in this new environment. The sleeping bag and flashlight ... sure. But food for three days? A one-man all-weather tent? When he stopped to think about his assignment the extra gear seemed like overkill. Furthermore, photographic evidence or not, he doubted the tracks his dad saw going into the woods were made by the people who'd killed Lena and Michael. Dad knew the gas business, not tread patterns and tire widths and wheelbases. Hell, if Gregory's memory served, before the fall, back when things were normal, the elder Dregan's eyes were capital O's every time he walked into a tire place and tried to tell the attendant what he was there for. Talking with an auto mechanic, as Gregory recollected, had been much worse, sending him into a tirade because he thought every little thing added to the bill was just the shop 'sticking it to him.' In hindsight, perhaps he was right. But that was then and this was now. In the nearly three months at Bear River, he, his family, and the others had had to learn things and do things they had never dreamt of in order to survive. To say the men of the Dregan family wore many hats would be a vast understatement.

Gregory took a few steps away from the sled and tried his hand at pissing his name in the snow. He made it to the R in his surname and could go no further. So he tucked his business away and paced back to the Yamaha, where he unzipped his hunter-green Arc'teryx jacket and pulled a neatly folded map from the inside mesh pocket. He carefully opened it and spread it out lengthwise on the sled's wide seat, weighing the corners down with a handful of rocks he scrounged from the dry ground under the low branches of a nearby tree.

He stood tall and looked across the vast expanse of a recent clear-cut. Mostly snow-covered, the upended stumps and gnarled roots snaking skyward looked oddly out of place. As he peered to the northeast across the sea of white at a flat rock mesa with a lonely finger of rock rising up, he got the sensation that he was on that alien planet Hoth from one of those Star Wars movies he'd watched on VHS when he was a kid.

He walked his gaze right-to-left, taking in every little point of reference on the northern horizon, then turned back to consult the map. With the GPS receivers the group had relied on earlier now acting strangely, or just plain not working at all, he had no choice but to orient this way. *Old school.* Everything was old school now, and he missed the old world terribly. Everything about it. Especially Mom and Magdalena.

He knelt down and removed his glove. Started tracing the squiggly line representing the State Route he had caught occasional glimpses of on the ride up. Triangulating between a hillock to the left and the mesa on his right, he found what he thought was his current position on the smaller dashed line that he guessed to be the fire road on the topo-map.

He refolded the map and was replacing it in his jacket when the long-range CB deep down in the pocket emitted a soft hiss followed by a voice he was very familiar with.

He fished the Cobra from the recesses of his parka, turned the volume up a couple of notches and thumbed the *Talk* button. "Yes?"

"What was yesterday's password?" asked the gravelly male voice.

"Why not today's? It's Jack and Jill."

"Yesterday's," said the man, his impatience clearly evident.

"Bart and Maggie."

The voice softened. "Hi, Gregory. It's me, Cleo."

Rolling his eyes, Gregory said, "You just hail me to say that? Or do you have a reason for making small talk over an open channel?"

"Boy ... you talk to your dad like that?"

Gregory made no reply.

"Are you there yet?"

"Not sure. I just stopped to check the map."

"Your dad tell you to stop short and walk in?"

"Yeah, a mile or so … but I was going to anyway," Gregory replied. "This sled is a noisy beast."

"Sound carries more than a mile now that nothing else is competing with it. If I were you, Gregory, I'd err on the side of caution. Maybe give yourself a *two* mile buffer." There was a brief silence then Gregory heard what clearly had to be Cleo spitting out a juicy wad of chewing tobacco. "Finished?" Gregory asked.

"Shit," Cleo exclaimed. "I'm all out of Copenhagen."

"Sucks to be you," Gregory said. He thought: *And me too. The walking man. In the snow. With all this gear.*

"If I were you, I'd take my advice," Cleo proffered.

If I were you, I'd give up the smokes and snuff and vodka. "Gotta go," Gregory said. "I'll check after I find this fabled camouflaged gate Dad's vengeance road is hiding behind."

"Your dad mention the cameras?"

"That he did," Gregory answered. "He says they're in the trees east of the road. Wish he would have had the time to take a picture."

"You'll figure it out," Cleo said. "And make sure to watch yer back while yer doing the watchin'."

"Will do. Thanks, Cleo." There was no response and Gregory heard a brief burst of squelch as Cleo silenced the call on his end. So he stowed the radio in his pocket. Put his arms through the pack straps and slung the scoped Winchester Model 70 across his back, barrel down. He donned the helmet and snugged on his glove. In the next beat, he spurred the sled to life just as snow began to fall again.

A blip of the throttle got the sled moving and in no time the fire lane dove back into the trees; in his mind's eye he saw the map and the imaginary X on it where he planned to stop and resume his approach on foot.

Chapter 32

Even with the massive plowing blade attached up front, the Mack truck's sloping hood made seeing the road ahead much easier than Cade had imagined. The air suspension smoothed out the ride, swallowing up the ruts and washboard-like channels in the roadbed that made the initial drive in to the UDOT yard a little harsh on the smaller vehicles. Furthermore, the automatic transmission mated to the power plant took all of the guesswork out of shifting, making the truck that seemed intimidating at first glance nearly as easy to operate as the F-650 he'd grown accustomed to driving.

After a three-minute's drive from the UDOT facility, Cade spotted Route 39 in the distance. Nearly perpendicular to the private feeder road, the snow-covered section of two-lane cut east to west through the countryside. On the far side of the road, to the south, were fields backed up by stands of firs and skeletal white aspens. Closer in, roadside businesses and a smattering of homes crowded 39's north flank.

Negotiating a gentle left-to-right S-turn, Cade saw the red and yellow Shell sign peeking above a stand of juvenile trees to the left. Coming out of the turn, he let off the accelerator to slowly bleed forward momentum. Not yet familiar with the vehicle's stopping distance, he let the engine compression do most of the work and then cautiously applied the air brakes a couple of truck lengths before the looming T-junction.

Hissing air and squealing subtly, the brakes engaged and the pads gripped the cold rotors, bringing the twenty-plus tons of

Pennsylvania metal and crushed Utah rock to a halt a dozen feet short of the junction.

He looked left and well off in the distance saw the black and white hulk of the burned-out Shell station.

He looked right and spied less than a mile distant the steeply rising hill preceding the edge of Huntsville proper. In his mind's eye he saw the ill-fated National Guard roadblock and the lined-up bodies of the unfortunate soldiers he knew had died at the base of that hill. Knowing the paved surface of 39 would be less forgiving than the gravel of the feeder road, he raised the plow slightly, hoping that once he turned onto the two-lane the minor adjustment would have it hovering just above the road's surface.

Out of habit he flicked the stalk up to start the right blinker strobing and, as soon as he could see the whites of Taryn's eyes in the wing mirror, pulled smoothly onto 39 westbound. Once the Mack was tracking straight and a thin fan of snow was painting the scratched and dinged guardrail on the right a brilliant white, he toggled the switch that started the gravel spilling from the spreader out back.

With the steep rise starting to fill the windshield, Cade took the Motorola from his pocket and thumbed the *Talk* button: "Taryn," he said. "How does the road look?"

As a long silence ensued, he listened to the different sounds made by the truck. In front the big diesel's growl was throaty and he could feel its subtle vibration in his bones. The plow blade, however, was strangely silent. Nothing like what he was expecting. There was no crazy bone-jarring vibration transferred from the road to the blade to the frame. The only evidence the plow was employed was a constant humming—which could as easily have been from the tires—and the bloom of white powdery overspray as it did what it was designed to do: scoop snow off the road and spit it out on the truck's passenger side.

Beginner's luck on getting the blade elevation correct, he was thinking when the radio finally crackled to life and Taryn said she was seeing patches of bare pavement and confirmed that the gravel spreader was attaining a lane-plus of coverage.

Cade smiled at the good news. Save for the crispy rotter in the Shell garage and his tweaked ankle as a result, it seemed to him that good old Mister Murphy had taken the day off.

Seeming to counter that thought, up ahead where 39 began its climb over the rise, Cade saw a group of twenty or so Zs, the majority of them stalled out upright in a ragged formation taking up most of the right lane. He looked at the passenger side mirror and saw through the hoary chaff caught in the truck's turbulence that the other four vehicles were lined up, each practicing a safe following distance.

So he veered slowly left and, using the top right corner of the blade as a reference point, aimed it for the four inert forms standing approximately where he guessed the centerline to be.

He gently applied more pedal. Simultaneously he heard a whine from the motor and felt the transmission gear down and then at once start ticking up incrementally. As the speedometer hit forty miles-per-hour, he thumbed the Motorola's *Talk* button and informed the others of the impending experiment.

He put the radio in his lap and gripped the wheel two-handed. Amazingly, he found the successive impacts less violent than he had anticipated. And as he exhaled slowly, the white showing on his knuckles was the only proof he'd been expecting worse. Though four forms met the blade, he discerned only three consecutive bangs, each sounding like a garbage man slamming galvanized cans around. And what transpired next happened so quickly it was mostly lost on Cade. He saw one snow-flocked body, mostly a pale white blur wrapped in a couple of scraps of blue and red fabric, enter his cone of vision; then, as quickly as it had, like a whirling dervish it flashed to the edge of his peripheral and was gone from sight.

There was a small fraction of a second between the first and last impact, which left a vague impression of ashen skin and fluttering fabric and maybe wisps of hair, of the latter Cade wasn't certain. And though he didn't see the faces of the dead in those action-filled seconds, he was certain they would be starring in his nightmares in the near future.

***

Hearing the warning and seeing Cade's truck closing with the dead, Lev slowed and slipped his plow truck far left, putting the driver's side wheels where he figured the white line tracing the shoulder would be. Last thing he wanted was a rotter going through his windshield and getting a face full of zombie guts—or worse—as a result.

***

At roughly the same time Cade's initial warning was tailing off and the truck in Taryn's left side mirror was dropping back, she had reflexively jinked her truck left a few inches in order to avoid the coming carnage. Then, as the ragdoll forms were careening away in different directions, she steered back on line and watched the lead truck's turbulent slipstream topple the rotters that had escaped the reach of the front-mounted blade.

***

Lagging the 4Runner a good distance behind the three plow trucks, Jamie gripped the wheel tight in anticipation of the show to come. "Here you go, Wilson," she said, edging the SUV a yard farther to the right, putting the tires on his side all the way on the shoulder. "Your wish just came true."

Wilson shifted his gaze from the field full of rotters he had been fixating on to the road dead ahead just in time to see the damage inflicted by Cade's plow truck. Instantly, like a circus performer shot out of a cannon, a rotter rocketed near horizontally to the road's surface before, inexplicably, it started a series of perfect cartwheels. Hands first, then nubs for legs, the extremities slapped the snow repeatedly and finally the perfectly proportioned corpse bounded gracefully over a distant fence without touching a thing.

The next meeting of metal and flesh was by no means graceful nor Olympic in caliber as a second creature, also with newly amputated legs, hit flat on its back and slid head first and face up along the shoulder, its severed legs painting two bold black stripes over the churned up snow.

***

Lost from everyone's view, the third rotter of the four was shortened at the ankles by the blade on Cade's plow. A millisecond later, like a smack down from God, it slammed flat on its back, spun a one-eighty, and its arm and ribcage and leg on the right side were instantly pinched and sucked into the sliver of space between tempered metal and snow-slickened asphalt. Trapped fast, the adult-sized corpse was rapidly disintegrating under tons of pressure, its friction-heated dermis and flesh becoming a wide and shiny red slug track in the lumbering truck's wake.

***

In the 4Runner, Wilson's jaw had hinged open while the first Z was settling beyond the fence and the second had just finished plowing snow of its own. Then he noticed the wide swath of red kick out the back of the lead plow truck and mingle with the bouncing gravel. And if things couldn't get any more macabre, the whole scene was punctuated by a third rotter making acquaintance with the unforgiving plow.

Child-sized and no match for the Mack's Gollum-like forward momentum, the pale runt of a corpse flipped up and was thrown off to the right likely without contacting the top of the blade. Arms and legs flopping like a sock monkey's, the tiny form flew through the air for what Wilson guessed to be twenty feet or more, closed with terra firma like a meat missile, skipped once, then jerked violently as the triple strands of a barbed wire fence arrested all forward travel.

"Flying fucking Cirque Du *Saa-lay*," cried Wilson. He looked at Jamie, his eyes capital O's. "You see that kid go airborne?"

"Wish I hadn't. And FYI ... the word you were looking for is *So-leil*," she said, correcting him.

"I meant to say *saa-lay*, slay … get it? That was so damn wicked." He rubbed his hands together excitedly. "Bowling with a big rig."

***

In the second truck, Taryn's radio broke squelch. She kept her eyes on gravel spilling and bouncing about the road. Found it soothing and mesmerizing at the same time. The spell was broken when Cade said, "Slow the gravel spread. We're taking both of these to the Ogden Canyon roadblock and I want them to be as heavy as possible."

***

Bringing up the rear in the Land Cruiser, Duncan was listening to Cade's chatter just as the first evidence of the damage a Mack Truck could do to the human body—living or undead—slid by on the right. Eyes taking in the trail of broken and toppled corpses, he scooped up the radio and in his characteristic drawl, said, "You better take it easy on that rig of yours, soldier. We'll be needing all three of them for what we talked about."

"Roger that," Cade replied. "No more experiments."

"Outcome?"

"She passed with flying colors," Cade replied.

Then as expected, Duncan quipped, "That's not all that was flying."

With the older man's cackle filling the Mack's cab, Cade took a breath and began to steel himself for what lay on the other side of the rise.

Chapter 33

Thankful for the full-face helmet, Gregory swiped the visor clean of snow and then nosed the sled off the fire lane and parked it under the low-hanging branches of a massive fir. He killed the engine, dismounted, and then shed his rifle, backpack, and helmet.

He sat with his back to the snow machine's paddle-shaped tread and ate a snack of venison jerky and dried berries given to him by Helen three days ago. After poring over the map again, he decided he was close enough to his imaginary X to strike out on foot.

Before setting out on the solitary trek, he policed up a dozen flat rocks and erected them into a conical pile he heard was called a cairn. He threw a shudder as he remembered a horror flick called the *Blair Witch Project.* What a bitch it would be if he had to deal with more than just the walking dead during his hike. Always a little superstitious, he scanned his surroundings and conceded they were strikingly similar to the woods the students were traipsing around when they came upon the trail markers that turned out to be harbingers of the evil they'd soon face. He regarded his cairn and thought the only harbinger this represented was cold food coupled with a long night alone in the woods. However, superstition or no, he left the foot-high cairn standing so he could find the sled if his tracks became completely snow-filled.

With vestiges of that jittery, fright-filled, docu-style movie running through his head, he pulled a green stocking cap on, hoisted the heavy pack up, and slipped his arms through the padded straps. He shouldered his rifle, then adjusting everything for the slog ahead, tightened straps and made sure the Glock semi-auto pistol was snugged securely in the drop-thigh holster on his leg. A cursory check told him that his boot prints and trio of tracks made by the sled were the only things pointing to his being here. And judging by the dark clouds slowly edging out the watery sun, that evidence was sure to be erased before long.

***

During this, her third trip upstairs in an hour, Helen saw something she couldn't write off as a figment of her imagination. It was a flare of light right in the center of Ray's brambles. It blossomed briefly like a struck match then was gone. As far as she knew, rocks didn't smoke.

"Ray … someone's smoking in your brambles."

"Are you sure, Helen?" he asked in a skeptic's voice. He put down the oiled rag. Set the AR-15 parts aside still disassembled and pushed away from the table. "Keep an eye out. I want to check the front property and the road before we do anything."

"I don't want you to go it alone, Ray."

"It'll be fine, dear," he called over his shoulder. He donned a coat and buttoned it up. Forgoing the shotgun, he grabbed a carbine off the hook by the door, snatched up his walking cane and left the house without another word.

He drove down to the State Route, the old Chevy pickup, carried by gravity, slipping, sliding, and steering itself as the snow-filled ruts grabbed the tires in their muddy embrace.

After making it the half-mile to the two-lane and adding only a few minor scrapes to the already fingernail-raked powder blue paint, Ray left 'Ol Blue running and, with his wooden and brass cane in one hand, stepped onto the firm level ground and slammed the door shut behind him. Looking left, he saw nothing but a white ribbon of road curling and rising south. To his right, he counted roughly a dozen bodies languishing in the right lane. A small amount of snow had collected in the creases of the dead's clothing. Their eye sockets and open mouths had accepted all the snow they could, leaving the pallid upturned faces looking like plaster of Paris death masks. Nearby and nearly covered over were two pairs of tire tracks, the ones running off to the north barely discernable. However, an identical pair following the road up and over the rise south looked fairly fresh.

With the ornate duck head cane poking neat little holes in the snow, Ray approached the tangle of death and saw that some of the corpses were cleaved in half while others had merely been decapitated. He approached a pair of severed heads. Strangely, like they had been arranged and left in view as a kind of warning, both rested with an ear to the ground, one peering east and the other west.

The sword came out of its oak scabbard with a *snik* and Ray used its needle-sharp tip to make certain the severed heads wouldn't become deadly Omega-carrying land mines once the thaw happened. There was a soft squelch and a grating sound of metal on bone as he ran the thin blade through each one, sticking it all the way into each upturned ear until he felt the point meet the unforgiving road. He left them as he found them, silent sentinels keeping watch for all eternity—or at least, he thought with a sad chuckle—until a passing vehicle pasted them to a slushy pulp.

He cleaned his blade by sticking the tip into the firm soil just beyond the shoulder. Then he sheathed the sword and, relying on it for balance, walked back to his truck with two of his questions answered. Based on the fair amount of snow drifted against the bodies, he concluded the monsters on the road were culled by Dregan prior to his unannounced and wholly unnecessary *welfare* check.

Before turning back to the idling truck, Ray inspected the tracks. The fact that the ones heading south towards Bear River held less snow than their identical northbound counterparts told him that Dregan was most likely back home and enduring the end to another day with no kind of closure.

He'd be back, of that Ray was certain. And he and Helen would remain neutral, of that Ray was unwavering.

So that left the identity of the watcher in the field the only unanswered question of the day. And if Helen had her way—as she usually did—Ray figured that by hook or by crook they'd be making the fella or gal's acquaintance before long and entirely on their own terms.

Chapter 34

As the Mack's transmission geared down for what seemed to Cade like the fifth time in as many yards, the extra weight in the box and angle of attack caused the plow blade to momentarily lift off the road. At the apex of the hill and finally free of gravity's strong embrace, he pulled the rig close to the right guardrail and engaged the air brakes. With the rattle clatter of the diesel serenading him, he looked out over downtown Huntsville and saw a scene that instantly reminded him of pictures he had seen in history books of cities firebombed in World War II. Albeit on a smaller scale, he conceded, much like Dresden or Tokyo or Nagasaki, very little in Huntsville was left standing. Down near the water, in the abbreviated business core, was an L-shaped building constructed with what from a distance looked like cement block. The yellow exterior was tinged black, yet the windows and steel roof were intact. Somehow it had escaped the conflagration that had engulfed most of the one- and two-story buildings for blocks around.

East of downtown, on a sparsely vegetated hill, a trio of grand houses—Painted Ladies was what he thought they called them in San Francisco—still stood defiantly. Untouched by fire and facing west, the windows fronting the two-story homes reflected the shimmering pewter waters of the Pineview Reservoir and the snow-covered Wasatch Range off to the west.

Taryn's voice came over the radio. "Should I shut it down here to save fuel?" she asked.

Not wanting to rely too much on the two-way radios in case someone was listening in, Cade rolled down his window and waved her forward. Once she had pulled up alongside, he met her eyes, wagged his head slowly side-to-side and mouthed, "We're not stopping here." He turned away and, as he did, heard brakes engaging and motor noise but focused his attention solely on the town itself. Because, from the moment he'd swept his gaze northwest, he was struck with a familiar and unshakable sensation, a cold chill that was spreading its tendrils from the pit of his stomach to the base of his neck. Other runners were caressing his rib cage and sending gooseflesh rippling back and forth there. And in that moment he'd never been more certain in his life that he was the watched, not the watcher. He ripped the binoculars from off the seat next to him then quickly scanned the town left-to-right starting with a trio of sailboats wallowing on the reservoir's choppy surface, moving over the bare concrete pads and skeletal remains of downtown before finally settling the Steiners on the houses on the hill.

Cade's swift recon produced nothing. Not a glint of sky off of glass—the telltale sign of optics being trained on the multi-vehicle spectacle clogging the road in plain sight. With his Spidey sense now tingling worse than ever, he set the brake, climbed down from the truck, and hustled back to the Land Cruiser in a combat crouch. Catching Duncan's eye, he said, "We're being watched."

Duncan answered immediately. "I feel it too."

"Time to go," Cade said.

On the way back to his ride, Cade stopped at each plow truck and—to a pair of confused looks—told Taryn and Lev to raise and retract the blades on their trucks.

Shaking his head, he loped around front of Taryn's truck and hopped in his. He clicked his seatbelt and worked the plow controls before him and, eavesdroppers be damned, with the hiss of hard-working hydraulics filtering into the cab, took up the radio and talked the others through the process.

In the third plow truck, Lev was listening intently and without a hitch managed to get the plow apparatus to fold up and out of the way.

Taryn, on the other hand, demanded to know why they couldn't just stop at the bottom and take the time now to dismantle the roadblock entirely.

"Just trust me," Cade said, as he put the blade on his own truck back into the lowered position.

After a short pause, Taryn was back on the radio. "You haven't failed us yet," she said. "Lead the way."

Realizing how big and tempting a target they were for whoever was watching them, Cade released the brake and goosed the throttle to get the truck rolling forward. Then, on the start of the downslope, as the truck picked up speed, he eased up off the gas and let it coast. Steering one-handed, he snatched up the radio and thumbed the *Talk* button. "Keep a generous following distance," was all he had to offer. He couldn't say: *These trucks might be too wide for the gap*. That would be wholly counterproductive.

Duncan came back on the radio. As if he'd been reading Cade's mind, with a touch of skepticism evident in his voice, he asked, "You sure these things are gonna fit?"

Trying to sound confident, Cade answered, "Brooke drove the F-650 through there on the way to the compound. I figure these can't be that much wider."

"If they prove to be," said Duncan, "y'all will soon find out … the hard way." For a brief second before he released the *Talk* key, the beginnings of one of his trademark cackles filtered over the air for all to hear.

Shaking his head, Cade set the radio in the console. He gripped the steering wheel tightly, squinted against the glare, and fixed his gaze on the National Guard roadblock dead ahead. It had been set up on the west end of a viaduct crossing, and Cade figured that the ink on the President's declaration of Martial Law wasn't even dry before the soldiers who died here had come under attack. Just a few short weeks ago, while traveling overland from Mack, Colorado to the Eden Compound, he, Brooke, Raven, and the Kids had happened upon this scene of carnage. Using the F-650's winch, and with Wilson's help and Brook driving, they had managed to clear a lane, but not before discovering the bodies of the dozen soldiers who had died there protecting it. At the time, without stating his intentions, Cade struck out on his own and with only a couple of cans of gas and a Bic lighter gave the fallen heroes a modified Viking's funeral.

Thankfully, due to the cement Jersey barriers and coverage of drifted snow, things were different this time around and he wouldn't have to look at the burnt and bullet-riddled bodies again. Nosed into the Jersey barriers in the eastbound lane was a long line of cars whose owners had failed to escape the horrors of Huntsville. Since morning, an inches-thick layer of snow had accumulated on their trunks, roofs, hoods and, to a certain extent, their side windows—obscuring the handful of Zs still locked inside.

The right lane, however, was a different story altogether. The cement barriers that had been blocking the westbound lane and shoulder were now resting in the ditch along with several cars, the latter of which were snow-covered and canted at odd angles, some listing to the point where their driver's sides were planted in the dirt, leaving the grime- and grease-streaked mechanical components exposed to daylight.

Just before the hill flattened out, and with only a couple of hundred yards or so to go before entering the narrow breach between the barriers and bridge rail, Cade flicked his eyes to the side mirror. He liked what he saw. He had a three-truck's-length lead and the other two plow trucks were a like distance apart. The 4Runner was partway down the hill and the Land Cruiser was just now moving off the flat spot atop the rise.

Here goes nothing, he thought, toggling his blade up and out of the way while simultaneously increasing the volume of rock falling through the spreader out back.

All at once, the blade up front juddered violently and there was a hollow twang, followed a tick later by the shrill keening of metal molecules being instantly reshaped.

***

In the 4Runner, Wilson was gripping the grab bar near his head with one hand and had the other, fingers splayed, planted on the dash right next to where the words *SR5 AIR BAG* were embossed in quarter-inch script into the pebbled gray vinyl. Praying that Jamie was half the driver Taryn was, he saw the horizon tilt in his side vision. As the two trucks in front tackled the decline, everything seemed to slow for him. He saw clearly the load shift in back of Cade's truck as it entered the level stretch of road running up to the roadblock. Then he noticed the massive plow blade lifting off the ground and simultaneously merging with the apparatus up front.

"Cade's big ass F-650 barely shot that gap before," Wilson said. "I don't think this one stands a chance."

Like a square peg fed into a round hole, Cade's plow truck, bouncing and slewing slightly to the left on the slick surface, entered the gap traveling at what looked to be north of forty miles-per-hour. Feeling slightly prophetic, Wilson witnessed the shower of sparks erupt from down low on the truck's left side the second the orange sheet metal came into contact with the thirty-five-hundred-pound Jersey barrier. Consequently, the equal and opposite reaction came in the form of the Mack truck caroming towards the right shoulder, where the truck impacted an incredibly small two-door car. Originally resting with its stunted front end jutting from the roadside ditch, the collision with the plow truck blasted every flake of snow off the compact car and sent it tumbling nose over tail. Wilson saw the running gear underneath show itself first; then, as the car neared one full revolution, clear as day, he saw the red and blue interconnecting bars of the Union Jack flag painted on its roof. Then the sound of the car—clearly a Mini Cooper—landing wheels down atop the sedan behind it was lost on Wilson; however, the resulting eruption of pebbled glass and powdery snow was not.

As the Mini settled into its final resting place, the UDOT truck veered back to the left at a shallow angle toward the static line of vehicles.

***

Taryn winced at the first sign of sparks, but there was nothing she could do. Already committed, she held the wheel straight and felt the air suspension swallow up the dip at the base of the hill. She looked at the speedometer and saw the needle creeping toward forty miles-per-hour. When she looked up again there was a flash of color and movement and an eruption of sparkling debris as a compact import went airborne then landed smack dab atop a much larger passenger car, causing every one of its windows to implode. The finale to the unexpected chain of events happened as she watched the truck driven by Cade veer back to the left and sideswipe the dozen or so static cars there. Consequently, like old-timey flash bulbs going off one after another, splintered plastic and shards of mirrored glass bloomed from every wing mirror down the line until the UDOT truck was rolling free.

"That should do it," Cade said glibly over the radio.

Taryn tensed as the blade on her truck came parallel with the Jersey barrier. To her relief, there were no sparks or sounds of rending metal as she saw it flit cleanly by on the left. The side mirrors on the row of cars that weren't sheared clean were now swinging wildly from their control wires. On her right, she saw the cars in the ditch flash by in a blur of white and red and black and maroon. She didn't allow herself to relax until her truck was clear of the roadblock and she saw the brake lights of Cade's truck flare red.

***

Immediately following the chain-reaction collisions with the line of cars, Cade watched a dozen prostrate Zs disappear under the vibrating blade. Next, the truck bucked slightly, and then a prolonged chorus of breaking bones assailed his ears until the rig literally *ground* to a halt atop the mangled bodies. He consulted the side mirror and saw that all of the vehicles were off the hill and three of the four had made it through the block. The Land Cruiser was just entering the widened opening and he caught a brief glimpse of the dead soldiers, the snow blown off of them by the passing slipstreams, their charred prostrate forms standing out in stark contrast against the white backdrop.

He sensed the truck driven by Taryn as it pulled even. Ignoring the movement in his peripheral, he manipulated the controls to get the blade moving. There was a hiss of hydraulics, but nothing else. He toggled the switch rapidly back and forth.

Nothing.

Then there was a loud banging followed by a high-pitched whine, and at the end of the sloped hood he saw the blade moving into position. When he looked left, he saw Taryn standing there, beaming at him, an eight-pound sledgehammer clutched in her gloved hands.

She walked around the driver's side and was looking up him just as the blade locked into position. He opened his window and thanked her.

"It was on the floor board when I got in the truck. Figured I'd put it to use," she said. "And hell, Cade. You said you'd get us through the block. And you sure did. Pretty impressive."

"Physics," he said, as the other vehicles formed up in a line stretching back. "Honestly ... I thought this thing would squeak through without making contact."

She smiled. "Nobody's perfect, Mister Grayson. Are you going to see if the blade is going to stay put before we get going?"

"No need," he said. "It's down now ... thanks to you. It's going to stay there until it won't. And it's Cade ... or Grayson. No Mister. And I've never answered to sir, never will."

She nodded and looked to her left at the static herd of dead, some standing, most not. "Are we going to take care of these now or later?"

He looked at his Suunto. Saw that it was nearing four o'clock and realized time was slipping away fast. He shook his head. "We've got a lot to do still. Mount up or we'll be driving home in the dark."

Just as Taryn nodded and turned toward her truck, Cade's radio blurted to life. He regarded the side mirror and saw the Land Cruiser coming to a halt at the back of the procession. In the next beat Duncan said, "We better stop and bury those soldiers back there."

"No time," Cade said. Full of remorse for having left them languishing in the elements the first time, and cursing under his breath at being forced to leave them now, he dumped the radio on the seat, released his foot from the brake, and pinned the pedal to the floor.

Chapter 35

Dregan's chest heaved as his body was wracked by a big, booming cough. He spit a thick rope of phlegm on the bark dust at his feet and stood up straight, trying to get his breath. Though he was telling his boys and anyone else who showed concern for him that the changing of the seasons and the fluctuations in weather that came with them was the reason for his worsening condition, deep down under the outer layers of voiced denial, he knew something was eating away at him from within.

He coughed once more, spat on the ground, and then removed the stake holding down the corner of the blue tarp. He walked counter-clockwise around the boxy shape and pulled up three more stakes, watching the edges of the tarp fluttering in the breeze coming up from the east. Mesmerized by the gentle movement, he held one corner and watched the thin tarp ripple for a few short seconds. Once the wind picked up, he pulled sharply on his corner and, like a magician performing the age-old tablecloth routine, jerked the waterproof covering clean off the squat desert-tan Humvee. After catching briefly on the matte-black barrel protruding from the top-mounted turret, the tarp fell quietly in a bunch on the ground.

Just as he'd been doing bi-weekly since late August when he, his brother, Gregory and Mikhail returned from the outskirts of Salt Lake City with this Humvee and three similar vehicles, he climbed aboard and started the diesel engine. He let it idle for a long while, and once the blue-gray smoke began to build under the boughs near his head, he silenced the engine and tapped out a random rhythm on the wheel.

"What are you doing, Dad?" asked Peter. He was standing in the snow equidistant from their house and picket of fir trees under which the vehicles were parked. He was wearing fur-lined Sorel winter boots with the sales tags still attached. His winter jacket and quilted heavy-duty pants were camouflaged in a typical tree pattern favored by hunters. On his head was a hat emblazoned with the words *Call of Duty Modern Warfare* and the silhouette of a soldier clutching a rifle.

"How long have you been there, Peter?" called Dregan. He hawked again and motioned the boy forward.

Peter replied, "The whole time the motor was running." He took his hat off and as he crunched across the snow, tucked his long blonde locks behind his ears and readjusted the clasp on back of the hat.

"Time for a haircut, boy. Maybe for your birthday I'll take you in to see Doc. Get your teeth checked and ears lowered all in one sitting."

Peter said nothing. Self-conscious of it, he hid his hair under his hat and snugged it down tight over ears that were already going red from the chill.

"You forgot about your *birthday*?" Dregan said, incredulous. "You've been crowing about the big one-three for most of the year."

Peter opened the heavy door—*up-armored* is what he'd heard his older brother Gregory call it—and climbed up into the passenger seat. He looked up at his dad, his azure eyes watery from the fluctuation in temperature between inside and out.

"Too much bad stuff happening," Peter said. "Yes … I forgot." He smiled, showing off his straight teeth. "But I won't forget Halloween, though."

Dregan tousled his head, setting the cap askew. "You already got your mom's short gene. Candy will just stunt your growth ... and ruin your teeth. She was always proud of how straight they came in, you know. Figured you were going to save us money on braces on account of it."

Peter made a face and looked away. "We were going to go to Disneyland if I didn't need them, remember?"

"How could I forget? And Peter—"

"Yes," the boy said, sweeping his gaze back.

"It's okay to forget your birthday." He went quiet for a tick. Covertly wiped a stray tear on his flannel sleeve then fixed his blue eyes on the boy. Slowly he said, "Don't you ever forget your mom."

Consciously changing the subject, Peter looked over his shoulder. He hooked a thumb at the weapon in the turret. "What's that?" he asked.

"That, my boy, is a Mark 19 grenade launcher."

"Do you have any bullets for it?"

"They're not bullets like our guns take. It shoots forty-millimeter grenades," Dregan absently corrected his son. He reached his long arm around between the seats and over the transmission hump. He removed the rectangular lid from a metal canister and walked his eyes across the ammunition lined up in the bottom. He counted the linked projectiles for the weapon. They were gun-metal gray with yellow/gold tips and about the size of a can of soda.

"We have eight rounds left," Dregan said.

"Is that enough to kill the people who murdered Lena?"

"Perhaps," Dregan said, the granite set to his jaw suddenly returning.

"And the other three ... are there guns on them too?"

"You know there are, boy. Don't play dumb with me." His demeanor softened and he said softly, "I've seen you under there and the tarps tenting up. Wasn't Casper the Friendly Ghost playing soldier, was it?"

"Uh, uh," Peter said, looking away.

"It's okay. I woulda done the same at your age. I did, actually."

Peter swept his gaze to his dad. "Can you tell me about your time in the Army?"

For the umpteenth time, Dregan shook his head. And for the umpteenth time he said, "Not today."

Peter frowned.

"Go … now. Get back inside the house," Dregan said with a shooing motion. "And close the door quick so the heat stays in."

"Are you coming, Papa?"

"After I start these other vehicles. Now go."

Dregan watched his youngest tear across the snow-covered lawn. The boy scaled the ladder like a spider monkey and went inside without looking back.

***

Forty minutes after the conversation that had left him choked up and thinking about his dead wife, Dregan was finished prepping the vehicles for war. The first round of eight was fed into the MK-19, the other seven resting in the attached ammo box. The other three Humvees were also armed, fueled up, and had started as easily as the first.

Heart heavy from thinking of his wife and daughter, Dregan staked down the last of the tarpaulins. He stood and breathed in deep, felt the cold stabbing his chest. And as he exhaled, the air around his head clouded from his breath and another coughing fit wracked his body.

The horizontal blinds in the upper-story window were parted, but Dregan had no idea he was being watched as he set off for the house. Halfway there, he convulsed again and spat over his shoulder, painting the snow with a smattering of bright crimson.

In the house, Peter drew his hand back from the horizontal blinds and let the dusty slats snap together. He lay down on his bed and said a small prayer to God, asking for his help so his dad would get better. He heard the *rattle-clank* of footfalls on the ladder treads then the door opening and closing downstairs.

"Come on down, Peter. Time to go and get your birthday haircut."

***

Leaving the Blazer in the carport, Dregan drove the Jackson Hole PD Tahoe into town. He decided that by flaunting the vehicle directly connected to the crime scene, he would send a silent message to anyone who might have gotten wind of his plan that snitching was not an option. Conversely, showing up on Main in the liberated vehicle would send the not-so-silent message to the men Gregory had lined up for him that the mission for tomorrow was still on.

He drove the half-mile to town, slow and deliberate. Along the way, he stopped at two different homes. At the first, when a young man came out onto the porch, he made eye contact and delivered a nod and hand signal. The second was different. He stopped the Tahoe in the drive behind a Humvee painted in woodland camouflage and when his brother Henry looked up from whatever maintenance he'd been embroiled in, eye contact was made and Dregan backed out of the snowy drive. With the details having already been agreed upon, nothing beyond that was needed.

Catching on after the second seemingly non-exchange of information, Peter looked at his dad, saying, "The hand signal to the first guy. Means we're leaving at noon ... when court is in session, right?"

"Very good, boy. I'm glad you picked up on that. But it's me and your uncle and the men me and your brother lined up who are going. You need to stay and guard our home. If the judge comes snooping around again, you tell him we went out to cull the roamers."

"They're not roaming anymore."

"Exactly. That's why the judge will buy the story if you have to lie to him."

Peter was thinking of a way to sway his dad to let him come along when a mud-splattered pick-up sped by on the right then reentered their lane, cutting them off.

"That's Mister Newman."

"Probably tied one on. I would if I were in his shoes."

"You told me Ford's going to get his."

"The judge's verdict only stopped Newman from killing Ford. No satisfaction in letting others avenge your kin. That's why I need to get to Lena's killers before the judge and court gets involved."

"We," corrected Peter.

Newman's truck swerved in the snow then jumped a curb directly across the street from the bookstore-cum-courthouse. It was at that moment when Dregan realized what was about to happen and could not help but watch. Part of him wanted to stop Newman, if only to keep the jailers from being injured or killed. But the other part of him—the majority—decided that Ford had already cast his own fate and then concluded that Pomeroy's men didn't deserve to be saved.

Like a slow-moving train wreck, the old truck sheared off one of the porch stanchions and the makeshift jail's porch roof came hinging down atop the full-size GMC, effectively blocking anyone inside from exiting through the double doors.

How I would have done it, thought Dregan as he pulled hard to the curb, telling Peter to get his head down. In his mind, he saw Ford in the cell and Pomeroy's men watching him. The initial noise would draw the jailers to the blocked front doors. In the ensuing confusion Ford would be all alone in the back room, unknowingly awaiting the reaper.

Dregan silently rooted for Newman as all five-foot-six of him, brandishing an AK-47 assault rifle, leaped from the wrecked truck like a man on a mission. With short precise strides, the wiry man, dressed only in a rumpled tee-shirt and jeans despite the cold, peeled around the corner just as there was movement behind the jail's clouded front windows. A tick later Dregan heard a pair of gunshots. *There goes the door lock,* he thought. *And here comes act three.*

No sooner had Dregan thought it than there was a long, drawn-out fusillade of gunfire. But only the ragged chatter of Mikhail Kalashnikov's lethal invention. There was no return fire. Not even a few sharp pops of a semi-auto pistol neutralizing the threat. There was only a brooding silence. Like time had ceased rolling forward and the world decided to take a break from spinning. Then there was the opposite. A flurry of activity behind the wavy glass. Then raised voices full of emotion and people were spilling from the buildings on either side of the darkened courthouse.

As the men and women who had no doubt been enjoying time off in the saloon ran behind the Tahoe, not one of them paying him any attention, Dregan, still holding Peter's head below the dash, let the idling engine pull the rig forward and, steering one-handed, turned left at the crossing street. Goosing the accelerator, he let Peter sit up and turned another left.

Behind the jail, Newman was sitting in the snow, the shattered wooden back door hinged open, fingers interlocked and his hands atop his head. On the sidewalk a yard away, where presumably Newman had dragged him, Ford was on his back, arms and legs spread wide like he had died right there making a snow angel. Runnels of blood were seeping out from the cannibal's pulped midsection, and around his misshapen head was a rapidly growing crimson halo.

Peter sat up in his seat and looked at the carnage. Though based on his dad's mood, he should have been elated by the sight, instead, he was feeling equal parts disgust and something he couldn't put a finger on. *Torn*, is what he'd heard adults call the inability to decide how they felt about a certain thing. Only this wasn't deciding what coat to wear or whether he wanted white meat or dark at Thanksgiving dinner. A man had died. Or was dying as he looked on. And to Peter it was all so surreal. Up until now Dad had sheltered him from the dirty work, as he called it. Skinning a deer. Cutting a rooster's head off. Or killing a man. To Alexander Dregan it was all the same—*dirty work*.

Right here and now, the deep red liquid pulsing from the multiple holes punched into Ford's chest and guts looked like the *black cherry* flavoring the concessions people spritzed onto his snow cone after a Little League game. And the way it steamed as it cooled and bloomed slowly in the snow around the prostrate body only served to reinforce Peter's initial impression.

Dregan clucked his tongue. "That's what happens when you cross the line, boy. And don't you forget it."

One of the men Dregan had motioned to a few blocks back sidled up to the idling Tahoe. The man pulled his hood back, revealing his slender face and high forehead. He looked over each shoulder and then fixed his stony gaze on the Tahoe.

Peter looked into those eyes, shuddered, and glanced away.

Dregan pulsed down his window. The man, blonde and blue eyed like the boy, said, "You better go or you're going to be called as a witness."

"Nobody saw me," Dregan lied. "We lucked out. Tomorrow is going to be a busy day at the courthouse. And at noon when

Newman goes to trial and Pomeroy is feeling useful, we'll be at the gate."

"A fifth of hard liquor per," said the man, glancing at the commotion.

"Each vehicle?" Dregan did the math. Almost a full case.

The man raised a brow.

Dregan nodded and pulsed up the window.

The man smiled and backed away from the Tahoe, watching as it cut a U-turn and sped away, slipping at first and then tracking straight before finally turning right and disappearing from sight a block distant.

The blonde man zipped his jacket up around his scraggly beard and watched and listened as the jailers—a big African American man and a smaller Caucasian fella—filtered among the dozen townspeople congregating around the condemned man's body. Not wanting to get swept up in the questioning, Eddy Swain tucked his stubby carbine under his arm and strolled slowly towards his Subaru. He got behind the wheel, dropped the all-wheel-drive WRX into gear, and drove away slowly following in the Tahoe's tracks.

Chapter 36

No shots were fired their way as the small convoy left the roadblock behind. They passed the trio of roads leading north off of 39 into town, wheeled south for a spell, then looped around and paralleled the reservoir heading west—still no bullets cleaved the air or spiderwebbed any windows.

All parties were breathing easy when Cade pulled over on the Ogden Canyon Highway a short drive west of where Trapper's Loop Road peeled off towards Morgan and the County airport of the same name, twenty-three miles through the rolling countryside due south.

While Duncan and Wilson wrapped all eight of the SUV's tires with the pain-in-the-ass cable chains and topped off the gas tanks, Cade, Daymon, Jamie, Lev, and Taryn waded into a throng of roughly two hundred eastbound Zs. Stretching about a hundred yards west, the shamblers were mostly frozen in their tracks upright, and by the time Duncan bellowed, declaring the vehicles *"Good to go,"* the small group wielding a dagger, machete, tomahawk, and pair of folding knives respectively had felled two-thirds of the dead and left them scattered and leaking onto the road from one shoulder to the other.

Walking between Lev and Cade, Daymon wiped blood from Kindness with a scrap of cotton tee-shirt taken off a fallen corpse. He sheathed the machete and hurled the soiled fabric to the ground. "Too bad we couldn't finish the job."

"Get used to it," said Cade. "This is nothing. I spotted a real big herd back a ways. They were a couple of hundred yards south on Trapper Road. Easy to miss if you weren't looking left."

"Doesn't matter," said Lev. "I did the math and it isn't encouraging. Before the shit hit the fan there were fifty thousand people residing in Ogden. Even if only twenty percent of them found their way through the canyon and were standing in a neat little line, we would need a bunch of snow days and every warm body from the compound in order to cull them all and dispose of the bodies."

Shaking his head and grumbling about math and snow, Daymon increased his already long stride and left the others behind.

Slipping her tomahawk into its scabbard, Jamie said, "No getting through to that man"

"We made our peace," Lev said. He removed his cap and one of his gloves and ran a hand through his sweaty, steaming, hair. "If I'm willing to cut him some slack after what happened back at the compound ... I think you should let a little bit of whining slide."

Jamie made a face.

Wisely, Taryn and Wilson also held their tongues. No use adding fuel to the fire, in case he was still within earshot.

With daylight a dwindling commodity, Cade said nothing. No use burning precious time debating or arguing about things he had no control over. Instead, letting his actions do the speaking, he hustled to the truck and clambered aboard.

Behind Ray and Helen's Home

The sun had dipped behind the distant trees and their shadows were seemingly growing longer by the minute. Ignoring the snow falling all around him, Cleo took a big drag off the unfiltered Camel and held the warm smoke in his lungs for a long five-count. With the fourth cigarette he'd lit since his willpower crumbled twenty minutes ago already burnt down to a nub, and the throbbing behind his eyes not reacting to the introduction of *real* nicotine into his system, he flicked the butt away and cursed himself for agreeing to help Dregan—no matter how much in the way of reciprocation he had milked the big man for.

He took out the pack and, seeing how few were left, cursed Dregan for allowing him to keep sweetening the pot to the point that it had been impossible to decline this little recon job.

Turning his attention to the job at hand, he put the binoculars to his face and though as repetitious as the routine had become, scanned the house from top to bottom, starting at the right and finishing off at the breezeway. Then he walked the binoculars over the big red barn and still found nothing out of the ordinary. Lastly, he glassed the turn-around in front of the house, following the rutted dirt road all the way to the State Route, and feeling a bit like Bill Murray in Groundhog Day, started humming *I Got You Babe*, swaying to an imaginary backbeat. Fearing he was getting a touch of hypothermia, he started into another set of seated calisthenics. Partway through his routine of stretching and rocking, he had an epiphany. His adrenaline surged and the warmth spread to his limbs as he calculated how many CDs and the newfangled digital downloads of Cleo's Calisthenics he would need to sell to become rich. To sock away a million dollars for a rainy day. The euphoria dissipated as fast as the thought had come when he remembered the world would never be the same. That he'd never have the feeling again of standing up from the poker table in the middle of a crowded casino and crowing about his latest win also pissed him off. It was the only time he felt comfortable in his own skin. And now, thanks to some egghead releasing a little microbial bug aptly named Omega, he would never again attain that level of bliss.

"Fuck you, God. And fuck you, Dregan." He rattled out another cigarette and—not giving a shit if he was made by the old couple—struck a match and puffed away on the stale and crumpled thing until a brilliant red cherry shone at its tip.

***

"Ray," called Helen from somewhere on the second floor, her voice just above a whisper as if whoever it was freezing their buns off in the back forty could actually hear across the distance, through the walls and over the sporadic patter of falling snow, and no doubt the chattering of their own teeth.

"Yes, dear. What is it?" he called back in a normal voice. He lovingly ran a lightly oiled rag over the M4 carbine he had just reassembled, being careful to give all of the metal parts a final pass. Finished, he inserted a loaded thirty-round magazine into the well and clicked it home. Expecting to have already heard some kind of reply from Helen, he looked up at the ceiling and squinted his eyes as if he had some kind of X-ray vision. And after decades of marriage, in a way, he did. He imagined her a dozen feet above the kitchen sink and sitting on her sewing chair in the spare room that overlooked the back yard. She would be in front of the window, her elbows on the sill and her rounded chin perched on the heels of her upturned hands. "What do you see now?" he asked, impatiently this time.

Ray had been partially right in his assumptions. A dozen feet above the kitchen sink in the spare room Helen was indeed sitting in her sewing chair by the window that overlooked the back yard and sloping pasture beyond. However, her chin wasn't cradled by her palms. Her liver-spotted hands were wrapped around the pair of military-issue field glasses that were trained on the distant tree line. Finished there, she swept them left-to-right down the gently sloping hill. Gave the whip-like river a onceover, then settled the optics on the brambles.

"Our watcher is smoking with impunity now," she called downstairs.

"Not a very good watcher, then." Ray rose from his chair and stowed one of the carbines, locked and loaded, behind the oddly shaped door to a small storage cubby under the stair landing. The second M4 he hung by its sling on a peg and replaced his moth-eaten Navy pea coat over top of it. Carbine number three was also an M4. It was painted in a tan camouflage scheme and was outfitted to the nines with doo dads. It had an extremely powerful optic on the top rail and sported a front grip complete with a rubberized thumb switch for the tactical light riding next to the slender tan suppressor at the end of the stubby barrel.

"I'm coming, Helen." Ray slung the rifle over his shoulder and made his way to the stairs. Gripping the bannister rail, worn smooth from thousands upon thousands of trips up and down, he took them slowly one at a time. A little winded, he made the landing and, without pause, turned the bend and tackled the next rise. Rosy cheeked and puffing, Ray made the second-floor two minutes after starting his ascent.

After catching his breath at the stair's summit, Ray took a few strides down the hall and entered the room unannounced. Instantly he was hit by the smell of gun oil and cordite and, underlying those familiar odors, thanks to Helen and her penchant for keeping in the nearby closet every coat, cape, and shawl she had ever owned, the ever-present chemical stench of mothballs.

Scrunching his nose, Ray took in the room. The place looked like a military surplus store, not an old woman's crafts room. He shook his head, amazed, because he didn't recall them hauling all of the gear up the stairs by themselves. However, the dozens of harrowing trips they had made to the towns and abandoned roadblocks south and east of here, and the faces of the dead men and women soldiers they had taken the gear from, were indelibly etched in his memory. Adrenaline had been their friend those first few days and weeks. Like squirrels getting squared away for winter, they had policed up everything they could, figuring the weapons would be better for protection than the old shotgun and thirty-ought-six rifle. And when the government went dark, and no UN vehicles showed up like the Wackadoos were predicting, Ray's gambit was validated in his eyes.

Propped up in one corner were a half-dozen nearly new black rifles, mostly M4s. Lying on the floor in front of the door to Helen's mothball-scented closet was an identical pair of black plastic hard-sided cases. Roughly four feet long and one across, the gun cases thick as a big-city phone book were filled with foam padding and contained high-dollar sniper rifles. The Leupold scopes alone, Ray guessed, once cost the taxpayers a thousand dollars or more. The whole ball of wax—two guns, two scopes, and the Pelican cases—probably cost more than a week-long Caribbean cruise for two and the accompanying bar tab.

"So the dummy is smoking now," Ray said, more of a statement than a question.

"Yep," said Helen. "Chain-smoking ... lighting the new off the old."

"Woulda got shot by my lieutenant if I'd have pulled that crap," said Ray, shaking his head. "Either that or the Chinese or North Koreans woulda done it for him."

Helen relinquished her chair and binoculars and, once Ray sat down, hovered over his right shoulder as he trained them out the window.

"If we can see him," she said, "what makes you think he can't see us?"

"Because the room is dark, Helen. And I'm sure he ... or she, has some kind of sunglasses on to combat the glare."

"What do you reckon he's doing out there?"

"Watching the road for Dregan. Probably has orders to let him know if the others come calling."

"We haven't done anything to make him suspicious." Helen looked out the window, squinting. She said, "Should we bring that boy in and tell him the rest of what Brook told us?"

"No, Helen. We don't know how many Brook and her gang are." Ray dropped the field glasses to his lap. Fixed his gaze on Helen. "My gut's been telling me that rage is clouding that poor man's judgment. Furthermore, we really don't know who else that young woman is rubbing elbows with."

Helen stood and paced the room. The boards underfoot creaked as she wound her way between mounds of tan-colored MRE packages and dark green ammo cans and military issue backpacks stuffed with all manner of gear.

"For all intents and purposes, we are Switzerland," Ray reminded her. He rubbed his eyes where the binoculars had been pressing against them. "Information is king, here, Helen. All we have to do is remain neutral and guard our hearth and home like we have been since those things started roaming around here. We do that and we will hold all of the cards if ... or *when* we have to choose sides."

Helen harumphed. She said, "I still think that young lady was being truthful."

"Everyone is trying to survive this thing," he reminded her. "Seems reasonable there were details she might have been holding back."

"And that's exactly what we're doing to Dregan," Helen conceded.

"Can't be helped." Ray removed his red felt hat and ran a hand through his closely cropped silver hair.

She sighed and began leafing through the MRE packets, reading the labels. "Well then, Ray. What do you want for dinner?"

Ray said nothing. His mind was screaming Switzerland while his every instinct was telling him to be proactive.

"Surprise me, hon," he said, sensing her presence at his back. "I'm going to stay right here and do some thinking."

Helen nodded and squeezed his shoulder. She thought: *You're just avoiding the stairs.* But she said, "Come on down when you're ready." As an afterthought, she paused in the doorway and added, "Leave the door open when you come down so that the gunpowder smell dissipates."

Beneath the binoculars, Ray's lips curled into a smile. *So says the mothball queen.*

Chapter 37

Cade reversed the Mack truck off the bodies it had come to rest upon. Then, intent on clearing a path through the twice-dead Zs, he let the truck roll slowly forward until he heard the hollow thunk of the bent plow making contact with flesh and bone. Feeling the resistance of Lord knows how many pounds of frigid meat building against the truck's forward momentum, he gave it more pedal.

In his wing mirror, he saw the diesel exhaust hanging heavy over the road. Dropping his gaze lower where the words OBJECTS IN THIS MIRROR ARE CLOSER THAN THEY MAY APPEAR were etched, he couldn't help but see the reddish-black ribbon of polished snow unfurling at his six. At first, as the plow truck picked up speed, the limp arms and legs of the fallen Zs flailed and banged into the curved metal blade, creating a morbid cadence that set his teeth to singing. Once enough of them were concentrated up front and the truck gained momentum, the discordant clanging stopped and the packed drift of dead meat simply slid along the road, emitting an awful squelching noise not unlike that of calloused fingers rubbing corduroy. What a sight this Zamboni of death must be to whoever had eyes on it at the moment, thought Cade as the transmission downshifted and there was a grunt from the hard-working power plant.

"Leaving a lot of chum in your wake," said Duncan over the two-way. "You should see it from our vantage."

"Saw it from mine," Cade said.

Thinking out loud, Duncan keyed the *Talk* button and shared with everyone. "Sure puts the blood trails in Nam to shame."

Ignoring the morbid observation, Cade flicked his gaze at the burned-out town off to his right. He still couldn't shake the feeling of eyes on him. Earlier, at the top of the hill overlooking Huntsville, he had been expecting shots to be fired their way but none came. Then the entire time they were exposed on the road culling the dead so they wouldn't have a hundred crawlers to deal with after the thaw, he had been anticipating the sonic crackle of hot lead cutting the air around them. And now, even after getting through all of that unscathed, as he was clearing a swath through the dead and the convoy began picking up speed, he half-expected to see a group of marauders roaring toward them from Huntsville as it passed on their right.

Shifting his gaze back to the road ahead, Cade keyed the two-way. "Just in case we've got breathers watching us, I want to use the plows as a rolling shield for the SUVs. Jamie and Daymon … I want you both to get ahead of Taryn's truck. Lev and Taryn … once they're in, you two slip right a little and tighten up the formation. Grills to bumpers until Huntsville is behind us." There were no replies back. Just actions taken. Flicking his eyes intermittently to the side mirror, Cade watched as the truck Lev was driving slowed and a gap was created between it and Taryn's. Then, slowly, like fighter planes escorting a bombing sortie, the smaller SUVs passed Lev's plow truck and tucked in tight behind Taryn's plow. And it wasn't until they had driven another half a mile in this tight grouping and the gradual sweeping left-to-right turn was behind them did the feeling of being watched go away.

Suddenly neglectful of radio silence, Duncan said, "Was everyone else's butt puckered as tight as mine through all that?"

"If I'd have had a piece of coal up there, I'd be shitting diamonds later," Taryn replied. "Felt like I was being watched on the hill, for sure. Same creepy sensation I felt twenty-four-seven at the airport with old Dickless eye-humping me."

"Should have said something to somebody," Cade said, as the dull gray reservoir and bordering picket of snow-dusted dogwoods drifted by on the right. "'Trust your gut *always'* is what my old friend Desantos preached."

She asked, "Did you feel it, too?"

Cade said, "Of course I did. But I didn't want to distract you and the others from the task at hand. So from now on, just act on the assumption that we are all being watched whenever we're outside the wire."

"Roger that," replied Taryn, having adopted Cade's vernacular, if not the ability to process at all times what her sixth sense was telling her.

In the lead vehicle, Cade put the radio aside and cracked a half-smile. Though they had been in constant peril and faced death on a daily basis, the small band of survivors had continually stared it down. Day-by-day they were becoming less of a frayed rope—only as strong as its weakest strand—and more of a cohesive unit, able to act without having to be micromanaged, as evidenced by Wilson, the least tactically seasoned of them, acting without instruction on two separate occasions so far.

Cade cast his gaze right, where on the reservoir's choppy surface, lolling and straining against their lines, he spotted three familiar sailboats staggered a few yards apart and at anchor a good distance from shore. The trio of angular bows were all pointed due east and nothing moved above deck on any of them. Judging by the razor-sharp shadows cast across their decks by main masts and the upper portion of their cabins, Cade deduced that the layer of snow there was untracked. And further pointing toward the likelihood there were no survivors aboard, like a shark's unblinking eyes, the oval portholes on all three vessels were darkened and there was no signs of movement below decks. Just seeing the vessels produced a sharp pang in his gut, for weeks ago on a trip from the compound to Morgan County Airport, from his seat in the DHS Black Hawk, he had witnessed a group of gleeful survivors waving at him from these same uninhabited teakwood decks.

Now, less than a minute since leaving Huntsville and the feeling of impending doom behind, he was experiencing emotions that normally would stay stuffed deep down in the back of his brain until he was wheels down and home in his family's loving embrace.

Maybe the time away from his Delta brothers was making him go soft again? Though the slim Thuraya sat-phone was tucked out of sight inside a pocket, he could still sense the missed call light strobing in there like a lonesome heartbeat he imagined was pounding a message in Morse from Major Freda Nash saying: "Come back into the fold, Wyatt. *I* need you. The *team* needs you. Your *country* needs you." *Country*, he thought, looking in the passenger side mirror at a rapidly shrinking Huntsville. *Not much of it left to fight for.*

The reservoir's wind-rippled waters slipped behind and soon Cade could only see the road and snow-flocked trees in his wing mirrors. The plow kept scraping the road ahead free of snow and the spreader continued dropping the sand-gravel mixture on the newly cleared asphalt; soon a natural slot appeared in the mountains ahead. He gently eased up on the gas pedal and pulled over, stopping adjacent to another large contingent of inanimate dead.

Keying the radio, he said, "Knock yourself out, Kids." He put the truck in *Park*, jumped from the cab and, employing the Gerber, dropped every single Z in his general vicinity with a swift jab to the eye. By the time the others had dismounted and come forward, a couple of dozen former humans were dead again and hopefully the souls of who they used to be were going in the correct direction for a happy rendezvous with those preceding them in death.

Cade walked toward Daymon, Jamie, and Lev, who were jawing with the Kids, and in passing said, "You all take care of rest of the dead while me and Old Man chain up the SUVs."

"You sure that's necessary, Boss?" Daymon asked, making a face. "They're four by fours."

"Just hoping to head 'ol Murphy off at the pass, that's all."

"Pardon the pun, right?" Daymon tugged his knit cap tight over his mini-dreads and then pulled *Kindness* from her sheath. He looked at Cade with a smile and a rare twinkle in his eye. "Thought you'd never ask." He turned and strode toward the small herd and, as he passed through the low-hanging exhaust, his black boots set the vapor swirling, giving the impression that he was walking on clouds.

Cade watched him go for a second then flicked his gaze to the others. They were arming themselves and chatting like they were getting ready for a night out—not fixing to take down a hundred former human beings: men, women, and children all represented within the eastbound procession. He called Wilson over and relieved him of the baseball bat. Then he drew the Gerber and held it out, pommel first. "Use this," he said, more order than request. "You'll find it's much more efficient."

Without a word, Wilson took the offering and started out after the others, who were already following closely in Daymon's footsteps.

Cade leaned the bat against the 4Runner. Then, favoring his tweaked left ankle, he walked to the Land Cruiser, where Duncan was bent over and rummaging through the gear in back.

Hearing the squeak of Cade's soles on the settled snow, Duncan poked his head around the rear of the SUV. "You prick," he said. "Volunteerin' *me* instead of Carrot Top to get down on the cold ground and monkey with these things?" He tossed the two plastic boxes unceremoniously to the road, breaking one wide open in the process. Grimacing, he hoisted a tangled tire chain from the box and held it up in front of his face like a metal veil. "Hell, I'd just as soon try to shove a hot buttered noodle up a cat's ass than shred my fingers putting these on."

"Gimme one of them," Cade said. "I wanted the Kid to get back to being used to seeing blood on his blade." He took the chain from Duncan and gestured at the dead crowding the road up ahead. "This is just the tip of the iceberg. There's bound to be thousands of them at the pass and in and around Huntsville and Eden."

"And?" Duncan drawled. "You obviously wanted some alone time with me, too. So spit it out."

Cade looked over his shoulder and saw the five survivors tearing into the immobilized herd. On the periphery, where he had asked that the corpses be deposited for ease of removal later, Wilson was jabbing the black dagger head-high then immediately dragging each kill to the shoulder where a small pile of them was building. Daymon and Jamie were out ahead of everyone. He had taken his hat off and his stunted dreads were bobbing with each methodical swipe of the machete. On the far side of Daymon, where Cade imagined the dashed yellow centerline to be, Jamie was bringing her tomahawk down in short efficient strokes, dropping the dead into vertical heaps on the road where they once stood.

All the while the unlikely duo were at work with their blades, Lev and Taryn were following in their footsteps and dragging the leaking sacks of pallid skin from their metal-flashing wake.

Cade regarded Duncan with a hard stare. All business-like, his hand touching the Glock strapped to his leg, he said, "What do you think about us staying the night in Huntsville when we're done in Ogden Canyon?"

Duncan's brow shot up. He hadn't been expecting this. Especially after the one-two punch the younger man's family took last time he was away for an extended period of time. "Sure . . . but what's Brooke gonna say?"

"I won't be asking her. This is for the good of the group and *needs* to be done. It's the first real advantage we have had ... hell, *all* of mankind has had over the dead without having to resort to the use of tactical nukes. I just hope the President and her people in Springs don't have so many irons in the fire that they throw away this first real opportunity to make a huge dent in their numbers."

With a look of confusion on his face, Duncan removed his glasses and a square of fabric from a pocket. "So what are you asking *me* for?"

"Because of where we'll be staying."

Not following, Duncan regarded the nonstop movement down the road.

Cade followed Duncan's gaze and, after they both watched the macabre happenings there for a couple of beats, he noticed the older man's shoulders droop.

Wearing a look of concern, Duncan turned to Cade. "You mean you want me to stay the night in Glenda's home."

Cade nodded. "If she's alright with it. You can call the compound and ask her first."

"Well, well. I'll get to meet Louie after all," Duncan said, the look of concern morphing to one of astonishment. He shook his head, cast his eyes down. "I don't think the old boy is going to have much to say about his wife's new man."

"I'm not following," Cade said.

"You'll see," Duncan replied, forcing a smile. "Let's get these chains on." As he bent down to grab the box of chains, the smile faded and, triggered by the fear that he might find out things about Glenda she had not yet divulged to him, that old familiar craving was back.

Chapter 38

A short while after adding a number of fresh lesions to his knuckles, Duncan was sitting in the passenger seat and pounding his fist on the dash in perfect time with the chains thrumming against the freshly plowed road.

"What's eating you?" asked Daymon, taking his eyes off the road for a long two-count.

Seemingly hypnotized by the shiny wood veneer fronting the glove compartment, Duncan stared and drummed, but made no reply.

Nonplussed by the lack of response, Daymon shook his head and shifted his gaze forward just as the 4Runner two car lengths ahead rolled over an adult-sized corpse, splitting it in half at the hips and sending the two pieces spinning off in entirely different directions. He muttered an expletive as the legs and pelvis went into a lazy flat spin across the snow and became hopelessly tangled up against the right-side guardrail. Then, in the blink of an eye, he was channeling a sailor and his muttered curse words were a full on verbal assault on his own bad luck. And though his reflexes were superb, due to the effect the chains had on both the steering and acceleration, when he tried to wheel around the three-foot-long chunk of legless upper torso, the maneuver was not entirely successful. Like hitting a speed bump at thirty-five miles per hour, the luxury sport-utility rose up on the left side, but only shortly, because the speed bump was a skull and, bone not having the same properties as cured asphalt, it imploded, sending a hollow sounding *pop* coursing up through the floorboards. In reaction to the sudden change in angle, in unison, both men listed left and then jerked back to the right as the rig settled back to earth and the metronomic cadence that had been vibrating the chassis and their teeth returned, as loud and annoying as ever.

Still grimacing from the imagined visual produced by the awful noise, Duncan answered the question. "What's eating me?" he said, voice rising an octave. "A whole bunch of little problems, that's what. And all of 'em put together is like a whole school of piranhas tearing me apart bit by bit."

"I feel ya," Daymon said just as one of the plow trucks delivered a metal hockey check that sent a dozen corpses careening against the canyon wall. "I'm dreading the moment my girl runs out of her pills. Ever since the shit happened in Robert Christian's mansion she's been a special flavor of crazy." He paused for a tick and then went on, "And when they do run out it is going to be ultimatum time for good 'ol Daymon."

"What do you mean?" Without conscious thought, Duncan popped open the glove compartment.

Daymon shot him a glare. "Why you goin' in there?" he asked.

"Habit," replied Duncan. "An old one that's dying hard."

Up ahead, the road took a sharp dip where it looked as if an unchecked stream had spilled down the opposite hillside and eroded the roadbed underneath. The four vehicles ahead of them slowed, entered the dip and then rounded the following right-hand sweeper, picking up speed along the way. As Daymon braked to navigate the beginnings of a major washout, his eyes were drawn down below to his left, where visible in places through the snow cover was a mosaic of color. After staring for a second, he realized what he was seeing was the clothing of the dead that had fallen or been pushed from the road. And as he steered nearer to the guardrail and got a closer look at the canyon bottom, from his elevated position he saw arms reaching up, the fingers frozen claw-like and seemingly taking desperate swipes at the sky.

"Gotta be a couple thousand of 'em down there," Duncan said.

Still gawking at the macabre sight, Daymon replied, "Double or triple that number ... at least."

Duncan rapped his shredded knuckles on the glove box door. "Better keep your eyes on the road," he said as brake lights flared red up ahead and the lead truck with Cade at the wheel swung a sudden right-to-left arc over three lanes.

Heeding Duncan's warning, Daymon slowed, and once the taller plow trucks pulled around the bend, got his first good look at the Ogden Canyon roadblock that up until now he had only seen from the air. To the right of the road rose a nearly vertical cliff face with scrub and gnarled trees clinging to it tenaciously. Opposite the steep face, beyond the guardrail, the canyon dropped off sharply an indeterminate number of feet to the logjam of dead bodies that a second ago had been the object of his fixation. And looming a dozen feet over Cade's now inert and inexplicably high-sided plow truck was a wall of rust-colored shipping containers. Best he could tell, they were still mostly blocking off the body-strewn four-lane.

Four abreast, three deep, and stacked two high, the containers looked to have originally been assembled in an inverted 'V.' The twelve on the side with the drop off had been pushed inward, presumably by the surging dead, and now sat nearly parallel with the guardrail. From Daymon's viewing angle, the breach there looked to be three feet wide and at the most ten feet deep. And, like cattle in a chute, dozens of unmoving corpses were stuck fast in it. Most were upright and had succumbed to the effects of the cold mid-stride. A handful of them teetered precariously over the guardrail, spared a trip to the bottom of the canyon due to Old Man Winter's sudden intervention.

Daymon steered the Land Cruiser around the 4Runner, leaned forward and looked across Duncan and saw that both Jamie and Wilson were staring slack-jawed at the scene they had all just happened upon. A little overwhelmed by the scope of things and just how close the truck Cade was driving had come to driving off the cliff face, he swallowed hard and said to Duncan in a low voice, "We've got our effin work cut out for us."

Always the optimist, Duncan replied dryly, "And two hours of light left in which to git-er-done."

Noting the sarcasm in the older man's voice, Daymon nodded and said agreeably, "We are fucked." He applied the brakes and, once the monotonous thrumming of the chains quieted, added, "And I have a sinking feeling we're all gonna be staying the night in Huntsville."

"I think you're onto something," replied Duncan, cryptically.

Daymon pulled the rig hard to the right and parked it with the passenger side tires on the soft shoulder. He pressed the Engine Stop/Start button, quieting the motor.

"Why don't you hail Sarge and see what he was thinking going balls-to-the-wall toward the drop off."

"No blood no foul," Duncan replied. "Besides ... he's the only one among us who's not acting like his panties are bunchin up. No sense in driving him there."

Daymon made no reply. He was looking at the listing plow truck with its horribly pranged blade up front and recalling Cade's prophetic words: *Just trying to head 'ol Murphy off at the pass.* "Mission accomplished," he muttered.

"What?" said Duncan, his fingers curling around the grab-bar near his head.

"Never mind," Daymon replied.

The doors on the Land Cruiser opened simultaneously and both men exited, Duncan wincing at the annoying metal-to-metal groan his produced. Eyes downcast, he made his way out of the deep snow-choked ditch and, sneering with disgust, kicked aside a severed leg blocking his path. Slipping, sliding, and cursing under his breath while using the vehicle for stability, he shuffled to the front of the SUV, stepped over the crushed cadaver the leg had apparently come off and, finally standing on flat ground, shook a fist at Daymon.

Without a trace of sincerity in the delivery, Daymon smiled, looked over the hood at Duncan standing ankles deep in gore, and said, "Sorry ... I had no idea the ditch was there."

***

Sitting in the listing truck, left cheek mashed against the side glass, Cade relived his near-death-experience. First he had felt the building mass of corpses working against the engine. Then he had eyed the looming wall of metal and tried to time his left turn so that the blade up front would clear as many of the Zs away from its base as possible. Finally, as he gave the truck more gas and straightened the wheel, two things happened simultaneously. First, the extra added weight bogged the truck down and there was the groan of rending metal. Then, as a gunshot-like bang of the plow trying to tear free from its mount rang out, all resistance of the bodies grinding against pavement gave way, the truck suddenly lurched forward and he felt a sudden weightlessness.

Ass off the seat and wrestling with the wheel and brake to get the combined tonnage of truck and load stopped, time slowed for Cade. A heartbeat away from impacting the guardrail and a fatal plummet over the ledge, he recalled grabbing the door handle and preparing to bail out. In the next half-beat, fingers touching the cool metal, inexplicably the sluggish handling truck hauled over to the left and ground to a complete stop, its once-straight plow blade bent into an "L" and periscoping over the hood.

Flashing back to the present, Cade took a deep breath and pried his fingers free of the door handle. He said a prayer, thanking his God as he looked past the sloped hood and saw the accumulation of bodies below. He regarded the blade and came to the conclusion that because of the way it was bent completely to vertical and rocking back and forth gently—thanks to his numbskull miscalculation at the first roadblock, and this new failure to foresee certain handling characteristics—it was now rendered all but worthless. So he set the brake and stilled the engine. *Time to make lemonade out of lemons.*

He hailed Taryn and Lev on the radio and asked one of them to pull close to the rock spreader attached to his truck. He climbed over the transmission tunnel and flung the passenger door open. Half-expecting gravity to send the fifty-some-odd pounds of metal, vinyl, and glass right back into his face, he immediately leaned back into the cab. But instead of the undesirable result, the door hit the break point and hinged wide open with the mirror hitting sheet metal and finally arresting it. After looking over the sill and judging the drop as doable—even with his tweaked ankle—Cade lowered himself slowly, facing the detritus-smeared undercarriage, until he felt his boots come into contact with the unusually spongy roadway. With the stench of decay assailing his nose, and fully aware of the dangers the splintered bone and body fluids presented, he limped through the minefield of body parts and around back of the truck where he was met by Lev.

Holding a nylon tow strap he'd scrounged from under the seat of his UDOT truck, Lev asked, "Where do you want it?"

A little embarrassed by the predicament he had gotten himself into, Cade said nothing. The only child in him coming out, he took the orange strap from Lev, duck-walked under the truck's passenger side and hooked it to the frame. When he turned back, Lev had the other end attached to his truck's bumper and was behind the wheel, hat off, and staring ahead with a stony set to his jaw.

Cade straightened the strap and backpedaled well away from the rig's exposed undercarriage. Flashing a thumbs up to Lev, he bellowed, "Go!"

There was a puff of black smoke and the Mack's big diesel howled. The strap produced an inharmonious twang as it snapped taut. Then, slowly but surely, Cade's *mistake* rolled off the crushed corpses, banged back onto all ten tires, and lolled side-to-side like a dinghy in a swell for a quick second until the load in back leveled and all movement ceased.

Grimacing, Cade looked at his mess. For one, he had drastically overestimated the amount of bodies the plow could handle. He studied the distance from the wall of cadavers and the guardrail dwarfed by it. Couldn't have been more than six feet from going over. Shaking his head, he shifted his gaze to the scraped and dinged white metal rail and the vertically ribbed wall of the nearest container and saw through the gap there what had to be thousands of Zs packed in tight.

Out of his truck and working to get the strap untied, Lev paused and said, "That was close."

Cade made no reply. Just stared at what almost was and what they were going to have to face if his plan here failed.

Having just walked up, Duncan said, "Lev … I think if our boy *Crash* here woulda somehow jammed just one more carcass under his truck, we'd be looking over that rail and saying sayonara to him."

Lev started to say something until he saw how shaken Cade appeared.

So Duncan did it for him. "Were you trying to commit vehicular hari-kari there, Cade?"

Cade was about to make a reply he would have probably regretted when Lev reentered the conversation. "What do you figure, a couple hundred new ones were showing up here daily until the weather stopped 'em?"

"At least," replied Cade, his glare softening as he looked away from Duncan and met Lev's gaze. "Good thing for us is it seems just as many end up below as actually squeeze through the gap."

"Quit yer jawin' about couldas and wouldas," Duncan said. "This *would* have all been avoided if *someone*"—he looked directly at Cade—"had let me dynamite this pass closed for good."

"But I didn't," Cade said. He locked eyes with Duncan. "And I told you my reasoning behind it. And you agreed."

"I was drunk."

"When weren't you?" Cade said.

Duncan had nothing to say to that. Instead, he shifted his weight and looked longingly up at the sheer rock face.

"Now gather round," Cade called, his voice carrying down the road to the others.

Chapter 39

Underneath the three-hundred dollar jacket that he could not have fathomed paying half as much for had he the money to burn, Gregory Dregan was sweating like a whore in church—as his highly religious, albeit none too politically correct mother had been fond of saying. The spot on the overgrown fire road he had chosen to take a break from walking was sheltered from the still-falling snow and in sight of yet another victim of the virus let loose on humanity by some dumbass in a supposedly secure facility somewhere on earth. That much he was certain of. The lies to the contrary had piled up early on, with leaders of every country on earth pointing fingers and, in some cases, nuclear-tipped missiles at each other. Rumors ran rampant that last week in July. And the first inkling that Gregory had that the President of the United States wasn't being totally honest with the people he served was when POTUS had urged everyone, except those in essential services, to stay home and ride it out even while news outlets were reporting that government bigwigs were fleeing D.C. like rats from a sinking ship. This was confirmed when a Russian language internet site Gregory liked to get the other side of the story from showed a still photo of Air Force One lifting off from Andrews and, in the background, clear as day on his computer monitor, he saw inert cars clogging the surface streets and highways and a background haze dotted with points of orange light that told him D.C. was burning. So much for *essential services*, he had thought at the time.

The part that really confused him, however,—to the point of making him think the photo might have been manipulated in Photoshop—was that after watching footage on television and online and then consequently seeing, in person and up close, armored personnel carriers on the streets of Salt Lake City—was the President's live message from the White House situation room in which he doubled down on his initial call for citizens to, in his words, 'shelter in place and ride the effects of this nasty virus out.'

The infected forty-something woman kneeling on the snow a yard from him was all the proof he needed that the President's words had been meaningless bullshit. Shelter in place or run for the hills, it didn't matter what you did—this immobilized monster was proof that Omega would find you regardless. And that aspect of how the virus was delivered was most insidious of all, for if this victim on the fire road was a decade older she might as well have been his mom. People's reluctance to confront the fact that a loved one could suddenly turn and immediately hunger for the nearest meat certainly hastened Omega's spread.

In the end—even with all that he had learned about the government's failed attempt at containment and seeing first-hand that there was no surviving a bite—he couldn't bring himself to put his own mom down. In the heat of the moment, nothing anyone said could convince him that who and what she had meant to him—which was the world—was no longer inside that ambulatory shell.

She's dead, Peter had screamed to him as the pistol wavered in his numb hand on that hot July day.

They were pulled off at a rest stop near Arsenal, Utah, where Dad had made the executive decision to bypass the burgeoning FEMA facility near there and 'head for the hills' as he put it then. The self-proclaimed Gas Baron's old overloaded Buick, threatening to overheat, was parked in the furthermost spot from the looted vending machines standing sentinel before the cinderblock bathrooms. Mom had been raving about how her head hurt one moment then was dead the next. *Flatline*, as the doctors on television called it. No pulse. No respiration. And all because they had listened to the President and sheltered in place in their two-story colonial at the end of a once quiet cul-de-sac while the world died outside their multi-paned windows. One tiny bite from a wandering neighbor kid did her in. She was a *slow burn,* as some of the scientists started calling the ones who didn't turn right away. Mom had taken sixteen hours to succumb, whereas the kid who bit her was dead in less than twenty minutes.

Just like the assholes who watch their dog leave a steaming dump in the middle of a park, then look over both shoulders before walking away without doing their civic duty—the grandmother warding over the recently turned kid wanted nothing further to do with him and released him onto the street like a feral dog. Then Silvie, always the kindhearted one, tried to round the infected boy up to do what was right. The 'compassionate thing' were her exact words. And that vein of compassion that ran so deep in her was what did her in.

At the rest stop, with Dad's revolver in hand and a stern 'just do it' echoing in his head, Gregory Dregan saw no kind of compassion in what he was being told to do … only murder. So he had walked away from the Buick, leaving Silvie thrashing and snapping at him like an animal. No amount of begging and pleading from him could convince his dad to do the same as the elderly neighbor had done with the neighbor boy—simply let her go. Just drive off and leave the rest up to fate.

The word 'coward' rang out at Gregory's back, then, a millisecond later, he flinched when his dad, Alexander Dregan, put a bullet into his mother's brain. The people at the rest stop didn't flinch like he had. Not a person. They just went about their business as if the woman *was* a rabid dog being put down.

That was the day the new normal hit Gregory Dregan.

And that was the day any respect he had had for his dad was at its lowest.

Now, weeks later, Dad still hadn't apologized for calling him a coward in front of his brother and all of those people at the rest stop. Pot calling the fucking kettle black. Send a boy to do a man's job and all that jazz. Therefore respect for the elder Dregan was nowhere near to where it had been before that day in Arsenal.

"Sorry, lady," Gregory said to the undead thing as he drew the long blade from his hip. Though this one, like all the others he'd encountered since the snow started to fall, was unmoving and unresponsive, he still approached the slight woman with caution and from the side. "I have to do this to you. It's my duty." He grabbed a handful of the thing's matted blonde hair and was startled by how it crackled in his grasp. It was slippery against his glove, so he pushed the thing onto its side and put his boot on its thin neck. And like every female roamer he'd dispatched since denying his mom sweet release, he said, "Bye Mom," before thrusting his dagger into the soft spot between ear and eye socket. Lips set in a thin white line, he pushed hard on the handle until the hilt struck bone, then continued applying pressure until the horrid sound of cracking skull made him ease up. He drew back the blade and, like the seven roamers he'd already come across and dispatched since leaving the snowmobile under the tree, no blood spilled from this kill. No maggots squirmed from the jagged gash. But best of all, somewhere, he knew Silvie was watching and proud of how far he'd come.

He dragged the corpse off to the side. Straightened the body out face up and arranged the arms so they crossed over where he guessed the heart to be.

After saying a prayer, which he did for every female regardless of age, he shed a glove and again consulted the map. Ten minutes studying the myriad roads and symbols only confused him further. The Ogden River and fire lane had taken divergent paths a mile back. Since then the fire lane had twisted and turned on him and made a big run in a direction he thought was south before abruptly turning back on itself.

As he stood there, his dim shadow falling over the dead woman, he realized several things were stacking up against him. One, the map taken from a car left behind a ransacked and burned-out Shell station just outside of Huntsville weeks ago predated the 9/11 attacks. Two, it had gotten wet the last time he had it out and as a result had started to tear at the creases, two of which intersected near where he thought he was. And three, with no compass and snow-laden clouds blocking out the sun, orienting himself west where he knew the missing orb would soon be setting was an exercise in futility.

Eden Compound

"Girls," Brook called. "Get your coats and gloves on. We're going topside."

"C'mon Mom," replied Raven, a defiant tone to her voice. "Can't we watch just *one* more episode?"

"Shut it off, *now*," shot Brook, a rare hint of anger creeping into her tone. "The fuel in the generators isn't there just so you two can binge watch the entire Twilight series."

After a bit of grumbling the girls assembled, dressed and ready to go, albeit a little blurry-eyed.

"What do you have in mind, Mrs. Grayson?"

"Sasha ... like I said, call me Brook or Mom. Mrs. only makes me feel old."

"But you are, Mom." Raven's eyes went wide, as if she couldn't believe the words that just spilled from her mouth. In the next beat, instead of atoning for the transgression, a chuckle escaped her lips and she looked to Sasha for approval.

Knowing it was normal for a newly minted twelve-year old to continue testing boundaries, Brook let it slide. She cast a glance at Sasha, who was older than Raven by nearly three years. The girl was standing silent, her eyes twinkling with a newfound intelligence. Either due to the recent deaths or simply time's effect on her maturity, the fourteen-year old had become steadily more respectful. The smart alecky outbursts were few and far between and she'd even softened her anti-gun stance. It was as if in some strange Jekyll and Hyde sort of way the two girls were switching poles. And Brook found it kind of refreshing. A little sass aimed in the proper direction never hurt anybody. In fact, she reasoned, it might be just what Raven needed to boost her confidence a little. She made a mental note to pick and choose her battles very carefully in the near future and let Bird win the ones that—though inconsequential in the big scheme of things—might be monumental in importance to the still maturing tween.

With both girls looking on, Brook opened a drawer and pulled out a pair of Beretta semi-auto pistols. They gleamed dully under the lone overhead bulb as she placed them side-by-side on the tabletop. She set the pair of loaded magazines next to the pistols and closed the drawer. She took one of the nine-millimeters in hand, pointed the muzzle at the floor and struggled to grip the slide fully with the forefinger and thumb of her right hand. Still lacking in that hand the motor skills and strength necessary to perform this very important task, she gripped the weighty pistol between her knees and easily pulled the slide back with her left. Visually, she verified the chamber was empty, let the slide snap shut, then holstered the pistol. She repeated the process with the other Beretta and handed one to each girl. "We're going to shoot off-hand again, today. That means with the hand you *don't* write with. One magazine each." She rose and grabbed her own Glock 19, which was in a holster and hanging off the corner post of the bunk near to her head. She strapped the drop-leg rig on and regarded Raven with a no-nonsense look. "Antiserum check."

Raven fished the metal canister from her jacket in front. Held it for all to see and rattled the contents. "Satisfied?" she said, letting go of the string securing it around her neck.

Brook went about tightening the thigh strap while out of the corner of her eye she watched the girls cinching their weapon belts on. Then to her surprise, like a scene unfolding before a mirror in a Gap fitting room, the girls looked one another up and down and smiled like they were doing something as innocuous as accessorizing new school clothes.

"Let's go, Max," she called. The dog appeared at her heel out of the gloom. She looked at the girls with an arched brow. "We're Oscar Mike, *fashionistas*." Walking with a slight limp and unaware of the funny looks being sent her way by both girls, Brook led them down the hall and when they reached the security desk, sent them ahead with Max. She craned towards the foyer and, once confident the girls were out of earshot, asked Seth, "Have they checked in?"

"Nope," he replied, munching on a stale Cheeto, the orange crumbs raining down on his black beard where too many to count already languished in the lengthening tangle. "I don't think we'll hear anything until they're on their way back."

Brook looked at her Timex. "Not a lot of daylight left."

"Probably will take them longer to hump their gear through the fallen trees than make the drive back from Huntsville."

Brook nodded, then grimaced as a dagger of pain shot through the taut skin around her healing wound.

Seth pushed the Cheetos bag away, rose and offered a steadying hand. "You OK?" he asked, his face gone tight with worry.

"Same 'ol, same 'ol." She gestured at the monitor and tensed up. After a second she relaxed and muttered an expletive at herself for forgetting so quickly that every sudden movement had its consequences. Steadying herself on the counter, she drew a deep breath and asked, "Is the road still clear?"

Seth wiped his hands on his pants, leaving orange tracks there from his fingers. He sat down and, while absentmindedly worrying his black beard with one hand, said cheerily, "Nothing. And I mean *nothing* is moving up there."

"The microphone working now?"

Seth shook his head. "Foley couldn't work his magic on it."

"Couldn't hear anything but wind in that piece of crap anyway," Brook said. "Is the shroud over the cameras doing what it's supposed to?"

"Don't know if it's the shroud, the WD-40 Foley shot on the dome, or a combination of the two. But whatever the case, the snow is avoiding it like the plague." Seth winced and then flashed a wan smile at Brook. "Sorry," he added. "Very bad choice of words."

"No worries," Brook said, returning the smile. "I'll be at the range with the girls if you need me."

Seth noticed that the corner of Brook's mouth and her cheek on the right side still drooped a little. Then, highlighted by the overhead bulb, the streaks of gray shot through her dark hair were suddenly evident. He looked away before she had a chance to catch him gawking. Locking his gaze on Chester the Cheetah on the Cheeto bag, he said, "Heidi's pulling watch for me in a few so I can take a pee break and get a little something more filling than these puffs of air."

The skin around her right eye and mouth still slack, Brook said, "Yellow the snow well away from the entrance, please."

Seth looked up, smiling. "Maybe we ought to yellow up a few snowballs for Lev to chuck at Daymon when he gets back."

"Better yet," she said over her shoulder. "You ought to write Lev's full name in the snow in front of Daymon's trailer."

"What is his full name?"

Already out of earshot, Brook made no reply.

Shrugging, Seth looked into the bag, picked an extra cheesy specimen, and turned his attention back to the monitor.

Once topside, Brook, Max, and the girls tromped across the snowy clearing, walked around the Winnebago and then entered the trees near the Black Hawk. With their every breath producing a churning white cloud, they followed the snowy path for thirty yards or so until reaching a small clearing where the ground rose sharply, creating a perfect backstop of packed earth and clay twenty-five feet across, and nearly half as high. Likely created instantly by some kind of violent seismic upheaval, it curled at the top like a dirt wave frozen mid-break. There were rusty cans scattered about, all misshapen and with jagged holes torn in their sides. Tatters of colorful paper still clung to some of them and quite a few remained stuck in the mud wall where they'd been placed as targets, each consecutive bullet burying them deeper. Brook's first impression, though she was partially responsible for the mess, was that someone had indiscriminately shot up a supermarket's entire canned goods aisle.

Obviously excited to be out of the compound, Raven and Sasha scurried ahead and assembled a dozen cans and plastic bottles of varying sizes against the backstop. Some they pressed into the mud. Others they arranged on horizontal slabs of bark inset into the mud here and there and acting as makeshift shelves.

"That's enough," Brook said. She looked over her shoulder and was pleased to see Max sitting on his haunches behind them all. She told the dog to stay then looked at the girls saying, "I want to go first." She donned the pair of shooters muffs and dragged the Glock from its holster.

Without being told, the girls formed up well behind her and stuck Day-Glo yellow earplugs into their ears.

With the Glock clutched in her off- hand, working the slide with her dominant right not only was unnatural but also next to impossible. Though she'd been working on her fine motor skills and strengthening her grip through a variety of exercises Glenda had taught her, it was apparent and humbling that a full recovery from the effects of the battle waged in her body between the Omega virus and the antiserum Cade had injected into her would take a lot of hard work and time, the latter of which, thankfully, she had an inordinate amount.

After a valiant ten-second struggle—exactly nine seconds too long to be effective in a true survival situation—she managed to finally cycle the slide back and release it, chambering a round with a metallic *snik*. A week ago she couldn't grasp a soda can let alone hold the pistol in the hand in question. *Progress, not perfection.* With sweat beading on her lip, she held the Glock in as tight a two-handed grip as she could muster, set her feet apart a little wider, and cast a surreptitious sidelong glance at the girls. Tracking her eyes straight, she drew a breath and exhaled slowly while simultaneously drawing the trigger pull in. The gun bucked, yet she kept it under control. The sharp report seemed to circle the small clearing then rolled over their heads like a mini sonic boom.

Already bouncing lightly on her toes, Raven beamed and clapped excitedly.

Strengthening her grip on the Glock, Brook took three or four calming breaths then repeatedly caressed the trigger. Three more thunderous booms, spaced seconds apart, crashed and banged the cold air around them.

The hot expended brass tumbled through space and disappeared down a trio of holes burned into the snow near the first.

Brook crinkled her nose at the result. Two of the four cans she had targeted were untouched. So in the interest of saving ammunition, she snugged the Glock into its holster. Once again forgetting her condition, she made a sweeping bowing movement to usher the girls forward, and suffered the consequences. Wanting nothing more than to numb the pain the easy way—with one of the opiates Cade brought back earlier—she instead bit her lip until the pain there took her mind off the sensation of what seemed to be a million pins and needles assaulting her back.

"Show me what you got, ladies."

Chapter 40

The crumpled cereal bar was poised an inch from Gregory Dregan's mouth and the previous bite was still mid-swallow when the first gunshot caught him completely by surprise. He swallowed, drew in a deep breath, and froze. At once a flurry of thoughts bombarded his brain: *One shot. Most likely a small caliber pistol. And very, very close.*

He rocketed off of his backpack which he'd been sitting on and cast his gaze upward, darting his eyes all around as if he could actually see the dissipating sound waves. When a second report didn't immediately follow the first, he clean-jerked his pack off the snow, thrust his muscled arms through the straps, and snugged the waist belt tight. He grabbed his rifle and calmed his body. Stood still, listening hard against his own breathing and was rewarded a few seconds into the vigil when another boom sounded off in the distance. His nylon jacket rustled softly as he swiveled his upper body and faced the retreating sound. He stood statue-still and just a handful of seconds later there came two more identical reports spaced apart like the other.

He waited a few long seconds and, when no fifth shot came, hiked off in the general direction of the gunfire with no more of an idea where he needed to be than when he had folded and stowed the ruined map.

***

Gregory walked in silence for a couple of minutes with the fire lane meandering away from where he thought the shooting had taken place. Not wanting to go breaking brush through the heavy forest—a move that would undoubtedly give him away and provide an inviting target for the shooter if he or she were still nearby—he stayed the course.

After slogging another hundred yards or so through the snow with the weight of the pack cutting into his shoulders, a single shot rang out deep in the woods off to his left. He paused and a few beats later there came another shot. Then a few seconds after that he heard a third and fourth. *Nine-millimeter*, he told himself. *Same as the others.* The fifth report was unexpected and caused him to start. He had assumed the four-and-done pattern would hold true. But it hadn't. And this changed everything. The shots continued coming. And they were methodical, like someone was taking aim, concentrating hard, presumably. No sane person would cruise about the countryside wasting good ammunition on the roamers when they were incapacitated and easy enough to kill with a blade. So he figured what he was hearing was one or more people engaged in a round of target practice.

Acting against the overwhelming urge to bolt in the other direction, instead he broke into a dead run towards the sound and began counting the shots. By the time his mental tally had hit fifteen and the shooting stopped, the fire lane was looping back around almost like it was encircling the shooters' position.

With the sound of the final shot still crashing through the firs overhead, he came to a complete stop, bent over, and braced his hands on his knees. Save for the noise of him greedily gulping lungfuls of crisp mountain air, a heavy silence returned to the forest. There were no hardy mountain birds calling to each other in the canopy above. As the sweat beaded on his brow found the path of least resistance and started the slow slide down his angular nose, he became acutely aware of the pressure building steadily between his ears and the accompanying noise of his own heartbeat throbbing inside his skull.

He remained that way, stooped over, his back arched and straining against the weight of the pack until another round of gunfire commenced. Acting on the assumption that this volley would peak at fifteen, he took a final deep breath, hinged up, and took off running down the road. With the gunshot tally in his head standing at twelve and the steady popping still off of his left shoulder and coming every couple of seconds, the road seemed to end and he found himself staring at a thick phalanx of ferns and ground-hugging undergrowth.

As shot number thirteen rang out, Gregory shed his right glove and drew his pistol. He quickly pulled the slide back and saw a glint of brass in the chamber. Using shot number fourteen as cover, and feeling a little like Indiana Jones entering some jungle-choked ancient temple, he bulled his way through the head-high wall of foliage to his fore. Spitting snow and batting creeper tendrils from his face, he stepped over ferns the size of small trees and inexplicably found himself standing an arm's reach from a single solitary upright rotter on the side of a two-lane road that had to be State Route 39.

Thoroughly disoriented, like a dog dizzy from chasing his tail, he looked left along the road and fixed his gaze on a spot where the forest canopy gave way and saw what looked like a wide-open meadow. The field of white was fenced near the road and rose gently up and away from the two-lane. Trying to get his bearings, he looked right down the natural tunnel created by the encroaching forest. The road there was straight and littered with fallen branches and needles and a light sprinkling of snow that had managed to infiltrate the thick canopy.

Though it had seemed much longer as Gregory stood there gaping at his surroundings and being gaped at by the thing in stasis, in reality he had only been in the open for a couple of seconds when the fifteenth and final shot sounded off in the distance. Not sure what to do, he ignored the creature and bolted across road to the other shoulder and froze in place, his breathing loud against the all-encompassing silence that followed. He stood unmoving for five long minutes and, when the shooting hadn't resumed, found a path through the flora to the point where the abandoned fire lane picked back up. He shrugged off his pack and laid it flat on a dry patch of ground amidst a huddle of massive firs. There he sat for another fifteen minutes and when a boisterous conversation between a couple of crows started up down by where he thought the shooting had originated, he took his gloves off and fished the Utah road map from the side pocket.

With the birds bringing their war of words nearer, he unfolded the map very carefully to keep it from tearing completely along the already damp creases. Using the pack as a table of sorts, he folded the flimsy edges in and placed the map flat on the pack so that the town of Huntsville was on the lower left corner and Bear River was on the right. Then, seeing as how he still didn't know which direction north was, he went about tracing the fire lane with his finger from its origination at the lower quarry and came to the same conclusion as before—the map was old and he was lost.

So he fished the CB radio from a pocket and powered it on.

***

Thirty argument-filled minutes later, with his dad on the other end juggling a radio of his own while consulting a more recent topographic map of the area, they concluded that sometime in the past another road that was not on either of their maps had been carved through the forest. And by comparing the stretch of 39 and retracing his steps on the fire lane in his head, Gregory realized that both the State Route and fire lane had dipped about a mile north before coming back on itself, nearly encircling a seemingly impenetrable tract of forest in the process.

Finally, after looking at the topo-map from every conceivable angle and estimating with a ruler and the mileage key just how far Gregory had come did his dad confirm that where the fire lane crossed 39 was a bit west of where he had spied the tracks and pair of black camera domes.

After once again arguing over compass points and then listening to his dad spew a litany of orders, Gregory turned the volume low on the long range CB and flipped it the bird.

***

As per Dad's orders, Gregory continued following the fire lane. A dozen yards from where he paused last, it started a slow rise in elevation and began a big lazy right-to-left arc. He walked through the snow with the Odd Couple crows and their argument keeping pace. After figuring he had travelled a quarter mile or so, just as his dad had predicted, the fire lane leveled slightly, then turned very minimally to the left and began a gradual descent.

"Shit, Dad," he said under his breath. "You were dead to rights about the road."

He paced left for a few yards, scrutinizing the brambles and low-hanging ferns, searching for a way through. Finding nothing, he retraced his steps and repeated the process a few yards in the other direction.

It was a scrap of fabric, red and checked like a lumberjack's flannel, that caught Gregory's attention first. Trapped waist-high by the bramble's sharp thorns, it seemed to be marking an opening just wide enough to fit a man, albeit one with much narrower shoulders than his.

He forced his way through, half-expecting to meet a hail of lead or at the least be looking down the barrel of a gun on the other side.

Though the briars grabbing at his jacket and pack slowed his progress, he didn't have to wait long to find out his fate. When the brush gave way, he found himself in a sheltered little alcove surrounded on three sides by a smattering of old growth and juvenile firs and aspens. Much like the foliage concealing the fire lane both times it crossed 39, the undergrowth in front of the little hide consisted of ferns and some kind of wild shrubs that came up to his waist.

He looked out from the sheltered pocket abutting the meadow and saw the road below. It ran left to right, and though his dad insisted the vehicle responsible for the tracks had turned north off of 39, he still wasn't entirely sold. The dense woods in which he was certain the gunfire had come from stretched out ahead of him beyond the gently curving stretch of 39. A triple strand of barbed wire bordered the road nearest him. Across the two-lane State Route an identical run of fencing stretched from left-to-right almost the entire run of road, but for some reason came to an abrupt end where the thick tree line took over.

Nothing moved in his field of view—living or undead. So he shed his pack and set it at his feet on the dry, packed earth. Laid his rifle atop the pack and his eye was drawn to a recurring pattern in the soil.

He went down on one knee and, like an umpire dusting off home plate, brushed aside the accumulation of dry needles and rotted leaves.

The pattern was left behind by someone wearing lug-soled boots. The marks were numerous and had mostly crumbled over time, the edges losing most of their definition.

For a moment Gregory contemplated digging out the CB and calling his dad and asking him to again describe the location where the tire tracks in the snow left the road. Instead, he took his binoculars from the pack, slipped the strap over his head, and stuck the rubber cups to his eyes. He walked the field glasses from left-to-right all the way to where the fence across the road ended, seeing nothing out of the ordinary until he got to the wall of foliage. For some reason he couldn't point to, when viewed under high magnification, it just didn't seem natural. Continuing on, seemingly hovering a dozen feet off the ground and reflecting a sliver of white that was the nearby State Route, he spotted the black plastic domes his dad had mentioned. Perched under a circular shroud affixed to a tall tree just inside the tree line, the shiny orbs looked like a pair of unblinking and all-seeing eyes.

Bingo.

Feeling a sense of accomplishment after overcoming the soggy map fiasco and more importantly, avoiding contact with his sister's gun-wielding murderers, Gregory Dregan set the binoculars aside and started preparing his hide for the long night ahead.

Chapter 41

Cade had called for the huddle, and once everyone was standing in a ragged semi-circle, he began doling out jobs. When he had finished assigning responsibilities, and to his amazement no questions—inane or otherwise—were lobbed in his direction, he picked a path through the morass of fallen dead, careful not to step on a hand or trip on a splayed-out leg and further aggravate his tweaked ankle, and then climbed aboard the damaged plow truck.

With the watery sun starting its slow slide behind the distant Wasatch Mountains and dusk not far off, the group set to their tasks with a newfound urgency that only being outside the wire among thousands upon thousands of undead things could instill.

Taryn and Lev boarded their plow trucks, started the motors, then waited until Cade's truck was rolling downhill towards the largest concentration of zombies before conducting three-point turns of their own and falling in behind.

In the cab of the lead truck, Cade thumbed his radio to life. "You two are going to have to do the majority of the work. I'll follow behind to mop up the ones you miss."

"With that busted up blade?" Taryn said.

"I plan on fixing it first," Cade replied. "Out." He put the radio aside and drove past the head of the stalled eastbound herd by three truck lengths. He wheeled left, looped around the handful of Zs that had been out ahead of the undead troop, and then nosed the truck forward until the pranged blade was parallel with the shoulder. Slowly he let the Mack roll forward, checking against the weight of the load with short stabs to the brake pedal until the top edge of the once-horizontal blade was scraping against the underside of a rocky shelf no doubt created when the highway was blasted from the side of the mountain decades ago.

In his wing mirror he saw the other two UDOT trucks finish wide turns and pull abreast of each other, their plows lowered and facing uphill.

Manipulating the controls, Cade kept the pressure building behind the blade despite the harsh whining coming from the hydraulics. The truck shuddered and crouched down up front as the air shocks compressed. He continued depressing the *Raise Blade* button until there was a drawn-out groaning of metal and the blade began to move in opposition to the static granite outcropping. As the pressure being exerted on both surfaces built further, the weaker of the two yielded first, with the blade bending from the near vertical "L" to something twisted up and resembling a cross between a flattened letter "V" and a fancy curly type of pasta of which Cade couldn't remember the name.

Roughly half a mile uphill, Jamie and Wilson had lined the two SUVs up against the rock wall and left them parked there bumper to bumper.

Having taken the Stihl from the back of the Land Cruiser, Daymon had it running and was working its sharp chain back and forth against the creosote-stained six-by-six wooden beams supporting the banged-up guardrail. With the pair of muffs covering his ears dulling the keen of the saw, he also failed to hear the sound of metal scraping bare pavement and thus remained oblivious of the goings on at his back until movement in his side vision drew his attention. However, before he was able to react to the incomprehensible sight, two things happened at once. The chainsaw blade chewed through the last couple of inches of the third and final six-by-six support beam. And then, feeling the chainsaw's bar break free, Daymon took his finger from the trigger, stilling the engine, and backpedaled just as gravity took hold of the twenty-four-foot run of newly severed guardrail. There was a groan of metal twisting under stress and then in a flash several hundred pounds of W-shaped steel and wood beam tore free and performed a lazy end over end tumble to the canyon floor below.

The dangerous part of his job done, Daymon shut off the chainsaw and set it down. With the steam produced by hot metal contacting snow swirling above the road, he removed his hearing protection and turned to see what the commotion behind him was.

"Holy hell," he shouted, taking a quick step back as half a lane away from him a slow moving head-high mound of death came to an abrupt stop, with many of the corpses on top spilling off the pile and landing with dull thuds near his feet. At first glance, Daymon thought maybe a world-record-setting game of undead Twister had occurred at his back while he'd been working. Many of the rotters were folded over on themselves, some face up, their backs obviously broken like twigs under pressure from the plow. Pasty, road-rash-covered arms and legs, bent at strange angles in relation to their intended travel, protruded here and there from within. Scores of lifeless eyes stared back at him as moist gassy sounds emanated from deep inside the warren of decayed flesh.

He thought it comical at first what he must have looked like crouched there on his haunches, ear muffs on and sawing away obliviously, while a couple of hundred zombie corpses slowly tumbled his way. The humor in it evaporated the second he realized that if the pile hadn't stopped where it did, he could have ended up down below amongst thousands more cadavers just like them.

Anger building, and not seeing Duncan walking his way from down the hill, Daymon stormed the plow, jumping on the running boards and trying to get at the driver.

Hands up, face wearing a look of incredulity, Lev cranked the window down, yelling for Daymon to relax. In fact 'Stand down' were the exact words and it took a couple of seconds for Daymon to come to the conclusion that Lev also found nothing funny in what had just happened.

Eyes wide, palms facing outward in a display of surrender, Lev said, "Duncan told me to put them right there. Said you were expecting them there."

"Duncan is full of shit," bellowed Daymon, loud enough to be heard above the racket coming from the two approaching plow trucks.

Duncan opened his mouth to shout out an amends for the miscalculation when the truck with Taryn behind the wheel turned directly in front of him and added another three dozen corpses to the growing mountain of arms and legs and staring death masks. He caught her eye and mouthed, "Back up."

Taryn immediately punched the transmission into *Reverse* and, like any experienced driver, consulted her mirrors and checked over her shoulder before backing. And it was a good thing she did, because Cade was driving his truck behind hers with the plow up and seemingly on a collision course with the inverted "V" where the containers making up the blockade came together. At the last moment, hearing the Mack truck's backup alert jangling across the entire highway, he swung the truck around Taryn's and, with the drawn-out protest of the metal plow again changing shape, wedged all sixty tons of truck and gravel hard against the Conex containers.

"That's the way you do it on the MTV," Duncan said to himself, riffing a little Dire Straits as he witnessed Taryn back up and nose her UDOT plow truck against the seam where the stacked Conex containers abutted the mountain.

Heated, Daymon had already forgotten about Lev and was down from the truck and loping towards Duncan, who was standing hands on hips equidistant between the pile of dead and the parked SUVs. Almost to a flat-out run, his long legs and arms pumping, Daymon only made it halfway across the twenty-foot-wide river of slush and guts left by the passing plows before his boots lost traction and the rug was pulled from under him. He was airborne briefly and then his tailbone and elbows met the unforgiving gore-coated asphalt.

Duncan hustled toward the fallen man, talking in soothing tones the entire way. "I didn't time the body delivery right, Daymon. Please accept my apology … consider this an immediate Tenth Step amends."

Now Duncan was the one with his hands in the air in full surrender mode as Daymon—moving slowly, like a drunk at last call—managed to clumsily work his way back to standing.

"Get the fuck away from me," Daymon said, slicking human detritus from his pants with his bare hands.

Duncan stopped his advance two full paces into the debris field. He looked down, saw the reddish-brown sludge lapping over the toes of his boots, and burst into laughter, which proved to be as infectious as the soup they were standing in when Daymon—realizing the absurdity of the situation—threw his sticky hands skyward and joined in himself.

Unaware of how close Duncan and Daymon had been from coming to blows, Lev cast a glance at the two. Standing in the morass and laughing like a couple of fools was a far cry from what he was expecting after seeing the rage on the younger man's face. Shrugging, he reversed and oriented the blade so it was aimed directly at the dead. He said a prayer for the men, women, and children all tangled up there. Then he tromped the pedal and winced as the first thud of metal meeting flesh resonated through the truck's frame. Singing the Star Spangled Banner loudly enough to mask the macabre sounds, he went about the grim task of plowing hundreds of bodies off the road and to the bottom of Ogden Canyon.

***

Twenty minutes after scraping every corpse and severed limb and scrap of flesh and bone off the road's edge, Lev was parking his truck sidelong against the pair of Conex containers now pushed back in place and hanging a foot or so over the cliff's edge. He killed the engine and set the brake. Then, just as Cade and Taryn had done before him, he broke the key off in the ignition, reached under the dash and sawed through the wires with his Kershaw's serrated edge.

Finished disabling the truck mechanically and electrically, he slid across the seat and let himself out through the passenger door.

Mission accomplished.

He walked a dozen steps away from the truck, drew his Sig Sauer P226, and to put the cherry on the sundae, methodically shot flat all ten of the truck's monstrous tires.

Chapter 42

Peter was sitting on a chair pulled in from the dining room and warming his hands by the fireplace. The red flicker thrown off the glowing logs had the cream-colored walls in the front living room looking like the inside of a forge, yet, save for a semicircle ranging just a few feet out from the tiled hearth, the rest of the house was, as he had heard his dad say more than once since summer had abruptly turned to fall, *'as cold as a witch's tit.'* In fact, it was so cold that when he exhaled he could clearly see his breath and, though he'd been inside for some time, he was still fully clothed and wearing his boots laced up tight, a practice that had become mandatory for everyone in the Dregan family since the dead things began to walk.

With the early evening light filtering in through the horizontal blinds not enough to read by, and television and portable devices a luxury of the not-too-distant past, Peter passed the time staring out the big picture window beside the fireplace.

In the field beyond the cement barriers that had been placed there some time after the outbreak were the same four roamers that had wandered in from the State Route the day before. At first, watching them dodder around the field, tripping over molehills and at times each other in reaction to engine sounds and voices carrying over the wall had provided Peter a little entertainment. He had especially liked watching them trudge along just outside the barrier, pausing now and then to scrabble futilely at its rough, textured surface. But now, standing still as store mannequins, having not moved for hours, all they did was make the young Dregan boy wonder about who they had been ... before.

The one among the four he found himself studying most was a young boy dressed in a shirt gone reddish black with blood congealed and dried long ago. Missing his left forearm and a majority of the skin and muscle near the soft underside of his jaw, the undead kid was frozen in place with a perpetual horrific sneer on his face. In his mind, Peter decided that the boy and trio of adult dead out there with him were somehow related. Why else would they stick together? He took his eyes off the biters and regarded the mesmerizing flames and soon his mind had drifted off to thoughts of his mom and sister. He could smell his mom's perfume, and for a second Lena was haranguing him to get ready for church, which he kind of enjoyed, because he was guaranteed to see a number of his friends from school there. Suddenly he realized they were all gone, Mom, Lena, and those friends and, just like that, as vividly as if he was watching a movie, he was reliving that last normal day.

Grass was swatting his fatigue pants as he sprinted through the soon-to-be-built subdivision near his home. He was leaping over freshly poured concrete foundations, wearing his camouflage and goggles and in the middle of a rowdy game of airsoft when the passenger jet screamed so low overhead that he saw the big black wheels and then, distinctly, the desperate passengers beating on the oval windows. He saw their white palms and splayed out fingers, then his breath was stolen by the explosion and he was thrown aside, losing his expensive airsoft gun.

The right side of his face was warm and, from where he was lying, flat on his back surrounded by brittle grass, he saw a fireball rising quickly over the end of the nearby airport. When he finally got to his feet, he was aware of only two things. There was a grassfire sweeping his way from the direction of the crash. And somewhere in the grass, about to be burned to death, his best friend, Liam, was screaming for help. It was a shrill scream, kind of like what you'd hear from a five-year-old girl who had seen a snake, he would later tell his dad.

Ignoring the flames, he ran forward to help Liam, whom he assumed had been hit by a part of the plane, only to come across the first biter (before anyone in his family had started calling them that) he had ever laid eyes on. It was wearing what looked like a fireman or ambulance driver's uniform. The uniform was covered with blood and then the snarling blank-eyed thing came up with a mouthful of guts. Slick and yellowish white. Then more screaming and kicking and blood. And the blood—Liam's blood—was turning the dry bed of grass and tiny clods of dirt from brown to almost black.

The second explosion warmed his face full on and he took one last look at Liam, who was beyond help. Even a twelve-year-old could see that. Liam's screaming stopped abruptly and Peter heard other friends calling his name.

"Peter"—there was laughter—"caught you daydreaming," his dad said. "If you would have leaned over any further I'd be scraping bits of your burnt face off the hot glass there."

After yawning wide, Peter flicked his eyes to the field. The four dead things were still there, the boy still gaping open-mouthed at the house. The snow hadn't melted and there was no burning wreckage anywhere to be seen. He put a hand on his right cheek and it was hot. In fact, he felt like a chicken that had become stuck in one spot on a rotisserie, the entire right side of his body, clothes and all, hot to the touch.

"Why don't you follow the heat upstairs," Dregan said. "Should be good sleeping up there tonight."

Peter protested.

"I have associates coming over. You can't be downstairs when they're here."

As soon as the order was issued, the front door was rattled by three dull thuds.

Dregan shot Peter a serious look. "Those were snowballs, I'm guessing. Go on now." He nodded towards the stairs. "I have to let the ladder down."

Peter rose and was halfway up the stairs when the rasping and wheezing indicative of another of his dad's coughing fits filled the front room. Soon it was echoing up the stairwell and, figuring he might be called down to help with the ladder, he stopped where he was, three stairs from the top, and sat down out of sight. A few seconds passed and more snowballs pelted the door. There was an awful hawking sound and in his mind's eye he saw his dad filling up the handkerchief he kept in a pocket with bloody spit and boogers. Finally his dad shouted, "Keep your shorts on ... will ya?" There was more spitting and nose blowing then Peter heard the door open followed by distant voices, all belonging to men, and none of them familiar. A tick after the squeaky hinges went silent, his question was answered by the distinctive rattle and clatter of the extension ladder being lowered to the ground.

But Peter didn't heed his dad's orders. Instead, he sat there while conscience and curiosity engaged in all-out war, the former screaming at him to go upstairs, while the latter, seductive temptress that she was, whispered in his ear, trying to convince him to stay hidden and eavesdrop on the clandestine meeting. In the end—aided by the arrival of someone whose voice he knew all too well—curiosity's sweet whisperings won out.

Peter heard his dad, in a voice made hoarse from coughing, welcome the men into his home and offer them seats on the couch. A short while later there came the sound of more footsteps coming up the ladder and then another round of greetings and introductions followed by the discordant screech of chairs being dragged across the dining room floor. The door slammed shut and a couple more minutes of small talk ensued before finally the serious negotiations got underway.

Peter's stomach churned as he learned some of the gory details of what his dad and the men downstairs were conspiring to do to Lena's killers. And though he wanted to stand up and creep to his room and pretend he hadn't heard a thing, he couldn't, because a familiar voice now had the floor, and he wanted to hear what his Uncle Henry had to say.

Chapter 43

Two birds with one stone, Cade thought, the second Daymon called '*shotgun.*' For one, during the downhill creep from the Ogden Canyon blockade, he figured sitting in back of the Land Cruiser where he could stretch out and elevate his bad wheel would go a long ways towards him being useful for the rest of the mission. And two, sitting in back with the chainsaw and the strong odor of oil and fuel wafting toward the headliner was a far cry from what Daymon smelled like after slipping and rolling around in zombie pulp. Besides, Cade thought, smiling inwardly, making Duncan drive and suffer up front with the walking biohazard seemed fitting. After all, it was the perennial prankster's fault Daymon had lost his cool in the first place. And Cade could see how unexpectedly coming face-to-face with a six-foot-tall pile of dead bodies could do that to a person—especially someone wound as tightly as the former BLM firefighter.

"Oh boy. Am I ever making amends for setting Lev up like that," Duncan said, holding his nose. "You smell like a bag of assholes left out in the sun for a day."

Daymon was leaning hard against his shoulder belt. His right hand was braced on the dash against the pull of the downhill grade. "You only got yourself to blame, Old Man. Who were you pranking, anyway?" he said, staring hard at the driver. "Were you busting *my* balls? Lev's? Or both ... for an epic effin twofer?"

"Whoever's were hanging out that needed busting," Duncan drawled. The Land Cruiser shimmied and bounced as it struck something small and snow-covered in the road. "I'm an equal opportunity button pusher. Y'all should know that by now."

The two-way radio hissed. "Taryn wants to know if we are going to stop at the same place and take the chains off," Wilson said, his voice oscillating. "All four of us are getting sick from the vibration."

"Tell Taryn to slow down a little," Duncan shot back.

"For her … this *is* slow," Wilson said. "She didn't think it necessary we chain up in the first place."

Cade stuck one arm between the seats and gestured for Duncan to hand him the radio.

In the same camp as Taryn where the need for chains was concerned, Daymon relaxed and sat back in his seat, arms crossed, content to watch this play itself out.

Cade thumbed the *Talk* button. "You ever heard the saying: An ounce of prevention is worth a pound of cure, Wilson?"

Wilson didn't respond.

So Cade said, "Prepare for the worst, hope for the best? Does that ring a bell?"

Still nothing.

Cade imagined Lev sitting in back of the 4Runner. Being former Army, the stoic young man no doubt had heard them all. Hell, Cade thought, Lev probably knew some that he had never heard. In the *Big Green Machine* everything centered around the *mission. Everything.* And there were procedures put in place to minimize human error. That's what the tire chains had been for. To minimize human error, of which Cade had been guilty of more than once today. Finished venting, he handed the radio forward to Daymon and told Duncan to pull over where they'd chained up earlier.

Dregan Home, Bear River, Utah

Peter had loitered on the steps, fighting sleep as his uncle and dad droned on. Promises were made and favors traded in. Bartering was happening on a grand scale downstairs, that was for sure. And though Peter had only seen and heard the action on the floor of the now worthless New York Stock Exchange on television—a Nickelodeon short that aired on take your kid to work day, to be exact—what was going on downstairs seemed one and the same, only on a much, much, smaller scale.

The *Dregan Home Exchange* had been in full swing for some time when a sudden hush fell over the downstairs living room and now only his dad was speaking. Peter noticed that the hard edge to his dad's voice was gone. *Good news.* That meant he was no longer in negotiation mode. In fact, Peter hadn't heard his dad sounding this happy since Lena's summer wedding.

Suddenly his dad went silent and Peter heard the static of a radio-breaking squelch followed closely by his older brother Gregory's voice, distant and hollow-sounding. It carried up the stairs, and though he couldn't make out every word, he caught enough to know Dad was going hunting tomorrow. So he rose from the step, his butt and right leg asleep and just starting to shoot through with pins and needles, and crept to his bedroom, a good deal of planning of his own yet to be done.

Chapter 44

The dead were right where they had left them earlier, laid out beside the road in various death poses, the fluids that had leaked from them now frozen. Cade shifted his gaze from the tangled bodies and shouldered open his door. As he knelt down on the road to take the passenger side chains off the Land Cruiser, he was hit with an odd sense of déjà vu. In an instant, he was back in Iraq, pulling dismounted patrol on a rutted litter-strewn dirt road out in front of a pair of Humvees. Separated by ten to twelve feet each, several of his brothers in arms trailed in a ragged line behind him.

In one of those defining moments of his deployments, he was hit in the face by the viciously sweet stench of death. Sticky and thick, it enveloped him and his squad. Then he saw the source and in a millisecond it was burned into his memory forever. One of those things that could never be unseen. In the ditch next to the road, rotting in the blistering hundred-and-twenty-degree heat, were twenty or thirty corpses, all beheaded, most women and children, their only crime: belonging to the wrong sect and being in the wrong place at the wrong time.

Strangely enough, that was the first and last time—save for the littlest kids—that he had ever felt sorry for those people over there. Reap what you sow, and all that. They didn't know peace. And they didn't seem to aspire to it, either. The callus that formed on his soul that day grew tougher every time a buddy was lost to a sniper round or scores of fellow soldiers were vaporized by a vehicle-borne IED or artillery shell deviously concealed in an animal carcass beside the road. That callus became a near-bulletproof suit of mental armor as he continued to lose fellow Rangers and Special Forces comrades during his multiple deployments in the 'Stan. And it wasn't until Cade made Delta and reunited with Mike 'Cowboy' Desantos that he started to experience feeling again. Hearts and minds, and all that jazz, *had* to be back in play to be a part of a team as compartmentalized as they were. Especially during interrogation sessions. For one got burned out quick always playing the role of bad cop.

While fighting to get the tire chain crammed into the plastic box with the ones already in there, Cade was struck at how in only a few short weeks his mental defenses had returned stronger than ever. Which he figured was a good thing seeing as how the good cop/bad cop routine didn't work on the dead. And when it came to the living, since all evidence pointed to so very few of them remaining, anyone willing to rob and kill instead of forage and fortify to survive the dead—deserved no mercy whatsoever.

Cade got the remaining tire chain in the box and tried closing it. "Why don't these things *ever* go back in as easy as they come out?" Shaking his head, he put a knee on the box and the plastic halves moved together. He added more weight to the endeavor then pitched forward, nearly hitting his head on the nearby running board as two of the corners collapsed with a sharp *crack*.

Like a foreman on the taxpayer's dime, Duncan had been standing over Cade and watching him struggle. "Hulk *smash*," he said, chuckling.

Cade glared but said nothing.

Suddenly changing the subject, Duncan stuck his index finger in the air. "Hey Delta. Does it feel like the temperature has buoyed a bit since we were here last?"

Cade nodded. "We'll have to keep a close tab on it. Wouldn't want to get stuck in a town full of these things when they come back alive."

Duncan threw a visible shudder at the prospect. "That big 'ol watch of yours tell the temperature?" he asked.

Shaking his head, Cade said, "It does a bunch of useful things ... but monitoring the air temp isn't one of them. It's got a barometer that is flatline right now. If the pressure starts dropping and the line on this thing takes a dive, I'm afraid the temperature's likely to spike big time." He looked over his shoulder and saw Taryn putting the boxed chains in the back of the 4Runner. Unlike his, the box hers had come out of looked to be intact, the chains, benefitting from a woman's touch, no doubt coiled neatly inside. Thirty or so yards east, Lev, Daymon, and Jamie—the self-anointed Clean Up Crew of this trip—were walking along the shoulder and kneeling here and there, presumably providing a swift second death to any of the fallen corpses they had missed earlier.

"Let's git," Duncan said, looking in Taryn and Wilson's direction. Then he whistled to get the others' attention and then waved them forward.

With the thin satellite phone in one hand, Cade caught Duncan's eye and nodded towards Daymon, who was now walking ahead of the others, the sheathed machete banging against his hip. "Go ahead and let him ride up front again. I'm going to call Brook." Without waiting for an acknowledgement, Cade thumbed the Thuraya alive and started out across the road, the new hitch in his step pretty obvious.

He stood on the road looking out across the rolling snow-covered grassland. The low bluffs to the right shone white on top, while the steep dirt flanks remained mostly reddish brown, shot through with white—like finely marbled steak—only where snow had settled in the vertical crevices.

The Thuraya's call-waiting indicator blinked steadily. The number indicating that the call had originated from Major Freda Nash's personal number now had a small numeral 3 next to it. *Persistent one, that lady*, thought Cade as he dialed Brook.

There were several electronic trills before she picked up. After they exchanged pleasantries, Cade filled her in on everything that had happened up until now, putting extra emphasis on how he thought the hundred-and-fifty tons of strategically placed gravel-laden plow trucks was going to hold for some time while conversely omitting the crispy critter in the Shell garage as well as his newly reinjured ankle. The former would have to take the spotlight. However, the latter two minor details—*no blood, no foul*, he figured.

She ran down the day's events for him, crowing proudly about how well the girls' off-hand shooting was improving. Then she spent a second or two lamenting the fact that she was still far from proficient with her off-hand and might as well just surrender if forced to rely on her dominant hand.

"It's going to take time," Cade said, telling her something she already knew. "Keep working with the ball and bands. It'll come."

"I know," she said. "It's just that I've got nobody else to complain to."

"That's what I signed up for, honey. For better or for worse ..." His voice trailed off into a long silence.

"What is it, Cade?" Brook asked calmly.

"I've got bad news."

Now there was silence on Brook's end.

"It's not *that* bad of news," Cade said.

Silence still.

"We're going to have to stay the night in Huntsville."

"Why?" she said, her voice rising a little.

"Took us longer than we thought to clear the road and seal the breach."

"What are you going to do now? It's not going to be dark for another hour or two."

Cade looked at his Suunto. "Ninety minutes ... give or take. Even with the cloud cover the moon should provide the ambient light we need to work. Brook ... we can't pass up the opportunity to clear as many dead from in and around Huntsville as we can."

"What about Eden?"

"We'll go check it out first thing in the morning." He went quiet again. Finally he said, "Brook, it just makes sense doing this now so we won't be hunting them down later in the countryside or woods. Less chance of one of us getting ambushed again." That last part he regretted saying the moment it left his lips.

There was dead air for a hard three-count. Brook finally said, "And we all know how that turned out."

"Can't go feeling sorry for yourself," Cade said. "Bad wing or not, it's on you to hold the fort down." Sensing someone watching him, Cade peered over his shoulder. Less than ten feet away,

Daymon was standing, hands up and opening and closing his fingers, mimicking a blabbering mouth.

"Don't worry, we'll all *stay frosty*," she said, erupting in laughter. "Say, the girls are going stir crazy in here."

Cade turned his back towards Daymon. "After one day?"

"They're burning through the DVDs at a furious pace."

"What are you proposing?"

"Let them explore a little while the things aren't ambulatory," she proffered.

"In layman's terms, Nurse Grayson."

More laughter on Brook's end.

Mission accomplished, Cade thought. "Might not hurt to give them a radio and let them explore a little *inside* the wire."

"Weapons?"

Automatically, Cade shook his head. "Not without you or me around. Not yet. They should be OK without ... if they stay close in."

"Stay safe, Cade Grayson."

"Always. I'll check in with you before noon tomorrow. Earlier if anything comes up."

"I love you," Brook said.

"Love you, too."

Cade took the phone from his ear and was about to thumb it locked when he heard Brook's tinny voice calling for him. So he put the phone back to his ear. "Yes," he said.

"Nash has called and left messages on both of the sat phones. Do you want me to check them?"

Cade thought for a minute. Finally he said, "No. What we're doing here is more important than anything she might need from me right now."

Incredulous, Brook said, "Anything?"

"Anything," he said matter-of-factly. "The troops are getting restless. Gotta go."

"Stay frosty and come home to me, Cade Grayson."

Cade said nothing. He thumbed the phone off and turned to see that Daymon had given up and Duncan was in his place and tapping his watch with big exaggerated motions while mouthing, "Let's go."

Cade pocketed the phone and raised his arms in mock surrender when he saw the 4Runner's occupants also shooting expectant looks his way. In spite of his troublesome ankle, he jogged across the westbound lane, wincing noticeably after every other footfall. Seeing Daymon in the passenger seat, Cade again clambered into the back of the Land Cruiser and sprawled out on the supple leather.

"Where to now?" Duncan asked.

"Downtown is a good a place as any, I suppose," Cade said. "From there we can work our way east to Glenda's place."

"Copy that," said Duncan. "Next stop ... downtown Huntsville." He shot Daymon a look that screamed 'you reek', then released the brake and started the Land Cruiser rolling smoothly eastbound with the 4Runner close to its rear bumper.

Chapter 45

Duncan slowed the Land Cruiser to a crawl on 39 near the T-junction with Trapper's Loop Road. He looked to the right out Daymon's side glass and whistled, low and ominous. A few hundred yards down the intersecting road, and mostly shielded from view from 39 westbound by an upthrust mound of earth, was a full-blown horde of walkers. And like most of the Zs they had encountered since the temperature dipped below freezing, these too were stalled out, upright and wedged shoulder-to-shoulder into the straight stretch of fenced-in two-lane splitting the jagged rocky knoll.

Duncan's stomach dropped at first sight of them. He guessed the mass of rotten flesh to number close to a thousand, their snow-dusted heads just little white dots going on and on southbound for as far as his old eyes could see.

"I spotted them on the way out of Huntsville," Cade said.

"I missed them," Duncan said unapologetically. He brought the Cruiser to a halt in the middle of 39.

The two-way warbled and Wilson asked, "Where the hell did all those come from?"

The radio remained untouched in the center console, the Land Cruiser's occupants all fixated on the dead.

The 4Runner pulled to a smooth stop alongside the bigger SUV. The passenger window pulsed down and Wilson was staring at Duncan, his hand forming the universal *Hang Loose* gesture, thumb and pinky finger extended, and pressed to his head like a telephone. He was mouthing, "Pick up your radio."

Ignoring the redhead, Duncan tapped his knuckles on the leather-wrapped steering wheel in time to the low music coming from the speakers. Voice thick with disappointment, he said, "No chance we're going to cull all of those today."

"Or tomorrow ... or even the next. Why don't we stop and do these ones right now?" Daymon pleaded, gesturing ahead to another throng of unmoving creatures hundreds strong. A few of them dotted the greenway between 39 and the cement boat ramp cutting the reservoir's sandy shore. The majority, however—no doubt attracted by the nonstop sound of water lapping the hulls of dozens of grounded watercraft and looking like faithful fans crowding the stage at a Phish concert—had congregated along the sandy shore down by the waterline.

"Hell, Urch's right. We're going to need a week of snow and ice and every last person from the compound poking eyes to put all of these down," Duncan agreed.

Wilson was now gesticulating wildly with both arms.

Duncan snatched up the radio. "Keep your shorts on, *Red*," he said, still not ready to give the twenty-year-old the courtesy of his attention.

"They're not our problem right now," Cade said. "If history proves"—he craned and looked out the rear quarter window at the horde—"when they do start wandering again they'll continue on south to Morgan."

"They'll be back ... eventually," Duncan said. "You know that."

"Yeah, they will," Cade agreed. "But now that we have the Ogden approach sealed off, we can winnow them down starting in Huntsville and keep at it until midnight or so. Turn in and get up early and work our way over to Eden while the weather holds."

"All in a day's work," Daymon said, rubbing his sore right shoulder.

Duncan pulsed down his window. Stared daggers at Wilson. "Just like an ankle biter … what was so goshdang important it couldn't wait a few seconds?"

Looking sheepish, Wilson said nothing.

Duncan cocked his head. "Come on. I'm sorry for callin you *Red.* Now spit it out."

"What about them," Wilson stammered, hitching a thumb at the distant horde.

The cloud cover parted momentarily. Duncan squinted against the glare, collecting his thoughts. "You get your baseball bat, hop out, and get started. We'll be back for ya in the morning."

Wilson stuck his hand in the window opening, first three fingers extended vertically. "Read between the lines." He smiled wanly and powered up his window. Then, thinking out loud, he added, "Wonder what the eff is eating Old Man?"

"He's a *dick* when he's not drinking," Taryn said, watching the Land Cruiser pull away. She looked Wilson square in the face. "If you haven't figured that out yet. You, my friend, are blind."

He looked at the dead standing three deep at the reservoir's edge. Cast his gaze farther out to a lonely cabin cruiser anchored offshore. He noticed a female form above deck, snow-covered and frozen in place, clutching the rail two-handed. Suddenly his feelings didn't factor into the equation. Remembering how his mom always drilled the *golden rule* concept into his head, he decided he didn't have anything to say.

In the back seat, Jamie leaned against Lev and in his ear, whispered, "See … I'm not the only one who has noticed the change in Duncan."

***

A short distance east on 39, where the straight stretch of State Route became a steady carving arc north toward downtown Huntsville, Duncan braked and nosed the truck perpendicular to the shoulder and parked there facing north.

"Is this good?" he asked Cade.

"Perfect," Cade answered. He punched his window down and flinched as a gust of east wind blasted him full on in the face. He reached back into the cargo area, rummaged in his pack, and came back with his Steiners in hand. He braced his elbows on the window channel and brought the military grade optics to his eyes, their 7x magnification instantly adding sharp detail to the panorama laid out before him.

With the stench coming off his clothing now invading every crevice of the vehicle thanks to the intermittent wind gusts, Daymon twisted his upper body around and faced Cade. "I could have sworn some of those deadheads down there by Main Street were standing when we took the bypass through here earlier."

Unable to see for himself, and eager to hear Cade's response, Duncan lowered the stereo volume, putting Hank Williams Junior's crooning about *country boys surviving* way into the background.

"Why don't you turn that all the way off," Cade said. "I'm getting a bad feeling about this."

Duncan killed the radio just as the 4Runner pulled up smartly outside his window. He looked and saw that all eyes were glued to the town across Pineview Reservoir's slate gray surface.

Duncan turned to Daymon. "How do you know there's a Main Street in Huntsville?" he asked. "No way you can read the signs from here."

"Yes I can," Daymon replied. "Next one over from Main is Gullible Lane. Then comes Naive Drive and the far one there is ... I'm Yanking Your Chain Boulevard."

Doing his best to ignore the banter, Cade swept the binoculars over the finger of land that curled west by south away from downtown. It was narrow, maybe a few hundred yards wide at most, and dotted with headstones of all different sizes and all with inches-high wedges of snow perched atop them. There was a black hearse parked sidelong among the grave markers, its last delivery, a gun-metal gray casket, still inside and visible behind the curtained side windows. He continued the sweep left-to-right over Huntsville, which was very small, encompassing no more than six blocks to a side. The destruction wrought on it by the runaway conflagration was near total. Save for the Queen Annes bordering the downtown core on high ground to the east and what looked like a gas station plus a couple of nearby houses rising above the ashes to the north, all that remained centrally was the same trio of buildings he recognized from the cursory recon taken earlier from atop the hill southeast of town. "Nope," Cade finally said, lowering the Steiners and clapping Daymon on the shoulder. "There is no Main Street. Nor is there a Naive Drive. But I did see one called *Daymon Talks Too Much Crap*

Lane. By the way"—Cade made a show of sniffing the air—"you, my friend, need a bath."

"Sheeit," said Daymon, feigning slapping his leg. "Captain America does have a funny bone in his body after all."

"Yeah, but my timing and delivery are all off," Cade replied, deadpan. "In all seriousness, though, looks like the streets are all numbered. If we keep going straight where 39 cuts east towards the compound, the road turns into the central drag that splits Huntsville, demarking east from west. That's where we need to be."

Now eschewing the radio in the event that anyone was listening in, Duncan lowered his window and, talking over the whipping wind, conveyed the information directly to the others. He finished by telling them to be on high alert because both he and Cade still had a feeling that they may not be the only humans in Huntsville.

With Wilson's wide-eyed look on his mind, Duncan backed away from the shoulder and pulled out on 39 ahead of the 4Runner. He caught Cade's eye in the rearview mirror. "Where to after we hit the center of town?"

"Let's start west at the cemetery and work our way east to those houses on the hill. Pause there at Glenda's place for some food and then do our best to mop up as much of downtown as we can before turning in."

"Solid plan," Daymon said, smiling. "Kindness likes a bedtime snack before I tuck her in for the night."

Duncan turned *Hank* back on. Then he caught Daymon's eye and winked. "You keep talking about that machete like she's your new girlfriend or something, and I'll be obligated to tell your current one about your infidelity."

"Fiancée," Daymon said, grinning.

"No shit?" Duncan and Cade said at once, seemingly in full-on Dolby surround-sound-stereo.

"Nah ... just me talkin crap."

Touché, thought Cade.

Chapter 46

Cade looked out his window and shook his head. There *was* a Main Street and it ran east/west. Then he gazed right and chuckled at the irony on display. Hanging out over the sidewalk and gently swaying was a sign adorned with red two-foot-high letters that read DAVE'S BBQ and, somehow, name withstanding, the joint had survived the fire. The storefront faced west and the reservoir was reflected in the small windows inset just above the thick sheets of overlapping plywood that looked to have spared the larger plate windows below them from falling to looters. That the place was still intact seemed a miracle to Cade given the surrounding blocks had been razed by fire.

Sharing the wall to the right of the BBQ place and running the length of the block was what used to be a bar called The Angle On Inn. The mirrored back bar was trashed and the furniture reduced to sticks. It looked as if one hell of a bar fight had broken out with the window glass and neon beer signs suffering the worst of it.

Sandwiching Dave's to the north was a sundry store called Rhonda's Reservoir Requisites. Cade especially liked the play on words here. The door was but an empty bent frame hanging ajar by the top hinge, which looked to be one loose screw from parting with the frame itself. Left of the entry, affixed to the wall at eye-level, were a pair of steadfast survivors of the apocalypse. The colorful cardboard sign advertising cold Budweiser twelve-packs for $13.99 was done up red, white, and blue with stars and stripes, a holdover from the final holiday America enjoyed free of death and destruction. Below the patriotic beer advertisement was a weathered cardboard sign that read: LIVE BAIT $1.99. Emblazoned on one flapping corner of the bait sign was a happy little worm wearing a fedora and flashing a grin suggesting he knew nothing about the fishhook and hungry predators in his future. *A fitting metaphor for mankind's upcoming tangle with the Omega virus, indeed.*

Judging by the mess inside the store, Cade figured Rhonda was all sold out on both of the advertised items. In fact, all he could see from his seat in the SUV through the windowless storefront were emptied shelves and a single cadaver standing in the lane designated *Express Checkout*. But things were going slow for this one. Like the one at the Shell station, it was charred black as night and rooted in place and, as if it knew something Cade did not, its lips curled back over its teeth to reveal an evil, ivory-hued grin.

Wasn't that the truth about all of humanity? Cade thought as the Land Cruiser turned a left. *We were all in effect the worm and little did we know that the hook called Omega was headed our way.*

***

In the five minutes it took the group to get from downtown to the entrance to the peninsula called Cemetery Point, as if God had grown tired of punishing them with drab hues of gray and frequent gusts of biting wind, the sun had broken through the clouds and the air had grown calm.

The single swinging gate, presumably used to block off vehicular access to both the Cemetery Point Marina and Huntsville Cemetery during off hours, was hanging wide open. Behind the useless gate and STOP sign was a lonely toll collection station. The way it had been abandoned, with its metal mesh window guards hinged up and battened in place, gave the impression that the last person manning it had no intention of ever returning.

Wary of there being tire-damaging spikes under the snow, Duncan stopped just short of the entry and, under Daymon's watchful gaze, put the SUV into *Park*. He exited the Land Cruiser, hustled forward and kicked at the snow, finding nothing. On his way back, he paused for a second and ran his gaze over the scraps of paper that covered every square inch of the little one-person shack.

They all contained desperate and very personal messages from people looking to reunite with missing loved ones. Scrawled big and bold in black Sharpie on one weather-beaten paper plate was a particularly poignant message. It read: JOE HUSTED WAS HERE 7-29 LOOKING FOR VALERIE HUSTED. SOMEHOW I MISSED YOU! LOVE YOU HONEY! LEFT FOR JACKSON HOLE 8-1. PS - MY MOM DID NOT PULL THROUGH. Before moving on, he read another note written in old folks' cursive on a piece of cardboard ripped from a box of Pampers. It was lengthy and penned by a mother named Sue Adler who revealed she was camping in her Volvo in a parking lot nearby. After detailing her escape from Ogden, she expressed her dismay that not one other Adler family member was here upon her arrival. She ended with a plea for whoever read her note that knew her to come and search her out. It was signed with a flourish and a bevy of X's and O's. There was no date on the one-sided correspondence, nor was there evidence suggestive of how it had turned out for the anonymous lady called Sue Adler.

When Duncan returned to the idling SUV, he was heavy of heart and lacking the energy to proceed. He took his seat behind the wheel and sighed.

Cade said, "Checking for spike strips?"

"Yep," Duncan drawled. "Found more than I was looking for."

"They're usually facing out on the exit side," proffered Daymon.

"An ounce of prevention ..." Duncan replied, sounding tired.

Swinging wide right and with the sound of snow squelching under tires, both vehicles left the guard shack behind. A hundred feet beyond the shack on the right side was a matching pair of institutional-sized dumpsters. They were brimming with all manner of trash and, taking dumpster diving to a new level, a moldering corpse that had been stuffed in head first with its horribly twisted legs sticking skyward.

"Damn," Daymon said. "Someone threw out a perfectly good white guy."

Chuckling, Duncan swung his gaze forward and said, "It's not like the cemetery is all the way across town."

***

From his seat in the 4Runner, Wilson noticed the macabre sight passing by outside his window. "Just when you think you've seen it all," he said, shaking his head.

Lev leaned between the front seats and pointed out the patchwork of colorful nylon tents through the smattering of trees to their left. There were too many to count and looked to have been set up some time ago among the trees near the reservoir's edge. He said, "That's some desperation right there ... camping damn near inside a cemetery."

"No, that's desperation there," Jamie said, pointing to an old maroon Volvo wagon stuffed to the gills with half a house worth of belongings. The side windows had been shored up with framed pictures of a large family posing together in happier times. Looked to her like a couple and what appeared to be their three adult daughters. And speaking to the normalcy bias that had been in play when the dead began to walk and led to many a person's downfall, brown leaves of long dead houseplants pushed up against the car's long side windows, filling in the gaps between the photos. "Treated the event like a simple cross-country move ... and paid the price for it."

"That could have been me and Sash if Mom hadn't been flying that day," Wilson said, his eyes glued to the overloaded car. "Hell, we even had a Volvo ... and an apartment full of pictures and plants."

"I'm sorry for your loss," Jamie said, putting her hand on his shoulder. Next to her, Lev was shaking his head and mouthing, "Don't dredge it up."

"It's OK," Wilson said. "I've let go of the idea she survived her layover and is out there looking for us. Sasha, on the other hand ... when Jenkins took off to find Pauline, she wouldn't leave the idea of us looking for Mom alone."

"I won't mention it again," Jamie said. "Around you or her."

Wilson turned forward. Saw Taryn's chest heaving. Tears were streaming down her cheeks, falling onto her parka and sliding off the Scotchgard-treated fabric.

She saw him eyeing her and immediately started the silent side-to-side headshake Wilson knew to mean she wanted her space.

***

Duncan saw the Volvo as soon as they passed the dumpsters. He instantly put two and two together, but said nothing. He'd already said a prayer for Sue Adler and her outcome and considered it out of his hands now. No reason to mention her plight and drag everyone else into his deepening emotional abyss. So he drove on without slowing. Without casting so much as a second glance at the Volvo, he wheeled the Land Cruiser along a gently curling drive that was choked with abandoned vehicles and trash and corpses, the latter both fallen and upright. To Duncan, who was old enough to remember seeing footage of the Woodstock Music Festival on TV, it looked like the aftermath of that orgy of drugs, drinking, and debauchery. Had he not been eyeing a career in the military at the time, he probably would have made the trek. Hell, who wouldn't have liked to spend a weekend awash in booze and get to see Jimi and Janis and one of his all-time favorite bands, CCR, live and in person?

***

When the two Toyotas finally passed through the yawning gates and onto the cemetery's hallowed ground, it was clear that the stiff wind gusts that blew through earlier had toppled all but a handful of the immobilized flesh-eaters. The tops of the tombstones had also been scoured of their crowns of snow and the boats out on the water were now bobbing aimlessly, their anchor lines no longer taut.

Duncan drove deeper into the graveyard and parked the Land Cruiser beside the forlorn-looking hearse. He killed the engine and craned back, looking at Cade. "What now, Boss?"

"We snuff them all," Cade said, no remorse in his voice.

"I'm down," Daymon said. He dug his whetstone from a pocket and passed it over Kindness's long curved blade. Examining the nicks and slight waves in the metal, he added, "I'm going to have to get a hatchet like Jamie's ... for when this girl gives up the ghost."

"Nothing wrong with a good old-fashioned lock blade like mine or some kind of a dagger like Cade's," Duncan said over the steady *schwicking* sound of Daymon applying a fresh edge to his blade.

Cade made no reply. He was consulting the barometer on his Suunto and hoping that Mother Nature wasn't getting ready to edge Glenda's parting words to the realm of prophecy. The doors opening his cue, he followed suit and once outside got the blood flowing back into his gimpy ankle with a quick set of jumping-jacks, followed by a few squat-lunges—all of which hurt more than they seemed to help.

Taryn rolled up in the 4Runner and parked adjacent to the Land Cruiser, the open grave and hearse taking up the space between the two.

Duncan and Daymon were already standing beside the open grave and looking down on the half-dozen Zs trapped there. Nearby was a snow-covered dirt mound, flashes of the green tarp covering it showing around the edges. All that remained of what once was a spray of sympathy flowers awaiting the unfinished ceremony were scattered stems and a bare wire stand lying on its side and partially covered with snow.

Cade emerged from behind the hearse and waved the occupants of the 4Runner over. After a brief huddle during which everyone had a say in where and with whom they wanted to start, they paired up and fanned out to all four points of the compass.

Daymon started on the southwest tip of the peninsula near where the majority of the dead had become mired.

Duncan and Cade cleared the inner shore of dead, starting south of the hearse and working their way north by east to an eventual rendezvous with Jamie and Lev, who were culling the dead twenty yards east, and on a mirror image tangent that also had them moving north by east.

Starting in the center of the cemetery near the vehicles, Taryn and Wilson picked their way among the tombstone maze. With no real method to their madness, they walked a counterclockwise spiral out from the hearse, kneeling next to each prostrate form. The routine was always the same. First locate the head and clear the snow from the face. Next, pierce the brain through the eye socket until hearing the telltale crunch of bone losing to steel. Wash, rinse, repeat.

"What do you think, Wil?" Taryn asked, taking a break to rub her sore shoulder. "Are we going to be able to appease Cade and get our five hundred kills before nightfall?"

"I figure I'm already a third of the way there."

"Sorry I asked," she said. "Let me rephrase that. Do you think we'll kill enough of these things to even make a difference before it warms up? Or are we just spinning our wheels here?"

He went to one knee and plunged his blade to the hilt into the eye socket of a terribly emaciated first-turn. Without a word nor rising to move, he pivoted to his right and repeated the motion, giving a child-sized Z the sweet mercy of final death. All in all, he put down four former fellow human beings in less time than it took for him to fulfill a drive-thru order at his last job. Fast Burger this was not. He was dealing death on a grand scale, and with every thrust of cold steel a little part of him died. He took a halfhearted swipe with the blade on some grass poking up through the snow. Eyes downcast, he said, "Wanna know the truth?"

About to deliver a coup de gras, Taryn's hand stopped in mid-air. "Yes," she said. "The honest to goodness truth. Lay it on me."

A bar of sunlight lanced down, painting a wide swath of land near the water's edge a brilliant saffron yellow.

Wilson drew a deep breath. Exhaled and said, "I think we're just delaying the inevitable."

She finished the motion, stroking her blade deep into a first turn's brain. "Death, or undeath?"

"Doesn't matter. Either way we lose each other."

A wild whoop carried from somewhere beyond their parked SUVs.

"Daymon's going crazy," Taryn said.

"Going? said Wilson, incredulous. "He's got a shit ton of issues."

"Better be careful where you cast your stones, Wilson. I think we're all in danger of losing some of our humanity."

The incredibly vivid image of a young couple, their heads caved in and liquid halos spreading on the carpet around them, flashed before Wilson's eyes. He smelled the blood, metallic and imparting a coppery tang on his tongue. He released his grip on the female rotter's neck. Looked the waifish young thing straight in its putrefying face. Lost himself staring into the darkened sockets.

"What is it?" Taryn asked, her voice gone soft, every syllable weighted with concern.

"I can't help but think for every one of these things I've killed today there's potentially a million more of them still roaming around out there." He crushed down his boonie hat only so that he could covertly swipe away some tears. He regarded her with red-rimmed eyes and then went on. "That's like two hundred and fifty million walking dead, Taryn. It makes me tired even thinking about it."

She said nothing. Went about putting another five rotters out of their misery.

Wilson turned in place. A slow circle, taking in the corpse-dotted landscape. He faced her and said, "That's what I meant by inevitable. The odds stacked against us are astronomical."

"We could move to somewhere that's cold all the time. What about Antarctica?"

Wilson cleaned his knife by stabbing it into the hard soil a few times and then finished the job by wiping the muddy blade on the dead girl's tattered tank top. "That's not living," he finally said, slipping the knife into a pocket. "We're done here."

Taryn watched him walk away, not quite sure in which context he meant the words to be taken. Cade walked up a second later and strangely enough uttered the same three words to her.

She cleaned her knife in the same manner as Wilson had and then struck out towards the vehicles, following the footsteps in the snow. Halfway there the wind picked up and a gust from the east slammed her from the side, slowing her gait momentarily. She put her head down, thrust her hands in her pockets and forged ahead. As she neared the vehicles and was deep in thought about her place in the cosmic order of things, suddenly from out of the blue—shockingly similar to the skull tattoos gracing her arms—she began seeing in her mind's eye the gaunt and hollow-eyed faces of the infected that she had just granted exit from this world. Only these visions visiting her without warning weren't a harmless facsimile of death like those which she had purposefully inked into her skin. Borne of parchment-thin skin drawn tight over angular bone, the indicting sneers she was imagining represented a real and final passage from this world and would no doubt haunt her for as long as she lived.

Chapter 47

The sunset was a sight to behold as the two SUVs pulled sharp U-turns and headed east back into Huntsville.

In the rearview, Duncan watched the withdrawing clouds go from burnt orange to bright red. The transformation transpired in just a matter of seconds and, as the cemetery gates fell quickly behind and his attention was drawn to the houses on the hill, he saw reflected in the windows there those same clouds abruptly turn a deep purple hue that he instantly interpreted as an ominous portent of things to come.

Physically and mentally tired, Duncan was easily mesmerized by the scattered clusters of skeletal trees and sooty light standards flicking by in the waning light. Sitting where they had been abandoned lining the streets shooting off of Main Street were the hulks of dozens of cars, windowless and sitting on pancaked rims. Here and there, zombies that had been present when the wind-driven fire jumped from Eden to Huntsville lay in the snow, their upthrust gnarled and blackened appendages a sharp contrast to the early season snowfall now covering the ground.

Main Street took them back past Dave's and Rhonda's and the long wooden bar with nobody bellied up to it. Instead of turning south and retracing their route to 39, Duncan held the wheel straight and continued east towards Glenda's house on the hill, the sky show at their backs still reflected in the windows and lighting it like a beacon. Three blocks removed from the business core, Main started a steady uphill climb. More trees seemed to have been spared on the terrace-like east-end of town.

"Stop here," Daymon said, an unusual sense of urgency in his tone.

The two-vehicle convoy stopped dead center of an intersection four blocks east of the L-shaped commercial building. Daymon stepped out and left his door hanging open. He strode quickly to the northeast corner of the four-way intersection and went to bent knee beside a two-door compact burnt to nothing but a shell and resting low to the ground on warped black rims. And resembling a tortilla left for too long in a hot pan, its once-white paint was bubbled in places and charred brown and black all over. In front of the car were four pallid corpses, two female adults and two kids, one of each sex. The summer attire—tattered shorts and tank tops and T-shirts—still clinging to the gaunt forms barely hid the roadmap of welts and open sores whose decomposition had been temporarily halted. And suggestive of many weeks spent roaming the countryside hunting the living, their feet were bare, the pads nearly worn down to bone.

Leaving Kindness in her scabbard, Daymon grabbed the long greasy locks of one of the Omega-affected women and turned its head until the death mask was squared up with him. He took a folding knife from his parka, flicked it open with a thumb, and started to probe one of the thing's once-blue eyes with its angled tip.

The soft orb gave way immediately, releasing a congealed mess of viscous fluid that seemed just south of its freezing point. The other eye—as he had noticed previously from his seat in the SUV as they drew near—was already punctured, the fluid definitely frozen. The wound there, when compared with the one from his knife point, was almost nonexistent. It was as if something very thin and with enough length to it to reach the brain had been thrust in quickly and extracted, leaving behind a tiny tell-tale puncture mark. But as liquid was wont to do, it always found a point of least resistance, and whatever the fluid contained in the human eye was called, this stuff had done just that. It looked to have leaked out in a slow trickle from the entry wound and then frozen dark and jagged, like a Mike Tyson tattoo, mostly around the outer eye socket.

He released his grip on the rotter's hair, letting the skull strike the roadway with a solid *thunk*.

The other adult Z was face down and had frozen to the pavement—also a victim to the same instrument used on the other.

The kids shared the same injuries to their eyes. However, judging by the minuscule purple pucker marks on their temples, their brains had also been skewered and scrambled from the side. *A clean through and through to the temple*, thought Daymon, *to make doubly sure they would never wake up*. Which to him was overkill that suggested whoever was responsible possessed a measure of compassion he didn't have for the already turned—kids or otherwise.

Over the intermittently gusting east wind he heard doors opening then thumping closed. During a lull, he detected footfalls squelching in the snow. Then in his peripheral he saw three pairs of scuffed boots; two were military issue with identical MultiCam fatigues tucked and bloused. The third pair were some expensive hiking models with snow-crusted blue jeans riding over their tops. He turned and peered over his shoulder and saw Cade, Lev, and Wilson standing between him and the vehicles.

"So Daymon, what's your finding? Cade asked.

"Great minds run on the same tracks," he answered. "Goldilocks seems to think someone's been culling our Zs for us."

"And they're still around here somewhere," Cade said.

Lev nodded. "I've had the feeling we were being watched ever since we came in off 39."

"I felt it, too," conceded Daymon. "Figure when it's my time to go ..."

Another door hinged open. There were more footsteps. Jamie said, "What's up?"

"We're being watched," Wilson answered. "And D here thinks that whoever it is has already been culling the dead here in town."

"What makes you say that?" she asked, her hand resting on the tomahawk, carbine held loosely in the other.

Again Daymon took a fistful of the female Z's hair and lifted and rotated its head off the ground so the group could fully see its slack face. With his knife, he probed the older of the two wounds and then chipped off a quarter-sized sample of the frozen fluids. Next, he moved the tip around in the other eye, a clockwise motion that showed there was still some viscosity to the milky fluid there. Without explanation, he let the cadaver down easy and stood tall. "The two little ones were done the same way." Then, pointing to the boy's temple with the blade, he added, "And they got a little *extra* attention when it came to the brain scrambling part."

"So they were all put down *before* the temperature dropped," Cade said, nodding. "That would explain why the fluid migrated before freezing."

"*Bingo*," Daymon said. "What is that *old ass* saying from that ancient tic-tac-toe game show Duncan is always dropping?"

"X gets a square," Duncan said as he formed up next to Wilson. He stared down on the dead for a second then looked up and met Daymon's gaze. "What made you think to stop and check 'em out?"

"It was obvious to me that the wind didn't knock these ones down in this perfect little pig pile," Daymon answered. "And I think whoever stacked them like that wanted them to stay together ... forever."

Like some kind of affirmation from on high, a vigorous gust of east wind swept in, clearing the roof of the once white car of several inches of snow. Covering the ten feet in the blink of an eye, the tiny razor-sharp crystals spread like buck shot and blasted the gathered crowd face-high.

Harsh words and snow spilt from Daymon's mouth as he reflexively turned away.

The others were dusting themselves off and angling for their respective rides when the first gunshot rang out.

Chapter 48

Thankful for finding a lonely bulging can of something other than sauerkraut hiding behind the Vienna sausages, Helen stirred the corned beef and hash with a spatula, added a few dashes of Tabasco and three generous shakes of ordinary everyday black pepper—just the way Ray liked it—and stirred it again. She divided it up three ways in the sizzling skillet and then carefully transferred the portions of steaming hash onto the three plates lined up on the counter. She placed a pale excuse for a sausage beside each serving of hash and dusted all three plates with ordinary everyday iodized salt. Nothing fancy in the Thagon household. Never was and never would be.

She thought back to her first date with Ray and the words he had uttered that at once had both appalled and endeared him to her. Being an East Coast city girl, never once in her young life had she heard a person say to a waitress, in as calm of a manner as he had, what Ray had said that day. After ordering a steak and potato dinner, the waitress inquired how Ray wanted his steak prepared. His reply was all country. Short and sweet and to the point. He had said: *Knock its horns off, wipe its ass, and bring it to me mooing.* Helen came to learn that day for Ray words weren't meant to be wasted. And that's what she loved about her simple man.

Still smiling at the memory, Helen bent over next to the stove and shut off the flow of propane with a quick clockwise twist of the knob. Yet another thing to be grateful for, she thought. For just days after martial law was declared, it seemed as if the utility folks up and discontinued natural gas service to the entire county without warning.

And without Ray and his shed full of tools and head full of knowledge gleaned from a lifetime of observing and listening, the conversion to propane would never have happened and she would be looking at a long winter subsisting on their stockpile of barely palatable MREs. No amount of seasoning or hot sauce, in her humble opinion, could make a meal of those things something to look forward to. What a catch that man was ... ingenious, and never afraid to get his hands dirty.

The propane, however, was a different story. Though Ray had scoured the county and outlying areas for a truck with a full load to *liberate* and bring back and stash in the barn, he had come up empty. Furthermore, every little store for miles around that had always had an ample supply of the ubiquitous white canisters (usually kept in a locked cage out front) had been picked clean when the first wave of survivors fleeing Ogden, Salt Lake City, and Jackson Hole breached the National Guard roadblocks established on the Interstates and State Routes and, like an invading army, swept through the high country, bringing their infected loved ones along with them. Once the motels and campgrounds were full, people took to staying in their vehicles or pitching tents on private property. A week later, the scourge the television talking heads had started calling Omega knocked those same stations off the air and dashed what little hope Ray and Helen still held for the government—FEMA, DHS, the military—to turn the tide on the dead. Remembering how his family had scratched out an existence during the Great Depression, Ray came up with a plan.

Before the dead had started roaming the countryside in herds, and later hordes, he and Helen had put that plan into action, making as many forays from the farm as daylight would allow, oftentimes coming back with the old truck sagging on its springs, the box brimming with everything *but* propane.

Then, one day roughly two months back, after the herds and hordes began roaming the countryside with impunity, Dregan and his boys came poking around the farm. But instead of coming with bad intentions, they had come as emissaries of sorts, offering sanctuary in Bear River. That day they had also learned that Dregan was the one who had beat Ray to both of the Bear Valley Propane trucks locked in the sprawling yard, as well as every pound of propane on the premises. In the old days that was called a *monopoly*. Even so, without a second's thought about leaving their farm, Ray and Helen had declined the offer; instead, they'd bartered three alpacas, each one a ten-thousand-dollar animal before the fall, for eight weeks' worth of fuel—amounting to about twelve canisters that would have cost all of one hundred and fifty dollars in the old world.

Now, with the last of their propane dwindling, and no more alpacas to trade for fuel, a new bargain needed to be struck. A bargain that might eventually boil down to someone either living or dying.

Helen scooped up the plates and, carrying them with all of the agility of that waitress Ray had offended all those years ago, delivered them to the dining room. She deposited one in her usual spot at the table and continued holding the other two in one hand close enough to Ray's face so that tendrils of steam curled about his nose.

"Smells good," he said. He moved his pocketknife aside and brushed the accumulation of ash from where his plate was to go. He set the corncob pipe he'd been cleaning on the table above his plate and regarded Helen, his face a mask of concern. "Are you sure this is what you want to do?"

"Positive," she answered. "What's that old Middle Eastern proverb? Keep your friends close and your enemies closer."

"No, honey ..." Ray said. "That, my dear, is a *Sun Tzu* quote."

"Well, I stand corrected." She smiled and made a play like the plate still in her hands was burning them.

"Tell me," Ray asked. "How do we know the difference between the two?"

"Exactly," she said, a smug smile forming on her lined face. "That's why we don't ever need to tell Dregan or anybody close to him what we know."

"That Brook girl had hard eyes," Ray said. "I'm certain Mikhail wasn't her first."

"And not her last," Helen stated, as if she were privy to future events. Again she nodded toward the side door and did the floating plate thing.

"He can wait," Ray said, sampling the hash. He motioned with the fork. "Sit. Eat."

She did.

And they talked some more.

Finished with the hash and just starting in on the sausage, Ray said, "What makes you so sure that if Dregan gets the best of those folk they won't tell him that we knew they killed those kids? Because if he does find out we withheld anything ... the fight we'll have with him and his kin, no matter what Pomeroy has to say about it, will require the application of a lot more of our friend Sun Tzu's rather unconventional wisdom." He sliced the sausage in two and stuffed one-half in his mouth while thinking how nice the addition of farm fresh eggs would be. *If only the monsters hadn't eaten the hens along with the alpacas.*

Helen made no reply. She went on chewing and swallowed, but still kept her thoughts to herself.

Behind her eyes, Ray could see the wheels turning. Processing everything he had just said. There was a long pause, then he added, "I'm just thinking aloud here, Helen. Did the negroes ever give up the people who hid them along the Underground Railroad?"

"Good point," Helen said at last. "Switzerland." She pushed her empty plate forward and rose with the full one in hand.

"Is it cold?" Ray asked.

She nodded. "It was never going to make it up there any other way. Now go on upstairs and cover me."

Ray rose from his seat, grumbling under his breath. The stairs were not his friend. Especially with a full stomach and loose bowels. Put forth as more of a statement than question, he said, "Darn it, Helen, why don't we just call 'ol Cleo on down for dinner with the radio. It's gotta be on the same frequency as ours."

"Because Dregan is no dummy. I'm sure they're all on a predetermined channel. Like the party lines of old. Remember those?"

"I'll cover you. Now git." He started grumbling again at the foot of the stairs and no doubt would still be bellyaching when he finally reached the top. And though she would be trudging through the snow when he did, the old coot would probably still be goin' on when he opened the window and placed the bolt-action rifle's crosshairs right on 'ol Cleo's poorly camouflaged sternum.

Chapter 49

Cade's first indication they were taking fire was the *crackle-hiss* of the rounds cutting the air, validated a millisecond later by the two puckered gray ovals appearing back-to-back and just inches apart on the nearby STOP sign. Blasting flakes of red from the sign's surface, two more hurtling bullets punched through the thin metal just inches from the others. Reacting instantly to the impacts and their following reports, he pushed off of the car he'd been leaning against and, with a handful of Taryn's parka, crashed to the ground, dragging her along with him. Their fall was cushioned partially by snow, but mostly by the quartet of corpses Daymon had just been examining.

The final two reports rolled over the leveled town like twin thunderclaps.

"Get down," Cade hollered at Wilson, who was rooted in place, totally exposed and panning his head dumbly left-to-right.

The barked order was enough to get the redhead moving; however, instead of making headway towards the vehicles, the young man did a clumsy shuffle on the snow, fell to his knees, and scooted off on all fours like a dog, quickly covering the fifteen feet to the 4Runner's rear bumper where Duncan and Lev were crouching.

On the passenger side of the car Cade and Taryn were using for cover, Daymon raised his head up off the snow and whistled softly a couple of times. Once he had Cade's eye, he hissed, "I told you we were being watched."

Cade said, "Where's Jamie?"

"I'm behind you," she said from afar.

Cade craned around. Below the stop sign that had just taken the hits was a bright orange fire hydrant. There were four gloved fingers waggling at him from behind its base and he could just make out the woman's slender frame stretched out long and pressed tight to the ground. *Everyone accounted for.*

"What are you gonna do, boss?" Daymon whispered.

His adrenaline now flowing furiously, Cade sensed the action slow as he snapped into an all too familiar state of hyper-awareness. Just as he was about to answer Daymon's question, the sonic signature of two more closely spaced shots crackled the air just yards over their heads, but struck nothing.

Same pattern and coming at them seconds after the first shots fired, a fourth volley struck the stop sign, the bullets punching through equidistant and an inch below the others. He peered through the corner of his eye and saw that the final three shots to hit the sign had created a sort of arced horizontal line below the other points of entry. *Six shots to the sign and two just to keep our heads down,* thought Cade as he dug the Motorola from his pocket and keyed the *Talk* button. Staring across the half-dozen yards of open ground between the burnt shell of a car and the east-facing SUVs, he said, "On three, one of you throw half a dozen rounds at Glenda's house. Aim for the circular windows above the upstairs porch."

"That's where the shooter is?" Taryn whispered, her face a foot from his, her breath hot and sour-smelling.

Cade nodded an affirmative. He thought, *Not exactly*. In his side vision he saw Lev flash a thumbs up, and when the count in his head hit three, two important things happened. First, brandishing his carbine off-handed, Lev leaned to his left around back of the SUV and squeezed off three quick shots along its flank. Then, following Wilson's tracks in the snow, his boots kicking up tiny white rooster tails, Cade crossed the open ground between the burned-out car and 4Runner without catching a bullet. In fact, even after Lev checked his fire and the glass had ceased raining down on the upstairs porch two country blocks distant, the anticipated fusillade of bullets didn't come.

Cade was breathing hard from the combination of pain radiating upward from his left ankle and the new surge of adrenaline introduced into his system. "Good work," he said, clapping Lev's shoulder. He looked at Duncan. "Are you good to go?"

"Me?" Duncan said, his head jerking to face Cade.

"Gotta have Lev's eyes down here. I want you on my six." Cade nodded and locked eyes with the older man. "Speak now or forever hold your peace."

In a rare display of humor, Lev turned his head and said, "You don't want me to tell Glenda you pussed out, do ya?"

Duncan made no reply. He pulled the Land Cruiser's fob from his pocket and triggered the automatic tailgate feature. Staying low, he disappeared around the 4Runner's passenger side.

Duncan was gone less than two seconds when a pair of shots rang out and the familiar metallic sounding *tang-tang* issued forth as the speeding lead passed through the stop sign, showering Daymon and Taryn with jagged white and red shards.

"I got a muzzle flash."

"Middle house ... Glenda's?" said Cade.

Lev nodded. "Second floor alcove. I'm guessing it's a covered veranda."

"Copy that," said Cade, just as Duncan returned with a stubby shotgun in one hand and the suppressed M4 slung over his shoulder. He went to one knee, shrugged the M4 off and handed it to Cade, who immediately began detailing how he wanted to take down the shooter.

Eden Compound

"Bedtime," Brook hollered. "And turn off the laptop … we need to conserve the batteries."

"Can Sasha stay over?" called Raven from the dark recesses of the Grayson quarters.

Though her fingers ached, Brook continued working the rubber therapy ball. "I don't see why not," she called back over her shoulder. "Question is ... which one of you is going to freeze your butt off and let Max out to make his obligatory yellow hole?"

"Or brown stink bomb," Sasha added, her giggles echoing up from the rear of the container.

"Or ... *that*," Brook said, smiling. "Better up there than in here."

There was the hollow double thump of the girls jumping down from Raven's bunk. Then footsteps on the plywood flooring. Raven rounded the corner first. Her face reflecting the dull yellow thrown off by the single hanging bulb, she said, "If he does, maybe we can get a couple of sticks and play a game of turd hockey with it."

"Gross," Brook cried. "Thanks for the visual, Bird."

"I'll take him out," Raven said. She slipped on her boots and jacket then clapped and called for Max to come.

There was a scrabble of nails on the wood floor as Max crawled from under Brook's bunk. He loitered for a second, stub tail going a mile a minute. In arm's reach of Brook, he spun a couple of circles and when the usual scratch between the ears never materialized, was out the door in hot pursuit of Raven.

Trying to ignore the dull ache deep in her shoulder, Brook started in on another set of ten, and when Raven's footfalls were out of earshot she put the ball on the bed and regarded Sasha. After an awkward silence, she thanked the teen for about the thousandth time since her near undead experience weeks ago. Mainly she was trying to show gratitude for Sasha being a positive influence on Raven. But how she really wanted to word it was: *Thanks for not continuing to act Raven's age. And thanks for not being a b-word to Wilson every waking moment. I'm happy to see you growing up ... let's keep it that way.* But she didn't. She had been fourteen once, and though conjuring up positive memories from those heady times was growing more difficult for her with each passing day, Brook was certain that when she was their age, the similarities far outweighed the differences.

"Hang out here for a sec."

Sasha nodded. Sat on the bunk and snatched up the discarded therapy ball. It was still warm and damp with sweat.

Brook rose and gave Sasha an affectionate squeeze on the shoulder. Then she left the Grayson quarters and struck off in the direction of the security container. The dim corridors seemed to be crushing down on her until she reached the security pod and Heidi greeted her warmly.

The young woman, whose blonde hair was now maintained in a short pixie cut, was illuminated by both the overhead bulb and the large flat-panel monitor to her fore. On the monitor, lit by the final light of day, was a number of partitions, each displaying a CCTV feed from one of the many cameras arranged about the compound's sprawling grounds.

"Raven's right here," Heidi said, pointing at the image from the camera trained on the clearing. "And Max is taking a dump."

"Mission accomplished," Brook said.

"And here they come," Heidi said. "Prepare for the cold draft." She grabbed a knit cap and snugged it on.

"How's 39?"

"Clear."

"The outer and inner gates?"

"Closed, locked, and clear." Beating Brook to the punch, Heidi continued, "Tran topped the generator. Foley filled all of the water bottles and shoveled snow into the water collection system ... just in case we wake up to a thaw like Glenda's been predicting. Oh ... and I also had him move the RV to the feeder road entrance. Figured since me and Daymon wouldn't be sleeping there ... putting it to use as a roadblock wouldn't hurt. Keys are on the shelf by the phones."

Brook shifted her gaze to the shelf and saw the keys. Then her eye was drawn to the message warning lights still flashing incessantly on the pair of sat-phones sitting there. "Did we get any new calls?" she asked.

Nodding, Heidi said, "Another one came in about an hour ago. For the record ... I feel like a turd not answering them."

"Out of my hands," Brook said. "Cade will address the elephant in the room when he's good and ready to. Hell, if Nash really needed him, she'd have already dispatched a team to come and pick him up." The moment the thought was fully voiced and out in the open, she wished she hadn't said it. For the truth of the matter was that it hurt her insides more than any amount of scar tissue could her outside.

Heidi made no reply. She took a bag of Cheetos from the counter and offered Brook some.

"No thanks," Brook said with a wan smile.

The cold air preceding Raven and Max came in as a *blast*, not a draft. As the pair brought the frigid air through the foyer with them, Brook noticed that her girl had more pep to her step than the dog. She looked at the wood flooring after the two passed on by and saw wet boot prints left there by Raven and, overlapping the minuscule bergs of melting snow, a trail of bloody paw prints. Lest the dog disappear under the bunk and she forgot to address the issue, she called after Raven, "Sweetie … we need to take a break from throwing the ball for Max. His paws are taking a beating from chasing the ball on the snow and ice."

Finally, against her better judgment, she snatched a Thuraya off the shelf and thumbed it on. The keys lit up and, with Heidi casting a watchful gaze her way, she found the heading for the phone Cade had taken and hit the *Send* button. The phone trilled in her ear, but there was no answer. Instead of leaving a message that would prove to be as confusing as her feelings, she ended the call before the voice-mail prompt sounded.

She put the phone on the shelf and attached the power cord. Before turning to leave, she put her hand on Heidi's shoulder and squeezed gently, wincing in pain as a result.

Heidi put her hand on Brook's. "Don't worry about me." She rattled the pill container in her breast pocket. "I've got these ... thanks to Cade. I've got coffee, also thanks to your man. And Seth's relieving me at midnight."

"I'm feeling up to pulling a shift tomorrow. The noon to six open?"

"It's all yours."

"Thanks," Brook said. She took a big handful of Cheetos. "For the girls."

"Sure they are," replied Heidi, grinning.

Brook said nothing. She turned and followed the crimson paw prints back to her quarters and along the way a single Cheeto made its way into her mouth.

Chapter 50

With Duncan and Wilson looking on, Cade checked the volume on his Motorola. He turned it down a notch and tucked it into an inside pocket. Addressing Lev, he said, "When I break squelch, give us a three-count, and if you're not taking fire send another half-dozen rounds into the siding *above* that veranda."

"I've got one question," Lev said. "Why don't you want me to shoot to kill?"

"I've got a hunch about this one," Cade answered. "However, if you're receiving direct fire ... *do not* think twice about taking them out."

Wilson broke his silence. "Seems like we got Stevie Wonder taking pot shots at us."

Duncan said, "Maybe. Maybe not."

His confidence slowly building due to the short lull in gunfire, Wilson said, "Can I come?"

In unison, each replying a little differently in inflection and verbiage, the other three men shot the redhead's idea down.

"You stay here and spot for Lev. Watch the buildings down the street. There may still be some slow movers in there." Cade nodded at the Beretta holstered on the kid's hip. "And Wilson, if you have to shoot ... I want you to shoot to kill."

"Roger that," was Wilson's reply. He unholstered the 9mm semi-auto pistol and went through the motions of checking its operation with practiced ease. "Good to go."

"He even sounds like a soldier," said Duncan with a soft chuckle.

Cade tapped his Suunto. Looked Lev in the eyes. "Shouldn't take but a few minutes for us to get into position."

Lev nodded. Flicked the Les Baer's safety off and shouldered the tricked-out M4. "Go, go, go," he called softly, swinging the suppressed rifle's muzzle up next to the 4Runner's quarter-panel and opening fire on the Painted Lady on the hill.

***

From his position on the curb next to the burned-out car, Daymon watched shell casings arcing from Lev's rifle, tumbling in front of Wilson's face, and settling in the snow behind the Toyotas. He also saw snow kicked up by Duncan and Cade's boots as they made a break for the cover of a low wall and picket of partially burned trees half a block southeast from the SUVs.

Crouched low to make as little a target of themselves for the shooter as possible, the two sprinted uphill and against a new blast of wind coming at them. When they reached the wall, Lev was ducking back behind the 4Runner and Wilson, happy and smiling about something, was flashing a thumbs up his way. The smile, however, evaporated like a breath in the cold the second the shooter resumed the inaccurate, yet seemingly systematically timed barrage. There were four shots, which strangely all missed the SUVs and instead shattered the globe of a light standard precisely one block west of Taryn and Daymon and the car they were still using as cover.

Cursing himself for leaving his rifle in back of the Land Cruiser, Daymon went for the pistol on his hip. He flicked the retaining strap off with his thumb and heard Taryn behind him whispering, "Don't do it."

He craned over a shoulder and shot her a glare hot enough to melt snow. In the next beat he thumbed the snap closed and flinched as Lev began firing uphill again. The gunfire ceased about the time Cade and Duncan skirted the front of the low wall and came to a skidding and slipping halt behind a wildly misshapen garden shed that looked to be constructed of some type of flimsy metal. *You win*, Daymon thought to himself, content for now to just watch Delta Boy, Fly Boy and the always silent Lev do their thing.

Thagon Farm

At first Cleo thought he was seeing things. The apparition coming at him was cloaked in white and its face was blurred by a shroud of fog that seemed to be following it. He wasn't drunk nor drinking now, and hadn't had a nip since breakfast. The fact that he was a firm nonbeliever in the occult or ghosts or things that go bump in the night led the rational part of his brain to initially dismiss the form as a byproduct of the combination of failing light and his old eyes playing tricks on him. That thought was barely fomented when the crunch of footfalls on the crusty snow reached his ears. He hadn't believed the dead could walk until they did. Now, what he was seeing approaching his hide was beginning to open his mind to the likelihood that specters and apparitions might be real.

With a cold chill tracing his spine and feeling like one of those soon-to-die guards in an old black and white World War Two film, in a booming voice he said, "Halt. Who goes there?"

"The password is sausage and hash, *Cleo*."

Momentarily confused, Cleo stammered, "What?" then leveled his rifle at the hooded being.

"I know you're cold," came the familiar voice. Then the form stopped a dozen feet away, reached up with one hand and folded the hood back, revealing a face he recognized. "I figure you're hungry as well," Helen added, tilting the plate forward to show off the tepid meal.

Cleo lowered the carbine. "Helen, what are you doing out here?"

"I was going to ask you the same thing. But now that the watcher in the field's identity has been confirmed ... the *what* and *why* component is crystal clear. And furthermore ... you can tell Dregan he just lost a measure of my respect for sending you out to spy on me and Ray."

"This is nothing personal, Helen. I'm just trying to get ahead like everyone else. It's not like I was sent to kill you two."

"Good for you," Helen said with a wolfish grin. "You'd have ended up like the others who tried and failed and are currently buried behind the barn."

Cleo's Adam's apple bobbed up and down. The emergency blanket crinkled as he reached for the plate.

"You *are* hungry."

He nodded.

"Come on in where it's warm then. I'll reheat this food and we can sip some brandy and you can tell us about Colorado Springs. Sure sounds promising what the *woman* president is doing there. Never thought I'd live to see the day ..."

Like someone else had control of his limbs, Cleo shed the sleeping bag and emergency blanket. Going through the motions without putting much thought to it, he grabbed his rifle and pack and started following Helen down the gentle slope towards the farmhouse and its inviting candlelit and no doubt toasty warm interior. Suddenly yanked back to reality, he halted dead in his tracks ten paces west of the brambles. His face screwed up for a tick. Then he was digging out the CB radio. Wearing a sheepish grin, he turned his back to Helen and called and checked in with Dregan. The information he relayed was all general and contained no mention of sausage and hash or an invitation to enjoy it in the house he was watching with the very people he was supposed to be spying on. Finished lying, he kept the radio to his ear and nodded a couple of times while offering up short one- and two-word answers to whatever Dregan's inquiries may have been. Finally, less than a minute from making the call, he ended it and stuffed the bulky CB in his pocket.

"Mum's the word?" said Helen, who had also stopped and waited while the act of subterfuge was being committed. She pantomimed zipping her lip by dragging a gloved finger horizontally across her mouth. Then for good measure she pretended to lock an invisible lock hanging there near the corner of her mouth, held up the invisible skeleton key, and tossed it away.

Satisfied that Cleo was in her pocket, Helen about-faced and resumed the slog toward the house, where in the upper window she could just make out Ray silhouetted by the diffuse light filtering in from the doorway at his back.

Seeing Helen's reaction to the spate of white lies, and knowing both her and Ray's character to be rock solid from trading with them in the past, Cleo kept up with the elderly woman and the aromatic plate of food, fully confident that this harmless little deviation would never be shared with Dregan.

Chapter 51

After cutting the corner, hustling south down the cross street and making it to the shed, all without hearing the angry hornet sound of bullets scything the air anywhere near him or Duncan, Cade figured one of two things to be true. Either Lev's last half-dozen rounds of 5.56 hardball striking around the windows and raining splinters and glass down on the veranda had convinced the shooter, or shooter's, to keep their heads down. Or, the less likely of the two scenarios, whoever was up there squirted just after the previous volley.

Shattering Cade's hypothesis, and the still that had settled over Huntsville, four more shots came from the middle house. From his new vantage point, the muzzle flash lancing out from the gloomy confines of the upstairs veranda was a star pattern of flame that looked a lot like it belonged to some sort of carbine. *Lots of them hanging around nowadays*, thought Cade. *And sadly, lots of dead National Guardsmen who wouldn't be needing their M4s any longer.* He caught Duncan's eye and broke squelch on the radio. "Anyone hit?"

For a brief second the radio crackled with white noise. "Negative," Lev finally said. "Another street sign is KIA, though."

"Check fire, then," Cade said quietly. He looked at his Suunto. *Seven on the nose.* That meant sunset was only a handful of minutes away. That also meant there would be a small window of time during which the sun would dip below the cloud cover and slide behind the curvature of the earth. And if all proceeded as it had without fail for millennia, the sunflare off the snow-covered mountains ringing the valley would be spectacular and short-lasting, and just the advantage they needed to safely cover the terraced block and a half to the southernmost home without catching a lethal lead overdose.

Hastily, so as not to miss the celestial bus, Cade relayed that part of his plan to Lev, following it up by giving him the green light to kill anything that threatened them once they were out in the open.

Listening in, just an arm's reach from Cade, Duncan nodded soberly. His jaw took a firm set as he jacked the shotgun's breach back a couple of inches to confirm a shell was ready and waiting. Slug, shot, slug, and so on is how he had loaded the shells into the pump gun prior to leaving the compound. Slug would do just fine for what he figured to be the opening shot in the upcoming engagement.

At three after seven by Cade's watch, the angry purple clouds to the west changed dramatically. Save for a thin horizontal band turning white at their base, the rest had gone coal black. Cade thought for a second he was looking at one-half of a giant Oreo cookie suspended in midair. One big enough to sate Godzilla and which extended all the way across the horizon from left to right, only the band of white was an optical illusion created by the rapidly changing play of light, not a layer of sweet creamy filling. The sun's rays were piercing the bottom of the clouds and they stayed lit up like that for a few short seconds until the dropping orb's aspect in relation to the horizon hit the sweet spot and the halo effect imparted on the Wasatch Mountains made them look as if they were cloaked in molten lava. The flare that quickly followed was brilliant—like that of a million diamonds twinkling around the jagged-edged range.

Cade was on the move when the clouds above the mountains were just turning color. By the time the mountain range bathed in coronal flare was mirrored in all of the west-facing windows to his right, he and Duncan were another block east and weaving their way northbound through the maze of corpses littering the streets running up to the homes.

The flare lasted only a handful of seconds and then a rapid transformation occurred. As if a switch had been flicked, the lower strata of clouds darkened and seemed to merge with the Wasatch and its shark's-teeth-like crags there lost all definition.

Crouched low and ready for combat, Cade continued north past a waist-high white picket fence and then made a ninety degree cut to his right. Head on a swivel, and with his ankle throbbing angrily, he made short jabbing steps in the snow and quickly ascended the slick driveway bordering the first house in line. After zippering through a number of corpses prostrate on the level stretch leading up to a one-car garage, he crab-walked to his right, keeping the M4s suppressor tracking with his eyes. As he cut the corner by degrees, left-to-right, thirty yards to the fore he spotted a snow-covered mound with a shovel speared into it vertically. To the left of the mound was Glenda's house. To the right was a one-car garage. The door was up, and sitting inside and out of the elements was the antique Austin Healy roadster he had heard Glenda telling Taryn all about.

With Duncan still close on his heels, Cade passed through the open gate and took a knee in the shadow of the two-story house, where, a tick later, his breathing ragged and labored, Duncan did the same.

"You OK?" Cade asked.

Holding a finger up, Duncan nodded and gulped air.

Taking the gesture to mean the older man needed a short breather, Cade rose and went through the swinging gate the way they'd come in. He scurried back and forth, inspecting a few of the corpses on the flat part of the drive near the garage and learned that they had already been granted a second death, their primitive brains scrambled by something long, thin, and sharp inserted into either an eye socket or temple.

Cade padded back through the gate and crouched next to Duncan. "The Zs on the driveway were all done just like the others," he whispered. "Whoever's claimed Glenda's place as their own has been cleaning up the hood."

"I seem to have missed the *neighborhood watch* sign," Duncan quipped.

***

Through the Leupold scope riding atop his M4, at the exact moment the sun had lit up the entire veranda and most of the elongated room behind it, Lev got a quick snapshot-in-time look at the shooter. Standing with his back wedged into a corner that a second prior had been fully ensconced in shadow, the man had been aiming some kind of a scoped rifle in his general direction. Whether the man had been able to see him through the 4Runner's smoked glass was unknown. And strangely enough, though the shooter had the high ground, which was a serious advantage in most battlefield scenarios, the look of indecision and fear etched on his youthful and clean-shaven face was anything but that of someone determined to make a stand.

Half a heartbeat from acting against Cade's wishes, and just when the sun slipped away and shadow again embraced the man two blocks distant, Lev listened to the gut that had saved his ass many times in the Sandbox and eased up on the trigger. Instead of putting a bullet into the gloomy corner in hopes of shattering the man's sternum and calling it a day, he swung his rifle to the right and watched Cade and Duncan scurrying up the snowy drive. Multitasking, he kept tracking his friends through the scope as they neared the garage and, once they disappeared around the corner behind the first house, he asked Wilson to get them on the two-way.

Chapter 52

Still crouched beside Duncan, Cade felt the radio vibrating against his thigh and fished it out with two fingers. He held it up equidistant between him and Duncan, its volume turned to a whisper, and together they listened to Wilson dictating a situation report via Lev.

When Wilson was finished, Cade turned the volume all the way down and, obviously contemplating something, looked left and walked his eyes up the steps, finally settling his gaze on the wooden four-panel door looming over them.

"Kind of figured there was maybe two at the most holed up in there," he said. "Based on what Lev saw and given that the potshots being lobbed our way were few and far between ... I'd be willing to bet we got ourselves a lone shooter. A novice shooter at that."

"And dollars to doughnuts," Duncan added, "that good ole boy is hoping to keep us at arm's reach until full dark. Then he's gonna squirt out the back and make a run for it."

Cade nodded, then, thinking out loud, said, "If we wait for him to make the next move, chances are he'll have already worked his courage up and then he'll no doubt be operating on a hair trigger and shooting to kill."

Duncan nodded.

"Right now," Cade said, "he has no idea he's been flanked. That makes me think he's probably just a Joe Citizen who scooped his rifle up at a roadblock."

Duncan said nothing.

Cade said, "Lev's convinced that our shooter's got some kind of a high-powered sniper rifle. It's not far out of the realm to think that he also has a pair of NVGs. That would really put us at a disadvantage if we wait until full dark."

"Let's take the house," Duncan said forcefully, his respiration now slow and steady.

Cade nodded. "Wait here." He scaled the four steps. Opened the screen door a few inches and tapped on the weathered door. A minute crawled by and nothing went bump inside, so Cade tried the knob and found it locked. He fished the lock gun from a pocket and had the deadbolt defeated with the sophisticated lock pick tool in seconds. Carbine leading the way, he entered through a mudroom of sorts. There were coats and galoshes and a multitude of cobwebs with a mosaic of bug husks trapped in the wispy strands. Ignoring everything save for any out-of-place noises, he traversed the kitchen and padded through the entire downstairs, memorizing the layout. Judging by the fact that two of the three houses, save for minor changes in the architectural detail—different dentil moldings and florets and such—looked to be identical in build on the outside, Cade figured their floor plans, though likely flipped for sake of avoiding monotony, would be strikingly similar in layout and room dimension. However, what he really wanted to know was where the stairs were in relation to the front and back doors.

All total, Cade burned ninety seconds between breaking in and his return to the back stoop. During that minute and a half, he came across nothing living, dead, or undead while inside.

Face screwed up in concentration, Cade said, "The stairs are sandwiched between the kitchen and dining room and are about twenty feet in from either door ... front or back."

"Makes sense. The same fella probably built all three of these Easter-egg-looking things."

"Copy that," Cade said. "That's what I'm banking on."

After drawing up a plan and hashing out all the ways it could go wrong—of which there were many—Cade was on the move north, through the expansive backyard to the waist-high picket fence bordering Glenda's place. The fence was easy enough to surmount, and once both men were on the other side they took refuge with the car in the garage, where they could observe both the south-facing side and rear of the towering home.

Leaning against the low-slung sports car, Cade scrutinized the house. The small window set high off the ground on the south side closest to them had its horizontal blinds parked at half-mast, while, as expected, the windows closer to the ground were all boarded over. The drapes in the upstairs windows were pulled tight save for the ones looking out on the backyard and garage. The smaller of the three, presumably inset in the bathroom wall, was darkened and looked to be shuttered from the inside. Near the corner closest to them, underneath a small overhang held up by wrought iron columns, was the newly reinforced back door. It was shored up with squares of plywood and, as if it had withstood a lengthy siege of hungry Zs, smeared bloody handprints marred every inch of its undulating surface.

***

Moving with the urgency of a tree sloth, Daymon had wormed his way in reverse along the gutter, with the charred car offering him minimal cover. The rough stone curb grated against his left side the entire way until he cleared the front tire and rolled to his right, putting the vehicle and stacked corpses between him and whomever was shooting at them. He locked eyes with Taryn, who had also crawled to cover from the opposite direction and was pressed flat next to the corpses, her head resting on the metal bumper just below the gaping opening where the car's plastic grill used to reside.

Seeing Lev looking his way and motioning with an open palm to the ground—universal semaphore for keep your head down—Daymon tore off his hat and erupted in anger. He was claustrophobic by nature, and though he wasn't underground or trapped within the fenced perimeter of a sprawling Air Force base, being pinned down by the shooter was no different. His freedom had been stolen and he was pissed.

The diatribe that spewed from Daymon's mouth was filled with epithets and death threats, all directed at the shooter. With cheeks gone redder than Wilson's, and the short wiry ends of his dreadlocks whipping wildly, he continued hollering at the top of his voice until the bullet zinging off an abandoned compact a stone's throw up the side street silenced him.

After the report dissipated and all Daymon could hear was his own heartbeat, he called out to Lev, "Cover us," while making his intention known by walking two fingers in the snow in the direction of the 4Runner.

Lev shook his head side-to-side. He whispered across the divide, "Not part of the plan. Keep your head down."

Still crouched by the 4Runner's bumper, Wilson mouthed, "I love you," to Taryn, who simply shook her head and pointed uphill as if saying *pay attention.*

Again Daymon called out across the open space. "I know you don't give a shit if I get my ass shot off, but"—he was jabbing a finger at Jamie—"don't you want your lady here over there with you?"

Glancing over, Lev said, "She can take care of herself. And regardless of what happened between us earlier ... I do give a shit about you. But right now, I need you to quit distracting me." He turned back toward the house and shouldered the scoped carbine.

Wilson had been shifting his gaze between Taryn and Jamie, but after the verbal sparring he glared at Daymon, who was silent for the moment, though his face was still wildly contorted. A few seconds went by and strangely enough the shooter took a page from Daymon's book.

Chapter 53

The second serving of sausage and hash lasted a little longer than the first, and Cleo was finishing his second snifter of brandy and completely sated and a little fuzzy of head when Helen began asking him questions. She poured him another two fingers of the amber liquor, set the bottle down close to their guest, and looked across the table at Ray. "Now I realize Alexander was going to call Cleo any minute, but I just couldn't see letting him sit out there any longer."

"There's not a single bone in my body that cares if that boy goes back out there in the cold or not," Ray said, laying the *bad cop* on real heavy. "Furthermore"—he dropped his fork on his plate, rose from his chair and shot a serious look at Cleo—"I don't care if Dregan offered this man free propane all winter, every winter, for life—from where I come from—neighbors *do not* spy on neighbors."

"Give him a break," Helen said. "Alexander Dregan is a convincing fellow." She refilled Cleo's snifter. "The poor boy was nearly freezing to death as it was."

Ray harumphed loudly. "I'm going to bed," he said, pushing his chair against the table. Muttering under his breath, he shuffled towards the stairs, leaving Helen and Cleo and the brandy alone in the dining room. Halfway up the stairs he heard Helen's voice. So he paused on the stairs just in time to hear the *good cop* say: "So what is our Ukrainian American neighbor to the south up to anyway?"

***

In his new hide overlooking State Route 39, Gregory Dregan was sweating under a pair of long johns, two fleece layers, and the

Arc'teryx jacket and snow pants worth more than two weeks' pay in the old world. Having set up the three-man four-season Vaude backpacking tent without an undue amount of cursing or breaking a pole or having a zipper malfunction, he was busy unrolling his sleeping bag when a mournful baying rolled up from the deep woods across the road. The hunt ensued for a couple of minutes, and by the time the rowdy pack had moved off to the east, his heart rate was back to normal and the little hide was all set up. *Tent, check. Thermarest pad, check. Sleeping bag, check. All that's missing*, he thought ruefully, *is a roaring fire and a warm lady.* Sadly enough, he'd almost forgotten what it was like to be with the latter. Truth be told, though he was loathe to admit it, he hadn't so much as held hands with, let alone bedded a woman, since before the fall. That silly little thing known as survival coupled with his strict moral upbringing had seen to that.

He tugged the handheld radio from his inside pocket. Powered it on and switched the channel to match Cleo's. He thumbed the *Talk* button. "In place," he said. Just the two words. No greeting or other formalities. This was strictly business, so none were necessary.

After hearing the soft click meaning message received, he selected the previous channel and hailed his dad. A few seconds of dead air ensued and then the elder Dregan answered. "Dregan here."

"I'm in place," Gregory said. He released the *Talk* button to a burst of squelch, probably caused by the double canopy tree cover.

"Have you seen anyone since the shooting?"

"Not a soul. Heard some coyotes, though."

"Watch your back, son," Dregan said. "Call me if anything changes. Out."

"Good night, Dad." Gregory left the unit on, with the volume turned low. He had more batteries. Besides, the white noise made him feel less alone.

Huntsville

"What the hell was that?" Cade exclaimed, shooting an incredulous stare at Duncan.

"Sounded to me like our friend Daymon just lost his temper and done went and got himself shot."

Cade shook his head. "There was no return fire from our side. I explicitly told Lev to let loose if any of our own started taking direct fire."

The two-way vibrated. "Scratch one Honda passenger side door," Wilson said. "Hurry the hell up and do whatever you're going to do. We're effin freezing down here."

"What's up with Daymon?" Cade asked.

"Oh, Daymon. He's on the verge of going postal. You know how he gets when he's feeling trapped."

"Do I ever," Cade answered back. He released the *Talk* button to consult his Suunto. *Twenty-five to eight.* The sky was darkening by the minute, and if the previous night between sunset and moonrise was any kind of barometer, this one, considering the layer of thick black clouds riding high in the sky, should prove to be just as inky black, if not darker—if that was at all possible. He flashed Duncan a tight smile.

Duncan shrugged, brows creasing.

Still holding down the radio's *Talk* button, Cade said, "Piss him off a little, would you?"

"What do you mean?" shot Wilson.

"Just get him cussing like that again. Have Lev return any fire ... same as before. High and non-lethal. Six rounds only. Two seconds between each."

"Lev's listening in," Wilson said. "He just flashed me … er, I mean, you, a thumbs-up."

Cade took the lock gun from a pocket. Letting his carbine dangle from its center-point sling, he scaled the back steps one at a time. He felt a tug on his jacket sleeve. Craning around, he saw Duncan point at his shotgun, then at the door.

Cade shook his head. Put a vertical finger to his lips. "Quiet," he said. "We use Daymon as the diversion and if need be, nonlethal means once we're inside."

"Why?" Duncan whispered.

"You'll see," Cade replied. He went to work on the doorknob and had the inset lock defeated in seconds. The newly installed deadbolt a few inches above the knob was another story altogether. It was a real heavy-duty item, like it had come off of a door serving one of the businesses in the town below. Gun sticking into the lock's guts, he paused until the dreadlocked former firefighter with the vocabulary of a pissed-off Marine started braying about something or other. The words, though unintelligible, were dripping with venom and spoken at full volume. Hearing the distraction ensue, Cade bit his lip and manipulated the pick deep into the lock's inner workings. A tick after the cursing began, the lock clicked open with a fairly audible report. "We're moving on the house now via the back door," Cade said into the Motorola even as he was stowing the pick tool and leaning a muscled shoulder into said door.

Someone had oiled the hinges recently, so it started the journey inward silently. However, something with substantial weight to it was hanging off the opposite side of the door and bumped and clanked against the lower panel.

Cade held his breath and listened hard while the noise subsided. *Nothing.* Nobody was shooting or moving around upstairs—yet.

"Let's go," Duncan said, his voice suddenly gone hoarse.

After determining that there was nothing dead awaiting them and that the item hanging off the inside of the door was just an overstuffed daypack in desert tan—probably the shooter's go-bag—Cade was on the move. The stench of standing water in the sink hit his nose as he passed it. Three strides later, he was at the west end of the kitchen, a mountain of dirty dishes and empty tin cans behind him.

Shaking his head at the poor display of sanitation, Duncan closed the door and then maintained a yard's separation between him and Cade, the stubby pump gun held at a low ready, its gaping muzzle pointed at the floor a foot-and-a-half in front of his boots.

Cade held his hand up, fingers curled into a fist, and took a knee by the stairway leading up and away off his right shoulder.

The gunfire resumed from upstairs. Like before, the pattern was the same, two quick shots followed by a pause of three or four seconds. Only this time, between the first and second volley, three things were added to the mix. There was the tinkling of shell casings bouncing off of the broken glass from the shot-out dormer windows. There was also a harsh crunching and grating sound of glass being ground into the veranda floor, presumably under the solo shooter's feet. Lastly, there was another volley of curse words, only this time clear as day and filtering down from upstairs. He heard only one man's voice. And that man was pissed off that the *dumbasses* wouldn't just leave him alone. "Pick another town," he said loud enough to be heard throughout the house and most assuredly blocks away.

Suddenly silencing the man, bullets were incoming. The first smacked glass in a window somewhere.

Cade counted in his head.

One-one-thousand.

He said to Duncan: "Stay here." Which Duncan correctly took to mean *watch our six.*

Two-one-thousand.

He started up the wood stairs, knees bent to keep his center of gravity low, while being careful to step only where he figured the treads were nailed to the stringer below. Less chance of a groan or squeak giving him away. By the time he was four steps committed, any noise rising from the stairwell didn't matter, because the man half a house length west of where Cade was had stopped cursing and instead was letting his carbine do the talking for him.

Not one to let a golden opportunity slip away, Cade pulled an olive drab metal cylinder from his parka pocket. Eschewing Hollywood's glamorized way of pulling the pin, he spared his teeth and wiggled it free the old-fashioned way—with his thumb and forefinger. The spoon flew one direction and, like Kareem Abdul-Jabbar delivered his famous skyhook, Cade lobbed the grenade over the railing, ducked and covered.

Seeing this, and knowing all it took from a grenade going off to ruin one's day was the tiniest bit of shrapnel, Duncan followed suit. However, as time slowed and he was privy to a preview of his own mortality, he shot a quick glance at Cade turning toward him and read the former Delta operator's lips: *Flashbang away.* Never before had those two words put him so at ease. Moving with a speed he didn't think was in him, Duncan set the pump gun on the floor and simultaneously squeezed his eyes shut to preserve night vision, opened his mouth wide, and clamped both hands over his ears. Last thing he wanted to be doing after the thing detonated was charging up the stairs, momentarily blinded, and sporting a hangover-like concussion.

The one-pound device hit the upstairs floor with a solid *kerchunk*, followed a half-beat later by a *whoompf!*

Like a freight train was passing outside, the windows in the three dormers rattled in their tracks, a seconds-long symphony of shaking glass and counterbalancing sash weights banging around inside their pockets.

The gunfire ceased in accordance with the breath-robbing concussion. With the acrid reek of accelerant hitting his noise, Cade keyed the radio and hissed, "Cease fire." In one fluid movement, he mounted the final three stairs, leaned forward, and was aiming around the bannister, his right elbow braced on the dusty wood floor. "Freeze," he bellowed. "Drop your weapon."

Because of a large queen-sized bed taking up the center of what he guessed to be the master suite, all Cade could see of the man was his profile from the waist up. He had his hands in the air and a stocking cap on his head. It was loose and drooping to one side, the fuzzy ball on top bringing it down to ear level. Judging by the way the man's stomach was rounded out and wavy in places, Cade guessed either he was in dire need of an abs workout regimen or was wearing one of those overly stuffed down vests. Considering the temperature inside the house was hovering somewhere in the mid to high thirties, if he had to wager on one or the other, he'd put his money on the latter.

There was a clatter of metal on wood. About seven pounds louder than the noise the tossed flashbang made when it hit the floor. Thankfully, this familiar sound didn't precede a bright flash and jarring explosion.

"Don't shoot me," the man hollered, his voice no doubt elevated on account of the sonic assault on his eardrums. "Ju-ju-just take all my stuff." He buried his face in his hands and a loudly mumbled, "Please don't ... shoot ... me," escaped through his fingers.

The man was of average height and weight. Cade figured he had about twenty pounds on the guy. The man's face was narrow and freshly shaved, and with the way it was framed between the low-riding hat and turned-up collar of his vest, guessing his age was a matter in futility.

Despite further aggravating his ankle from rocketing up the final handful of stairs, the instant the man's rifle had clattered to the floor, Cade was up and rushing forward, the bed between him and the man, bellowing "Hands up!" with the M4 trained on the stammering man's sternum.

Chapter 54

By the time Duncan had finished scaling the stairs, he saw only the smartly made-up bed and the upper third of Cade's body rising up behind it. The younger man's jaw was set in deep concentration, the rifle hung from its sling, and his hands were out of sight, busy zipping ties on the shooter's wrists, Duncan presumed. Shotgun shouldered and trained on the shooter's legs, he stepped over the spent flashbang cylinder, a gossamer thin wisp of smoke still curling out of one end, and cut past the foot of the bed. Seeing Cade's knee still planted in the cuffed shooter's back, he slung the pump gun and hustled forward to help.

"His weapon is out on the veranda," Cade said, nodding to his left. Then he rifled through the man's vest pockets, finding a couple of half-eaten sticks of jerky, a half-dozen granola bars, and a fistful of loose cartridges for the rifle. The man was wearing a pair of catcher's combination-shin-and-knee-guards over cold weather snow pants. Cade unsnapped the gear and resumed frisking the man, working both hands down his legs, one at a time, then proceeded up under his arms before rolling him over and helping him to sit.

On the porch, in a corner, was the rest of the man's catcher's gear. Duncan saw a helmet and chest protector that went with the leg protection. There were some arm pieces, flexible at the elbows, that looked like they belonged to a correctional facility's Cell Extraction Team. All of the black gear looked to have been heavily modified. Rattle-can painted a flat black and duct taped lengthwise on the shin and forearm pieces were thin runners of reinforcing steel. And no doubt to keep the swivels and clasps from squeaking when he moved, all of the moving parts were wrapped with black electrician's tape. Cade called an all clear over the radio and stepped back into the bedroom.

"Puts my magazine armor to shame," he said to Duncan, casting his gaze about the room. Unfurled on the floor and sitting atop a thin inflatable mattress was an extreme temperature sleeping bag. Propped against the wall next to the bag was a well-used internal frame REI pack in dark green. It had bulging pockets on all sides and more black tape had been utilized here.

Sitting cross-legged on the floor, the man craned his head around. His eyes met Cade's at a crazy angle. "I wasn't trying to hurt anybody," he said in a near whisper.

Still holding the man down with a hand on one shoulder, Cade said, matter-of-factly, "I know. But you were shooting at us all the same."

"Tell me about the gear," Duncan said. "You planning on going as Johnny Bench for Halloween?"

"That *gear* has saved my ass more times than I can count."

"So you just walk around like one of them ... all stiff and clumsy?" Duncan asked, his eyes wandering to a host of framed pictures arranged atop the vanity near the stairs.

"I only move at night. I have a pair of night vision goggles that tend to keep unwanted encounters few and far between. And I'm not real proud of this ... but I've taken to wearing coveralls over my armor. I smear them with innards and such and when I get to where I'm going I toss them. I've got a couple of spare sets in my pack."

"Apple doesn't fall far from the tree," Duncan said under his breath.

"Huh?" the man said.

"Never mind," Duncan said, a sad chuckle riding the tails of his reply.

"Help me with him," Cade said. Grimacing, he pushed off of the prisoner, stood up, and grabbed hold of the man's left elbow. Following Cade's lead, Duncan grabbed a handful of the fluffy vest and together they helped the man to his feet.

"Over here," Cade said, leading him by the elbow towards the bed.

"Not there," said the man, his voice wavering. Then, in a panicked state, he twisted his torso away from the bed in an attempt to avoid even the slightest contact.

"Stand down," Cade said, letting go of the man's vest. "We just want to talk to you."

The words were lost on the man as he continued twisting his body so that he fell hard to the floor instead of atop the queen-sized bed.

Duncan crouched down next to the man. Looked into his red-rimmed hazel eyes and, judging from the gathered folds and crow's feet there, got the impression that the guy was closer to forty than thirty. He stripped the man of his hat, releasing a tangle of curly brown hair shot through with gray that, along with the age lines, all but confirmed his earlier assumption. *Signs of the times*, thought Duncan, stroking his own silver goatee. "I know why you don't want to sit on the bed. And I can't say that I blame ya."

The man nodded, then seemed to relax a bit.

"We saw the grave out back," Duncan said. "Quite a mound of dirt ya dug up." He pulled out his folding knife. Thumbed the blade loose from the handle and flicked it open with a practiced snap of the wrist.

Watching from near the head of the bed, Cade saw the man's narrow-set eyes go wide, making him resemble a character in one of those British clay animation shows Raven used to like to watch. For some reason the names Wallace and Gromit immediately popped into his head. Strange how inconsequential minutiae liked to resurface at the oddest of times, he thought, pushing the memory to the corner of his mind where it belonged. "How long have you been home?" he asked the man.

Though the man's eyelids still seemed stretched to their anatomical limits, somehow, upon hearing Cade utter that one short sentence, more bloodshot whites of his eyes were revealed. "How did you know ...?" he asked, breathless.

"Better call the others forward," Duncan said to Cade. "I'll handle this." He cut the zip ties from the man's wrists, folded the knife and put it away in its sheath on his belt. He sighed and turned to sit on the foot of the bed and suddenly the man was rushing at him.

While he was busy on the two-way, out of the corner of one eye, Cade saw the flash of movement. Mid-sentence, he dropped the radio and, before it had covered the distance to the floor, was drawing the Glock from its drop-leg holster.

Not expecting the suddenness of the younger man's movement, Duncan tried to parry the perceived attack and instead fell sideways, arms flailing, and got a real close look and whiff of the soiled bedspread on his way to the floor. Falling face up and tensing in anticipation of the bone-jarring impact, he turned his head left and his gaze locked on the black suppressor, muzzle the size of a manhole cover, as it traced an arc across his breadbasket. And just when he expected the muffled reports and tinkling brass to reach his ears, strong hands grabbed his upper bicep and coat front and he experienced an unexpected and rapid deceleration as his body was let down slowly and without injury to the hardwood floor. As if in slow motion, Duncan looked away from Cade, who was lowering his weapon nearly as fast as he'd drawn it, then walked his gaze back across the ceiling and settled it on the younger man's smiling face. What came next surprised him more than the abrupt hockey check. The man let go of his coat and arm and said: "I'm sorry, but I just reacted. That bed is soaked with God only knows what. Would've moved it out of here already if it wasn't for the bend in the stairs."

Bewildered and wanting a drink now more than ever, Duncan rolled over to his stomach and, with the younger man's help, got up on his aching knees and finally rose creakily to his feet.

"Why the hell didn't you just say so, Pete? I could've easily broken a hip there."

There was a slight tilt to the man's head and now *his* face was a mask of confusion.

"He's Oliver," Cade said. "Pete is the older of the two."

Duncan planted his hands on his hips and stared at the man Cade had just called Oliver. "Glenda said Oliver was *thirty*."

The air seemed to leave the room as the man drew in a deep breath and sat on the foot of the bed. He buried his face in his hands.

"My mom isn't dead?" he said, the words coming out muffled against his palms.

Duncan looked to Cade while pointing at the man sitting on the end of the once forbidden bed. "How do you know who this man is?" he asked.

Cade said nothing. He simply pointed at the framed photos arranged in a neat row and standing upright atop the vanity.

The man on the bed was sobbing now, but instead of consoling him Duncan stalked over to the vanity. He looked closely at the different photos. One front and center clearly showed Glenda and a rail-thin man that had to be her husband Louie. In the photo they were dressed to the nines, he wearing a three-piece suit and her in a long flowing burgundy dress. Duncan had never met the man so there was no way for him to put his age into perspective with the here and now. Glenda, however, looked a hundred years younger than she did now. In the back row were a dozen framed pictures of younger kids, grandchildren, he presumed. There were a few more of Glenda and Louie in happier times and taken long ago—when black and white film was the norm.

The photo in question was leaning up against the mirror. Duncan had no idea how Cade spotted it in the first place. Then again, there were a lot of things that man did that seemed utterly unconventional until all of the puzzle pieces fell together and the big old lightbulb illuminated the method to his madness for all to see.

The 8x10 was in full color and in it were two men, one nearly a head taller than the other. The taller man was bald as a billiard ball, while the other was endowed with a full head of dark, curly hair and wore a bushy beard. And peering out from the locks hanging over his forehead were familiar hazel-green eyes. The eyes Oliver Gladson had inherited from Glenda Gladson thirty-plus years ago.

Cade was on the veranda talking into the radio and out of earshot.

Duncan turned away from the vanity. He parked his gaze on Oliver. "That fella out there yappin' on the radio is Cade Grayson. He's a hell of a good guy. Brash at times. But to know him is to love him." Finally he offered his hand and introduced himself. Then, against his better judgment, he added, "I'm really sorry about your father. Glenda talks fondly about him, still."

Still, Oliver thought. Hit with the sudden realization of where he was sitting and that the body—his father's corpse—that had soiled the bed was now buried under several feet of dirt out back, he rose from the bed and sat down heavily on the floor.

"I get it now," Duncan conceded. "Your mom told me what she did to make it out of here alive." He paused for a moment. When he finally went on, Oliver was staring at him through eyes shot with red. "I'm so sorry you had to find your father that way."

Oliver nodded. He palmed the tears from his eyes and stared at the photos on the vanity. "She left me a note. It was in with the pictures. She waited for me or Pete to come home for as long as she could. And I did … a little bit late, though." He smiled. It was pained, though not forced in any way. "Mom said she was going to Woodruff. As if there's anything or anyone she knows in Woodruff. Sure wasn't before the dead started walking."

"She never made it to Woodruff."

Oliver made a face.

Feeling like an ass because of how he'd worded that last part, Duncan blurted, "No. It's not what you think. She didn't *continue on* to Woodruff. She's safe, though. We have a compound east of here. We have solar power, water, food, and plenty of arms and ammo. Most importantly, Oliver ... your mom, she's with good people."

Oliver's entire body went slack like all of his bones had liquefied. He slumped back against the foot of the bed, gazing at the vaulted ceiling.

The sound of engines roaring to life broke the stillness.

Cade poked his head inside. "They're coming up now. Wilson said Daymon's real pissed. I'll head him off at the pass for you."

Duncan grunted. "Me? It was your idea," he mouthed. Shaking his head, he took a seat on the floor, knees popping as he did so. He handed the cap back to Oliver and looked him in the eye. "I can't imagine what you went through to get here. If you want to talk about it ... I'm a good listener."

"Cannibals. Killers. And the dead," Oliver said, still staring off into space. "But I'm still a good man." He donned his cap as his lower lip began to quiver. "I never thought in a million years that I'd see any of my family alive again."

"You have Glenda back in your life now. Or you will soon. If you want to tag along with us, that is."

Oliver nodded. Eyes gone glassy, he cupped his chin with his palms and stared out the French doors toward the reservoir.

Changing the subject, Duncan said, "You better let Cade zero that rifle of yours in."

"Oh, it's zeroed," Cade called from the veranda. "Come take a look."

After hauling his old bones off the hard floor, Duncan trudged out to the veranda. Without a word, he accepted Oliver's rifle from Cade. Lev had been correct in his observation. It was an AR-style carbine with a heavy barrel and a massive scope that took up two-thirds of the top rail. Up front was a foldaway bipod and out back the cheek rest on the butt stock was adjustable in seemingly a dozen different directions. Duncan checked and found the rifle's selector already set to *Safe*. He flicked the bipod legs down and snugged the stock to his shoulder. The view through the scope made it seem like he could touch whatever he trained it on. First off, he tracked down and left, settling his gaze on the two vehicles as they neared the corner a block south. The Land Cruiser was in the lead with Daymon behind the wheel and alone. Wilson was riding next to Taryn in the front of the 4Runner. There was movement in the gloomy back seat which Duncan presumed to be Lev and Jamie. Suddenly, brake lights flared red off the snow. Both rigs slowed through the left turn and the brake lights continued painting the street red as the SUVs crept through the maze of prone corpses.

"Stop sign," Cade said, pointing west.

Duncan lowered the rifle and found the sign with his naked eye. He raised the rifle and looked through the scope. Everything in the foreground snapped into sharp detail. He tracked right and saw the red of the sign fill up the reticle and then the word STOP, big and blocky and white, was framed by the crosshairs.

"Down," Cade said.

"Holy shit," Duncan replied. Below the letter P was a smiley face. Not the perfectly round yellow thing made popular in the sixties. This one-dimensional face was rendered by bullets impacting the sign in a tight little grouping. Nine precisely punched-out holes made up the circle. There were two identical holes for eyes, closely spaced. Below was a tiny puckered dot representing a nose. The mouth was more of the same, three holes below the nose shot into the sign in a small upturned arc. Speaking to the power of the sniper rifle, they were all through and throughs. Fifteen total. And they stood out starkly on the sign's darkened face thanks to the ambient light reflecting off the reservoir in the background.

"Blue Ford compact. Half a block north of the sign. About your one o'clock," Cade said, exhibiting all the emotion of a fast food worker sick of his job.

Duncan shifted his aim by a few degrees right, the bipod feet flaking orange paint off the porch rail in the process. Whistled. "Kid is good."

"That's a peace sign if I ever saw one," Cade said. "And to punch that tight of a group at three, maybe four hundred yards … on a down angle with a slight right to left tail wind ..." He nodded and made a clucking sound.

Duncan looked up briefly. "You're leaving out one thing, Delta. Nobody was shooting at him."

"That was coming and he knew it. Still, he acted instead of ran," Cade replied, his voice hushed. "Bravery is one of those intangible things that can't be taught."

"Nor true discretion," said Duncan. He looked over his shoulder, past Cade, and saw that Oliver hadn't moved. So he looked to the fore and aimed the rifle a little left and focused on the beach and boat ramp beyond the cemetery. In the gathering dark, he could just make out the legions of inert dead gathered there. Though less than half the numbers of the horde still clogging Trapper's Loop Road a few hundred yards due south of there, they would still have to be dealt with while the conditions still favored the living.

Cade strode inside.

Oliver looked up. His eyes were red, but dry. "I'll pull it together," he said, sitting up straight. "I've been stuffing these emotions for going on … what seems like forever."

"It's been a crazy couple of months, that's for sure," Cade conceded. "It's gonna get far worse before it gets better, I'm afraid."

The sound of the SUVs pulling up out front filtered in through the open doors. Then, near simultaneously, the engines went quiet. Duncan closed the French doors against the cold and the sounds of doors opening and closing. He propped the rifle in the corner beside a lamp with a stained-glass-style shade. On a table next to it were a dozen differently colored candles. Rising vertically from a hardened lake of wax, each burned down to a different height, they resembled a metropolis's jagged skyline.

There was a knock on the back door.

Duncan crossed the room, but paused in front of Oliver. They locked eyes. "That was some good shooting. Your dad would've been proud of how you handled the situation." For the first time in a long time, Oliver smiled. For one, he was happy a reunion with his mom was in the near future. Secondly, he was kind of proud of himself for checking his fire the way he had. Like the butterfly effect, had he not, he probably never would have heard those three words: *She's safe, though.*

Such sweet words, indeed.

Chapter 55

Amazingly, Daymon was no longer heated when he got to Glenda's house and finished battling the driveway's slick surface. And during the long slow walk from the Land Cruiser to the back door, Lev was explaining to Daymon why his buttons were pushed. The realization that the shooter was merely trying to run them off helped to cool him down. Then the disclosure of the shooter's identity washed away any residual anger. However, before joining the others upstairs, the two conspired to prank Wilson, who was the conduit between Cade's order and the disparaging words that led to one hell of a brilliant diversion.

Using the low murmur of conversation as a beacon, Lev and Daymon transited the kitchen and found the staircase leading up. Stifling a laugh, Lev pointed to Daymon and said, "He's already upstairs. Mean mug activate."

Instantly Daymon's face made a complete one-eighty, going from his usual placid affect to the mask of rage it was the second Wilson had called him an adopted dumpster baby.

"Perfect," said Lev. "Now ball up your fists."

Daymon stuffed his stocking cap in a pocket and shook out his dreadlocks. "I have a better idea." He started up the stairs, slowly, stomping his lug soled boots on each tread. He paused mid-run and out came Kindness. "Where's that ginger-haired skinny-ass good for nothing waste of skin!" he bellowed. He continued muttering about perceived slights and then paused on the fourth stair from the top. With the flickering light from the candles adding a rather sinister effect to his scowling face, he looked over his shoulder and shot Lev a conspiratorial wink.

Upstairs, Wilson was sitting on the chair by the vanity with Taryn taking up space on the floor between his legs. Duncan, Oliver, and Jamie were sitting on the floor nearby, facing one another, and engaged in conversation.

Out of those congregated in the master bedroom, Cade was the farthest from the top of the stairs, near the French doors and looking out over the town and reservoir. Upon hearing Daymon's booming voice, he turned and double-timed it across the room. The limp was more pronounced now as he picked his way through the gear and guns strewn about the floor. With all eyes glued to him, he took up station between Wilson and the top of the stairs. "What did you say to piss D off?" he whispered.

Wilson cupped a hand near his mouth and beckoned for Cade to come closer.

Grimacing from shifting his weight to the bad ankle too quickly, Cade hinged at the waist and lent an ear. He stayed like that for a handful of seconds as the sound of Daymon's grousing and footsteps drew nearer. Then, just when Wilson was finished whispering into his ear, Cade heard the footfalls stop. Right behind him. He could almost feel Daymon's breath on the back of his neck. So he rose up, turned slowly and found Daymon one stair from the top, which, considering the height difference, put the two men nearly eye-to-eye. Cade recoiled when he saw the swollen eye up close. He could also smell the man's breath and it was no kind of pleasant. And strangely, behind Daymon, in the gloom of the landing below, Lev was gesticulating with his arms. Cade squinted hard, focusing on Lev's mouth moving, and read his lips: *Daymon is not mad. Practical joke*. Lev mouthed it three times and Cade finally figured out they were messing with Wilson for something he'd initiated. And he was fine with that. The less drama, the better.

Cade nodded to Lev. Then he winked at Daymon. Left eye, so Wilson wouldn't catch on.

Suppressing smiles, Cade and Daymon stood there, eyes locked and exchanging put-on and wildly exaggerated angry glares like a couple of boxers at a weigh in.

Out of the corner of his eye, Cade saw movement. He broke eye contact with Daymon just long enough to flick his gaze right to see Wilson backing away from the impending confrontation.

"Move, motherfucker," Daymon said.

"If you're going after Wilson … then you're going through me," Cade shot back.

Ten seconds had passed since the stare-down began. Lev was on the landing below, a huge grin on his face, holding his sides and craning to see what was going on.

A dozen feet away from the standoff, Duncan was up and already angling to intervene.

Taryn was also standing now, her hands curled into fists and coming up defensively. She had a smoldering glare fixed on Daymon.

Oliver remained seated. He had no dog in this fight and wished he hadn't been part and parcel to the drama that preceded it. He thought about slinking around the stairwell rail and going down behind the faceoff. In fact, at the moment he wanted to be back on the Pacific Crest Trail away from any and all humans. Surviving was much easier when he only had himself to worry about. As soon as the initial thought of bolting diminished, he got a sick feeling in his gut and wondered just how his mom was faring after spending three weeks with this group of crazies. And just when the tension in the room seemed to have reached critical mass and he thought all hell was about to break loose, the bearded guy named Cade, and the dreadlocked guy he'd heard someone refer to as Daymon, turned toward Wilson and blurted: "*Gotcha!*"

Wilson flopped over onto his back like a turtle and lay there, eyes fixed on the ceiling. "Thought I was a frickin dead man," he said, his chest rising and falling rapidly.

Taryn jabbed a finger at Daymon. "*You,* motherfucker, were almost a dead man," she said, a little wild-eyed. No sooner had she said the words than her face broke into a half-smile.

Daymon peered around her. "Dumpster baby? Really?"

A sheepish look fell on Wilson's face. "They were your own words."

"Tell some momma jokes. Make fun of my hair like Old Man does. Call me Urch." He wagged his head side-to-side. The dreads kept pace, the handful of longer ones whipping his neck. "*All* of those things get my goat. Sometimes they even piss me off ... when *I* let them. But don't bring up that sore subject ever again? Last guy who did ... a ski patrol cat full of Rumple Minze and attitude. He got a broken nose courtesy of my thick forehead."

"Cade said we needed a diversion. He told me to piss you off. I figured ..."

Cade nodded. "He speaks the truth."

"I figure I still owe Cade for all the crazy shit he's done for us up to now. I'll let it slide. You're both forgiven. Ends to a means and all that." Like a switch was flipped, Daymon went quiet. His eyes were fixed on something across the room. He stepped up and crabbed past Cade. "Who's this dude? And what's that I see on his head ... does that say *Powder Mountain* on there? I've always wanted to ski that hill and never got around to it. *Park City*, yes. *Grand Targhee*, yes. *Solitude*, ditto. All over the Grand Tetons ... resort and backcountry galore." His eyes were glazing over just talking about it. He went on, "But never *Pow-Pow Mountain*. We gotta talk, my man." He slid Kindness into her sheath and crossed the room eyes, locked on Oliver as if they were the only two people left on earth.

Chapter 56

In the end, the pretend fisticuffs, though disconcerting at first, served to break the emotional dam that had been building within the group for weeks. Though Cade hadn't seen this coming anytime soon, it seemed as if Daymon was slowly returning to his old self—the fella he'd reunited with back in Jackson Hole before that city finally fell to the dead. The metamorphosis that Cade was witness to began with the apology following the snowball fight that actual *did* lead to a couple of landed blows. And now, hours later, Daymon was acting like an adult—playing nice with others—even after having just been used as a pawn.

Cade grinned inwardly, recalling the look on Wilson's face. Sheer unadulterated terror. He was also amazed the scrawny redhead hadn't drawn his pistol to even the odds. It's what he would have done. No doubt about it.

He was witnessing growing pains every thrown-together group experienced. A pecking order was being established. Flaws and strengths were being exposed and cultivated, respectively.

"Time to punch the clock," said Cade. He tipped his head back and funneled the crumbled remains of a granola bar into his mouth. Crumpled the foil wrapper and stowed it away in a pocket for use later, in the garden Tran had planned to plant come spring. *Keeps the birds away*, the usually quiet man had said after posing the strange request for anything shiny, foil or otherwise.

Taryn and Jamie were already zipping their coats and donning hats. Weapons were passed around. Boots were laced up tight.

Flashlights were checked and spare batteries transferred from backpacks to pockets.

"Hand warmers? Duncan said. Several hands shot up. He passed a couple of the little squares to each person. "Daymon? Oliver?"

"I'm good," said Daymon.

"My pack is full of them," said Oliver. "Raided a ski shop in Eden. Mostly just the vacation homes burned. A lot of the town close in survived the fire."

"The rotters?" asked Duncan.

Shaking his head, Oliver said, "Most of them were burned beyond recognition. I figure like the ones packed in by the water here, the burning subdivisions north and east of downtown Eden literally drew the roamers in like moths to a flame."

Duncan slung his pump gun over his shoulder and creakily rose from the floor. "Did you see any breathers?" he asked.

Again Oliver shook his head. "Not a one. Didn't even feel any eyes on me … except for the dead's."

There was a chorus of boots clomping down the stairs as the room emptied.

Duncan followed after the others and paused at the top of the stairs next to Cade. "You coming, Daymon?"

"Go on ahead without me. Oliver was just about to tell me about all of the dead he culled over in Eden."

"So that's a no?"

"I figure I'll roam around the Huntsville outskirts and let Kindness eat."

"Suit yourself," said Duncan as he started down the stairs. "Take a radio if you two head out. And don't forget about the critter in the *Shell* station."

"I'll keep my guard up, *Dad*."

Oliver snickered.

Before descending the stairs, Cade zipped his jacket up and arranged the collar to accommodate his beard. He shrugged on his pack and checked the mags in the pouches on his chest. Satisfied he was good to go, he slung his M4 and shot Daymon a look that the other man could interpret only one way: *Don't make us come looking for you.*

***

Twenty minutes after leaving Glenda's house and the deathly quiet town of Huntsville in the rearview, Duncan slowed the Land Cruiser at the end of the long and familiar winding drive and let Cade out.

The snow on the ground here felt different under his boots when he stepped onto the roadway. It no longer had that squeak of powdery crystals being compacted together under his hundred-and-eighty pounds. It kind of reminded him of the wet snow that often fell on Mount Hood. Known to the locals as Cascade Concrete, it had a tendency to grab and pull on the bases of all but the more recently waxed skis and snowboards.

He could still see his breath coming out white as he walked, and he noted the air here offered less of a sting to his lungs. The night sky was inky black and he couldn't see his hand at arm's length when the rig's dome light snapped off. Working in the cone of light thrown by the SUV's headlights, he removed the length of chain and pushed the gate to the UDOT yard aside. Eschewing the warmth of the truck, he switched on the tactical light affixed to his M4 and waved Duncan forward, then closed them and the Land Cruiser inside with the heavy equipment and piles of gravel.

With the bouncing white beam preceding him, he hustled on foot to the trailer where the keys to the vehicles were kept. He turned the knob and nudged the door open with the suppressor. Carbine tucked tight to his shoulder, he swept the room first then found the keys. Thirty seconds after entering the darkened pre-fab trailer, he was climbing into the SUV's passenger seat with not one, but the entire assortment of keys that had been hanging on pins pressed into the corkboard inside.

Cade had Duncan shuttle him to one of the Mack Granite trucks already fitted with a plow. Only this plow wasn't the type that shot the snow off to the right like the rigs they'd left shoring up the roadblock. This monster was fitted with a bi-directional plow more than twice the size of the others. Rising from the ground to just above the top of the hood in an aggressive upswept arc, both halves dove down and met in the middle, creating a sharp vertical leading edge. A student of military history, Cade's first impression was that the truck had been fitted with a mine-clearing device. However, this shiny item up front was good for clearing a road of snow in one high-speed pass—not deadly high explosives at a crawl.

Chapter 57

Approaching the turn-off to Trapper's Loop Road, Cade's attention was drawn to the boat ramp and day use area up ahead and off to his right. There were flashlight beams bouncing and swinging back and forth. Occasionally a single shaft of light would illuminate one of the many nylon tents and make it glow like a grounded Chinese funeral lantern. Unlike the cemetery where everyone split up, the stabbing bars of white light were clustered together and seemed to be moving left-to-right, near the shore, the beams flaring brilliantly every time they hit the water's surface. That the group was quite a distance removed from the parking lot where they said they would leave the 4Runner suggested to Cade that Jamie, Taryn, Lev, and Wilson had wasted no time getting underway and their late night culling session was moving ahead nicely.

He flicked his gaze to the tracked-up surface of 39, eased off the pedal, and let the Mack's transmission gearing down do the job of slowing the lumbering vehicle. At the T-junction he made a wide arcing left turn, and in the rearview saw the Land Cruiser's headlights sweep through the snow churned up by the eight massive tires on the double axle out back. Half a beat later, the plow's lights revealed a scene yanked right out of Cade's worst nightmare. Though he'd already seen the immobilized mass of Zs in their entirety in full daylight, that was nothing like seeing them suddenly snap from the dark like some kind of ambush rising straight out of hell.

The dead were stalled out heading south, so thankfully Cade was spared falling under the hungry gaze of a thousand pairs of staring, lifeless eyes. Throwing a hard shudder at the prospect of getting caught in this kind of a jam with the mercury north of thirty-two, he pulled the plow truck hard to the side of the road and shut the rig down. Leaving headlights burning, he lowered himself to the ground and shut the door just as the Land Cruiser rolled up and parked beside the plow truck.

Since the hostile takeover of Glenda's house, the wind had died to nothing. Still, as Cade stood on the lonely stretch of two-lane with his breath coming out in ever lessening detail, he felt a subtle vibration coming from the gathered dead. It wasn't physical. It was almost the same sensation he had gotten earlier when he was being watched. Only this was more ethereal, like a premonition he couldn't quite put his finger on.

Still lit up by the quad shafts thrown out by the trucks, the horde remained rooted. There was not so much as an eye twitch to confirm they were actually still undead.

The Land Cruiser's engine shut off and the driver's door slammed somewhere off Cade's left shoulder. Still he continued to stare. *Where to start? Front or back?*

Duncan's footfalls drew near. Gone was the initial crunch of boot soles plunging through the frozen veneer. As was the soft squeak and squelch of the powder-like snow under the mantle being compacted. Hearing this dispelled Cade's hunch that the lower elevation of the UDOT depot was responsible for similar conditions there. Given that and the fact that the road here was slowly rising from the level of the Pineville reservoir, there was only one explanation for the changing conditions. The temperature was climbing. He glanced at his Suunto and saw that the barometer rendered in the LCD display was flatlined, meaning it was probably going to get warmer from here on out.

"Where we gonna to start? Front or back?" Duncan asked, his hoarse voice and drawl making him sound as tired as he appeared.

Great minds, thought Cade. He didn't answer at once. He was busy trying to decide who looked worse, Duncan, or the dead thing lying face up in the snow a few paces away. Magnified by his spec's thick lenses, Duncan's red-rimmed eyes and the puffy bags under them made him look like a junkie who had been up and riding the dragon non-stop for days. Then it dawned on Cade that the older man wore the same look as every soldier he'd survived the Special Forces Qualification Course alongside of so long ago—dog tired and running on fumes.

"Are you up to this?"

"I was born ready," Duncan said. He plucked his knife from the belt sheath and flicked it open. "I'll start in the back. You start here. We'll meet in the middle."

Cade donned a headlamp and adjusted the beam so it hit head-high to him wherever his eyes tracked. "Sounds like a plan," he said, inadvertently blasting Duncan's eyes with its hundred-and-thirty lumen beam.

Mumbling something that began along the lines of *with friends like you,* Duncan stalked off south, wending between the tightly packed dead and stopping a dozen feet in. "I'm at an impasse. Let's both start here. I'll go right."

"Roger that," Cade agreed, his Gerber already tainted with the first victim's viscous black blood.

***

Two hours after they started, Cade and Duncan were nearly three-quarters of the way through their grim task of thinning out the *maxi-herd*—a name Duncan coined, and every time he uttered it in a forced high falsetto made both he and Cade think of a Kotex commercial.

Cade made his way to the middle of the two-lane. A hump of earth rose up more than head-high to him a dozen yards beyond the shoulder. It wasn't a gradual rise, but more of a vertical wall shot through with various horizontal layers of sediment, mostly reds and oranges which, like the quarry to the east, indicated soil rich in iron. And like stubble after a hasty shave, lonely sage and scrub clung to its top.

He treaded through a warren of twisted corpses and leaned with his back to the cut in the earth. He took a long pull from a bottled water and passed the remainder to Duncan, who was sitting in the snow, his breathing labored.

Hand shaking with a perceptible palsy, Duncan accepted the bottle. He downed the water in one gulp and tossed the bottle aside. "Chief's shedding a tear somewhere," he joked.

"I'm not following," Cade conceded, cracking a second oft-refilled bottle open.

Duncan chuckled. "Just referencing a commercial that was on television before you were a gleam in someone's eye."

Cade shrugged and handed the water over. Then, again utilizing the skill recently taught to him by former SEAL and Special Agent to the President, Adam Cross, he stood atop a morbidly obese corpse and looked south down the length of the road. He did a quick calculation and decided two hundred was a fairly accurate headcount of the dead they had left to cull. "Almost done," he said. "I'm going to move the plow up again. Watch yourself."

"Going to get me back on Daymon's behalf?"

"No," replied Cade. "But you and Lev better give him a break. Why don't you take your passive aggressive aggression out on Wilson?"

"Called out by Cade." Duncan rose, shakily. "I've been expecting this. And the answer is no. I'm working with Glenda on my character defects."

"I know, I know," Cade said. "Progress, not perfection. You guys keep it up, though, that last strand is going to snap and we'll lose him."

Awash in the headlights, his shadow a hundred feet long, Duncan said nothing.

"Why I wanted to end the standoff peacefully," Cade said. "We need all of the living we can get because there's a war brewing, and I'm pretty certain we'll be fighting more than just the dead."

"What makes you say that?"

"For one … I've been seeing lots of vapor trails. High up."

"You jumping on the chemtrail bandwagon?"

"No. Hardly." Cade shook his head. "However, Nash keeps calling. She's called each of the sat-phones. Gotta be something to them."

Incredulous, Duncan said, "Phones … plural?"

Cade nodded. "All three."

"That's what you're basing your assumption on?"

"No. There's more." Cade relayed to Duncan everything the Navy SEAL Griffin had told him during the flight to Los Angeles aboard Jedi One. About how the Chinese and Russians were both trying to exploit the United States while she was on the ropes.

"We're fucked if the Bear and Dragon both fared better than us."

Again Cade nodded. "First things first. We've got these to go through. Then I'll plow them off the road."

"Lookie who's spouting the AA lingo now."

"I don't follow."

"Of course you don't, Cade. I wouldn't expect you to. *You*, my friend, are what *we* like to call … a *normie*."

Cade said nothing to that. He was already on his way to the plow truck and wolfing down an energy bar.

"You'll never understand," mumbled Duncan. He watched Cade hop into the truck and followed it with his gaze as it pulled forward three or four lengths.

Cade poked his head out the window. "Good?"

"Good!" Duncan flashed a thumbs up that cast a sword-sized shadow on the bodies in front of him. "Time to make the doughnuts," he mumbled, parroting yet another pop culture reference from his era that'd probably be lost on the thirty-five-year-old.

The diesel engine cut off and there was a little backfire, which was followed by that same crushing silence that reminded Duncan of the end of every one of his failed relationships. He was stewing in melancholy thoughts when he heard from somewhere south of him what sounded like the peep a baby chick makes. Just one. Could have been a figment of his imagination. He was about to delve back in with his blade when he heard it again. *Definitely from somewhere deep in the pack*, he thought. Making the drawstrings on his parka lash his face, a stiff wind gust whipped out of the east.

Cade limped over and saw the older man standing there seemingly bewildered. "You OK?" he asked.

Duncan shook his head. "Not if what I just heard is what I think it was."

Cade shot a look that said: *Go on.*

"It didn't sound like what you described earlier. Wasn't a scream by any stretch. But it did remind me of someone choking back a scream."

Panning his head slowly left then back to the right, Cade listened hard. *Nothing.* There was only the steady three to five mile per hour wind out of the east that had just picked back up and was sending puffs of snow from the scrub lining the top of the knoll. "You're hearing things now. Should I bust your balls … or believe you?"

"I heard what I heard."

There was a lull in the wind and the sound was back, louder this time, and from more than one spot in the throng of dead yet to be culled.

Cade shook his head. *Effin Body Snatchers.* With a granite set to his jaw, he said, "Let's finish this."

***

Forty-five minutes later, with the big numerals on Cade's Suunto reading a quarter of eleven and the newly risen moon casting a blue glow over the killing fields, he and Duncan took a short break from sending the dead to their final rest.

Cade stood on the frost-heaved shoulder, rubbing his neck with one hand. Taken root in his lower back was a knot the size of a golf ball. His hips hurt from stepping over bodies while favoring his left ankle. Something to do with his pelvis in a constant state of misalignment, most likely. And though not as bad as when he had injured it in the chopper crash outside of Draper, his ankle was throbbing and the leather upper and laces of his boot were stretched to their limit.

Sitting cross-legged on an oval of blacktop he had scraped free of snow, Duncan stared at a nearby corpse. The legs were twitching and the constant movement was slowly eroding the snow underneath it down to the blacktop. And even though the half-dozen creatures were now prone, they would occasionally emit a very eerie half-whistle, half-moan type of sound. Apart from this, all of them had one more thing in common that body-type, age, race, and sex had nothing to do with. All of the Zs laid out on the road in front of

Cade and Duncan were fairly recent turns that had died fully clothed and with hats of one kind or another covering their heads.

Two of the six were middle-aged. A man and a woman who, by Cade's estimation, which he based on the light wear and tear on their expensive matching outerwear and boots, had been walking the earth in an undead state for less than a week. Though the two were found nowhere near each other in the throng, Cade and Duncan were of like mind that they had been husband and wife in life. Their thin sterling wedding bands looked to have been worked by the same artisan's hand. Furthermore, cementing the shared hunch, the pair's clothing, though different in style and color, bore the easily distinguishable Mountain Hardware logo.

Another of the 'whistlers,' as Cade had taken to calling them, had died just a normal teenaged girl dressed in gothic attire: leather boots, ripped jeans, and a black leather jacket with spikes and anti-conformist logos plastered all over it. Pulled down real low, almost to her eyes, was a wool watch cap also in basic black. Save for a few facial piercings, the brunette wore no jewelry. Several fingers on one hand bore bite marks, while the rest had been cleanly stripped of flesh, leaving glistening white phalanges throwing the pale moonlight. Riding up the left side of the teen's ravaged neck were angry raised welts, the dark purple ridges contrasting sharply with the pasty white dermis and yellowed trachea on display for all to see. Cade gathered that the injuries to her hands had been suffered while fighting off the hungry dead. The neck wound was a direct result of her losing that life-and-death battle, which he imagined had happened, judging by the lack of real decomposition, no less than three days ago.

The other three whistlers lay sprawled out on their backs on the shoulder closest to Duncan. All were males in their twenties or early thirties and of Asian descent. The uniforms peeking out from under their cold weather gear sported a tan camouflage pattern nearly identical to the fatigues he was wearing now. The low-rise helmets still snugged tight to their heads were close in design to the Kevlar bump-style tactical helmet he favored. He walked his gaze lower and saw that, like the helmets and uniforms, the knee protection still strapped on the bodies were knockoffs of American designs.

He unzipped one of the cadaver's parkas and, in addition to finding a number of bite wounds suffered to its shoulder through the ripstop fabric, there was a black pistol and several magazines for a rifle riding in a chest rig slung over lightweight body armor—all glaringly similar to western products. Hell, he thought, the bastards copied our latest fifth-generation jets from plans stolen from various DoD contractors' computer servers. Why not mine private sector databases for anything else they didn't want to design themselves?

He pulled the coat back and slipped a small black radio from an inside pocket. One quick glance and it went into his pocket. Then he yanked the coat off the Z's shoulder and stared at the olive patch affixed to the uniform there. No surprise. The stylized sword complete with pommel and lightning bolt wrapping the blade, at a quick glance, could easily be confused with the SF patch worn by American Green Berets.

Shaking his head, and not liking this new finding one bit, he regarded Duncan, who was staring at the Chinese soldier and slowly chewing a bite of energy bar. "Chinese Special Forces," Cade said. "Probably part of a scout recon team."

"Where's their weapons?"

"Probably with their vehicles."

"Why'd they dismount?"

"They were riding motorcycles."

"That's stupid," Duncan said, chuckling. He took another bite and stuffed the rest of the uneaten bar in a pocket.

"Yes it was," conceded Cade, thinking back to his own two-wheeled flight from Camp Williams and the subsequent collision with the young Z that earned him a dose of road rash and almost got him killed. "Yes … it … was."

Duncan grunted and shifted to his knees. "Give me a hand," he said. "I'm stiffening up like a pecker in a Viagra factory."

Smiling at the joke, Cade put his hand on the older man's shoulder. "Why don't you take a load off," he stated. "I'll finish what we started here."

"I'm tired … not dead," drawled Duncan.

"I need you to try to get the kids on the horn," Cade said. "Tell them to wrap it up and head on back to the house."

"What if they're not finished?"

"It's a short distance to the boat launch from the house. Figure we can tackle whatever is left there tomorrow." Cade cast his gaze on the six corpses, one of which was again making that hair-raising sound. He narrowed it down to the teenaged girl or the older man. He knelt beside the man and slid the Gerber into his eye socket all the way to the hilt, silencing the faint whistling. "Once we're done in Eden," he went on. "We can come back and mop up the leftovers."

Duncan swallowed. "Copy that, Boss." He watched, emotionless, while the former Delta operator added five more souls to his black Gerber. Teenaged girl, older lady, and all three of what he guessed to be People's Liberation Army SF scout soldiers who had been caught by the Zs with their pants around their proverbial ankles.

As Cade cut across the road, his legs chopped through the headlight beams, creating a strange strobe light effect that made the handful of cadavers left standing look all the more like props straight out of a Halloween house of horrors. Duncan watched him go and dug out the two-way radio. He made the call and relayed the order in a manner so that it sounded more like a suggestion. Finished listening to Wilson yammer on about how many they'd culled and assuring the kid their work was far from done, he stowed the Motorola and, curiosity getting the best of him, stripped the coat from one of the Chinese soldiers.

***

By the time Cade had finished putting down the last of the dead, he was feeling like Duncan looked. He threaded his way through the sea of bodies, avoiding the obvious collections of fluids that had pooled here and there on the road's undulating surface.

He found Duncan in the Land Cruiser. The engine was running, that much was clear. Wisps of exhaust curled up and were scattered with each new gust from the east. The driver's side window pulsed down when he was even with the front bumper. He put a hand on the rig's b-pillar, and when he leaned forward the heated air escaping the rig warmed his face.

"You done?" asked Duncan.

"For today." He rubbed his shoulders one at a time. Then, working the kinks out of his neck, he said, "Strange house and hard floor be damned. I'm going to sleep like a rock tonight."

"Not after I show you this." He took something from the passenger seat and passed it out the window.

Cade removed his glove and took the item. Turned it over in his hand. It was a laminated sheet of paper roughly eight-by-ten and had a crease in the middle for ease of folding. Both sides were filled with symbols that looked like stick-houses to Cade. Opposite the strings of Chinese characters were English translations. The one that caught his eye first was front and center. It said: *Surrender and you may live*. Another disturbing phrase farther down the sheet, near the crease, read: *Are you infected?* Lastly, he read the words, *We are here to help you*, and lost it. "Bullshit," he said. "They're here to finish what they started."

"On a lighter note," said Duncan, "the Kids put down most of their Zs. Some of them that were still inside their tents started making noises and moving."

"I was afraid of that," Cade said. "Temps should drop back down again tonight. That'll buy us some time tomorrow before they fully reanimate." In his head he heard Glenda going on about the snow. *It's too early for this,* she had said. Then her warning: *Be careful out there. It might be shorts and tank top weather by tomorrow.* Though he knew she was being a little facetious with the last part, she wasn't joking about how the weather was prone to have wild fluctuations this early in the season. She was speaking from experience. But, she was only speculating. And that meant that Cade had a little wiggle room in the decision-making department.

Interrupting Cade's train of thought, Duncan said, "One more thing … while we've been out here, Urch and Oliver were clearing out the buildings downtown. They wanted me to tell you they're going to get a jump on Eden just before first light. Apparently Oliver's already gotten a headstart culling the rotters over there."

"Knowing Daymon, he's got something percolating he's not letting on about."

"Give the kid a break. Do those words sound familiar, Delta?"

"Yes they do, Army." Cade clapped Duncan's shoulder. "Go ahead and turn in. I'm going to give the road a quick plowing. I'll be back at the house in twenty minutes … tops."

Without a word, Duncan pulled the Land Cruiser around in a three-point turn. He stopped near the opposite shoulder and fixed his gaze on Cade. "Watch your six, friend."

Cade nodded and climbed into the Mack. As soon as the SUV began to slowly pull away, out came the Thuraya and he banged away at the keypad, composing a quick text message to Brook. Then, repeating a Duncanism, he said to himself, "Time to make the doughnuts," and started the gory task of clearing the two-lane of the twice-dead corpses.

Chapter 58

When Cade turned the plow truck onto the street dominated by the towering Queen Annes, both of the SUVs were parked against the curb out front. There was no flicker of candles behind the panes of the French doors up above, and on the ground floor not so much as a stray bar of light escaped around the front door or the boarded windows. All in all, the house seemed just as dead as the hundreds of corpses he'd put down this day.

With every muscle in his body afire and the pressure in his ankle growing to the point that it was almost numb, he grabbed his backpack and M4 and, using the grab bar situated behind the doorframe, lowered himself from the truck's cab.

He opted to take the front steps instead of trying his luck on the sloped driveway. At the top landing where the snow had been scoured away by heavy traffic, he paused to put his arm through his pack's other shoulder strap. Sensing movement directly above him, he looked up and caught a tangerine-sized snowball square on the forehead.

"Good shot," he whispered to Lev, who was peering down from the veranda and shaking his head, no doubt in disbelief at making the one in a million shot.

"You looked like you needed a little something to wake you up," Lev whispered down. "Meet you in the kitchen with a towel."

Wiping his face on his sleeve, Cade said, "Don't bother," and hiked off to his right around the side of the house. Limping a serpentine path through the bodies, he heard a sound he couldn't quite place. It was coming from above and to his left and he was hesitant to look up in case a window was open and he was about to catch another snowball.

Curiosity piqued, he stopped and looked anyway. There was no window open. And no snowballs came raining down. There was, however, a build-up of snow on the gutter. And though he couldn't be sure, it looked as if the gutter had just arrested a slab that had broken free from raining down on him.

If he didn't know any better, he'd have chalked the incident up to a roof warmed by the heat rising off the seven bodies taking refuge underneath it. But he did know better, because the last time he had consulted the thermometer on the Land Cruiser's trip computer, the temperature *was* rising and the wind was dying down. Now, two hours later, the air over Huntsville was calm and moist—almost humid. This was one of those swings Glenda had warned him about. Tackle it head on was how he planned on following through with his decision to stay another day.

Cade was so tired when he got to the short stack of stairs leading into the back of the house that they may as well have been Kilimanjaro. He paused at the door and knocked. A moment passed, and when the door hinged inward, a helping hand was thrust in his face. Noncommittal, he glared at the hand for a second, then tracked his gaze up and saw Lev staring him down.

"Take it, you martyr," said the younger man.

Stealing Duncan's line, he said, "I'm tired, not dead."

"All the same … take my effin hand."

And he did. Once in the kitchen, with the boarded backdoor closed and locked, he also accepted a towel and dried the beaded sweat from his face. Then he went about shedding his weapons, pack, and parka. He toweled sweat from his neck and ran the floral scrap of threadbare fabric meant for drying dishes over his skin under his shirt. Using his Gerber, he cut through the silver tape securing the makeshift armor of magazines to his forearms.

Lev slid a low stool Cade's way. "Why don't you take a load off," he said, putting a hand on Cade's shoulder.

Cade sat down heavily. He put an elbow on the marble-topped island and ran his fingers through his damp beard. Eyes narrowing, he settled his gaze on Lev. "You and Duncan been talking?"

"No. Why?"

Cade shook his head.

Taking the nonverbal cue to mean *never mind*, Lev set his carbine aside and sat on a stool himself. Now eye-to-eye with the operator, he said, "We've got a lot of leftovers to get to tomorrow. A thousand or so—"

"And?" said Cade, cutting him off.

"It's going to be fifty degrees out there by sunup. I'm guessing—best case scenario—it'll be sixty by noon."

"Someone get their junior weatherman's badge?"

Lev shook his head. "Nope. Couldn't tell you it was gonna rain until it's hitting my face. This … this is coming straight out of Oliver's mouth. He worked the ski hills here for years. Apparently the first snow of the season only gins up season pass sales. It *never* gets the lifts running. And it never stays around for long. This, he says, will melt by tomorrow afternoon and the valley won't see any accumulation for another few weeks. Maybe not even until Thanksgiving."

"Guess we have to make the most of it while we can," Cade said. He pushed back from the table. "In the morning, you and Jamie and the kids ought to go back and finish up at the campground."

"What are *your* plans for tomorrow?"

"I want to give Eden a look see while the Zs are less of a threat. Get a feel for what needs to be done there next time we are blessed with another day like today."

"While you're at it," Lev said, standing up. "You should send someone up the North Ogden Canyon to make sure the barrier Oliver mentioned hasn't been compromised. Maybe leave some vehicles shoring it up too."

"I was planning on that. Shouldn't be far from Eden."

Lev nodded. "It's just a couple of miles if my memory serves. By then the roads will be clearing and you won't need to fix chains. Hell of a plus there. Save time and knuckles all at once."

"I'm hitting the rack," Cade said, a hangdog look on his face. "You have anything for this?" He pointed at his left boot. The laces were taut and the leather wrapping his ankle below where his fatigue pants were bloused was stretched to its limit and seemingly twice the size of the other.

"Wait one." Lev disappeared into the gloomy dining room and returned a few seconds later holding a white plastic pill bottle. "Once again, Glenda comes through in the clutch."

"In absentia no less," replied Cade. He couldn't read the label. Based on the muted colors on it, he gathered they were some kind of generic brand. "Whatcha got?"

"Ibuprofen." Lev popped the cap and rattled a trio of brown pills into Cade's palm.

Cade wiggled his fingers on the other hand, the universal sign for *keep them coming.*

"Twelve hundred milligrams … you sure?"

Again with the fingers.

Lev tapped out three more and watched as Cade dry swallowed all six. Then he handed over the entire bottle. "I got first watch. You take care of yourself."

"You're a good man, Lev," Cade said to the man's back as he started for the stairs.

"You've earned a break," Lev called back. "Take advantage of it."

Cade nodded to himself. He looked at the stairs disapprovingly. Shifted his gaze to the dining room and its barely penetrable gloom. He regarded the stairs once again and decided, for once, to take the path of least resistance.

Flicking on the headlamp, and feeling a little like a spelunker tackling a cave, he delved deeper into the innards of Glenda's home. He found the dining room crowded with a three-leaf walnut table and chairs for eight. On the far wall was a china hutch brimming with an antique store's worth of fine bone china and a highly polished box, yawning open and filled with what looked like service for an army, also polished to a high luster and reflecting his headlamp beam back at him. On through the arched entry was a sitting room with a pair of antique chairs, sofa and love seat all wrapped in plastic. The rugs on the floor were thick pile and Persian and did nothing to lessen the throbbing moving its way up the outside of his left leg.

After the short recon, he hung his head and, exhibiting a clumsiness that would have earned him a hundred pushups in basic, about-faced on the expensive rug in the front room. The place was so inundated with end tables, an ottoman, and a heavy wood coffee table that there was no room for him to sleep on the floor. Furthermore, the love seat and couch were both vastly undersized and wouldn't allow for him to lie in a fetal position let alone stretch out.

He backtracked through the dining room, hooked a left before the kitchen, and stood glaring at the seventeen steps running up to the landing. If the stairs out back were Kilimanjaro, he was standing in the shadow of K2. Knowing that beyond the landing shrouded in shadow was another stack of steps, he took a deep breath and began his ascent.

Three minutes after leaving *base camp* he was at the turn. Another handful of seconds later, and wishing he had a Sherpa to lug his gear, he mounted the four additional stairs and was in the master bedroom and surrounded by half a dozen bodies, some snoring, some farting, and all out cold after a full day's worth of manual labor in not so ideal conditions.

Cade collapsed to his knees by the vanity. Shrugged his pack off and stowed it where the chair normally lived in the kneehole under the tabletop. His rifle went by his side and, using his parka as a pillow, he stretched out fully clothed and propped his left foot up on his pack, *toes above the nose*, as Brook was wont to say.

His last thought after saying a short prayer for his family's safety was to set his Suunto to wake him at seven, which would afford him six hours of shuteye while leaving a good chunk of the day to tend to business before heading back to the compound.

Unfortunately, the thought never made it to the action phase as his leaden lids—exhibiting a mind of their own—fluttered once, twice, and then stayed closed.

Chapter 59

Throughout the night, Brook's sleep was interrupted by all manner of ghouls. It had started like it always did with her father's leering face, ashen and slack and scarfing down a slimy rope of her mother's intestine. Then she saw her brother, Carl, only he was never one of them. He was burned beyond recognition and trudging towards her, relentlessly, and cutting off her every avenue of retreat. Like bergs calving from a glacier, glistening hunks of pink meat cleaved off his bones and fell to the floor where they struck with heavy wet slaps. And just when she had convinced herself it wasn't really him, her name was carried on a labored breath rising from the depths of his fire-ravaged lungs.

She awoke with a start, shivering and wrapped in her thin, sweat-soaked sheet. "Raven," she called. *Nothing.* "Raven. Sasha." Her words carried an urgency with them.

There was a knock on the door.

"Who is it?" she croaked.

"Glenda."

"Wait one," Brook said. She cast the sheet aside and pulled the string, setting the single sixty-watt bulb burning. She threw on an ARMY sweatshirt, stepped into her boots and rose from the bunk. Crossing the plywood floor, she looked into the gloom and saw that Raven and Sasha's bunks were empty. The thrown latch on the plate door confirmed the girls were elsewhere, in the Kids' quarters watching movies or listening to music, she presumed.

Glenda was looking her usual spry self, smiling, gray hair tucked under a hat with writing on it that read *I'd Rather Be Gardening.* Wouldn't we all, thought Brook. Eschewing a good morning or hello she said, "Have you seen the girls?"

"They're in the Kids' room tending to Max's paws. Poor guy. I doubt if he had ever been exposed to snow like this before."

"I bet he has," said Brook. "He's a hard charger. I'll make sure he takes it easy today."

"The girls want to go topside and play in the snow before it all melts."

"Melts?"

"Yesterday's storm was just a tease of what's to come. Blew right through late evening, I would guess, and was supplanted by warmer air moving in from the south."

Brook looked at her Timex. *Quarter of eleven.* "I slept in."

"Raven said you needed it."

"Did they eat?" Brook asked, suddenly realizing her concern for Sasha was growing with each passing minute that Wilson and Taryn were gone.

"Cold scones and powdered milk. Did I do good?"

"Perfect." Brook strapped on her thigh rig and slipped the Glock home. Grimacing as the scar tissue stretched, she scooped her carbine off the floor and followed Glenda out the door and to the right down the cramped hall.

Seth was manning the security pod and tethered to the HAM radio by a pair of headphones. The Nintendo Game Boy Cade had given him sat on the desk in front of him. When he saw the ladies coming through, he slipped the headset off and greeted them warmly.

"Hi Seth," said Brook, squeezing his shoulder with her good hand. Her right arm was slow to wake up and hung at her side, pins and needles still shooting through it. A by-product of the Z attack, anti-serum, or a combination thereof. "Did you pick up any more of those strange radio transmissions?"

He pulled his long hair back and pinned it behind his ears. "Not since last night," he said, a pained look crossing his face. "I'll keep checking all of the obscure frequencies, though. If it's any consolation … I still think it was a bounce … some kind of anomaly that let us hear something transmitted half a world away. I keep asking myself … why would survivors not even try to pronounce a few well-known English words? I mean … even if they were Chinese speakers fresh off the boat when the shit hit the fan, don't you think they'd throw in a *help us* or *we're alive* now and again?"

"You'd think," Brook said. "How about the road?"

"Still desolate. The snow is starting to melt."

"Already?"

Glenda was about to recount a similar weather swing in the nineties when Foley and Tran edged around the corner and came to a halt. The security container was now filled to brimming with warm bodies, a couple of them in need of washing and at least a two-minute stint with a toothbrush.

Wiping sleep from his eyes, Foley said, "Mornin."

As usual, Tran said nothing. Just smiled that toothy grin that had gone slightly yellow overnight.

Brook leaned away from the wall of halitosis. "Going topside?"

Foley nodded. Then his gaze swung to the monitor. "Is the road steaming?"

Seth leaned back in his chair and nodded.

Taking advantage of the brief pause, Glenda launched into her story. "I remember one particular day in early October back in '97. It was already a real scorcher of a summer … prolonged through September on into October … classic Indian. I remember my youngest, Oliver, bellyaching about the ski season never arriving. About how he'd never get to meet the Ski Patrol folks before the Ogden crowd invaded the place. He was set to start at the resort that fall … probably food service or something. But … the $5.15 an hour came with a pass good for several different ski areas—"

"Where's Oliver now?" asked Foley, taking his eyes off the flat panel monitor and meeting Glenda's watery gaze. "You don't talk about your kids much."

Brook shot the man a steely glare that shut him up and caused him to look away and subconsciously start to stroke his lengthening beard.

Glenda swallowed. Her lips were making that dry smacking sound as she went on, "I believe it was ninety degrees that day and only two weeks from Halloween. Louie made a crack about Oliver going trick-or-treating as the Devil. Oliver spouted back about how he's sixteen and would rather be skiing in a Devil costume. Anyway"—she paused and wiped her eyes on a sleeve—"it started getting real cold just after dinner and was snowing before Buffy the Vampire Slayer was over. Hell of a swing."

All eyes were on Glenda and it was getting hot in the cramped confines. There was a clomp of boots on wood and Heidi was there, craning over Tran's shoulder to see what was going on.

"Glenda's telling us a story," Brook whispered.

Glenda smiled at Heidi, than winked at the woman she had recently started to think of as a kindred spirit. A real survivor.

"Go on," Heidi said. "Sorry for the interruption."

And she did. "It snowed all night," Glenda said. "Got about double the accumulation we saw yesterday"—she smiled and looked at the low ceiling—"but alas, it melted the next day. All gone. I think it was seventy degrees before noon. The look on Oliver's face." She shook her head. "He spent hours waxing his skis and getting the edges razor-sharp. His gear was laid out and he woke to sunshine and drips off the eaves. And adding insult to injury, school didn't even get canceled." She chuckled, The chuckle petered off, her back heaved, and a mournful wail escaped her lips.

"Cry it out," Brook said, wrapping an arm around the woman's shoulder. "Cry it out."

Foley saw Glenda lean forward and bury her face in the shallow curve of Brook's neck and shoulder. He crabbed forward, dodged the hanging light, then paused next to Seth to let him know he and Tran were going to clear the snow off the solar panels and then top off the generators.

Tran also slinked by the two women, who were still locked in an embrace and having a private conversation. He slid past Foley and then under the hanging bulb, clearing it by half an inch. He continued past Heidi, offering only a nod, and disappeared into the gloom of the foyer.

Being nearly a full head taller and much heavier than Tran, Foley was forced to wait a moment in the breach. He spent the time looking at the different feeds coming though what seemed like miles of new cable he had reeled out to the CCTV cameras in the weeks following his unexpected arrival at the compound. He could see that the road was indeed clear. Clear of vehicles. Clear of wandering monsters. And by the looks of it, clear of snow by noon. Sitting in the shadow cast by the firs and pines ringing the clearing, the helicopter and wheeled vehicles parked in what was commonly known as the *motor pool* were still coated with three or four inches of snow. The same heavy accumulation flocked the branches and tops of the trees, causing some of them to list over like the Grinch's sad little Christmas tree. Also affected by the previous day's dump, the Black Hawk's static blades—already weighted down by the camouflage netting—were drooping so much so that Foley wondered if even the diminutive Tran could walk underneath them without receiving a haircut.

Glenda's cry lasted a couple of minutes until she suddenly stood up straight, dried her eyes and went about smoothing her shirt and jeans. From embarrassment more so than a desire to rid them of wrinkles, thought Foley. Then, feeling a little uneasy, and probably more embarrassed than the older woman, he scooted past her and put a little squeeze on her shoulder, a move that instantly seemed inappropriate in such close quarters, and one that he immediately regretted. He had wanted to offer a word of condolence to go along with the physical gesture, but it had gotten trapped between conception and verbalization. He looked away sheepishly. He was no good at this type of thing and he knew it. He didn't cry. Never had.

"She'll be alright, Foley," said Brook, thankfully letting him off the hook. "She's a tough ol' broad."

Wiping her eyes, Glenda chuckled. "Carry on," she told Foley. "What you do is more important than consoling this"—she smiled, a twinkle in her eyes—"ol' broad."

Foley disappeared through the foyer with Heidi following after. A handful of seconds passed and the sound of two doors opening simultaneously echoed back to the security container. The creak of the front entry was one as the three adults filed outside. The second was the sonorous hum of the door to the Kids' quarters swinging wide, the hinges of which had purposefully gone unoiled. Kind of an early warning system for any adults who might be standing around and jawing about subjects not appropriate for a twelve-year-old's ears, and probably questionable for even someone two years senior.

Both doors closed at the same time. Then sounds: Footfalls on plywood. Giggles filtering around the corner. And the clop of boots coming to a halt by the foyer.

Brook craned around. "Where you going, girls?"

"Topside," replied Sasha, her bright red hair peeking from under a yellow stocking cap sporting a golf-ball-sized tuft of white fluff up top.

Brook suppressed a smile. The teen, from the ears up, reminded her of a Candy Corn—Brook's least favorite Halloween candy, by a country mile. She caught Raven's gaze. Held it and said, "You know the rules."

Raven nodded. Her black stocking cap was foraged from somewhere. Maybe a stalled-out car on the road, Brook thought. At any rate, the skull and crossbones emblazoned on it was more Taryn's style than her little girl's.

"Be careful. The dead are going to start stirring sooner or later. Watch your six."

"I will, Mom."

Sasha was looking on, a question hanging on her slightly parted lips.

"You too, Sash. You're the oldest. Do you remember what that entails?"

"Yes, ma'am. I'm in charge. Therefore the responsibility for whatever happens lies square on my shoulders."

"That's correct. And that's where the trust part comes in. I am entrusting you with my Bird."

Raven smiled at the sound of her nickname.

"Mrs. Grayson," Sasha said. "May we take a gun?"

Brook shook her head. "Shouldn't need one if you stay inside the wire and keep your runabout short. You have your knives, I see."

Glenda was following the exchange with rapt attention. Her head moved as if on a swivel. Left, right and then back again, taking in every word.

"We'll keep it short," said Sasha, setting the ball on her confection-looking-hat bobbing to-and-fro. "Promise."

"Go along then, girls."

"Max?"

"No, Raven." Brook pointed toward her feet.

Message received. Raven turned to follow Sasha out, the corners of her mouth turned down. Not a full-blown pout, thought Brook. But close.

"Raven," called Brook. When the girl looked over her shoulder, Mom arched a brow and made like she was tugging an imaginary item hanging from her neck.

Raven nodded. Reached her hand into her jacket, grasped the nylon cord and displayed the slender metal tube hanging there.

"Have fun, ladies," Brook said as the girls scampered off. She turned back and caught Seth looking at her. "What?"

"You sure?"

"Says the eye in the sky. They have blades. Besides … what could happen to them?"

"They're kids with cabin fever," he replied. "A lot." At that, he turned his eyes to the monitor and saw the girls already across the clearing and threading their way past Daymon's Winnebago.

"Well played, Mom," Glenda said. "Let's go now, young Brooklyn Grayson. It's time for your daily treatment."

Chapter 60

Cade awoke just as a slab of wet snow broke free from the steeply canted roof a dozen feet overhead. In his mind's eye he saw it drawn by gravity down the steep steel pitch, the swishing sound the granular crystals made as they picked up speed reminding him of a barber's straight razor taking a pass over a leather strap. The noise lasted but a split second then silence ensued and a blocky man-sized shadow hurtling towards the ground flashed in front of the south-facing window.

Look out below, thought Cade, a half-beat before hearing the resulting wet plops of the moisture-laden snow impacting the driveway.

There were no curse words rising up from below the window. Which was a good thing, considering everybody was pretty much irritable and on edge anyway. However, the next slab to take the plunge did so nearer the front of the house, creating enough of a racket from beginning to end to put a stop to Duncan's snoring—momentarily.

The acrid stench of flashbang residue was first to hit Cade's nose. Then the pong of death coming from the bed a yard from his head. Though noticeable, it had no effect on him. He had been surrounded by it for what seemed like ten lifetimes now. It was in his pores and hair and clothes. The same had been true in the Sand Box. After spending any length of time over there, one got used to the combination of unwashed bodies, human waste runoff, and the distinct smells of locals cooking with different staples and spices.

Coming home that first time had really thrown him for a loop. Though familiar, the sights and sounds and smells he'd taken for granted before were at times disconcerting. The thought of which helped him place the one odor overlying it all—the rancid smell of old man farts. Easily pinnable on Duncan, who continued snoring away somewhere near the front of the house.

He looked at his watch. *Ten of eleven. Shit!*

More snow lost out to the rising temperature outside and crashed to the driveway below, causing Duncan to go silent for a long three-count before the snoring resumed. It was a kind of wet rattle, interspersed with the inane and indecipherable mutterings of someone suffering from PTSD as well as a handful of undiagnosed problems of the head brought about by the day-to-day horror surviving the zombie apocalypse had become.

After staring at the ceiling and cursing himself for failing to rise at daybreak, Cade looked the length of his body and saw that his foot was still *toes above his nose* and parked atop his pack which he had wedged in the walnut vanity's kneehole. He wiggled his toes inside his left boot. Saw the leather give a little on the sides where the foot normally hinged and then a barely perceptible ripple of the metatarsals pressing against the hard leather toecap. Expecting a flare of pain, he felt only a dull throb emanating from deep inside. He imagined the angry purple bruising that he knew was there just underneath his bloused pants leg. He hadn't let injury stop him in South Dakota, and he wasn't about to let it stop him from making the most out of however much time was left of the brief gift the previous day's inclement weather had bestowed upon the living.

Before enduring the pain he knew extricating himself from his prone position was sure to bring about, he propped his body up on his left elbow. Craning his head back, he cast his gaze the length of the master suite past the perfectly made up bed, Duncan's legs—boots to knees—which were sticking out past the foot of said bed, and onward to the veranda where silhouetted in the flat light filtering in was a form holding a scoped rifle he immediately pegged as Lev.

Cade gritted his teeth as a sharp stab of breath-robbing pain took hold where the multitude of tiny bones came together inside his ballooned ankle. Sweat forming on his brow, he rolled over onto his stomach and sucked wind. Who had he been trying to fool earlier? This one *was* as bad as the Dakota injury. Using the vanity for support, he rose shakily. Wiped his brow and then dug out another half-dozen little brown pills. He swallowed them dry, then grabbed the handrail and made his way down the short run of stairs leading to the landing. Took them down, gripping the handrail, crossed to the other side and scaled their counterparts in a like fashion. Feeling the cold sheen of sweat reforming on his brow, he continued on down the narrow hall leading to the master bath.

Squinting against the light streaming in through the shuttered east-facing window, he bypassed the inoperable toilet and sidled up to the old white clawfoot tub. He leaned with his knees pressed to the tub's lip, parted his fly and let loose. The stream was slow at first, but when it got going he saw that his urine was the color of bile—a muddy shade of yellow like one of those expensive upper-shelf mustards. There was a hamster banging around in his head and his lips were crisscrossed with tiny cracks, and through the night, little beads of white froth had dried at the corners. He didn't need his wife here to tell him he was showing symptoms of dehydration. He'd been so focused on culling the dead that he'd neglected his own body's needs.

He finished his business, and once the last of the oily looking yellow liquid had trickled down the drain, he replaced the stopper.

He retraced his steps, testing the ankle by descending and then ascending the stairs without relying on the handrail. *Good to go.* He didn't pass out. Nor did he collapse. Mike Desantos would have barked, *Rub some dirt on it, pussy!*

Smiling at the thought of his old friend, Cade corralled his rifle and proceeded towards the veranda, where he saw Lev in virtually the same pose as before. As he passed by Duncan, who was still sound asleep but no longer snoring, he thumped the rifle against the soles of his boots and in his best DI voice hollered, "Private Winters … you *maggot* … we missed you at morning roll. Wake up, you pond-scum sucking gutter-dweller!"

Duncan's eyes fluttered and then his boot heels clicked together. Whether it was an involuntary reaction in response to the authoritative voice, muscle memory still ingrained from snapping to attention at a moment's notice during basic training, or a direct result from the carbine stock coming into contact with his boots, Cade could care less. Sand was slipping through the hourglass and he wanted to get to Eden before the monsters regained full mobility.

Without stopping to confirm that his rude move had produced the desired effect, Cade limped ahead to the veranda.

When he parted the sheer curtains and opened the left side of the French door, he was struck instantly by the temperature swing. Glenda knew her stuff. In only twenty-four hours the weather had turned from darn near arctic to balmy in comparison.

He craned around the door divider and saw that from where Lev was standing the Iraq war veteran had a clear view of all of downtown Huntsville, the cemetery due west of there, and the corpse-strewn green-space and beach across the thin blue-green finger of Pineville Reservoir coming between the two.

The milled metal forestock of Lev's inherited carbine was resting on his makeshift shooter's pad of folded-up blue jeans arranged on the veranda rail. He was sitting on the purloined walnut vanity stool with the five-thousand-dollar rifle snugged to his shoulder, eye close to the massive scope and one arm wrapped around the stock, holding it rock steady. A two-way radio was clutched in his other hand and he was talking to someone presumably near the boat launch where the carbine's substantial barrel was trained.

"Whatcha got?" Cade asked.

Lev didn't change his posture nor did he attempt to make eye contact. "I have eyes on Jamie and the Kids. They've been at it for about ninety minutes. I figure they're two or three hundred shy of being finished."

"How are they taking it?"

"Better now that the whistling has stopped. Creepy shit. I watched Wilson lose his cookies first. Then a little later Taryn and Jamie blew chunks all over the snow."

Duncan edged up to the railing. "Last night I got a little teaser of what Cade heard yesterday morning." He went on to describe the Chinese scouts they came across and what he heard coming from their maws.

"Good thing we let you two sleep through it, then," Lev stated.

Cade said, "Hey," to get Lev's attention. Lev raised up from the rest and sat straight, one hand holding the rifle in check against gravity. "Yes?" he said in as calm a tone as a man about to face a hurricane head on could muster.

"It's cool you didn't wake me," Cade said. "My body was trying to tell me something anyway." He took a bottled water from the side table and spun the cap off. Drank it in one long pull and didn't stop until the bottle crinkled in on itself. Before opening a much-needed second bottle he went on, "What time did everyone head out?"

"The Kids and Jamie … around oh-eight-hundred."

"Urch and Oliver?" asked Duncan.

"You mean Daymon and his new buddy, *O.G.*?"

"O.G.," said Cade. "Isn't that some gang thing? Original Gangster … I think."

"Correct—" began Lev.

"—Or Oliver Gladson," finished Duncan.

Cade said nothing.

Lev said, "They left for Eden at first light in the Land Cruiser." He paused for a second, a laugh trapped in his chest and threatening to bust out. Cade was looking at him intently, now. Sensing something was being withheld he said, "And?"

Lips pursed, Lev choked out, "Seemed like they were on a mission."

"What's so dang funny?" drawled Duncan.

Shaking his head, cheeks blushing red, Lev maintained a forced quiet.

"Spit … it … out," Duncan ordered. "Or I'll tell Jamie what you told me about her prowess in the *sack*."

"That's *fucking* blackmail. I didn't tell you shit."

The radio crackled. Jamie said, "You coming, Lev?"

Cade smiled big at the timing of that one.

Duncan said, "I know you didn't. But your little lady doesn't know what I do or don't know." He smiled.

Deciding the Old Man's bullshit arm-twisting only warranted a fraction of the information, Lev said, "When those two left they had to step *over* you."

"And?" Cade asked.

"Oliver made it over with no problems." Lev's nostrils flared. He shook his head, a twinkle in his eyes regarding some yet to be divulged detail banging around in his head.

"We don't have time for this," said Cade. "Divulge. Now. What are they up to?"

Lev fixed his gaze on Cade. "So … Daymon is stepping over you and out of nowhere you flinch and your arms fly up in front of your face and you're in some Rocky Marciano boxing pose in your sleep. Then … Oliver is chanting softly, 'tea bag, tea bag, tea bag' … on and on, like that."

"And?" the look on Cade's face still passive.

Now Duncan is pursing his lips and harboring a belly laugh of his own.

"Did he … tea bag? Whatever that is." Cade looked over at Duncan. "What's a tea bag? I'm guessing it's not Darjeeling blend."

Both men were holding their sides now. Lev had put the rifle down. Then, as if he were playing a game of charades, he went into great detail what a proper tea bagging entailed.

With a look of utter disgust parked on his face, Cade asked, "And why didn't you stop him from following through, *Lev*?"

"Didn't need to. Right when he grew a pair and was about to drop trou, your hands relaxed and went back to your sides … one of them near your Glock. That was when Daymon said 'Hell no … motherfucker will blow my balls off in his sleep' and pulled his drawers up quicker than shit."

Cade faked a laugh. "Ha ha. One brush of ball sack … hell, one little pubic hair hits my nose and the owner gets a free neutering compliments of my Gerber."

"If it's a woman pube?" said Duncan, tears streaming from the corners of his eyes.

In a moment of levity, Cade played along, saying, "We'll cross that bridge when we come to it."

Being left hanging in limbo on the radio for Jamie became unacceptable after roughly ninety seconds. “Are you coming or not?” she asked again, her tone, delivered through the small speaker, shrill and demanding.

Chapter 61
Eden Compound, Utah

The crown of Raven's head barely reached the top of the gnarled wooden post. She stood there, one hand gripping the top strand of wire, head craned and looking through the trees towards the feeder road.

Sasha was already on the other side, having scaled the fence without a word. Now the fourteen-year-old was staring a silent dare Raven's way.

"You're outside the wire." Raven jiggled the post as if checking its steadfastness. It did not move; however, her resolve wavered a little.

"Technically, I'm inside the wire," replied Sasha. She removed her stocking cap, letting her hair erupt to its normal volume. It was warming up, so the hat went in a pocket and she unzipped her jacket.

"What do you mean?" asked Raven, casting a furtive glance over her shoulder and trying to pick out the all-seeing-eye perched on the post somewhere through the trees to her right. Because if she could see the plastic globe, then the camera inside the globe could also see her. Thankfully, it was blocked entirely from view by the picket of juvenile trees lining the road just inside the middle gate.

"As far as I'm concerned," said Sasha. "The fence at the main road *is* the wire. Then, if we cross the road and climb the fence on the other side of the main road … we're right back *inside* the wire. Technically."

Raven put her hands on her hips. *Define technically*, she thought. Then right after that she heard in her head Sasha saying to Brook: *The responsibility for whatever happens lies square on my shoulders.* That was enough to erode her resolve, and as if someone outside of herself was manipulating a string attached to her head, it bobbed up and down once, then before she could stop herself, she was slipping between the stretched wires to Sasha's side.

"That's my girl," said Sasha, a devilish gleam in her eye.

It's your butt, babysitter, thought Raven as her namesake started to caw somewhere nearby. Instinctively her hand went to the knife on her hip. She rested her palm on its antler pommel. "What about the rotters?" she asked, shifting her sixty-five-pound frame nervously side-to-side.

"We don't have anything to worry about. Besides, it's still not warm enough for them to move with any kind of speed."

There was a brief silence as Raven shot her a look that seemed to say *are you sure?*

"Trust me," said Sasha. "C'mon. What are you waiting for? Let's go."

Raven said nothing. Her mind was going a mile a minute and in her head was a little voice trying to talk her into climbing back through the fence and letting Sasha go ahead by herself. But just as her muscles started to act on the impulse, a pair of east-facing firs, having grown up so closely together that a good deal of their branches had become interwoven, shed several huge chunks of wet snow in one fell swoop.

The roar was tremendous, shattering the silence, and the sight of the snow hammering the ground with immense force made any kind of walk, whether towards the State Route or back to the compound, seem to Raven too dangerous a thing to attempt alone. Again, as if something outside of herself was in control, first her left foot moved forward and planted on the narrow path, then the right grudgingly followed suit. Soon she was walking in Sasha's footsteps, all thought of consequence trumped by a heaping pile of age-old peer pressure. A hundred paces from the inner fence, as the forest went from mainly firs and opened up into a grove of birch and oaks, the latter whose orange and red leaves were not completely shed, the two girls cut a ninety-degree turn to their right. A minute later they were standing by the side of the feeder road, out of sight of the middle gate camera, and, to pass the time—while also keeping Raven's mind off of the fact that they were both playing with fire—Sasha proposed they play a game she called *Island Hoppers.*

"The snow is the water and the spots of gravel where it has melted are the islands," she explained. "The navigator goes *island hopping* until she gets stuck and cannot reach another island."

"What happens then?" asked Raven, no longer giving much thought to her mom or whether they were out of range of the camera or not.

"Easy," said Sasha. "Then the next person is the navigator until they get stuck."

"How does someone win?"

"Whoever is navigating when we get to the graves is the winner."

"Graves?" said Raven. She stopped abruptly, swung her gaze to Sasha and thrust her hands into her pockets.

Bear River North Gate

Dregan was in the lead driving the Tahoe. Lined up behind him was the surplus Blazer once belonging to Mikhail and three Humvees, the first two driven by men who were acquaintances and only along due to one negotiated transaction or another. The Humvee bringing up the rear sprouted the turret-mounted MK-19 grenade launcher and was driven by Dregan's brother, Henry.

At exactly eleven-thirty the black and white former Jackson Hole Police cruiser rolled to a stop near the rear gate, a twelve-foot-tall monstrosity clad with rust-streaked corrugated metal and strung through every which way with what had to be a mile-long strand of equally rusted barbed wire.

As heads panned up from what they were doing, the rain resumed, pelting the windshield and putting new pockmarks in the diminishing blanket of snow.

The pair of armed men guarding the gate—both having already been promised certain things by Dregan to look the other way—nodded at him conspiratorially then rolled the wheeled gate open and stepped aside.

After making eye contact with both men—one of whom was Eddie Swain—and nodding subtly their way, Dregan started the Tahoe rolling slowly over the threshold. A few dozen feet on the other side of the gate, just as the single-lane road entered an orchard, he stopped and waited while the other vehicles passed on through.

With the gnarled branches of the skeletal trees reaching for the jouncing trucks from both sides, and clumps of snow heavy with rain pelting the Tahoe's roof, Dregan led the convoy north. They drove through the orchard for half a mile until the road cut a sharp ninety-degree left, where it followed the contour of the land on a gentle downslope west to an eventual merger with the laser-straight stretch of State Route 16 off in the distance.

With the four-wheel-drive still engaged, Dregan drove one-handed through the muddy snow for a spell while he fished Lena's iPhone from his jacket's inner pocket. He reached to the dash and worked the phone lengthwise into a device that looked to either have at one time held a book of tickets or a wide pad of paper positioned nearby for taking notes on the fly. Secured left-of-center on the dash, the apparatus's rubberized arms held the phone firmly in place, almost like it had been designed by Steve Jobs himself. Nearing the bottom of the dip, where the road flattened out prior to the T-junction, Dregan again took his eyes off the road to thumb the device on.

While he waited at the "T" for the four military vehicles to close ranks, he tapped the Video icon and started Lena's wedding montage playing.

The tuned suspension complained as the slightly lowered SUV turned onto the snow-covered two-lane heading northbound. Once forward momentum was established, Dregan looked at the clock on the dash and learned it was a quarter to noon. In his mind's eye he saw Newman being escorted across the rutted street from the makeshift jail to the bookstore-turned-courthouse. In a way he envied the man. Whoever said revenge was a dish best served cold was either fucked in the head or had never been in either of their shoes. Norman got drunk and acted, and from that there was no escaping. There were far too many witnesses. And Ford's warm body to boot. The trial would be quick and the vigilante would be swinging from the hanging tree by one o'clock.

Dregan thought about how it must have felt to gun Ford down with the AK-47. After a second he decided, though very effective, it just wasn't quite as up close and personal as cleaving a sharpened length of steel into the deserving dirtbag's cranium and watching the light ebb from his eyes.

There was no doubt in Dregan's mind. He had been there and done that with his sword. It *was* satisfying, and that was how Lena's murderer needed to go out. Death by ancestral sword. Fitting and final. Peaceful and accepting or kicking and screaming. Either way, he would have closure and life could go on.

He pictured the bailiffs helping Newman through the double doors. He saw the judge in his *chambers,* just a glorified storeroom filled with dusty paperbacks. Right about now, he figured, Pomeroy would be draining the liquid courage from his flask, stuffing random papers under his arm, and standing in the gloom—all anticipatory moves preceding his title and name being barked from beyond the door.

Realizing he had been daydreaming, Dregan cast a glance at the drama playing out on the glossy screen. Pissed that he had missed out seeing Lena on the proposal portion of the strung-together footage, he kept one eye on the road and one on the screen as the bachelor party scene unfolded. Mikhail was pacing back and forth in front of the groomsmen-to-be, his mouth moving and gesticulating with his arms. He was drunk and his slurred words barely rose above the hot air blasting from the Tahoe's vents. Dregan did nothing to remedy this. He knew what was being said. He had been there that night and had bristled as the insecure young man pointed out everything that was wrong with the men—his supposed friends—sitting in a line on the barstools. A portent of what was to come; the bartender was in the background drying and stacking glassware and watching the drunk groom surreptitiously via the mirrored backbar.

There was a sharp jolt as the Tahoe ran over a prone form on the road. He took his eyes from the phone and fixed them dead ahead where the road would soon begin a long uphill climb.

At the top of the rise, the entire white landscape spread out before him. To the left were low foothills, the spiny ridges reaching down towards the road looking like bony fingers filling out a white glove. Straight ahead, miles in the distance was Woodruff looking every bit as dead as it was. To the right of Woodruff, foothills rose up, quickly culminating in the nine-thousand-foot-tall snow-covered peaks of the Bear River Mountain Range. And closer in, on that side, was the big red barn and two-story house with Helen and Ray snugged warmly inside. He flicked his eyes right a few more degrees and walked his gaze over the snowy field all the way to the snaking Bear River's slow-moving waters. There, somewhere between the house and river, was Cleo, the battery in his two-way radio no doubt sapped dead by the cold, freezing his ass off and earning every single thing Dregan had promised.

The radio in the console crackled to life. The voice that came through the speaker was a smoker's, gravelly and booming. "We were talking back here and Peter wants to know if we're picking up Cleo."

Dregan's knuckles suddenly went white as his grip on the steering wheel tightened. A steady throb started at both temples as he pulled to the shoulder and set the brake. On the iPhone's screen, the action was just getting to the part where the bartender shut the party down and singled Mikhail out by calling him 'Mister Rashovic.' Feeling a flush of heat spread to his cheeks, Dregan shut off the heater blower and let the embarrassing moment play through, every word coming out of the tiny speaker suddenly loud and clear. He put his thumb in front of Mikhail's moving image so he didn't have to see his face again. With the other hand, he picked up the two-way, and just when Mikhail was meeting the bartender toe-to-toe on the customer side of the bar and seconds from delivering his trademark line, Dregan spared himself from hearing it again by stabbing his thumb down on the iPhone's power button.

He sat in silence for a few seconds while the Blazer and three Humvees labored up the hill. As they pulled off the road behind the Tahoe, he saw in the rearview another half-dozen trucks and SUVs materialize over a distant rise. Mostly held together with rust and painted the same woodland camouflage pattern as the Blazer, Dregan had gifted them to a Bear River resident named Larry in exchange for a day's worth of armed backup. He watched them for a short while as they slowly closed the distance with the Humvees.

The sun high in the sky glinted off the passenger side windows as the vehicles hit the straight. A tick later as they picked up speed, Dregan saw the prearranged signal delivered when the lead vehicle flashed its high beams three times.

"Peter wants to know ... " Dregan said to himself, the sight of the older military surplus vehicles suddenly making him wish he had eschewed the Tahoe for the Blazer just so he could flick on the stereo and let the flowing notes of Bach or Beethoven bring his stress level down. But he hadn't and, seeing as how there was no way to send Peter back through the gate without racking up more favors than he wished to fulfill, Dregan had no choice but to bring him along.

Clenching his teeth and in as calm a voice as he could summon, he said, "I've got a call to place, Hank. Please send my blonde-haired blue-eyed devil up front. Our plans have just changed."

Chapter 62

Cleo was in the throes of ecstasy … in his dream. If he had been a bystander looking down on his own body stretched out on the old davenport, he would have laughed out loud. Deep in an REM sleep cycle, his eyes were moving rapidly under the lids. Judging by the disconcerting ripple his corneas made as they swept back and forth, pushing against the thin skin there, one would think that in his dream he was on the sidelines and watching an Olympic-caliber game of Ping-Pong.

A thin strand of drool broke free from the corner of his mouth and fell to the small puddle forming next to his head. His long johns were tented in front and he was in the process of giving himself a thorough, albeit, unconscious scratching down there.

Just when the thirty-something woman was about to apply leather to his backside, Cleo felt something altogether different. Had she gone rogue on him? Was that a stun gun crackling back there and about to deliver him into oblivion? His mind reeled. A tick after the initial sensation hit him, his eyes snapped open and he was wondering where in the hell he was.

He remembered a snifter being filled repeatedly. He'd lost count after five, but was pretty sure he hadn't been drugged. Two reasons: One, his own personal rule: he didn't drink with people he didn't know and, more importantly, trust. And two, that he was still alive meant he hadn't been traded away to someone intent on putting him into their stew. He knew enough to stay away from Bear River's seedy underbelly, where things of that nature, though not common, had been known to happen.

The sensation was back. Something vibrating against his backside. He was up in a flash as where he was and why he was here came rushing back to him. Wearing only a dirty wife beater riding high over the red long johns, he was up and stepping into his boots, the radio vibrating madly in his hand.

"Lunch is served," called Helen from the kitchen.

Cleo said nothing. If he didn't answer this he was going to end up as somebody's *lunch*—living or possibly undead. He rushed out the front door and was hit instantly by a sideways-driving drizzle. It was coming in from the northeast and dripping off the porch overhang. And it was still cold, even though the mercury in the old enamel thermometer tacked next to the front door showed the temperature had inexplicably climbed into the low fifties in less than twelve hours.

He thumbed the *Talk* key. "Cleo here," he said, wheezing a little.

"For Christ's sake," barked Dregan. "What took you so long to answer? And why are you breathing like you just left the whorehouse?"

"Feet got tangled in my sleeping bag when I stood up, that's all," he lied.

"You were *sleeping* on the job?"

The lies piled on. "No, Dregan," he said. "I was staying warm and couldn't find the radio."

"What did Ray and Helen do? Did they leave the house?"

Cleo paused for a second, radio clutched in his hand, mind reeling. The further invested in the lies he became, the higher his anxiety level climbed. At the moment he was embroiled in a massive Catch 22. On one hand he wanted to fire up a cigarette. He wanted one so badly he could actually taste the stale, month-old tobacco. However, at the moment, it seemed as if an elephant had parked its substantial backside on his sternum. Breathing was a chore. And the more he lied, the bigger the elephant got.

"Change your batteries," Dregan bawled.

"I'm here," stammered Cleo. "Ray and Helen were inside all night." *A half-truth.*

"And nobody came by?"

"Nope," Cleo said, casting a nervous glance at the door behind him. He released the *Talk* key. A few seconds of dead air. Now Dregan was leaving him hanging. He opened his mouth to ask whether he should get his vehicle and drive to the 39 junction or if he should just walk down and wait by the end of the Thagons' drive. But he didn't get the chance to. Instead, wholly unexpectedly, Dregan let him off the hook. The big man said, "I have enough men. You did a good job. Go on back and warm your old bones by a fire."

"But if I don't go … I don't fulfill *my* part of the deal," Cleo protested.

"Don't worry, old friend. I won't dock you, I'll add an extra couple of tins of snuff. Consider it a tip." There was a pause. Just a handful of seconds. Dregan went on, "Go. I insist."

The last transmission sent the elephant scurrying from Cleo's chest. In his mind, the hangover was gone and he was already at Smead's Tavern, hoisting one, and about to try and lure his favorite brunette back to his place with a fifth of the vodka he had been promised. But he played it cool. He said, "Are you sure you don't need an extra gun? I'm a little stiff and numb from a night out in the elements … I could still—"

Dregan cut him off. "I don't have room for you *anyway*. I just picked up another passenger." His thumb was still depressing the *Talk* key. Cleo heard a rattle and then a kid's voice followed at once by the solid *thunk* of a door closing. He took a deep breath. Fumbled in a nonexistent pocket for a smoke. Realized he was outside, damp and cold, and in his underwear.

"If you insist," Cleo replied. There was another rattle and then the creak of a screen door opening behind him. He craned over his shoulder and quickly powered down the radio.

"What's the word?" Ray asked. He was holding a red felt hat two-fisted and wringing it like a hunk of saltwater taffy.

"I've been relieved."

"Well then I'm relieved. Means neither one of us gets to face Dregan. I was going to give him a piece of my mind for sending you to spy on me." He thought: *Shut up Ray. Switzerland.*

Like an Etch A Sketch given a good hard shake, the look of elation instantly drained from Cleo's face. "You're not going to—"

"Tell Dregan you spent the night under the enemy's roof?" Ray put the hat on his head and cracked a mirthless smile. "I won't spill if you don't. Deal?"

Cleo's face lit back up. He was flashing the rotting picket of teeth again. "Deal," he said. "Now *I* need a smoke."

***

Dregan had just set the radio aside and the tail end of one of his famous one-minute staring sessions was drawing near. Counting down from sixty in his head had saved him from half a dozen murder charges over the course of his lifetime. Murder wasn't necessarily on the table here—a good old-fashioned ass whipping was.

The boy tried to speak.

Dregan held a hand up to silence him. Took the brake off and wheeled them north, the sweet taste of revenge oh so close to being realized instantly edging out the anger he was feeling toward his boy.

Chapter 63

From working a garden nearly year-round, Glenda's hands were sinewy and didn't tire easily—two attributes that came in handy with the task at hand. She began working Brook's lower back—softening her up for the pain to come—with what the younger nurse had affectionately dubbed her *'man's touch.'* While painful at the onset, Glenda's self-taught technique worked wonders at breaking down the built-up collagen fibers, which in turn was helping to increase the range of motion in Brook's right shoulder and neck.

For the first few seconds, as her hips were pushed hard into the thin mattress and the bones there made soft popping noises, Brook was swept away from all of the madness of the last few months, and she imagined she was in a high-end spa, enjoying a soothing soundtrack of new-age music accompanied by the sweet aroma of jasmine and sandalwood. Then, in her mind's eye—not in a sexual way at all—she envisioned some guy named *Sven's* muscled hands digging into corded tissue on the periphery of the shiny dinner-plate-sized mass.

She closed her eyes, enduring the initial discomfort until the nerve endings deep within the old wound woke up screaming bloody murder and sent a tsunami of pain signals flooding her brain. No stranger to this part of her rehab, with both hands she grabbed the horizontal bar by her head—the same bar she had zip-tied herself to that fateful day—and, grunting into her pillow, rode the initial wave out.

Thirty minutes of deep tissue work later, Glenda had transitioned from *man's touch* mode and was delivering feathery caresses on pressure points where energy was supposed to transit the body. This went on for fifteen minutes, during which Brook drifted off into a near trance-like state.

The final fifteen minutes or so of the now bi-weekly hour-long session were dedicated to something Glenda called *reiki* that Brook had learned just the basics about from one of her coworkers back at the hospital in Portland. Never one to really deviate from conventional medicine, she initially had no idea if it was some kind of mumbo jumbo or an established and accepted alternate therapy. With nothing to lose and a long way to go to getting back to normal, she had kept her mind open and was the better for it. For this had become the part of Glenda's efforts—totally devoid of touch or pressure or penetrating oils—that seemed most therapeutic.

Now, Brook's eyes were open and she watched Glenda move her open hands over certain areas on her body, letting them hover there, her face a mask of concentration. Before the first session, the older woman had confided in Brook that she had been practicing reiki for a number of years and, though she was loath to admit it to her AA fellowship—which didn't matter now because, sadly, she figured them to all be dead or undead—she believed it to have been a great help in her recovery from alcohol addiction.

"Almost finished," said Glenda. "Once you're one hundred per cent I want you to learn this so you can return the favor."

Brook smiled. "I owe you so much, Glenda. Without your calming influence on this group, I think we would have disintegrated. Maybe even ended up all going our separate ways."

"I was a soccer coach and den mother for the boys. Louie didn't want any part of it." Glenda smiled and sat back in the folding chair. "I guess it's in my blood."

Brook said nothing. She had pulled a tee on and rolled over onto her stomach.

Glenda covered her with a thin sheet. She looked at Max, who was curled up on the floor by the door, his bony ribs rising and falling, a steady rhythm to his breathing. "Get some rest," she said. "When should I reel the girls in?"

"Give them a little more time," mumbled Brook. "Half an hour or so."

"Max?"

The dog perked up.

"He stays," said Brook. "Thanks again for nursing a nurse."

"Sleep tight," Glenda said, unclipping the two-way radio from Brook's pants that were balled up on the floor by the foot of the bed. Before she had risen and pocketed the Motorola and halved the distance to the door, Brook was making snorting noises. And by the time she had let herself out and was closing the steel door to the Grayson quarters behind her, the chainsaw-like rattle of Brook snoring was in full swing.

***

Sasha hadn't been joking about visiting the graves of the fallen. Her reasoning for venturing up on the sloping hillside was to take a peek at the flowers Raven had recently adorned them with.

The two spent the better part of thirty minutes playing *island hopper*. Then, with the back side of the hidden gate in sight, abruptly and without warning, Sasha abandoned the game and cut another ninety-degree turn to her right and led Raven on a wild goose chase through the forest just inside the tree line.

Ten or fifteen minutes spent chasing the redhead around trees and through thick undergrowth had taken a toll on Raven. When she finally caught up to Sasha, she found the older girl sitting high up on the corner post where the fence stopped its parallel run with 89 and at a right angle snaked back into the forest in the compound's general direction.

Translucent bars of sunlight filtered in from above. Save for Raven's labored breathing, it was quiet here. There wasn't even a bickering blackbird or chattering wren to be heard in this lonely corner of the property.

Hands planted on her knees, Raven gulped air until the throbbing in her head subsided enough so that she could stand up straight. But when she did so she was met with the much sharper pain of her still knitting ribs telling her to slow down and take it easy.

"Why did you run away like that?" she asked.

"Would you have followed me if I hadn't?"

"Probably not."

"Are you glad you did?"

"Yes," Raven admitted, a toothy smile creasing her face. The exhilaration from being alone outside the wire … well, not *technically* outside the wire, but away from all of the adults—her parents especially—was a feeling unlike any she had ever experienced. The only thing she could remember that was even close to it was when she and Mom escaped the zombies overrunning Fort Bragg aboard the hulking twin-rotor helicopter. That wasn't quite the same, she supposed. Sure, the danger had been real, but at Bragg there were five or six armed soldiers and another twenty women and children aboard the '*bird*', as her dad liked to call helicopters, no matter the number of blades spinning over it.

Her nerves had been afire then, and she was feeling that same nervous energy crackling through her body now.

"C'mon," said Sasha. "I saw something over here by the road I want to show you." She reached down and offered her hand. Helped Raven up and over and then swung her own legs past the top post and lowered herself to the ground.

Once again, Sasha took the lead. Staying inside the tree line, they continued paralleling the 39, and after ten or so paces the redhead stopped and pointed through the thinning trees in the direction of the road.

By now, snow was falling off the trees like sailors jumping a sinking ship. Both girls donned their stocking caps as the fat white clumps splashed to the ground with audible wet plops.

Raven smelled the corpse before she saw it. Crinkling her nose against the sweet carrion stench, she parted a spray of ferns bigger than her and came face to butt with an adult zombie. It was stalled out, kind of like an ancient Egyptian hieroglyph, arms seemingly in motion, both bent at the elbow but hanging down at its sides. Its ashen white face was stuck in a permanent scowl, teeth bared and eyes '*peeled wide*' as silly old Duncan would have said if he were here.

"Told you they aren't moving yet," said Sasha, sliding her knife from its sheath.

Yet, thought Raven. Made her think of Glenda constantly telling Duncan about the *'yets'* he hadn't quite gotten around to. She didn't quite understand where the term came from, but this thing in front of her had moved recently. Behind each of its bare heels was a two-inch scuff in the snow. And as she exited the bushes first to get a closer look, she could have sworn its milky eyeballs moved ever so slightly.

"Kill it," said Sasha, thrusting her knife in Raven's direction, handle first as Wilson had taught her.

Raven said nothing. Eyes gone as wide as the smelly zombie's, she regarded the offered blade and shook her head side-to-side, delivering a vehement *'no way Jose'*, charades style.

Arm at full extension and knife held rather delicately—kind of like a diaper containing an especially juicy load—Sasha's body language said: *I'm not doing it.*

"We've been gone about an hour," said Raven. "Let's go back."

Putting the knife away, Sasha said, "I still want to see the graves. Real quick … then we'll call your mom and tell her we're coming back."

"The clearing is that way," Raven said, pointing to her left at the oval of light thirty feet down the road.

Once again, Sasha took off without stating her intention. This time she stalked off across the road at a diagonal in the direction of the clearing, parted more ferns and disappeared into the forested gloom.

Thankful Sasha didn't haul into a sprint this time, Raven shot a final worried look at the putrefying corpse and followed her new friend dutifully and without question as she delved into the woods opposite of where they had just emerged.

Sasha had fought through the undergrowth like she had an idea of where she was going. When the two parted the final phalanx of drooping ferns and ground-hugging scrub, they were standing on a muddy, snow-dotted, single-lane road. Left for nature to reclaim long ago, the uneven track rose up slowly while simultaneously curving right-to-left, where it was eventually swallowed up by the trees lining it.

***

After a fifty- or sixty-yard uphill slog, where the road began to level out, Sasha came to a halt and pointed out a scrap of fabric someone had tied to a low branch of a juvenile tree growing up on their left.

Raven looked at it and shrugged as if to say: *So?*

"Do you know where we are?"

"Behind the place where Phillip got bit," stated Raven, confidently.

"Nope."

"Where then? Cut out the spy routine and tell me." Raven's cheeks were flushed, her breathing rapid. She didn't know it yet, but she was one cryptic response away from experiencing her first ever full-blown anxiety attack.

"Jamie brought me up here not long after we all arrived from Colorado Springs. She said this is where her and Jordan got the jump on someone who was spying on them. Led to Duncan and Logan setting an ambush down there on the road. She said they took out a bunch of bandits some bad guy she called Chance brought back here from Huntsville."

"I remember hearing about that," said Raven. "Why didn't we just cross the road down below and climb the hill directly?"

"The camera, duh." Sasha slipped by the tree and her elbow brushed the fabric, sending it bobbing like a worm on the end of a fish hook. "If we're not seen outside the wire … were we outside the wire?

Chewing on that nugget of teen wisdom, Raven followed after, dodging left and right to avoid clumps of snow suddenly letting loose as Sasha threaded her way forward.

The hide was half a dozen of Sasha's long strides from the forest road. Raven reached it in ten of her own and a couple of seconds after losing sight of the bobbing yellow and white cap. When the packed dirt trail went soft underfoot, the instinct to see why drew her eyes toward the dry patch of ground opening up before her. However, when she looked back up to survey the graves through the portal in the foliage, there was a green-eyed man with a dark bushy beard towering over her. One of his large hands was already clamped over Sasha's nose and mouth and he was holding her off the ground. The older girl's cap was pulled down, partially covering her widened eyes. In the man's other balled fist was a black pistol, its barrel pointing right at Raven. The sight of Sasha in peril and kicking at the man's legs started Raven's heart battering her ribcage and the old injury there aching. In the next beat, her first real anxiety attack was robbing her breath and choking off any chance of the developing scream ever escaping her throat. The rest was a blur as her knees buckled and stars popped and flashed in front of her eyes like a fireworks display. The last thing she remembered was the cool ground pressing her cheek and hearing the man telling someone out of sight in rapid-fire delivery about *capturing two girls.*

Chapter 64

The gunfire had lasted all of twenty seconds. There were three or four staccato ripples as the three survivors chose their targets and fired. Cade had watched it go down through the high power scope, wincing with every report, which in his mind equated to one wasted bullet. Kick 'em when they're down is how he had been trained to take the fight to the enemy. With the enemies of his old life, violence of action applied swiftly and without mercy had been what kept him tap dancing on the right side of the dirt. However, in this new world where there would be no factories churning out 5.56 or 9mm rounds by the millions, (at least not in the near future, by any stretch of the imagination) survival would depend on scrimping and stockpiling, using the ammo sparingly to train the kids or throwing lead downrange only when there was no other viable option. And with the arrival of the Chinese scouts on American soil, the latter, he feared, may happen sooner rather than later.

A dozen Zs coming to life and making that nerve-jangling noise all at once, while disconcerting as hell, by no means constituted a clear and present danger to the young trio. But he wasn't there in the midst of the dead, so who was he to judge? He wasn't their leader, that was established the day he hung his hat at the compound. He made a mental note to bring it up again at dinner when everyone could contribute to the conversation. A little reminder, he figured, would be better than an ass chewing. Live and learn—another motto Mike Desantos favored—would have to suffice.

Five short minutes after leaving the house on the hill and letting Lev off on the shoulder of Ogden Canyon Road, Cade found himself lugging the plow truck around in an ungainly three-point-turn. Bones snapped under the weight of the partially loaded truck, and flesh and internals were ground into a paste as he man-handled the front wheels over the soft shoulder to get them facing in the desired direction. Once the wicked blade was facing east, he reversed the rig a dozen yards until the feeder road to the boat launch/day use area was off his left shoulder. The 4Runner was just a handful of yards away, backed up the entry road a short distance, the sun glare winking off its windshield.

Cars, trucks, and SUVs took up every available slot on the blacktop sprawl. Surrounding the inert vehicles and cinderblock structure rising up in their midst were tents of every shape and color, a good number of them collapsed under the weight of the snow. Sprawled out in death poses, the now twice-dead putrefying cadavers crowded every available square inch of real estate.

Duncan lowered the Steiners and looked to Cade. "Lev made it to the others." He set the binoculars aside and stretched his bowed legs in the footwell. "East to Eden, young man."

"Eden is north of our twenty," Cade replied, not bothering to look at the older man. "Or mightn't you be talking about the Steinbeck novel *East of Eden*?"

"Never mind, *Socrates*," grumbled Duncan. "Just get us there before the rest of the rotters come back to life. If I remember right, mister ... *we'll cull them on the way back* ... there's still a few hundred we left standing on the State Route between here and the compound."

"Would have had to deal with them regardless," Cade stated. He selected *Drive*, lowered the polished plow to within an inch of the steaming blacktop and, holding the wheel straight, started the multi-ton snowplow rolling.

The engine whined and Cade imagined the gray-black exhaust belching from the vertical stacks. As the rig picked up speed, a mixture of slush and body parts, frothy and reddish-black, shot from the blade in two different directions. In less time than it had taken him to turn the truck around, there was a straight path plowed through the dead and nothing but a steaming stretch of body-free blacktop laid out before them.

"What was that all about?" asked Duncan loud enough to be heard over the sharp jangling racket that was entering the cab.

Cade worked the controls, bringing the blade up a few inches. The metallic pinging ceased.

"Last thing I want is for us to have to come back to this side of the reservoir and help the Kids change a tire."

"Ounce of prevention ..." mumbled Duncan.

"Exactly." Cade maneuvered the plow truck through the sweeping left-hander at just under the posted fifty, then swept his gaze northbound at Huntsville as the Ogden River, glittering silver and gold, flashed under them. After the river crossing, with Dave's BBQ and Rhonda's Reservoir Requisites standing out like sore thumbs a few blocks west, 39 became Highway 166 where Cade wheeled the rumbling truck through yet another sweeping left-hand turn.

"I hope Oliver and Daymon made a big dent in the Eden dead," Duncan said. "Because this fella's knees are about shot."

"My pack," Cade said. "Side pocket right you'll find 200 milligram Ibuprofen. Take what you need."

They kept to a long and scenic straight stretch west with the Pineville Reservoir filling up the window on the left, and Duncan popping pills with a real good view of the snow-peppered foothills ringing Eden to the right. He was washing the half-dozen little pills down with a bottled water when 166 jogged back to the north and some unknown mountains, craggy and white, filled up the windshield. "Eden's seen better days," he noted as the fire-ravaged town became visible ahead.

"Misery loves company," Cade said. "I saw the fire from the air. Eden was throwing off embers like crazy and ended up taking Huntsville down with it."

"Glenda did say this was the hottest summer they had seen in a long time."

"Global warming at work," Cade said, knowing it would elicit a response from Duncan.

"Bullshit," the older man bellowed. "Manufactured fear so that that loud-mouthed, private-jet-owning enviropuke could jam us up with more taxes and restrictions. Don't get me started."

"Looks like I just did. So, why don't you tell me how you really feel," Cade said, the beginnings of a laugh bouncing around in his ribcage.

"Look out," wailed Duncan, as a pair of Zs rose up from the roadside a truck's length ahead and loped a couple of paces toward the plow's edge.

Cade jerked the wheel right. "Got 'em." The twin impacts sounded like gong strikes, deep and sonorous and lasting for a couple of seconds. The top of the blade vibrated briefly and then, like a big orange whale that had swallowed something disagreeable, the walking corpses were catapulted left and right, respectively.

Duncan grimaced. "You missed the point. I was trying to warn you in time to *avoid* them."

"I wanted to see what it could handle," Cade said. "Just in case."

Duncan said nothing. He pressed his back into the seat, arms folded, and looked out the window at the damage wrought on the town by the out of control wildfire. Charred foundations and skeletal remnants of humans and vehicles slid by on both sides. The street signs remained, but they had accumulated so much creosote that reading what was on them was nearly impossible. *The Earth abides*, he thought darkly.

Cade eased off the gas and looked toward what he guessed had been the town center. "I don't see the Land Cruiser."

Duncan put a hand on the dash and leaned forward. "I've got nothing," he said.

"Try the two-way."

Duncan dug it out and thumbed the *Talk* button. *Nothing.* He tried one more time and when there was still no answer, Lev broke over the channel sounding concerned.

Duncan brought Lev up to speed and told him to stay put while he and Cade went to check the one obvious place the missing pair might be.

Chapter 65

The junction where 39 and 16 came to a "T" was for the most part unchanged from the day before when Dregan had come through. The bus was still on its side. The ditch where he had found Lena and Mikhail, though no longer filled in with drifted snow, served both as a reminder to them all as to what went down here weeks ago, and what *he* still had to accomplish before he could finally achieve that sense of closure he longed for.

Driving one-handed, he crossed himself and looked out his side window to the blue sky above. The prayer he said was a simple one. Merely a request to God to make sure Lena was taken care of and would rest well with the angels for all of eternity. For he knew that if he carried out this mission the way he had played it out over and over in his mind hundreds of times already, the justice meted out by him under God's watchful eye, based on his firm beliefs from decades of being reminded of the Commandments, would amount to nothing less for him than a one-way ticket to eternal damnation.

With that gloomy thought settling in, he slowed and pulled the Tahoe just to the right of the decaying drift of corpses the former police cruiser had been high-centered on when he had found it already stripped of the radio and drained of most of its gasoline. Not a bad find considering the circumstances. All he had to do was scrape the former owner's brains off the headliner and put a square of foam over the cloth driver's seat where several pints of the man's blood had soaked in.

He rattled the shifter into *Park*. He looked sidelong at Peter. "Stay here," he growled as he shouldered the door open and stepped out onto the blacktop.

He strode down the two-lane past the Blazer and the two middle Humvees and stopped beside the Humvee driven by his brother, Henry. The door was ajar and an awful smelling gray whorl of cigarette smoke was wafting out.

"Why are we stopping here?' asked Henry. Smoke curled from his nostrils as he stared his older brother down.

"Equipment check," said Dregan gruffly. "Get the launcher manned. I want a round dropped into the middle of the herd."

"Futile," said Henry. "Sure the concussion'll drop the lot of 'em, but they're going to get right back up. Most of them at least." He blew smoke from his nose. "Chances of a little piece of shrapnel piercing skull and scrambling brain … highly unlikely."

"Hank … let me do the thinking. I simply asked that you make sure the thing isn't going to jam up on us when we get to where we're going."

"You're planning on using this on breathers?"

"If I have to," said Dregan. He stepped back as Henry blew another plume of smoke between the door pillar and flicked the butt past his face.

"Step back a few more paces, then." Henry closed his door, jockeyed the Humvee back and forth and pulled the squat rig out of the five-slot and to the head of the column.

Dregan watched this and then bent his gaze to the herd. It was clear that since he'd dismounted and the dead had become aware of the convoy, the ones still standing were beginning to turn in place, moving about half as fast as normal—which wasn't saying much, unless you were directly in their path and had no way of changing that part of the equation.

There was a squeal of brakes as the Humvee with Henry at the wheel came to a halt near the overturned school bus. A figure emerged from the turret. Shoulders and a stocking cap, mostly. A handful of seconds passed before Dregan heard his brother bellow, "Going hot." This caused a lot of heads at the far away front of the herd to begin a slow swivel his way.

Three more seconds passed and, in the same gravelly voice, Henry hollered, "Fire in the hole." There was a hollow *thwomp* and with his naked eye Dregan saw the projectile arc up—trailing a wisp of smoke in its wake for the first thirty feet or so—and then come down in the middle of the gathered dead. There was a concussive *whoomp* and bodies toppled in a sort of concentric ring as the middle third of the shuffling procession was slapped to the wet blacktop by the expanding shockwave.

Dregan put the two-way radio to his mouth. He wanted to get an idea of what he had to work with. He thumbed the *Talk* button. "Give me one more straight north down the centerline"—nearly all of the solid yellow stripe was visible by now—"maximum range."

Henry went through the same procedure, calling out *going hot* and then *fire in the hole*. Something he probably lifted from an actor's dialogue in *Band of Brothers* or something similar, mused Dregan. He heard the *thwomp* but failed to track the projectile. However, a handful of seconds later the explosion was impossible to miss as the grenade landed near a stalled-out car and window glass was sent flying to all points of the compass, glittering like chaff kicked out of a fighter jet, before falling to earth and skittering across the roadway.

Dregan liked what he saw. Though he was no expert with this weapon, he gathered the launcher's maximum range to be two thousand yards, give or take a few.

He smiled. "I've seen enough," he said into the radio, even as he was climbing back into the Tahoe.

***

Ten minutes removed from the impromptu firepower display, with the Tahoe back in the lead, the eleven-vehicle convoy had squeezed by the blockage at the junction single file, every one of them trading a little paint with the bus's undercarriage.

***

Another ten minutes slipped into the past and the convoy was a few miles west of the junction when Dregan slowed the Tahoe and let it coast to a stop adjacent to the lower and upper quarry roads. With Peter looking on expectantly, he called up Gregory on the two-way radio to see what, if anything, he had learned from his captives.

***

A handful of miles west of the quarry, Gregory was dividing a Hershey's bar into thirds. Keeping the smallest piece for himself—a calculated move he hoped wouldn't go unnoticed—he offered the two larger squares of milk chocolate to the girls.

Nose curled, Sasha said, "What's the white stuff?"

"It's past its sell by date … sorry," said the bearded man. "Most everything is getting that way now."

"I'll pass on being hand-fed by Paul Bunyon," said Sasha, turning her head away.

Raven shook her head vehemently at the offering.

The man shrugged and smiled, big and toothy.

Fake, thought Raven.

He wrapped the chocolate in the foil. "I'll save it in case you change your mind." The wedge of foil went into his pocket and no sooner had he shifted and scooped up his rifle, there was a soft little chirp emanating from inside the same pocket.

A phone, thought Raven as she watched with rapt attention. About all she *could* do. Her arms, like Sasha's, were bound behind her with a piece of rope the man had unraveled and cut from the bracelet he had been wearing. It was the same kind of thing her dad wore on his wrist, only the man's was a bright hunter's orange and Dad's was olive green. Amazingly, she could feel her fingers. So far this—her first experience as a hostage—was nothing like she had seen on television. A few minutes after she had walked in on Sasha being taken forcibly, the notion that they were in immediate danger of unspeakable things happening to them vanished.

In fact, both she and Sasha had already begun trying to work free of their bonds and it seemed as if he was none the wiser. Not exactly the sharpest knife in the drawer, Sasha had mouthed just a minute ago while the man rooted around in his backpack for the chocolate, with his rifle propped on the dead snag and his back facing them.

So as the man who called himself Gregory dug into his pocket for whatever was making the electronic noise, Raven situated herself so that her hands were near the jagged end of a broken branch sticking vertically from the fallen log she was seated on.

The man pulled out a radio similar in size to the Motorola he had confiscated from Sasha—aside from tying them up—the only smart move on his part thus far. He pressed a button on the chirping device and answered with a simple *yes*. At once a voice emanated from the speaker: "What have you learned?"

"The girls say they are orphans," Gregory answered. "They were taken in by missionaries who started mistreating them. They say they were running away when they stumbled onto my position."

Watching Sasha bury her face in her knees, Raven suppressed a smile.

"What?" said the raspy voice, incredulous.

"That's what they told me, Dad. The older one … says she's seventeen. She had a radio and a knife. The younger one … says she's ten. She had a knife and says she is allergic to bees."

Again Raven pushed back against the urge to laugh out loud. She felt the cord hot against her wrists and continued to move it back and forth, short sawing motions, applying as much pressure as she dared.

"Allergic to bees?" said the voice. "What the hell does that have to do with Lena?"

"The younger girl … she has one of those EpiPen-looking things hanging around her neck. I let her keep it, though. Just in case she gets stung."

"They're tied up, right?"

"Yep."

"First off, there's no bees out collecting pollen this time of year. Secondly, you dolt, how's she going to use it if she's tied up." The last part wasn't posed as a question. Gregory, though, didn't catch it. He was about to talk but was cut off. "What about Lena?" The voice was gruff and direct and there was no mistaking this as anything other than a question.

"I didn't ask about Lena," answered Gregory, eyes darting to the girls. "I figured I'd leave that to you."

"Take the EpiPen thing from the girl and keep your eye on them."

The call dropped off.

"Zombie apocalypse or not ... aren't you a little old to still be living with your *dad*?" asked Raven.

Gregory said nothing. He rose and stretched then took Sasha's knife from high up where he had stabbed it into the towering pine's trunk. He wiped the pitch from the blade onto his pants. Then, careful not to nick skin, he cut the EpiPen from Raven's neck, and without inspecting the metallic cylinder, stowed it in his right front jacket pocket.

After the blade was no longer near her neck, Raven stared up at him, the look in her eyes more like one she reserved for a stray animal dead in the road or a toddler Z who never had a chance to experience living. Her eyes tracked his hand as he stuck the knife back into the tree next to hers. She figured even if she was standing on a pair of stilts there would be no way for her to reach either one of them—the guy was just that big.

"This should be over in no time," the man finally said. "Then you two can go back to wherever you came from." He smiled and Raven took note, thinking it to be genuine.

"Why the fuck are you holding us then?" Sasha spat. "Let us go and you won't *die* like all the others."

"Shut up," Raven blurted. "You got us into this hole, Sash. No need to keep on digging."

"Quit fighting," said the man, a pained look on his face. "I promise I won't hurt you as long as you don't give me any reason to. Just be patient ... you are not our problem. Whoever killed my sister is our problem." The man turned his attention to the curved stretch of road beyond the clearing.

Sasha and Raven locked eyes for a second. Then Sasha flicked her gaze to her knife, an unspoken message Raven took to mean they weren't just going to run if given the chance. So, with the cold finger of dread tickling the short hairs at the nape of her neck, she went back to work dragging the rope along the jagged protrusion at her back.

Chapter 66

Sitting on a berm of slowly melting snow eight thousand feet above sea level and roughly eight miles northwest of downtown Eden, Utah, Oliver Gladson inhaled mightily and then passed the feather-adorned roach clip to his new partner in crime. Hands now free, he put the tips of both index fingers to his lips and crossed his eyes. Pretending he was new at this, he bobbled his head back and forth like one of those dolls given out as souvenirs at a Jazz game. Finished clowning, he moved his mouth fish-like, producing one ever-growing smoke ring after another.

Meanwhile, Daymon was simultaneously relighting the joint and puffing on the little nub, trying to get it to spark. "Roll another," he said, suddenly feeling light-headed from the trifecta of altitude, heavy cardio—the most he'd done in weeks—and good 'ol Mary Jane, which he had not partaken in since the earliest days of the Omega outbreak.

"All gone," said Oliver, choking the words out along with the last little curls of smoke he had been holding back. "There's some in my bag in the truck. And even more at the house"—his eyes went wide and he smiled—"lots more."

Daymon pulled his goggles down over his eyes, more so to guard against the blazing noon sun than the intermittent wind gusts. The temperature was still hovering near freezing at the top of Eden View where they were sitting. Not so much though a third of the way down the black diamond run, where the air had an almost physical presence to it. Inversion layer, he thought it was called. He snugged his new gloves on and picked up his poles. He crossed the poles, speared the tips into the topsoil and lifted himself off the snow. Standing, he turned his head and fixed a stare on Oliver, who was still sitting with his back propped against one of the three Powder Canyon snowmobiles they had liberated from an equipment shed in order to ferry themselves up the ski hill. "Last night you kind of dodged my question," Daymon said, feeling even more light-headed after standing. "Never did hear how you made it all the way from Oregon to Huntsville unscathed."

Oliver pushed off of the snowmobile and stood on his battered skis. "I avoided the *deadheads* by traveling only at night." A little buzzed, he laughed at the irony in the name he'd chosen to call the infected. "Ogden was real hairy. If it wasn't for the night vision goggles along with the rifle and bags of weed I found in a dead redneck's SUV … I'd be dead myself now, or worse … I'd be a *deadhead* like them. After making it through the city on foot, I rode a bike up the North Ogden Canyon highway and found it blocked."

"Glenda escaped by bike, too," Daymon said, indifferently. "So you backtracked to the south pass."

"Yep," admitted Oliver. "And lucky for me the deadheads had somehow breached it—"

"It's sealed up now," said Daymon, explaining how they'd left the gravel-filled plow trucks shoring up the containers. He went on, "And your mind's gonna be blown when you see the setup we have going on at the compound."

"I just want to see my mom again. That'll make everything I went through to get here all worthwhile." He smiled a dumb stoner's smile and donned his goggles. They were the two-lens type that made him look like a World War I fighter ace. All he needed to complete the look was a flowing scarf and a Sopwith Camel biplane. He opened his mouth to say something, then closed it and pointed down mountain with his poles.

The blaze-orange plow truck was impossible to miss. The plow was in the down position and twin feathery plumes were spewing off to the sides, painting the guardrails and trees with dirty brown snow.

"Shit!" Daymon exclaimed. He looked at his watch. *Quarter of noon. Fuck.* He had totally lost track of time. Being high hadn't helped at all. The plan had been to get one or two runs in and return to Eden and begin clearing dead from the remaining houses. The first part had gone off without a hitch. During the two hours between sunup and when their decision to check out the resort was fomented, they had left ten city blocks strewn with Z corpses. The latter part of their hastily constructed and ill-advised plan, not so much. He reached into his new jacket and pulled the radio from an inner pocket. Found the volume turned way down. *Shit, shit, shit.* He turned it up halfway and shook his head. "They'll call when they see the rig in the lot."

Pushing off with his poles, Daymon launched down the hill, planted the once-pristine pair of thousand-dollar skis perpendicular to the fifty-five degree incline, and shot for a patch of virgin snow drifted deep between two stunted pines. The skis were parabolic twin-tip models, lightweight and highly maneuverable—all of which didn't matter one bit with only half a foot of accumulated snow in places and a lot less everywhere else. Sparks lanced from his edges with each rock strike, and the racket of the juddering bases grinding over hidden obstacles was earsplitting. But Daymon was in heaven doing something he thought never again possible.

The weathered tree trunks whipped by in his peripheral vision, one on each side, and he was making quick turns toward a small outcropping he had been working his nerve up to drop from. In deep powder conditions and on his home mountain he would not have thought twice before hucking off a similar cliff band and attempting the maneuver his newly acquired Salomon 1080 skis were named for. But today, in these conditions and with none of his old Ski Patrol buddies around to scrape him off the hillside if he fucked up, pulling a ten-eighty—with, or without sticking a sick grab—was not going to happen. And there wasn't enough weed in the Land Cruiser below to get him high enough to take one more run and follow through. So instead he tucked his poles and shot off the outcropping at an angle parallel to the mountain and let his knees absorb the rather hard landing.

Now on the second pair of identical skis, and tacking a second high speed run onto them, he could literally feel the base layer being abraded away, and started catching chemical-laced whiffs off the melting P-Tex. So to ensure he didn't have to walk the rest of the way down, he tucked again and rode the second half of the hill without getting air while staying away from the ever-growing patches where the rocks and dirt and grass was showing through.

With no idea if Oliver was behind him or not, Daymon hit the end of the marked trail and, just like the old days, rode his momentum all the way into the parking lot and came to a grinding halt beside the looming orange plow truck where he received a well-earned double dose of stink eye from Cade and Duncan.

Duncan was standing near the gore-encrusted plow blade, arms crossed and looking like he had something to say.

Daymon tossed his poles down, clicked out of the thrashed skis, and kicked them aside. Sweating profusely, he unzipped the jacket to his waist. Feeling eyes boring into him, he ignored Cade, who was looking down on him from behind the big rig's steering wheel, and instead took the path of least resistance. He looked over to Duncan, who was standing by the driver's side door, and knitted a brow. "What?" he said rather sheepishly.

Before Duncan could unload one barrel, let alone both on the dreadlocked man, there was a harsh grating racket and Oliver skied onto the parking lot with sparks flying off his edges. Following Daymon's line, he made it to within a dozen feet of the UDOT truck where his momentum bled off and he stepped out of the still smoking skis.

"What in the hell," exclaimed Duncan, "do we have here?" He gave the two a quick once over then answered his own question. "Let's see, there's a black guy with dreadlocks and a white guy wearing a hat sprouting fake dreadlocks"—Oliver flashed a lopsided smile at that and peeled off the novelty ski cap—"and if I didn't know any better I would have thought I was looking at two-thirds of the Jamaican bobsled team. Only you two are dressed nowhere like that class act. Wearing all that neon makes you look like a couple of Technicolor dildos who've lost their way and ended up on the mountain." He pointed in the general direction of Eden. "The porno convention is down there. You dolts must have taken a wrong turn in that four-by-wanna-be Cadillac."

Skis, poles, and gloves shed, Oliver, still clad in a neon green ski ensemble and clunky boots, approached cautiously.

Daymon said nothing but looked to Oliver, a stupid pot-affected grin spreading across his face.

"Why yes, yes we did," said Oliver, sounding rather disingenuous.

Finally, somewhat composed, Daymon peeled off his goggles. "How'd you find us?" he asked.

Duncan shifted his weight and leaned against the truck. "The first dead giveaway was the SUV-sized hole in the front of the ski shop at the base of the hill."

"The accordion security gate was closed and locked," Daymon protested. "The Kids have the bolt cutters so we had to improvise."

Duncan said, "Cade here put two and two together and we followed the Powder Mountain Ski Resort signs. Hell, they've got one every hundred feet leading up to here like breadcrumbs. Must have had a hell of an advertising budget."

"Nope … just steep lift ticket prices," Oliver proffered, stoned eyes glittering. "And the Salt Lake and Ogden douchebags don't even blink at paying them."

"Didn't," added Daymon. "Past tense. They're *all* gone now."

Duncan changed the subject. "We drove through what's left of Eden. Good job coming in. What'd it take you, all of an hour to put them down?"

"Thirty minutes," said Oliver, his grin fading. "I already started in on them yesterday."

Arm and head hanging out the plow truck window, Cade asked, "And the North Ogden Pass … is it still blocked?"

"Real good," Oliver said. "I got a car running a while back, waited until full dark and drove up to get a look at it from this side. Even glowing green you could tell whoever threw it up meant business. In addition to the shipping containers—kind of what Daymon said you all did up at the south pass—these folks left the trucks they used to haul the containers up there nosed in against the barricade. Tires weren't flattened, though." He looked up at Cade. "That was genius."

"Well, hell," drawled Duncan. "Why didn't you *boys* answer the radio then?"

Like a mountain lion waiting to pounce, Oliver began, "Just cause you're doinking my mom—"

Cutting him off at the pass, Duncan said, "Whoever told you that is full of shit."

"Daymon told me all about you two," Oliver said, fingers on both hands curling into fists. "Don't think you're going to slide in and try and fulfill some father-figure fantasy of yours using me as a stand in for little boy lost"—as the man talked, Duncan's shoulders slumped and he began to worry his silver goatee—"in case it slipped your mind already … I just buried *my* dad behind that house."

Daymon looked away as Duncan pushed off the truck and took a step toward Oliver. "You don't have a thing to worry about, Oliver. I am the farthest thing from Louie you will ever encounter. Drunken degenerate gamblers just do not make good father material. That's why I never had any kids of my own … that I know of, anyway." He chuckled at his own funny. Then the chuckle became the full-blown crazy man cackle he was known to belt out now and again, which drove Oliver back to the Land Cruiser where he promptly lit up a joint and started changing from the ski gear back into his makeshift armor and hiking boots.

"Let's go, mon," Daymon said in a passable Jamaican accent. "Best be getting before all of deese dead be wakin up." He clapped Duncan on the shoulder, whispered in his ear, "You can be my daddy anytime." Now Daymon's pot-fueled crazy man laugh was on display.

"You gonna be alright to drive?" Duncan asked.

"Yes, Daddy …" Daymon said as he turned and clomped off towards the Land Cruiser, shedding the Day-Glo ski garb as he went.

Chapter 67

Gregory had relocated the girls to a patch of damp ground opposite the log where he could see them as he took down his tent. To Raven, the thing looked like something one would get in the Kid's section at *Ikea*. God, how she missed going there and getting all of those little containers and stationaries that she used to keep her desk back home so organized. She hated it when thoughts of the way things used to be crept in out of the blue on account of some stupid unrelated observation. Worst of all was the day she came to the realization that she would never again hear the familiar tune of the ice cream truck. Nor would she ever again have to battle the Pavlovian response it triggered in her. *Ice cream*, she thought. What she wouldn't give for one scoop of salted caramel in a waffle cone.

Gregory had just cinched up the stuff sack and was on one knee and turning at the waist with it in his hands when he froze. Went completely still and cast a sidelong glance at the girls. "You hear that?" he asked.

Raven snapped out of her daydream and shook her head. She looked to Sasha, who also indicated *'no'* with a quick roll of the eyes.

The only thing Raven *had* noticed when she gave it a second thought was that the pair of black birds—*mountain birds*, to Mom or Dad—that had been calling back-and-forth from somewhere behind her, in the general direction of the fire lane, had recently gone silent.

Then there was a crash from the woods as, presumably, another tree or two shed their early season coat of snow. The sound hadn't yet faded when from the opposite direction, downhill and across the clearing, the growl of engines in low-gear tackling an incline floated up to the hide.

Sasha could not resist. "I heard *that*," she said. "I bet it's Cade and the others coming back from wherever they went ... and when they find out we're gone they are going to hunt us down and kill you."

Wincing, Raven blurted, "They came back hours ago, Sasha. Remember?"

Smiling inwardly at this un-coerced tidbit of information, Gregory put a vertical finger to his lips and shushed the girls.

Hating nothing more than being shushed, Sasha stared daggers at the back of the man's head, and though there was nothing to work the cord against but dirt and pine needles, she continued trying to loosen it by forcing her wrists apart against the slight give.

Expecting nothing less than to hear a bugle call hailing the Calvary's arrival, Raven went to her knees as the motor sounds reached a crescendo. She smiled and glanced at Sasha when the black and white Tahoe she associated with Jackson Hole Police Chief Charlie Jenkins swung into view. Then her brow furrowed when she saw that it was followed closely by a number of other vehicles, including a trio of Humvees similar to the one parked in the motor pool near the compound.

Being a full head taller than Raven gave Sasha a better vantage of the road below. She looked for a second and regarded Raven. "That's not them," she whispered.

Raven knew this a half-beat before it was voiced. The vehicles were coming from the direction of the quarry, not the roadblock. Her heart was already sinking when Gregory raised the black radio to his lips. Then he spoke the words: *I see you. I'm at your ten o'clock inside the tree line,* and like it had never left in the first place, the finger of dread was back and a knot was forming in the pit of her stomach.

"Anything more from the girls?" a disembodied voice answered back.

Gregory nodded and a knowing smile rippled the whiskers ringing his mouth. "I have it on good word that whoever has set up camp down that road is sitting a little, or maybe even a lot undermanned right now."

Raven was watching her captor and started feeling the cord begin to flex against the constant pressure she was putting on it. Finally sensing that the thumb on her right hand was close to slipping free, she halted her effort long enough to shoot a glare at Sasha. "*Keep your trap shut*," she mouthed, then resumed her silent struggle.

Coming to see what her slip of the tongue might have ultimately cost them all, Sasha blinked against the tears forming in her eyes and hung her head between her knees.

Wondering where she had picked up '*shut your trap*' from—a Duncanism she supposed—Raven took advantage of Gregory's preoccupation with the new arrivals, got up onto her knees, and craned her head towards the road. Now head-high with Sasha, who was staring intently at the road, Raven saw the Tahoe's door open and a man just as tall as her captor—if not taller—unfold from the vehicle. Walking a little stooped over, he looped around the SUV and approached the front gate, where he stopped a few feet from the black camera domes. Then, as if the man already knew about them, he held up one of those large yellow pads of legal paper—whatever that was—and started stabbing his finger at it.

As the man continued pointing and flipping pages, a sound, kind of like the lift mechanism at work on a garbage truck, came from the second vehicle in line as the round part on top started swiveling slowly to the right. There was a younger man with a red beard standing straight up in it and holding onto something that looked like a smaller version of one of those cannons sticking from the side of a pirate ship. As the faint garbage-truck-sound ceased Raven saw that the *cannon* barrel was trained away from the road and in the direction of the compound where her mom and the others were. In the next instant, just as she and Sasha both figured out what that likely meant, Red Beard tilted the black barrel up and the big man with the pad backed away from the gate and went to one knee behind the Humvee.

Eden Compound

Brook selected the book she was reading at random from the pillowcase full of them Cade had brought home the day before. Letting the hand of fate do the choosing, she just reached right in and grabbed one.

The title had revealed little, and since she was the type of person who usually skipped reading the back blurb—especially when sci-fi and dystopian books were concerned, as she always got those two mixed up anyway—she cracked the cover and was hooked from the first page.

Having lost all track of time, she was at a part in the book where the protagonist and his young son were hiding under the floorboards of an old farmhouse, in the dark, and thinking they were alone. Then, just a few paragraphs in, she came to learn that the pair she had been rooting so hard for to survive had stumbled onto a cellar that was a larder of sorts, and the *provisions* were humans and still alive—albeit missing parts of limbs, the choicest cuts, perhaps.

Though she had yet to come across evidence of, nor hear about, the living eating the living, *yet*, the winter-like setting and all of the running and hiding from bad guys the two protagonists in the book were facing was starting to hit a little too close to home for her.

Suddenly hungry, she threw a shiver and looked at her watch. Saw that it was quarter past noon and immediately began to wonder why the girls weren't already pestering her for lunch, or, at the very least, sniffing around for some MRE pound cake, which seemed to be a big hit among the younger survivors.

She stepped into her boots and laced them tight. Grabbed her carbine and looked around for her gun belt before realizing she had been wearing it throughout her *treatment,* the brief nap, and all hundred some odd pages of one hell of a spooky read.

Heidi was watching the monitors when Brook stepped into the security container. The young blonde looked up at the sound of boots on plywood and smiled, which to Brook was a good thing that meant her medication dosage was working. Had she stayed glued to the monitor for a little too long and then presented her old flat affect, there would have been cause to worry.

Brook unfolded a metal chair and sat backwards on it. "How are things?" she asked, cheerily.

"It has been eerily quiet."

"Better than the alternative."

"Truer words have never been spoken." Heidi rolled her shoulders, her back popping as a result. "Are you taking over?" she asked.

Brook took a second to answer. She was looking past Heidi, at the monitor. On the partition showing the entrance from 39, save for rivulets of snowmelt coursing off the steaming two-lane, nothing moved up there. On another panel, she saw that the middle gate was closed and only dual strips of white remained on the road's shoulders where the undergrowth had shielded the snow from the effects of the high noon sun. Her eyes flicked over the other incoming feeds. The clearing was once again a sea of grass, now broken and bent over to reveal the muddy landing strip running down its center. On the far side of the clearing, the vehicles sat silent, sun glare lancing off all of their angled glass and chrome surfaces. And lastly, she saw that the camera trained on the compound's hidden entrance showed only the camouflage panel surrounded by a grove of small- to medium-sized trees that cast shadows in all different directions, rendering it hard to see even if one knew where to look.

"Everything looks great topside," replied Brook. "Want to trade me chairs? I think I've dropped a few pounds since the …" She still couldn't bring herself to verbalize what had happened to her. The weight of embarrassment she still shouldered and carried around as a result of losing Chief and nearly her own life had almost sent her running the couple of times she'd actually opened up and talked about *that day in September* to anyone who hadn't been there. "Any way … my butt's so bony I bet it looks like two razorblades wrapped with parchment paper. I've got my pants cinched all the way down and still they want to fall off me."

"Better than the alternative," replied Heidi, for the second time in as many minutes. "Those pills you gave me have got me eating like a horse. I think I may have taken on the weight you lost."

She removed the headphones and powered off the shortwave set. Absentmindedly she ran a hand through her spiked blonde hair as she relinquished the *'comfortable chair,'* which in her opinion was little more than a folding chair on rollers with a stadium seat jammed under cheap fabric—forty dollars, tops, at the Office Depot.

"Thank you," Brook said, sliding over and taking the seat. "Sorry I'm late." She grabbed a two-way from the shelf, and once she saw it was tuned to the proper channel and sub-channel, keyed the side button. "Sasha … Raven. Pick up. It's lunch time." She released the key to a little bit of squelch—par for the course considering the thin layer of dirt covering the roof. "Raven. Sasha." Nothing. Just static.

"Maybe they're out of range."

"Shouldn't be. I explicitly told them to remain inside the inner perimeter."

"Batteries?"

"Could be," said Brook agreeably. She made a face and was about to hail Foley and Tran, whose radios were tuned to the same frequency, when someone broke squelch and then Foley's voice emanated from the speaker. "Did you find them yet?"

"No. They aren't answering."

"I'm over here by the solar array. Me and Tran are gonna drop everything and go looking for them."

"He's not going to be happy … but I'm going to wake Seth and send him and Glenda out to help you."

"Copy that," Foley said.

"I'll get a coat and head on out," Heidi said through pursed lips, her smile long gone.

Brook made no reply because movement on the monitor to her left caught her attention. In her side vision flashes of yellow and black registered, making her think at first that a fat bumblebee had taken interest in its own reflection in the camera's dome. But once she focused on the panel where the movement was, two things dawned on her. One, the camera recording the movement was the one watching the east approach on 39. And two, the movement was no bumblebee ogling itself, that was for sure. Filling up almost the entire partition on the flat screen was a yellow sheet of lined paper filled with bold, black, handwriting. The letters were all capitalized, punctuation was nonexistent, and the grammar was horrible.

With Heidi reading over her shoulder, Brook leaned in and devoured every word, sentence, and paragraph on all five pages. After speed-reading the first page, when she saw a hand fill up the screen and turn it over, she knew from the thick fingers and knobby knuckles that a man was stating his case. He had started with evidence first. Apparently whoever had found the feeder road cameras had matched tread patterns from the scene of the perceived crime with identical ones owned by a vehicle he had tracked here the day before. He stated in writing that he had '*half an army*' and demanded the killer of a person he identified as Lena be brought out to the road. Ten minutes was allotted for the transfer. The last page was filled with instructions that ended with the phrase: "You have ten minutes. If ten minutes passes, a 'message' will be sent." The word *message* on the sheet had been underlined—twice.

Brook didn't like the implication the word carried. Hell, the man calling himself Alexander Dregan was pissed, and she sympathized with him. If she lost Raven the same way she wouldn't rest until the person responsible was dead by her hand and she was the one dumping the last shovelful of dirt on their grave. Unfortunately for the man, that kind of closure would never be achieved. Because the person who had killed his daughter, Lena, was already dead and buried.

What Brook couldn't wrap her head around as she read the last sentence on the final sheet was why this Alexander Dregan had made no mention of the young man *she* had killed that day.

Bootsteps sounded and a sleepy voice said, "What's going on?"

"Come with me, Seth," said Heidi, grabbing a coat off a hook and tossing it to him. On the way through the foyer, she snatched up one of the backup carbines and passed it back to him. Donning a coat of her own, she caught his eye and began spilling the bad news.

Wasting no more time worrying about the hows and whys, Brook snatched one of the satellite phones off the shelf and, ignoring the new message there—*probably Nash again*— thumbed it on. She yanked the charging cord off and hit the proper keys to raise Cade on it.

Leaning back in the chair and staring at the lined-up vehicles on the monitor, their contours slightly distorted by distance, she waited for the electronic handshake to happen. There was a series of clicks as the signal cycled through a DoD satellite somewhere far above Earth and there came a hollow and distant sounding ring. The electronic trill went on for three agonizing cycles until a familiar voice answered.

***

With the distinct trilling of the Thuraya sat-phone filling the cab, Cade brought the plow truck to a halt in the exact intersection and adjacent to the car and road sign Oliver had shot up the previous night. As he fumbled in his pocket to retrieve the noisily chirping handset, his gaze was drawn to the houses on the hill where the reservoir and snow-capped Wasatch were reflected in miniature in the west-facing windows. The feeling of being watched he had experienced the day before was gone; however, a creeping feeling of doom had taken root the second the phone began to vibrate and make that ominous sound.

He thumbed the rubber *Talk* key. "Cade here," he said under Oliver's watchful eye. He said nothing more. Just listened without interjecting, his normally stoic expression going stony.

Oliver noticed the transformation and suddenly, like something with leathery wings had taken flight in his stomach, he knew that a good day had just been shot to hell.

"No," Cade said slow and crisp, enunciating every syllable. "Under no circumstances do you leave the compound on the feeder road. Gather the girls and take the Ford and Humvee and punch a hole through the forest to the old fire road."

Oliver watched Cade's brow knit and his grip on the wheel tighten as a response was delivered from the other end.

"It's your only chance to get away," Cade answered, exasperation showing. "Arm yourselves and go. Follow the road back to Woodruff. I'll meet you there and then we'll find another place to call home." He listened for a handful of seconds then grunted and said, "Yes," and ended the call.

The Land Cruiser slid to a stop on the plow truck's left side.

Oliver sat up in the passenger seat rod-straight, eyes glued to Cade, who was now staring at him directly.

"Coming or going?" Cade asked curtly. He flicked his eyes away long enough to note the time on his big black watch.

"What?" said Oliver. "Going … where?"

There was a light tapping on the driver's side window. Cade rolled it down and found himself face-to-face with Daymon, who was standing on the running board and gripping the vertical grab bar one-handed for balance.

Eyes red-rimmed and bloodshot, Daymon asked, "What's the plan, Boss?"

Cade closed his eyes and let his head fall back into the headrest. "Get Duncan for me," he said slowly, the words enunciated perfectly.

One brow hitched, Daymon said, "O … K." He turned his head. Cupped his hands and bellowed, "Duncan … you're needed in the boardroom!" He turned back to see that Cade was talking into a two-way radio and heard him calling the rest of the group back to the house.

Duncan was out of the SUV now and shooing Daymon off the truck. He opened the Mack's slab of a door and stared up at Cade. The look on the younger man's face struck him right away. Fact is, it puckered him up and set his stomach roiling. He'd seen the steely gaze on many an occasion and it usually preceded a shit ton of Zs and humans both meeting their makers. Already knowing he was not going to like the answer, reluctantly he asked, "What's up?"

Eden Compound

Eyeing her watch every minute or so, Brook gathered the essentials: Weapons, magazines filled with 5.56 and 9mm, and both her and Raven's bug out bags containing food, medicine, and more loose ammo. Shouldering the pack with considerable pain, she called out on the two-way to see if the girls had been located yet.

Foley's response hit her like a mule kick. She'd been expecting to hear a resounding: *Yes*. Instead, she received a solemn: *No, ma'am. There's no sign of them … anywhere.*

Still filling her cargo pockets with spare mags, she asked, "Did you at least track them? Find any footsteps in the snow?"

"It's mostly melted. What Glenda predicted happened. It's pushing sixty out here."

Not liking any of these answers, Brook shook her head. "Are there Zs on the wire?"

"Negative," answered Foley. "I'm here with Glenda, Heidi, and Tran. I've already moved Daymon's RV and the Humvee started right up, first try. What now?"

Finally a positive among all the negatives. Brook took a deep breath and stole another peek at her watch. "Keep your eyes peeled for the girls," she said. "I'll be out in ten."

"Will do," replied Foley. "Out."

"Out," Brook said, her gaze glued to the tall bearded man whom she had no desire to tangle with. She watched him pacing back and forth and talking into a two-way radio.

Hurry up Cade.

Chapter 68

Cade filled Duncan in about the siege at the compound, closed his door, then drove a couple of blocks east and let Oliver out at the intersection near his house. Seconds later Cade had already looped back around onto Main Street and was steering the truck left to get back to 39. He saw the sun glare from the approaching 4Runner, but didn't bother to stop. Duncan's job was to rendezvous with the Kids at the house, load up the smaller vehicles, and catch up with him on down the road.

Ten minutes, he thought to himself. He looked at his watch. *Two down, eight to go. Not enough time. Not by a long shot.*

He saw the National Guard roadblock and ditch full of half-turtled cars and did two things at once. He uttered a little prayer for his family and the others, asking for them to get to safety unscathed. He also tacked on a little rider, asking God to allow the pranged plow up front to fit through the narrow opening dead ahead.

As bent and battered as it had become from plowing the Zs off Trapper's Loop Road the night before, Cade wasn't at all confident the dual blade would clear the Jersey barriers at the blown Guard roadblock. He figured the thing had to accept more adjustments—angle, camber, pitch all came to mind—but he hadn't taken the time earlier to acquaint himself with all of the control's intricacies, and had no time to do so now.

So he opted to raise the blade to the point where it looked as if the barriers would pass underneath and hope for the best. He heard an odd pneumatic whine overriding the hiss of the radials on the wet pavement. Next came a painful groan of metal on metal when he actuated the *Up* lever. The hydraulic whine rose in volume and there was a loud bang and the blade started to rise ever so slowly. Once the blade stopped moving, he released the lever, thinking to himself: *That's as good as she's going to get.*

Closing rapidly with the narrow gap, and feeling the diesel engine's vibration through the firewall a foot from his throbbing ankle, he suddenly reflected back to the hours following Jedi One-One going down in the church graveyard outside of Draper, South Dakota. The similarities between that awful day and the one this was shaping up to be were striking: Ballooned left ankle … check! Unfamiliar and battered truck … check! Having to get to a predetermined location traveling a Z-choked road and precious minutes in which to make it happen … check!

Gripping the wheel two-handed, and entering the cattle chute made up of stalled cars, burned bodies and unforgiving concrete Jersey barriers, he put the pedal to the metal—or in this instance a high-wearing rubber floor mat—and aimed the shiny chromed bulldog hood ornament at a point in the road beyond it all.

There was a gunshot-like bang from the right and the plow vibrated like a grain silo in a cat-5 twister. A little micro-car on the left was peeled open like a sardine can from gas tank to the front door-pillar by the left side of the blade. Then, concurrent with another pair of discordant bangs, two noticeable bends suddenly appeared at the midpoint on each half of the blade.

A tick later, save for the low engine growl, metallic meshing of gears, and steady thudding of his heart, silence ensued until he opened the gravel spreader out back to its most liberal setting and the deluge of rocks began to pummel the pavement at his six.

Fields, fence, and the occasional ambulatory Z flashed by as the rig picked up speed. Nearly emptied of gravel, it ate up the nearby grade, crested the hill, and sped downhill with the blade vibrating wildly and pushing a wind vortex ahead of it.

The road to the UDOT yard blipped by on the left. A half-beat later, the Shell sign and burned-out husk of a gas station was in the rearview mirror and fading into the background clutter.

He alternated between checking the wing mirror for the other two vehicles and the road ahead for the larger groups of walking dead. He knew the latter were somewhere up ahead. He only hoped they had not all resumed their march east and amassed into one big rotting knot of death. Last thing he needed was for the two herds they ignored earlier to have combined into a nearly impassable roving horde. No, actually, as he thought hard on it, the last thing he needed was for the reanimated throng to have made it all the way to Daymon's fallen tree roadblock and choke off all access to the bridge.

At just under sixty-miles-per-hour, the distance to the bridge rapidly melted away. Cade checked his speed by a third on the corners and pushed the rig hard on the straightaways. On one particularly long stretch, he glimpsed a glint of sun in the vibrating side mirror. Slowing to the point where the mirror stopped vibrating, he soon saw that the others were catching up to him, the bulkier Land Cruiser in the lead and the 4Runner riding close in its slipstream—Taryn at the wheel, no doubt. Damn, that girl could drive, he thought, casting a glance at his Suunto. Five minutes until *surprise* time—whatever that meant—and the two-way radio, CB, and sat-phone still had not made a sound. Whether that was good or bad, he didn't have time to decide, for when he looked up and slowed a little more for the next right-hander—the one where he thought the minivan and its long dead human cargo lay—he saw a sea of jostling bodies.

His own words came back to haunt: *There's less than two hundred here … we need to move on.*

But there were more now. Crushed against each other, several hundred deep, were the two groups of dead he'd feared would reanimate and eventually converge. *Eff you Murphy … why here and now?* he mused, as the full scope of the mess he was in came into view.

The blackened corpses from the two burned-out cities were intermingled with the fresher corpses he presumed had at one time ventured east from Ogden either in search of fertile hunting grounds or in hot pursuit of prey. Didn't matter now, because at the moment they were doing neither. Though he didn't want to stop, the threat of becoming mired like the minivan was real, leaving him no other recourse. Quickly, he applied the brakes slowing the rig right on the centerline. There was a hissing of air from the hard-working brakes and the tires juddered and chirped—alerting the monsters to his presence. He plucked the two-way off the seat just as Wilson's voice emanated from the speaker. "What are you stopping for? We're just catching up with you," said the redhead.

Grimacing, Cade eyeballed the horde and saw that they were amassed against a sizeable tree that had recently fallen across both lanes of 39. Beyond both shoulders the guardrails were bowed down under its weight, and though the dead were partially obscuring its trunk, he could see its massive and once far-reaching root system reaching skyward. It hadn't been brought down deliberately, that much was clear. Probably had just succumbed to the heavy snow and high winds of the previous day.

Worst timing ever.

Cade pressed the *Talk* button on the Motorola. "Lock and load," he said. "We have a few hundred bouncers guarding the door." As an afterthought, he added, "Have Daymon start prepping the chainsaw."

He took another peek at his watch. The LCD numerals indicated less than three minutes remained until the hostiles at the compound were to send Brook and the others whatever *message* they had planned. He shouldered open his door, planted his boot on the running board, and was hit by a wave of pain. It shot up his leg and started a galaxy of sweat beading on his brow. Grinding his teeth, he braced his M4 against the jam, engaged the EOTech 3X magnifier, and started punching holes in zombie skulls.

A split-second after he began firing, he heard between pulls of the trigger the reassuring sound of approaching engines. And as he dropped a spent magazine and grabbed a fresh one from his chest rig, the noise grew louder. He jammed the mag into the well, released the bolt and shouldered the rifle. In his left and right side vision, the two trucks pulled up, bookending the idling plow truck.

Knowing the others needed no prodding, he continued picking off the advancing wall of snarling flesh. As he dropped one after another, some of the rounds passed through the Zs, causing sparks to fly off the minivan trapped in their midst.

***

Inside the 4Runner, Wilson was thrown against his shoulder belt as Taryn jammed on the brakes. "I knew this was going to happen," he cried. He tossed the radio aside and grabbed his rifle from between his legs. Drumming up a little courage, he turned his gaze on Taryn and blurted out what he had been thinking. "Stay here … watch the truck. Please …"

Unaware of the drama playing out inches to their fore, Lev and Jamie were already piling out of the SUV.

"I can't," said Taryn, shaking her head. "The girls … Brook, Glenda, Heidi, I care about them. I *have* to give a hundred and ten percent on everything. If something were to happen to any of them and I didn't ... I don't know how I'd live with myself."

Wilson leaned in and kissed her hard on the mouth. For the first time—other than a couple of instances in the throes of ecstasy when he's uttered the words under his breath—he looked her square in the eyes and told her he loved her.

"I know," she mouthed. There was a short pause. "I love you too, burger boy."

A handful of seconds after the rear doors had slammed shut, Taryn and Wilson were armed and joining the others near the plow truck's right front wheel.

***

With the Land Cruiser parked and idling a yard off the plow truck's left side, Duncan actuated the tailgate lift and looked over at Daymon. "Better be channeling some kind of lumberjack-superhero chainsaw work, bud. Flannel Man activate." He turned and stared hard at Oliver. "Time to bury the hatchet, you and I. Go on out there and get yerself some more notches on that fancy rifle of yours, O.G."

Duncan reached back and grabbed the nearest rifle and a couple of magazines. The sound of carbines hammering away at the dead filtered in as doors opened and closed around him. He pocketed the mags and exited the vehicle, rifle in hand and pulling back on the charging handle.

Warily eyeing the target-rich expanse of highway laid out before the picket of idling trucks, he crabbed a few feet to his left, climbed over the guardrail, and took a knee behind it. With a clutch of undergrowth tickling his back, and the rifle steadied against the rust-streaked barrier, he said a silent prayer and then opened fire.

Chapter 69

While their captor, Gregory, continued breaking down his camp, Raven and Sasha remained seated and directed their attention to the armed men milling about the line of vehicles down on the road. All at once there was a burst of static coming from the radio in Gregory's pocket, the posture of the men down below changed from relaxed to vigilant, and the nervous chatter drifting up to their location all but ceased.

As Raven craned to see over the ferns in front of her, the silence was broken by a pair of closely spaced *thunks* coming from the cannon-looking thing. Whatever had caused the hollow sounds seemed to have left the elevated barrel at the same instant. A second later, that notion was dispelled when two separate and distinct explosions rattled the distant trees, sending a dozen birds fleeing upward into the hazy blue afternoon sky.

"What was that?" Sasha asked, her brow knitted.

Raven said nothing. She had turned away from the road and refocused all of her attention on Gregory, who at the moment was standing and holding the two-way Motorola he had taken away from Sasha. He thumbed the button and moved the radio to his mouth. Then, for a long moment, he stood rooted with his mouth open and no words spilling forth.

Collecting his thoughts, is all Raven could come up with. So with him preoccupied, she went back to working the cord farther down her clasped hands. And though she couldn't see the progress made, based on the lack of feeling in her fingertips, the knotted cord had to have worked down past the first knuckle on both thumbs.

Eden Compound

Precisely ten minutes after the Dregan guy had delivered his written ultimatum/warning, Brook felt a sharp jolt travel through the rolling chair. Then, as if she'd just been in a rear-end collision and had not seen it coming, whatever just exploded topside vibrated every bone in her body. More reflex than conscious thought, she grabbed onto the shelf in front of her as phones and walkie talkies were spilling off of it.

Even as a pair of low rumbles and the distant fireworks-like crackle made its way through the foyer, behind Brook's eyelids the capillaries flared red as a bolt of pain originating in her old wound shot through her entire body. Once the noise dissipated, a frantic voice came over the radio that had fallen onto the floor. "Fucking lobbing grenades at us," Foley exclaimed.

A dull throb still in her temples, Brook bent over gingerly, snatched up the radio, and cast her gaze to the monitor. "Are you all right?"

There was a foreboding silence and then movement on the motor pool feed caught her eye as one-by-one she saw a line of heads gopher-up between the vehicles. There was Foley, with his balding head standing next to the much shorter and dark-haired Tran. Heidi was there as well, bracing herself against the black F-650, her contrasting blonde hairdo the dead giveaway. Next to her was Glenda. Though thinner than the rest, she still had a couple of inches on them all. Missing was Seth—and the girls.

Finally Foley answered. "We're all right. Seth ran off to see where the grenades fell."

Grenades? thought Brook. She said, "Where in the hell are the girls?"

Another voice came over the radio. It was strained and a little raspy. *A smoker's voice*? "I have your girls. Send out the killer and I'll let them go. No negotiations. No brokering. A straight trade is what we want."

Like a line of sails being dropped on a tall-masted vessel, Brook saw the other survivors slump against the big Ford's sheet metal flank.

"Brook … you heard that, right?" Foley asked over the radio.

Brook said nothing. The radio was compromised and she was kicking herself for not thinking of it ahead of time. Plus, the Thuraya sat-phone was to her ear and the clicks indicating the connection to Cade's phone was being established had already begun.

***

Six miles west of the Eden Compound, still slugging it out with the undead horde, at first Cade failed to hear the phone trilling away in his pocket. But by the third ring, as he was leaning into his M4 as it hammered away against his shoulder, he became aware of the phone's vibration coursing up his right thigh.

He looked left and saw Oliver with the scoped rifle and firing controlled single shots down range. Forty feet or so ahead of Glenda's youngest son, the fruits of his labor lay tangled on the shoulder, piled three deep with a frothy soup of blood and snowmelt spreading around them. Passing his gaze left-to-right while he dug the vibrating phone from his pocket, Cade saw Daymon and Duncan standing shoulder-to-shoulder by the guardrail and reloading their carbines, thin licks of gun smoke curling from the hot muzzles.

Next, his eyes fell on Jamie, who had advanced on the right. Her tomahawk appeared as a black blur at the end of big angry chopping motions as she cleaved through Z skulls, Ian Bishop's visage no doubt transposed mentally on each and every one of them. Finally, as he blindly thumbed the Thuraya's *Talk* button and brought the phone to his ear, he saw Taryn, Wilson, and Lev moving and firing, and dozens of spent shells arcing up from their bucking carbines spinning and tumbling end over end and glinting the sun along the way.

With the stench of gunpowder and death assaulting his nostrils, Cade dropped the magazine from his M4 and listened to Brook's voice mingling with the ringing in his ear. As the click of the fresh magazine seating home registered, the words *They're holding Raven hostage* wormed their way into his ear.

The female first turn bracketed in his sights earned a momentary reprieve as he drew his carbine back through the window and slumped heavily on the seat. Though he heard her loud and clear the first time, he still shot back, "Come again?"

Brook repeated the ultimatum verbatim, then added, "I'm trading myself for both of them."

Cade wanted to scream, but held it in check. Instead, he said, "Have someone get to the road right now and get eyes on the convoy's six. Make sure they can also provide cover for you at the gate if it comes to that."

"Seth's already on the way."

"Good." There was a long silence. Just the nascent background hiss of radio waves flying into space. "Stall them at every turn," Cade finally added. "Take your time getting to the road. Once you're there … get the girls if you can and send them back to the compound right away."

"I'll have someone waiting for them."

"OK," Cade said.

"I'm going to have Foley bring the fifty cal into play if they don't honor their end of the deal," she said.

"No," Cade said. "That'll just escalate things." He looked over the hood and saw Daymon, chainsaw perched on his shoulder, crabbing over the fallen creatures. To the right the Kids were fanning out and putting their blades to great use, killing anything that still moved.

"What do I do then?"

"You are not to go with them, that's for sure. Stall. Reason. Lie. Do everything in your power to buy me the twenty minutes I need to get there."

Voice wavering, she asked, "What then?"

"I'll tell them I killed the girl ... *and* the young man. And they can have me in your place."

Now there was a long silence on Brook's end.

"Promise me, Brooklyn Grayson," Cade said.

"I can't," she said. "And I won't."

Before Cade could protest, there was a click and the connection was lost. He tried calling back, but after the requisite rings got only the strange robotic female voice telling him to leave a message after the tone. Intent on keeping all of this to himself for the time being, he thumbed the phone off, laid his rifle on the floor, and worked the control to lower the oddly misshapen plow blade to the road.

Chapter 70

Brook whistled and called for Max to come. A handful of seconds later there was a ticking of nails on plywood. Then, tail twitching and with a noticeable hitch in his normally peppy gait, the shepherd entered the light splash on the floor, sat on his haunches at her feet, and regarded her with an inquisitive gaze.

"Come on, boy," she said gathering up the two-way Motorola and Thuraya. Before heading to the exit, in case they all had to rabbit, she also grabbed the mate to the long-range multi-channel CB radio Cade had with him.

She took one long last look at the place she had called home for quite some time now. In doing so, her gaze fell on the monitor and she saw a new scrawled message from the bearded man filling up the screen. Written in black on the legal pad in the same stilted hand were the words: YOU HAVE FIVE MINUTES TO COMPLY BEFORE THE REDHEAD DIES.

"Fuck you." Brook set the stopwatch on her Timex scrolling forward, then, steeling herself against the pain to come, grabbed her carbine and Raven's go bag. With the shooting pain ebbing, she paused in the foyer and went through the pockets of a jacket hanging there. The item she was looking for was tucked deeply into an inside pocket. Her fingers brushed the knurled grip and she brought the Beretta pistol out into the light. She checked the magazine. *Full.* Braced the pistol between clenched knees and drew the slide back an inch. *One in the pipe.* Satisfied the weapon was as she had left it, she thumbed back the hammer and tucked it into her pants by the small of her back. One deep breath later, with Max at her heels, she was headed topside.

All eyes were on her and Max as they crossed the clearing, both walking gingerly, and burning forty-five seconds of the allotted five minutes. She wasted another precious twenty seconds doling out tasks and issuing contingency plans in case things went sideways. After making doubly sure everyone was on the same page, she ushered the shepherd into the F-650 and, with her left hand, threw her carbine, pack, and Raven's go bag onto the seat.

With the numerals on her watch indicating Sasha had three minutes to live, Brook fired up the big V10, dropped the transmission into *Drive*, and sped off towards the feeder road with a pair of muddy rooster tails sprouting behind the fishtailing Ford. Entering the break in the forest with the truck nearly sideways, the last thing she saw when the gravel started its usual symphony of pings was Foley and Tran sprinting for the Humvee.

State Route 39

Daymon had the trunk cut away from the left guardrail fairly quickly. Once he had waded through the thick boughs, it took him three minutes from the chain's first bite until the trunk was resting on the roadside. With the Stihl's motor throbbing at idle, he extricated himself and trudged six or seven paces to his right, looking for a thin spot in the branches to get to the trunk.

Seeing movement on the far side of the fallen tree, Cade shouldered his rifle and settled his crosshairs on the lone burnt corpse. He caressed the trigger and heard the brass banging around inside the UDOT truck even before the pink halo blossomed around the thing's head. He shifted aim and walked his fire right-to-left, away from Daymon, the sizzling rounds passing harmlessly over the section of corpse-choked road that lay between the oblivious firefighter and the others, who were now gathered near the vehicles now parked bumper-to-bumper on the far left shoulder.

While Daymon worked, Cade kept acquiring and engaging targets on the far side of the toppled tree. An elderly woman wearing a blood-streaked blouse and apron—a cartoonish-looking steaming berry pie and the words COME AND GET IT stitched across her bosom—was first. She fell behind the fallen tree as if yanked to hell by a demon. A tow-headed little boy was next, losing his face and top third of the mussed hairdo to a sizzling 5.56 round.

Daymon was tearing into the trunk and a quarter of the way through when one unfortunate creature tangled with the whirring chainsaw. A spritz of flesh and brackish blood erupted a dozen feet into the air as the already one-armed first turn disemboweled itself on the howling Stihl.

Cade flicked his eyes to the scene and noted the grim determination on his friend's face as he went on about his task. *Business as usual.* He dropped three more dead approaching Daymon from the left and then his weapon was empty, the bolt locked open, a curl of cordite heavy smoke wafting to the headliner.

After reloading, he stepped down from the cab and was looking at his watch just as the chainsaw won the battle with the trunk and the solid thunk of the twenty-foot-long piece of log striking the road reverberated through his boot soles. With Daymon making a quick pass of the saw over the upthrust branches to his fore, the grim fact registered in Cade's mind that only one minute remained on the countdown.

Wrapping one hand around the grab bar, he shot a thumbs up to Daymon and made a clearing motion with his arm while hollering for everyone to mount up.

The next part of the plan had already been discussed, and though there was still a number of miles and a bridge crossing ahead of them, if it went off without a hitch Cade figured they just might make it to the compound in time to make a difference in the outcome.

He climbed back into the truck and dropped it into its lowest gear. There was a grating of metal from up front as he applied a little throttle. Then, as the weight of the prone corpses built against the blade, it vibrated madly one time and bent to the point where it was nearly straight. Confident that the plow was not going to buckle and fail completely, Cade tightened his grip on the wheel and pinned the pedal to the floor.

Like a cresting wave, the flaccid drift of death consisting of meat and bone and detritus curled up in front of the charging vehicle. Though the blade—no longer an inverted "V"—merely shoved the corpses forward, it still had the intended outcome as their combined weight hit the severed length of log and sent it rolling forward. The staccato crackle of the remaining branches shearing off went on until the trunk had completed one full revolution and began to roll freely.

Cade eased off the gas and took his eyes from the road long enough to hit the button to disengage the low gearing. When he brought his gaze up, he saw the chunk of tree spin away like a Lincoln Log tossed aside by a petulant child. Next, with nothing pressing them against the blade, he watched the corpses spill off the blade to both sides of the truck in a mad final tumble of flailing arms and legs.

Another glance at the Suunto told Cade the time was up and there was nothing he could do at that moment but trust Brook and trust God.

State Route 39
Near the Eden Compound

Dregan checked the time. *Four minutes down and seconds to go.* The words in his head sounded like something a football announcer would say. Only there was nothing sporting about what he was being forced to do. Shaking his head, he reluctantly motioned his brother Henry from the Humvee.

Muttering under his breath, Henry unfolded his large frame and stood on the steaming road. He took a long drag off his cigarette and placed the still-smoking butt on the vehicle's flat hood for later. He walked across the road, transited the ditch without getting too muddy, and was bending down to slip through the fence when the low thrum of a strong-running engine met his ears. Hinging up, he looked to his brother and shrugged, arms out palms up, universal semaphore for *what now*?

Suddenly at alert, every nerve ending in his body afire, Dregan backed away from the hidden gate. Hearing the engine noise as well as a strange recurring sound of metal striking metal, he put the radio to his lips and barked orders to his hired help. He ended the call after ordering Gregory to get the girls ready for the transfer if it were to transpire.

Brook didn't know what was worse … the continuous ear-splitting *thunka-thunka-thunka* of the entangled strand of barbed wire battering the passenger mirror, hood and fender—in that order, over and over again—or the deafening silence from the electronic devices jostling together in the center console. The noise would soon stop, that was for sure. The middle gate she had just destroyed with the F-650's beefy front bumper could be fixed. The barbed wire could also be removed from where it had become embedded in the huge off-road tire. But if further instructions didn't come through the radio's speaker, what was she to do?

The radio remained silent as the F-650 cut a wide swath down the feeder road. Soon a branch or something stole the piece of wire and length of fence post and the *thunka-thunka-thunka* ceased.

Still, the radio didn't emit so much as a burst of scratchy static.

Though she prayed to hear the electronic trill she so despised, the Thuraya sat-phone remained silent. However, she did notice a message on the screen that she had been too preoccupied earlier to heed. On the final straightaway, while holding the wheel one-handed, she read the short message sent from Cade's phone: **Glenda's son Oliver is alive. Shhhhh … he wants to surprise her. Back soon.** *Good news amongst all the bad,* she supposed. "Well, well, won't Glenda be happy." Her face went slack as the back side of the hidden gate materialized out of the distance. She thought: *Here* I *am possibly about to lose a child and the old broad wins the maternal lottery.* She smiled at the lady's good fortune. "What kind of name is Oliver?" she wondered aloud. With so much death and suffering befalling her circle in the last few weeks, suddenly she wanted nothing more than to meet the guy. Hear his story of hope. Who he was. What he was like. And how he'd survived all these months, alone.

But first she had some surviving of her own to see to.

Gravel spattered the undercarriage like shotgun pellets as she jammed the Ford to a halt thirty feet from the gate and hard to the right side of the road. Up ahead in a break in the foliage she could see the light bar and needle antennas of the patrol Tahoe. And though it was painted woodland camouflage and blended in with the trees atop the rise, the roof of some other older model SUV was also visible. "Stay," she said to Max. She grabbed her carbine, flicked the selector to *Fire*, and climbed down from the truck.

***

Raven watched and listened intently as Gregory wrapped up the call and stowed his radio in a pocket. Strangely enough, she noted, even after the man stopped talking in his gruff smoker's voice, the black birds hadn't resumed their catty back and forth calls. Save for the occasional thump of snow hitting the forest floor, the woods surrounding them on three sides as well as the assemblage of men and machine on the road below was deathly quiet—and remained that way right up until the final seconds were about to tick off of the new five-minute deadline. Then, from somewhere across the road, deep in the thick forest, there was a muffled bang, almost like a minor fender bender had taken place. Immediately following the sudden noise was a ticking of metal striking metal, and then overriding that was a constant banging mixed in with a third vaguely familiar sound, mechanical in nature.

The second Raven realized the familiar sound was the distinctive throaty exhaust note and deep V10 rumble of her dad's truck emanating from somewhere along the feeder road, she sat up tall and craned at the road until her neck hurt. Having just overheard the man on the road telling Gregory via the radio to ready her and Sasha for release, her hopes were soaring. And now, hearing the engine noise below growing nearer, she was bubbling over with nervous energy and could barely sit still. Thus, when the engine finally shut off and the sound of a single door opening, then closing, reached her ears, she was on the verge of having her second anxiety attack of the day.

Keying in on Raven's body language, Sasha kicked the younger girl's boot. Once eye contact was established, she mouthed: *What?*

My mom is down there, I think, Raven mouthed back.

Gregory was now standing at the rear of the hide, fully loaded pack on his back, radio in one hand and the rifle in the other. Raven's eyes flicked from the rifle over to the pistol on the man's hip, and then moved up and settled on his bearded face for a brief second. Noticing all of his attention was focused on the goings on down below, she put extra effort into somehow channeling Harry Houdini so she could finally slip her hands free from the knotted cord.

Chapter 71

Five miles west on State Route 39, Cade was not only coming up against the growing number of reanimated walkers he had opted *not* to put down on the way in, but he was also having to keep the rig's speed down because the blade up front was on its last legs. With each new jarring impact, the twisted slab of metal slid lower to the road blurring by underneath it, worrying Cade that it might shear off and flatten a couple of tires as a result.

Less than a mile from the fallen log blockade, Cade swerved to avoid a group of first turns and clipped a number of them, starting a series of irreversible chain reactions. The first application of cause and effect slapped half a dozen Zs to the pavement, where they were promptly run over and pulped underneath the trailing Land Cruiser's undercarriage.

The second instance was more Newton's Law of Motion than anything when, as if made of tinfoil, the plow blade folded under the front bumper and broke free of its mounts. Hell—after all of the battering it had endured since the night before—Cade was amazed it had seen him this far.

The rising crescendo of metal on pavement ceased instantly and the rig bucked like a spurred bronco as the massive plow became wedged in its dual rear axles. Surprising Cade completely, the brakes locked up and the Mack veered right and ran up onto the guardrail before coming to a complete and jarring stop, high-sided, leaning hard to the left, and spewing steam from what he guessed was a punctured radiator. The run from the crash site in Draper, South

Dakota was again on his mind as he watched the under-hood geyser continue. He collected his radio, phone, and CB and filled his pockets with them. He shrugged on his pack and grabbed the carbine. Then, with the failed dismount from the night before fresh on his mind, he eschewed jumping down to the shoulder from the high side of the cab and instead took the chance of becoming a Darwin Award winner by throwing open the driver's side door and sliding from the seat to the wet pavement.

He rolled free from the open door of the dangerously listing truck and was engaging the nearby Zs with his Glock when the already loaded-up 4Runner ground to a halt a yard away and its rear passenger-side door was flung open.

A chorus of voices urging him inside rose over the silenced reports from his Glock. So Cade rose from his kneeling position, doubled-tapped a pair of rotters, and relinquished his pack and carbine to Wilson's waiting hands. Firing one-handed, he walked/half-limped backwards to the open rear passenger door, where he quickly holstered his pistol and planted his butt on the bench seat next to Jamie. Grimacing, he hauled his leg with the damaged ankle over the door sill.

"That was close," said Lev, as Cade closed the door and the vehicle lurched forward over top of the fallen and leaking corpses.

Leaning forward to make eye contact, Cade said, "The rig had to die sometime."

"Duncan's driving the Cruiser like a little old lady," exclaimed Taryn as a pair of Zs slapped at the 4Runner's right side.

"Pass him when you can," Cade said matter-of-factly. "Do it on the right. Then drive like it's your first race and your dad is watching you."

Wilson poked his head around the edge of his seat. "You planning on telling us how this is going to go down when we get there?"

"There is no *we*," Cade said gruffly. "We get across the roadblock and back to the truck and pile in. Then I'm going to have you drive me to within limping distance of the compound and I'll go it alone from there." He looked out the window at the carnage. Zombie bodies, twisted grotesque forms, many of them burned horribly—lay on the road every couple of feet or so. He swung his eyes all around, pausing briefly to scan the woods flanking the road, and couldn't believe the transformation. In less than twenty-four hours, all of this had gone from a winter wonderland postcard scene Bing Crosby would have crooned about back to a canyon of emerald green firs and pines shot through with lonely stands of white-trunked alder and aspen. Shaking his head, Cade consulted his Suunto and his fear was realized when he saw that that the deadline dictated to Brook and the Eden group had come and gone and the comms devices in his pockets remained quiet.

Eden Compound's Hidden Gate

Standing in the F-650's shadow, Brook noted the time on her watch. Then, holding her carbine at the low-ready with a round chambered and the selector set to *Fire*—locked and loaded, as Cade would say—she looped around the front of the truck and covered the distance to the gate on the far shoulder.

Head on a swivel—another practice Cade advocated as useful to surviving contact with the enemy—she heel-and-toed it forward, stopping every few feet to look and assess. Due to the height of the gate and the encroaching canopy overhead, she couldn't see the enemy's vehicles from where she was on the road.

When she finally reached the gate, she heard a low murmur of conversation in the distance and, nearby, the sound of boots squelching on gravel—quite possibly produced by the nervous foot-to-foot shifting of men grown tired of waiting.

"Drop your weapon and step to your right so I can see you."

The voice was gravelly and belonged to a smoker. It sounded very much like the voice that had spoken to her over Raven's radio. Close but no cigar. In her mind's eye, the voice of the person calling to her from the direction of the vehicles matched perfectly with the man who had been issuing ultimatums in writing on the legal pad.

Brook complied with only the latter part of the barked order. She moved farther right where the fencing was chest-high on her and the thick undergrowth and forest nearly pressed against her back.

The bearded man was standing a dozen feet away, dead center on the road, with a line of vehicles and expectant faces trailing away behind him. He was dressed in 1980's-era camouflage fatigues in a woodland pattern—browns and greens shot through with black. Over the surplus uniform and hanging open was a knee-length Western-style duster. Once black and now faded to dark gray, the coat's fabric could be canvas or cotton for all Brook knew. The man's hair covered his ears and merged with a full beard, both of which, like the duster, were once black and now graying considerably. His eyes were hidden behind a pair of dark glasses and on his head was a black watch cap, also surplus, she presumed.

The man had three weapons that Brook could clearly see. Held comfortably in one hand was a carbine, tan and not much different from hers. In a holster on the man's hip was a black pistol, and strangely, protruding above one shoulder was the intricately carved ivory pommel of some kind of two-handed sword.

The man said nothing. He removed his dark glasses and fixed his steely gaze on her.

Returning the hard look with one of her own, Brook saw the man's green eyes flick down to her weapon. So she took a step back from the fence and regarded the line of vehicles, letting her gaze float from vehicle to vehicle and face to face.

Feeling the bearded man's eyes boring into her, she scrutinized the vehicles and men one-by-one again, only in reverse order. The first two vehicles—Jenkins' Tahoe and the camouflage SUV she recognized as having belonged to the kids—were of no concern to her. But the next four in line did. They were sprouting enough manned firepower to shred the gun truck and all of the other vehicles in her group's motor pool. Seeing this made her contemplate saving Seth and Foley's lives by calling them off—an idea she shelved for the time being.

The expressions on the faces of the people manning the weapons and driving the vehicles weren't quite what she had been expecting. To a person—except for a young kid staring doe-eyed from the front passenger seat of the Tahoe and a bearded man strongly resembling the leader—every one of them wore the same bored visage she had seen draped on a person stuck in a menial job and wanting badly to get out.

The blue-eyed boy beaming the bland look of someone waiting out a TV commercial wasn't a killer, of that she was sure. And the rest of the posse—*if the shoe fits*, she thought—seemingly punching the time clock, weren't either. She heard Cade's voice in her head saying: *Trust your gut.*

She kept her eyes trained on the dozen or so men and their war machines. Sure, she figured, they would rise to the occasion if need be. After all, they had already survived nearly a dozen weeks of hell on earth since the dead rose. So, gritting her teeth, she locked eyes with the giant of a man and approached the fence, M4 still at the low-ready and every muscle in her body rippling under her clothing.

Gripping the fence with one hand, the rifle barrel conveniently resting on the middle strand of wire, Brook ran her plan through her mind one more time.

Fuck it, she thought. Take the initiative, and try to hit them flat-footed and backpedaling. Another one of Cade's sayings from the teams entered her head: *Speed, surprise, and violence of action.* She didn't know if this was the way to go about this one, but, damn it, she had gotten them into this mess and she was determined to get them out.

The man opened his mouth to speak.

The *speed* part of Cade's credo came into play as Brook beat the man to the punch. "Who in the *fuck* do you think you are, coming here and taking a couple of kids hostage and then throwing around ultimatums based on presumptions I'm guessing you gleaned from watching CSI before everything went to shit?"

Rendered momentarily speechless, even though his mouth was clamped shut, inwardly Alexander gaped at the petite brunette woman who had just emerged from the biggest truck he had ever seen. The black Ford made the Tahoe and Blazer look like toys by comparison. How this woman managed to drive the thing—let alone climb into it—spun through his mind. Clutched in her hands, held southpaw and looking normal-sized given her stature, was a compact version of the M4 carbine.

Where the woman was concerned, his presumptions had been way off base. Fully expecting some kind of toothless, double-chinned, Bubba-looking character in tobacco-stained coveralls to be driving the vehicle behind her, he was thrown a completely unexpected curveball.

Like drawing a face card on a hard sixteen, he was sadly disappointed this attractive woman had anything remotely to do with Lena's murder. A bust, in blackjack parlance.

"I don't know this CSI you speak of. Your vehicle"—he nodded toward her truck—"*that* vehicle, as described by eyewitnesses, was in the area when my Lena and her new husband, Mikhail Rashovic, were killed in cold blood. *I*"—he pounded his chest, strands of spittle flying from his mouth—"I found her body. The smile had been blasted off of her face. Lena's lovely smile was just a bloody hole. No lips. No teeth. Your people erased her face and her life on that road. All I have of her now is memories and a few pictures and video clips stored on a pair of phones."

"Listen—" Brook began.

"No ... *you* listen to me," bellowed the man. "Who killed my *Lena*?" The tan carbine's muzzle rose a few degrees and in Brook's side vision she saw the turret-mounted machine guns being trained solely on her. On the bright side, she mused, at least death would be instantaneous and final being shredded apart by those things. She let go of the fence and gestured in the general direction of the graves up the hill. "They're hard to see ... but, second grave from the right is where the man who shot Lena ... *in self-defense* ... is buried. He died that day too."

Shaking his head, the man said, "Lena was not a killer."

"Once again with the assumptions," Brook said. "Chief was bit earlier in the day. My daughter was hurt as well. We were just trying to go south on 16. Those two you're speaking of stood between us and what we needed. They were armed and assertive and they fired first. That's the truth. And as we all know ... especially in the current climate, violence begets violence."

"Live by the sword, die by the sword," said the man, his stance shifting, the muzzle rising yet another degree or two. "Matthew 26:52, I believe."

Brook nodded.

"Still doesn't bring Lena back."

"Why didn't you mention the boy in your makeshift Sharpie Power Point presentation?"

"Lena was my everything."

"You're not at all curious how Mikhail died?"

Shaking his head, the man said, "No." The carbine barrel tracked upward. "Drop your rifle. You and your people ambushed and killed two of ours. Someone has to pay."

Brook glanced at her watch. Stalling, she said, "Fuck you. I want proof of life. Show me the girls. In fact, let them go and you all live. Go back to wherever you came from and tell your people this is still the United States. We *will* travel anywhere in this state or any other with impunity. Is that clear?"

"OK," Dregan said. "Who killed Mikhail?"

Brook stared the man down for a full minute. As soon as she heard the rising engine sounds at her back, she said slowly, "I did. But after he shot at me first." She raised her right hand slow and deliberate to her cheek and traced with one finger the half-moon scar there. "I caught a piece of lead from his first volley. In addition to this"—she jabbed the thin pink scar, flashing a wicked half-smile as she did—"there are three dimples on my truck's bumper where the bullets that did this broke apart."

Looking past Brook, at the feeder road, Dregan said, "Whoever is coming, have them turn back or I'll send grenades raining down on them."

"That's the Tenth Special Forces Group returning from a mission upstate ... my husband is with them." She saw a flash of doubt in the man's eyes. "Bring me my daughter, *now*."

"You are bluffing young lady. That's only one Humvee ... maybe two, and they don't stand a chance against us."

"You people already fucked us once," Brook spat. "The firefight with your kids kept Chief from getting the treatment he needed."

The man's brow arched. "A bite is fatal, *no*?"

Brook went on, "We got trapped by a horde and sought refuge on a farm off the road."

Helen and Ray's, thought Dregan, nodding subconsciously. "And you let *them* live?"

Brook visibly started. "*They* let us live," she said. She saw two of the men nearby nod in agreement.

"Drop the weapon, and the girls get to go back with the"—he smiled wickedly, this time—"your husband. And hey! They'll have the protection of the entire Tenth Special Forces Group."

Hearing the engine noise drawing nearer and feeling her blood beginning to boil, Brook hissed, "Bring me the girls, now."

He shook his head, carbine barrel still unwavering.

Now or never. Keeping her eyes locked with the man's, Brook opened both hands and let gravity have the carbine. As it fell toward the ground, she uncurled her cramping fingers and started her right arm on an upward arc. Then, *bingo!* she saw confusion on the man's face and his eyes broke contact with hers to track the black rifle already near her knees. *Bad move on his part.* Because, you see, a person's hands usually follow their eyes. And this man's hands were no exception. And the carbine muzzle followed where they went … to the ground in front of her boots.

Moving lightning quick in spite of the weakness in her right arm, she darted her left hand behind her back and a fraction of a second later—just as the metal clatter of the M4 hitting the ground reached her ears—her left was sweeping back up with the black Beretta clutched in it. Even before her fingers found the knurled polymer grip and wrapped around it, in a vernacular she hoped would make her case, she bellowed, "Fuck you and the horse you rode in on! Does that sound familiar?" Pistol held steady and aimed at center mass, as Cade had taught her to do when tangling with the living, she let the words hang, then went on. "Those were Mikhail's last words … brayed right before I got hit in the face. He shot first … you need to get that through your thick fucking skull. Then, and only then, with blood already running down my face, did I return his fire. I gut shot him through the door of that SUV on the road behind you. It would have been over then and there if your Lena wasn't hell bent on playing Mallory to Mikhail's Mickey. For some reason. Love. Youthful indiscretion. She decided to go all Natural Born Killer and follow his lead and poked her rifle barrel out." Brook felt her face flush, but continued. "Chief was a prison guard in the other world. He was trained to check his fire until a target presented itself. And it did in the form of her face near the SUV's rear bumper." Beard notwithstanding, Brook could tell by the softening of his jaw and the look in his eyes that she was getting through to him. However, in order to underline her resolve, and against the voice in her head telling her not to, she tracked the pistol up, her finger drawing up some of the trigger pull—*just in case.*

He took a half-step back, his carbine still aimed at the road.

"I mourned them both then," she went on. "And I've mourned them both many times since. They were just kids who were out of their element." Her face softened even as the sound of tires crunching to a halt drifted up from the direction of the feeder road.

West of the Eden Compound on State Route 39

Just when Cade thought Mister Murphy was giving them all a much-needed break, and with the bridge preceding the fallen tree roadblock oh so close, they rounded a bend in the road and found both lanes blocked by a sizeable gathering of mostly burnt creatures. With no chance of bulling through the press of the dead, Duncan and Taryn reversed both vehicles to a standoff distance, where everyone dismounted and began engaging the nearest of the crispy critters.

"These ones are moving faster than the others," said Cade, referring to the Zs left twice-dead on the road along with the disabled plow truck some miles back. He dumped an entire magazine of 5.56 through his M4 in a matter of seconds, resulting in a mess of sooty dead things jumbled together on the double-solid centerlines up ahead.

To the right of Cade, who was steadying himself on the 4Runner's open rear passenger-side door, his rifle braced on the window, the Kids were lighting up the charred abominations with fairly accurate fire.

"Good job! Just keep firing and reloading," Lev said, his words of encouragement—aimed at Wilson and Taryn mostly—nearly drowned out by the raspy moans of the dead.

Shell casings pinged the road all around the four of them. Assembled in a ragged semi-circle a dozen feet off the 4Runner's right front fender, they, along with Cade's precision shooting, had succeeded in making a sizable dent in the throng moving towards them.

Left of the centerlines, the trio of Oliver, Duncan, and Daymon were embroiled in a battle with the dead that had rapidly devolved from a one-sided gunfight to a hasty retreat.

"Mount up," hollered Duncan, his shotgun booming twice, the buckshot sending big chunks of charred flesh and splintered bone skyward and two headless corpses to the roadway. He fired into the advancing assemblage head-high until the stubby pump gun was empty and smoking, then clambered aboard the Land Cruiser.

"Get your ass in here, Daymon," bellowed Oliver as he slid into the back seat and banged the door shut.

The dreadlocked firefighter—who was back to his old surly self now that the pot buzz had worn off—ignored the plea long enough to decapitate a trio of Zs with Kindness.

Duncan dropped the transmission into *Reverse* and watched Daymon backpedaling and swinging away with the polished machete. Once the kid's skinny butt was in the passenger seat, he passed some shells for the shotgun over and reversed again to create a buffer.

Juggling the shells, Daymon said, "You shoot 'em, you reload 'em. Isn't that the old rule?"

Duncan didn't indulge the man with an answer.

***

Cade guessed the three minutes burned on the stretch of road fighting the Zs crawled by normally for the others, but to him, knowing how many bad actors were on the road outside the compound, the hundred and eighty seconds had seemed like an eternity. With the horizontal trees in view and the 4Runner weaving through the fallen human shells, he swapped mags in both the M4 and Glock, then tapped the Gerber on his hip to make certain it hadn't been knocked loose in the midst of battle. Satisfied he was ready as he'd ever be, he gripped the door handle, ready to bail the second the rig stopped at the far end of the distant span.

Chapter 72

Staring into the gaping muzzle, Dregan relived the last couple of minutes in his head. First, kind of like Eastwood playing Harry Callahan, the woman's hard-set brown eyes narrowed. The death flinch, he had thought at the time. Then, as if she'd come to some kind of conclusion, he saw a change in the windows to her soul. They went impossibly dark and narrowed to slits. Next he heard the words *'Fuck you and the horse you rode in on,'* but didn't immediately associate them with the situation at hand. In the seconds between hearing those words, all crawling by at a glacial pace, and that piece of the puzzle locking into place, he took his eyes from hers and swept them down and saw her right hand let go of the carbine's foregrip. The fingers uncurled one at a time, kind of like a cat flicking out its claws. Just as he realized the raised hand looked a little crippled, the stubby black rifle was slipping from her other hand and on the way to the ground.

Naturally, his attention was drawn there and his rifle barrel followed suit. In the next half-beat, like some kind of David Copperfield sleight-of-hand shit, her left hand swept up and suddenly a black pistol was pointed at his sternum. He remembered flicking his eyes from the gun on the ground to the pistol, impossibly large in her hand. At that moment the words *fuck you and the horse you rode in on* replayed in his mind in Mikhail's voice, and as they sank in a huge weight slid off his shoulders and he relaxed his grip on his rifle.

Bring me the girls, or you die, the woman had hissed, believably.

He remembered mumbling something about it all being a big misunderstanding.

He remembered his brother Henry moving forward, rifle trained on the woman, screaming for her to lower the weapon.

He remembered the woman's eyes, glittering ... *tears?* Then the pistol swung up to his face close enough that he smelled cordite off the muzzle.

Now, Henry still screaming "Drop the gun," the other men all bristling and bringing rifles to bear, he heard over it all the distinct sound of a round the size of a baby's arm being chambered into the .50 caliber machine gun atop the Humvee that had just bulled past the Ford and ground to a halt behind the gate. Realizing the turret-mounted weapon was trained on the assembled men, Henry and Peter included, he said, louder this time, "This was all just a big misunderstanding."

A man will say almost anything in order to keep from getting shot, Cade had told Brook once. Anything to stay on the right side of the dirt. Robert Christian had. Pug had. As had countless others Cade had used as examples. Funny thing was, thought Brook. Though her man was probably still miles away, the words in her head came to her in his voice with the usual crisp delivery and even tone.

"Misunderstanding, my ass. Bring the girls out or you get a third eye," she hissed, still holding the pistol rock steady.

He said nothing. Just put his tan rifle down on the steaming pavement. Real slow, he hinged up and put a raised palm towards the other bearded man, silencing him. Then he turned towards the convoy and motioned for his men to stand down.

The radio in Brook's pocket broke squelch. "I've got you covered," said Seth.

Brook's eyes moved along the convoy, and far off down the road past the trailing vehicle she saw movement and a man's head and shoulders sticking out from behind a canted fence post. Protruding from the shin-high grass next to it was the long barrel of Logan's Barrett sniper rifle, easily recognizable by the boxy muzzle brake and Hubble-telescope-sized optics perched atop the long gun.

"My name is Alexander," said the man. "I'm going to reach into my pocket for my phone and radio."

Brook nodded. Her eyes remained locked on the man as he reached into the left pocket of the well-worn duster and came out with a two-way radio, its case scratched up and weathered from constant use. Then, slowly, he plucked a shiny slim smart phone from the opposite pocket and handed it across the fence.

"Thumb it on and start the video playing."

The gun was growing heavy in Brook's hand. She wanted this all to be over, but she shook her head. "Release the girls first."

The man called Alexander brought the radio to his mouth and ordered a man he addressed as Gregory to bring the girls out.

Out, thought Brook. She flashed a glance at the convoy. *Nothing.* The doors remained closed.

Seeing this, Dregan said, "My oldest son has them in the woods behind me. Play the video … please."

Brook lifted her gaze to the woods behind the clearing and saw nothing moving there. Then, to humor the man still staring into the business end of her Beretta, she took the phone from him, powered it on, and hit the translucent play arrow hovering there on the small screen.

There was sound first, laughter and the clinking of glasses. She was watching the bar scene unfold with one eye and Alexander with the other. She saw the boy she had killed. He was being an asshole to the bartender. *True colors.* Then he said it: *Fuck you and the horse you rode in on.* Half-expecting the hail of bullets that followed those words the first time she heard them, Brook flinched. Her eyes went from the screen to the bearded man's face—and on it was an expression of complete resignation. His posture had changed as well, shoulders and back slumping like a Macy's Parade float slowly deflating.

Guilt eating away at her, Brook was about to offer her condolences when she heard a chorus of piercing screams. They came from the tree line beyond the row of graves and died out quickly. Then, before she could say or do anything, she nearly blew the top of Alexander's head off when, from the same grove of trees, two closely spaced gunshots crashed the stillness.

***

Grateful that the ongoing shouting match between her mom and a man she assumed to be Gregory's father had ceased before ending in gunfire and screams, Raven was delivered a second miracle when she felt her right hand slip free from the blood-slickened paracord wound about her wrists. As she fought the overwhelming urge to look and see what kind of damage was causing the wild throbbing on primarily her right wrist, she heard the distinct soft warble of Gregory's radio emanating from inside his pocket.

Raven mouthed, "I'm free," to Sasha. Keeping her hands behind her back, and thus the illusion that she was still captive alive for the moment, she turned back to eavesdrop on the conversation. She heard broadcast through the tiny speaker details about a shooting on the Woodruff Highway that she knew nothing about. Next, just when the conversation seemed to be steering to the part pertaining to her and Sasha's freedom, she heard a racket in the bushes behind Gregory that was *not* falling snow.

Gregory Dregan was standing with his back to the foliage and stuffing the radio in his pocket when he saw the younger girl named Raven visibly stiffen then roll backwards off the log. Strangely, his first impression was that the girl looked like a scuba diver falling from a boat's gunwale. And in the next half-beat, as she worked to right herself from the clearly deliberate maneuver, he witnessed her face twist into a wide-eyed mask of terror and one of her tiny blood-slicked hands slip free of her bonds.

Simultaneously, the redhead, Sasha, rocketed up from the log, her jaw hinging open and closed with no words coming out.

The stench of decay entered the small hide right behind the initial sound Gregory had pegged as more snow falling off the trees. Everything after that from the girls' impromptu display of acrobatics to them both belting out horrific screams lasted two short heartbeats. Immediately following the auditory assault, Gregory Dregan felt something deathly cold brush his face and he was hit blindside by roughly two hundred pounds of damp dead weight.

Newton's Law of motion was in full effect at that point, and the loaded-down pack on his back precipitated and sped up his crashing to the ground. His head brushed the log and suddenly he was facedown with a mouthful of dirt and twigs choking off the startled yelp building in his throat.

***

From her vantage point, kneeling behind the log in a clutch of ferns, Raven saw the same rotten creature from the nearby road hit Gregory amidships and drive the larger man into the ground, face first by the log. At that point she forgot all about the blood painting her forearms from wrist to elbow and focused solely on surviving the encounter. Flicking her eyes right, she saw Sasha, arms still trussed behind her back and staring at the hissing creature like she was under some kind of hypnotic spell.

With nothing to lose but everything, Raven dove over the crumbling log with one objective: yank the boxy pistol from the holster on Gregory's belt. Mid-flight, she twisted to her right and the second she hit the ground, with her shoulder and hip absorbing the impact, both hands went to work. With her right, she stripped the pistol from the holster. At the same time she shot her left hand out, laced her fingers in the monster's hair, and pulled back mightily.

Too little, too late. The coppery smell of freshly spilt blood hit her nose and Gregory started grunting and spitting mud and kicking her in the side with one of his thick-soled boots.

Time slowed further and three things seemed to happen all at once. Realizing the pistol was a Glock like her mom's, she didn't bother looking for a safety, because she knew it was built into the trigger. So she swung the pistol up and pressed it to the snarling zombie's temple and in one motion rolled onto her back, let go of its stringy hair and squeezed the trigger two times. Real quick. Back to back. And they blended together, sounding as one, like the cannon thing going off earlier.

The first bullet entered the thing's head and its eyes bulged out under pressure. One of the jaundiced orbs launched out, splatted on its cheek, and dangled there from a thin ropy membrane. Raven's eyes were squeezed shut by the time the second report hit her ears, and she totally missed seeing the top of the Z's skull separate and spin away into the undergrowth. The spritz of putrid gray matter and flecked bone following nearly the same trajectory was also lost on her.

When she opened her eyes, Gregory was already wriggling out from under the twice-dead human, the damage done instantly apparent. There was a single deep fissure on the side of Gregory's neck. It was oozing hot sticky blood. Raven pushed up off the ground and spotted the fist-sized plug of flesh on the ground near the rotter's still gaping mouth.

"I'm dead," stammered Gregory, his face gone slack and ashen. He stole a glance to the pistol still clutched in Raven's hand.

"Mom," Raven hollered over her shoulder. "I'm OK."

"Shoot me. Please," Gregory pleaded in a funereal voice.

Raven looked at the pistol and shook her head. "Sasha, help me roll him over."

There was the sound of boots thudding the ground and her mom and the man with the beard burst through the opening, caromed off each other like bowling pins, and came to an abrupt stop beside Sasha.

Brook pushed past the redhead, looked down, and saw the bloody wound. "Help me," she said to the bearded man.

Together they tore off the backpack and rifle then succeeded in getting Gregory rolled over flat on his back.

"It's going to be close," said Brook, her hand outstretched toward Raven. "Antiserum."

Raven went into the stricken man's pockets and came out with the cylinder.

Dregan's mouth fell open. With the noise of the others scrabbling to a halt outside the hide, he crabbed out of the woman's way and fixed his gaze on his dying boy.

"Fucking guys and their beards," said Brook as she parted the thicket searching for the proper site. "Got it." In the next instant, like the trained professional that she was, the auto injector was out of the cylinder and she was jabbing the short needle into the man's neck.

Peering over Brook's shoulder, the elder Dregan asked, "Is that for real?"

Brook nodded and tossed the spent injector aside.

"Will he live?"

Showing little emotion, Brook replied, "Fifty-fifty … at best."

"I owe you," he said, tears rolling over his cheeks and into his bushy beard.

From the direction of the compound feeder road came the sound of a couple of hard-working engines.

"On your way back to wherever you came from, stop in and see if Helen and Ray are getting along. I haven't been able to. So I figure sending you is the least I can do … after all they did for us."

"I still owe you a life debt," Dregan said. "And you needn't worry, I won't mention another word about you or your people to anybody."

Brook nodded to the men assembling at her back. "And them?"

"I'll make sure they don't talk."

Just then, the youngest Dregan, blonde and blue eyed, crashed through the brush and slid on his knees next to the stricken man. He looked closely at the wound and, oblivious to the antiserum working its way through the man's system, said, "How do you feel, brother?"

"Hot," replied, Gregory, weakly. "I'm burning up."

"That's a good sign," said Brook. She removed his stocking cap and pressed it against the wound as a makeshift bandage. "Somebody get this man some water."

"Got it," said a man. Another came forward and offered to hold the cap in place.

Breathing deeply and looking around at the dozen faces wearing worried looks, Brook went from her knees to her butt, then suddenly was flattened by sixty-some-odd pounds of twelve-year-old and found herself suffocating in Raven's iron embrace.

After savoring the attention and returning it tenfold for a couple of minutes, Brook sat up and looked around. "I heard engines. Glenda. Is Glenda out there yet?"

The crowd parted and the older woman stepped up and shot Brook a bewildered look.

No reason to beat around the bush. Brook said, "Oliver is alive. He and the others should be back any time now."

Hearing this, Glenda fell to her knees. "How?"

Brook checked her patient's pulse. Smiling and looking at Glenda, she said, "That's all I know. And Mister Dregan … this one's not out of the woods yet but, based on firsthand knowledge, I think he's going to pull through."

She dug the Thuraya from her pocket. After dredging the code word for *safe* from her memory, she tapped out a short message and sent it to Cade's sat-phone. It read simply: Stand down. We are **peachy.**

Epilogue

The first part of the promised *life debt* arrived an hour after the convoy of mostly military vehicles turned around and headed back to Bear River with Gregory Dregan's feet still firmly planted in the realm of the living.

Now, hours later, Brook gazed to her left at the tanker truck partially blocking Daymon's Winnebago from view. Emblazoned on its polished stainless flank, barely discernable because of the licking flames of the roaring campfire being reflected there, were the words BEAR VALLEY PROPANE. And not to be missed beneath those two-foot-high red letters was rattle-canned writing in black that read: Alexander Dregan – Gas Baron of Salt Lake City.

"That will easily outlast winter," she said to Cade, who was sitting on the grass in front of her with his left ankle entombed in snow that once made up the main body of Raven and Sasha's snowman.

"You did good," Cade said, following her gaze to the tractor-trailer and shiny tank hitched to it.

"I learned from the best," she answered, fumbling left-handed to shovel some rice and beans into her mouth off an enameled metal camp plate.

Casting long shadows across the clearing, Daymon and Heidi rose from camp chairs and headed off toward the Winnebago, heads down and chuckling at something. A tick later, under Glenda's disapproving glare, Oliver set his metal plate down atop the ones left behind by the departing couple and followed after them.

"Gotta admit," said Cade, "The marijuana Oliver found sure has smoothed the rough edges off our resident logger extraordinaire."

Brook said nothing to that. She was still watching Glenda watch the trio leave. Then she snickered at seeing Duncan, who was obviously taking advantage of Oliver's absence, boost the woman up and lead her off toward the compound. "Yeah," she finally said. "Everyone seems to be getting along real well."

Making a racket, Cade scraped the beans into a neat little pile on his plate with his fork. Not caring if anyone was watching, he leaned forward and, with a wet slurping sound, hoovered them up.

Making Cade start and dump his fork in his lap, Brook called across the fire at Raven and Sasha. "Girls," she said, "welcome to Day One of punishment for going AWOL. Police up everyone's plates and silverware and get to washing."

Raven blew on her marshmallow until the bluish flame died out. "How many days does punishment last?" she asked just prior to jamming the blackened morsel into her mouth.

"Ninety days," Cade said in a no nonsense tone. "Breakfast, lunch"—

—"and dinner," Brook said, finishing for him.

Cade watched the girls begin their sentence. He tracked them around the fire as they relieved Tran, Foley, and Seth of their plates and utensils. "And they better be clean," he added, maintaining a straight face.

"And we've been appointed official quality control officers," Wilson said, nudging Taryn— who was snuggling underneath a blanket on the same camp chair with him—to go along with his ruse.

"Yeah … that's the ticket," Taryn said, not very convincingly, as Raven took a pair of dirty plates from her outstretched hand.

Happy to see a sense of community returning to the tiny group, Cade caught the attention of his daughter and her co-conspirator. "It takes a village," he said jokingly. "So from here on out, we are all watching you two like hawks." Then suddenly, as if a switch had been thrown, his smile evaporated and his face took on a hard set. He plucked the Thuraya from his pocket and thumbed it on. As soon as the sat phone's screen lit up, turning his face a cool shade of blue, he scrolled to the messages and selected the most recent. Seeing Nash's number and time stamp attached to the recording, he pressed the *Talk* button and listened intently.

Sensing her man's every muscle tense, Brook leaned forward and whispered into his ear, "What is it?"

Cade thumbed the phone off. "Raven," he called out. "Go inside and get my laptop." He craned around and caught Lev's eye. "I need you to get me the satellite dish from the Black Hawk."

Brook watched both Raven and Lev spring to action. "That urgent?" she asked.

Cade leaned back and looked into her brown eyes. "Words cannot begin to describe what Nash just divulged to me."

"Humor me," she said, meeting his upside-down gaze.

Cade shook his head. "You're just going to have to watch the screen over my shoulder and see it for yourself."

###

Thanks for reading *Frayed!* Reviews help. Please consider leaving yours at the place of purchase. Cade rejoins his former Delta team on a new mission in the forthcoming novel in my bestselling *Surviving the Zombie Apocalypse* series. Look for it in 2016. Please feel free to Friend Shawn Chesser on Facebook. To receive the latest information on upcoming releases first, please join my mailing list at ShawnChesser.com. Find all of my books on my Amazon Author Page.

ABOUT THE AUTHOR

Shawn Chesser, a practicing father, has been a zombie fanatic for decades. He likes his creatures shambling, trudging and moaning. As for fast, agile, screaming specimens... not so much. He lives in Portland, Oregon, with his wife, two kids and three fish. This is his ninth novel.

CUSTOMERS ALSO PURCHASED:

JOHN O'BRIEN
NEW WORLD
SERIES

JAMES N. COOK
SURVIVING THE DEAD
SERIES

MARK TUFO
ZOMBIE FALLOUT
SERIES

ARMAND ROSAMILLIA
DYING DAYS
SERIES

HEATH STALLCUP
THE MONSTER
SQUAD

Made in the USA
Lexington, KY
03 October 2018